MARGARET LEROY

Some Girls Do

Why Women Do – and Don't –
Make the First Move

HarperCollins*Publishers*

HarperCollins*Publishers*
77–85 Fulham Palace Road,
Hammersmith, London W6 8JB

Published by HarperCollins*Publishers* 1998
9 8 7 6 5 4 3 2 1

First published in Great Britain by
HarperCollins*Publishers* 1997

Copyright © Margaret Leroy 1997

The Author asserts the moral right to
be identified as the author of this work

A catalogue record for this book
is available from the British Library

ISBN 0 00 638450 1

Printed and bound in Great Britain by
Caledonian International Book Manufacturing Ltd, Glasgow

CONTENTS

ACKNOWLEDGEMENTS

My thanks are due to these people.

Michael Fishwick for his inspirational advice and guidance. Rebecca Lloyd, who was my best ever editor: working with her has been a great pleasure. Lisa Eveleigh for being unfailingly perceptive and supportive. Roy Umney of Bookstall Services and Martin Shaw for invaluable help at the research stage. Mick and Becky and Isabel for their love and patience, as always.

Above all, I'd like to thank all the women and men who talked to me, and who were so open about the things that usually stay unsaid. I'm deeply grateful for their generosity.

CHAPTER 1
COURTSHIP TODAY

'**I ASK** men out,' said Emma. 'I'm doing my bit. I can't understand why more women don't do it. It feels so good to go out with somebody you've chosen.'

Emma is a teacher in her early twenties. She's warm and friendly – but not unusually assertive. She's pretty – but not particularly confident about her appearance: like so many women, she's forever struggling to lose weight. She enjoys her sex-life – but she's not particularly sexually self-assured. In most ways, she's as full of self-doubt as the rest of us. Yet she asks men out: she finds it easy: and making the first move is a source of real pleasure in her life. She relishes her sense of achievement when she thinks, I chose him.

My conversation with Emma was the genesis of this book. It set me thinking how extraordinary it is that so few women make this move. Why is it still so difficult? What could help us to change?

Since talking to Emma, I've asked all the women I've met if they've ever asked a man out. All of them have wanted to – but few have ever done so: most said, 'I simply couldn't . . .'. Some of these women edit glossy magazines or manage social services teams or work in busy casualty departments. They feel strong, autonomous, entitled. In every other area of their lives, they're in control: they shape what happens to them. But this they wouldn't do. Unlike Emma, they don't think it would feel good, and they *can* understand why more women don't do it.

Even women in the age-group where it's often assumed that sexual patterns are changing most rapidly said the same. Nineteen-year-old Natalie told me: 'I do leave it up to the lad to make the first move – with telephone calls, the first kiss, everything – and if they don't do it, well then it's tough cheese isn't it?' Lucy, aged fifteen, said: 'Girls could, yeah – they don't though . . . It's just that nobody does. I think it would be good but no-one has the courage to.'

There are a few Emmas in every age group, of course. Most of the men I talked to had been asked out by a woman – but usually only once or twice.

Women's reluctance to ask men out does seem amazing. Over the past few decades, so much has changed in our sexual behaviour. Women have been setting limits and drawing lines in the sand. We've said no to male sexual violence and attempted to outlaw the darker expressions of male sexual initiative by establishing rape-crisis centres, taking action on child sexual abuse, legislating against sexual harassment. Some women have sought to set the sexual agenda with that effective act of vengeance, the kiss and tell, with its 'That's no way to treat a lady' subtext. And many of us have been exploring our own sexuality – by reading collections of female fantasies, or going to orgasm workshops, or buying 'Black Lace' books, or photographing the male nude, or queuing up to scream at the Chippendales.

Most notably for this book, women have been imposing their own agenda on courtship by highlighting the risk of sexual violence within a dating relationship. This is the sexual change that is causing most controversy. It's been suggested, most notably by Katie Roiphe in her book *The Morning After*, that awareness of the possibility of date rape creates a climate of fear which makes it harder for men and women to get close. As Martin Amis told an audience at Princeton University, 'As far as I'm concerned, you can change your mind before, even during, but just not after sex'.[1] The worry is that now women *are* changing their minds afterwards, and that sometimes the men involved will be wrongfully blamed – like Austen Donellan, who was threatened with expulsion from university after a woman he'd slept with claimed he'd raped her. Wisely he chose to be tried in a public court, and was acquitted.

But there were certainly casualties too under the old dispensation. And by and large it surely makes sense to see the date-rape panic as part of something bigger, and something to be celebrated. Our questioning of the old sexual certainties is part of a general move towards more egalitarian ways of relating, as we strive for gender equality in so many areas of our lives.

Yet the puzzling fact remains that one piece of the new pattern is missing. Few women are like Emma: few women ask men out. This simply doesn't fit with the rest of our sexual behaviour. We no longer see men as creatures who always have to be in control. We know that men like their regular partners to initiate sex: we know that they sometimes prefer to lie back and let us do all the work in bed. Our reticence also seems at odds with other aspects of our social behaviour – because once a couple have got together, it's usually the woman who makes all the social arrangements. Yet mostly we still believe to the bottom of our hearts that men don't like us to make the social and sexual moves at the very start of courtship.

When I gave women a list of sexual assertions and asked how hard they'd find them, a clear hierarchy emerged. Women find it easy to initiate sex with a man with whom they have a steady relationship – whether by dropping hints and touching suggestively, or by asking directly. Telling him what you want in bed is more difficult: some women say 'I just couldn't', but others are happy to suggest a new position or ask for a different kind of touch. Initiating the first sex in a new relationship – deciding when to turn up with a toothbrush – is also something many of us manage. But asking a man out comes right at the top of the list: it's by far the most problematic assertion. It's during the very first moves that women are at their most tentative and indirect and feminine. 'I'd never do that', we say, or 'I'd love to but I simply wouldn't dare', or even 'Well, we aren't equal, are we?'

COURTSHIP SCRIPTS: The hundred and fifty initiatives

In the past few years, US 'close relationships researchers' have looked at our courtship scripts – the behaviour we expect of ourselves and others when we go on a date. The results of their studies confirm that tradition still shapes our behaviour right at the start of our sexual relationships.

Psychologists Suzanna Rose and Irene Friez asked men and women to list the things they'd expect to do as they prepared for a date with someone new, and through the evening.[2] They found that men and women largely agreed on the scripts. On a first date a woman expects to: tell her friends and family, check her appearance, wait for the man, welcome him to her home and introduce her parents or room-mates, keep the conversation going and control the rate of sexual intimacy. A man expects to: ask the woman for a date, decide what to do, prepare his car and flat, check his money, go to the woman's house, meet her parents or room-mates, open the car door, pay, initiate sexual contact, take her home, and tell her he'll be in touch. Here, men are making the arrangements and taking the sexual initiatives, while women set the scene and have a right of veto – they worry about what to wear and what to say, and they tell him when to stop. In their commentary, Rose and Friez acknowledge that 'many young women today pay date expenses, and a majority of young men report having been asked for a date by a woman'. But the more dating experience the participants had, the more important they felt it was to stick to the time-honoured roles.

Other researchers have found the same. According to psychologist Susan Sprecher, men are still much more likely than women to take direct steps – to ask the other out, plan what to do on the first date, pay, and initiate the second date.[3] Susan Green and Philip Sandos found that both men and women feel it's more acceptable for the man to take the initiative – whether he's simply starting a conversation or asking a person out.[4]

Less academic writers reiterate the theme. In her book *Hot and Bothered*, a 'guide to sexual etiquette in the 1990s', based on hundreds of interviews with men and women in Canada, Wendy Dennis says she's found that women still aren't taking the lead at the start of relationships. 'Most women realize that many men still find the notion of a sexually assertive woman distasteful,' she writes.[5]

US writer and researcher Warren Farrell runs mixed workshops on gender issues. In his book, *Why Men Are The Way They Are*, he describes how he asks people to simulate meeting at a party. He says, 'That's how I discovered how rare it is for a woman ever to take the hand of a man who had never before taken her hand, or to kiss a man for the very first time, or to take any of the hundred and fifty initiatives between eye contact and sexual contact I found are typically expected of a man if the relationship is ever to be sexual.'[6]

COURTSHIP LIBERALS: Passive – *moi?*

Men still make the arrangements. Women still wait to be asked. Yet many of us would like things to be different. There were hints of this hunger for change in the way both men and women described their dating behaviour to me. Almost invariably, they played down the gender differences.

When women talk about the moves they do make, they strive to show that they have some control over what happens. A woman will emphasize the potency of her glances, gestures, smiles. She'll claim her signals are crystal clear. She'll describe how she'll cross a crowded room to talk to an appealing stranger, and how she'll touch the man before he touches her, or put her arm round him.

The behaviours that women present as examples of making the first move usually fall within the parameters of the traditional script. For instance, touching first – a light touch on the shoulder or arm – has tended to be the woman's prerogative. Initiatives like this that women do take are often open to interpretation. She goes up to him and starts talking. Is it flirtation or friendship? She puts her arm round his shoulders. A sexual move – or a warm affectionate hug? These initiatives are *indirect*: it's not obvious what they mean. And because they're ambiguous, they're a lot less risky than the traditional male initiatives – an invitation to dinner, a kiss on the lips. This distinction was clearly recognized by Rowena, who said, 'If you open your eyes wide at someone, you can pretend it wasn't really happening if it all goes wrong. But if you went and said, "Can you come to the cinema with me on Friday?" and he said no, you'd feel pathetic.'

Yet the fact that women highlight the moves that we do make shows how ready we are to move on. Women today are well aware of the rewards for sexual assertion. 'Passive' is a dirty word: no woman wants to be seen as passive in her sexual behaviour, and many of us would love to be more confident and innovative in our sex lives. I suspect that we put such stress on the active parts of our courtship behaviour because we yearn for more control at the start of our sexual relationships.

Men also tended to present themselves as thoroughly egalitarian. Men told me that yes, of course, it was fine for women to ask them out, it was a thoroughly good thing, they didn't go in for this man-the-hunter act anyway. They said they were sure it was happening a lot, because it had happened to them – though, on probing, I usually found that they'd been approached only once or twice, while they'd approached large numbers of women themselves. They also stressed how tentative they were in their traditional male role and how difficult they found it: they told me how few risks they took, how shy they were, how they waited till they were sure.

Younger men in particular played down the amount of planning they did. Geoff, twenty-six, said, 'I think planning spoils it. I take it as it comes, play it by ear according to the situation. With some girls you genuinely just want to have a coffee and a chat and see what happens . . . .' He mused on this, then added, 'Subconsciously I probably do plan what's the best way to go about it.'

Our attitudes to courtship are Janus-faced. Like Geoff, we look to both the past and the future. People talk first about how things *should* be – women should initiate, men should welcome women's initiatives, we should all be as clear as day in our sexual dealings, no-one should scheme. It's only later in the conversation that they reveal, like Geoff, what they actually do – which may well be less open and egalitarian than they'd at first implied. It's all very encouraging for those of us who'd welcome a new kind of courtship. In our heads we've invented a whole new world: we're just not living there yet, because we're not quite ready to risk it. In courtship the stakes are so high. And when we're approaching someone we'd love to get into bed with, we do what seems safest – and for now that so often means looking back to the past and taking our lines from the familiar script.

COURTSHIP CONSERVATIVES: From the Stone Age

But I also talked to people who felt that the pattern simply couldn't be changed, however much they might want it to be changed. These courtship conservatives were always women. To explain why men should always do the asking, they referred back to the ultimate authority – their mothers – or invoked the concept of the 'natural' and pointed to the sexual behaviour of their children's pet hamsters.

Jessica was one of these sexual conservatives:

'I've wanted to ask men out, but I wouldn't have done, ever, ever. I've always used other ways to invite them out, to do with one's behaviour, as I think most women do. You don't use words, you play a game.

'I don't think men like to be asked, I really don't. I think they do like to have a woman come and make sexual passes at them, I think that's lovely for them. I think what you get then is the one-night stand – where he says, "Ooh, that was great fun, wasn't it? Bye, maybe see you next year . . .". But I was never into doing that because I was never that into sex, I was into long-term relationships. I think they like to play a game of chase, where it looks like they're doing the chasing – and it may well be you're doing the chasing but no-one's going to admit to that.

'It's probably based on what my mother said, "Don't chase them, they hate it . . .", so there's all that kind of feminine lore from the past which I think there are seeds of truth in. Of course, women *should* be able to ask men out – but I just can't see it happening, the game is so set.

'My brothers have had streams of girls whom they laughed at. One of them actually booked a flight on the same aeroplane to Canada – he got on the plane and there she was, booked a seat next to him – and as far as he was concerned she was just a one-night fling – and it's been a joke ever since. So the horror of that sort of thing – realizing it was not a tactic that worked, and it was far better to pine by the telephone for a few days and then get over it than to make a fool of oneself – "hurling yourself at a man" as my mother would say.'

Jessica refers back to the past, to female lore, to the way things have always been. It's because this is how the game has always been that she feels it can't be changed.

Yet this belief that 'the game is so set' is worth examining. Because in fact Jessica is wrong. There are crucial elements in our present courtship patterns that don't go back as far as we imagine. Conventions about who initiates have changed radically within living memory.

In her study of courtship in the US from 1900 to 1950, *From Front Porch to Back Seat*, Beth Bailey describes how before the First World War, in the calling system that preceded the dating system, it was women who took the initiative at the start of romantic relationships.[7] The behaviour required of the genders at the beginning of a relationship was then quite different. Even though women had little power in the public world, they did have complete responsibility for making arrangements at the start of courtship. At first the young girl's mother invited men to call. Later the young woman herself could invite round any unmarried man to whom she had been properly introduced. These initial encounters took place in a social milieu controlled by women. It all happened in the parlour, in the women's sphere, and even the patterns of consumption were quintessentially feminine – little cakes and hot chocolate. This is the world of T.S. Eliot's *J. Alfred Prufrock* – written in 1915 – whose life was measured out in coffee spoons in rooms full of the rustle of women's skirts.

And in this world, male initiative at the start of sexual relationships was very differently viewed. In 1909 a worried young man wrote to an agony aunt of the time, the US *Ladies Home Journal* adviser, Mrs Kingsland. He asked, 'May I call upon a young woman whom I greatly admire, although she had not given me the permission? Would she be flattered at my eagerness, even to the setting aside of conventions, or would she think me impertinent?' A man making the first move? Absolutely not, said Mrs Kingsland: 'I think that you would risk her just displeasure and frustrate your object of finding favour with her.'[8]

But after the First World War, courtship changed. It moved out from the private female world into the public male-controlled sphere. Under the dating system, the couple went out – to a meal, to a dance, to the pictures – and the man took all the initiatives: he asked her out, planned the evening, bought the tickets, booked the table, paid the bill, opened the car door. And once the required behaviour had changed, people rapidly came to believe that the new convention was the way it had always been. In our thinking about sex, we have very short memories and no sense of history. A mere fifty years later, advice books were giving precisely opposite advice to that offered by Mrs Kingsland – and referring back to the palaeolithic as their authority. 'Girls who try to usurp the right of boys to choose their own dates' will 'ruin a good dating career. Fair or not, it is the way of life. From the Stone Age, when men chased and captured their women, comes the yen of a boy to do the pursuing.'[9]

COURTSHIP LIFE-CYCLES: Looking for love

For people today, the very word 'courtship' can be alienating. It seems to come from another era. Courtship is for Elizabeth Bennet and Mr Darcy, eyeing each other lecherously while doing the most decorous of dances. Yet surprisingly we have no other term for that sequence of behaviour through which we indicate our sexual interest in a more or less stereotyped way.

'Courtship' also implies quite a narrow range of relationships as the goal of the behaviour. As in *Pride and Prejudice*, we take the purpose of courtship to be the formation of the pair-bonds that lead to marriage. In this analysis, it's the marriage that defines it as courtship in retrospect. This is the kind of courtship that's examined in much US close relationships research. But in this book I'll include every type of relationship – casual sex, adultery, passionate and troubled affairs lasting six and a half weeks – all the many and various kinds of sexual activity or connection which are preceded by some kind of courtship process, however truncated, elliptical or secret it may be.

Courtship isn't only for the young, either. It's obviously young people who are most involved in this process, and the US research on the subject is all about people aged between about eighteen and twenty-three for purely pragmatic reasons: psychology students on US campuses get extra credits for participating in experiments. But this is behaviour that we may engage in at any time in our lives after puberty. There are love affairs even in old people's homes. In my interviewing for this book, the people I talked to ranged in age from the early teens to the mid–fifties.

Courtship doesn't follow a similar pattern right through the life cycle. Our courtship behaviour, and the kinds of relationship we seek to achieve through that behaviour, vary with age. In particular, as we get older our sexual negotiations gradually move out of the public into the private domain. Eventually, for many of those people for whom courtship continues, it becomes one of the most secret parts of their lives. To get a clearer picture of courtship, let's look at how our behaviour changes through the life-cycle.

The first bits of courtship behaviour are enacted in a very public arena. Chloe at thirteen says, 'These ten- and eleven-year-olds will see Eve Taylor on the bus, and they'll say, "Ooh isn't she gorgeous, isn't she hot" – and they don't really mean it, they're just doing it to show their mates they're cool. I've heard these little ten-year-old boys say to their friends, "I got off with Eve Taylor last night!" I'll think, oh yeah I'm sure you did. She's fifteen, I don't think so . . . Even your friend when it comes to a boy – well, you might think she's your friend, but she isn't really – if they thought someone was going to ask me out, they'd sort of sabotage it a bit and spread different messages and rumours.'

In a sense, young people at the start of adolescence are playing at courtship. Most of the time, it's rather like ITV's 'Blind Date' – the form without the content of sexual behaviour. There's talk about who you fancy – even if you don't. Passions are communicated via go-betweens, though the message may get distorted in the telling. Love letters are written and sent: some express real feelings, some are fake and may have a group authorship, and any of them may get read out on the school bus.

The public nature of this courting can cause distress. Young people of this age tell cautionary tales about the risks of using go-betweens. As Chloe points out, friends entrusted with messages may have their own jealous or malicious agendas. And in the tabloid culture of the school cloakroom, everyone knows how far you went: girls get given marks out of ten and a fourteen-year-old who admits to still being a virgin may be consigned to the 'V-group'. Rumours are spread and reputations destroyed: and a girl who's been out with too many boys will be cornered by girl bullies in the toilets and called a slag or a dog.

But the public nature of this behaviour also has a protective role. Friends are used as a source of courage: a boy who goes to visit a girl he likes may take his best mate too – rather like working-class adults in the eighteenth century, who often went 'a-wooing' together.[10] And the social group protects by establishing the norms, however cruel its effect on an individual young person. For instance, though there may be sexual harassment – and boys' early attempts to show interest in girls are often crude and intrusive – there will also be social support for coping with the harassment. Girls are by no means the voiceless and innocent victims of boys' playful or bullying expressions of sexual interest that they are sometimes made out to be. Kieran's approaches to Lydia mixed romantic offerings like letters saying how much he fancied her with more harassing approaches: he offered her a pepperami from his lunch – 'I cut it off just for you' – to which she responded with a well-rehearsed gagging routine, to the delight of her friends.

As people reach their mid- and late teens and early twenties, they move into the kind of courtship territory with which most of the existing research is concerned. Courtship is now a more private affair but the resulting relationships are highly public, and may be recognized with public ritual. Pairing-off may lead to a one-night stand or life-long marriage and parenting or anything in between.

Recently there have been some fascinating changes in courtship customs for this life stage – and there's a 'back to the future' theme to several of these developments. Some of our new customs – cohabitation, the rave, and sharing a bed without intercourse – revert to older ways of doing things. We're returning to courtship patterns that predate that era, lasting roughly from Queen Victoria's accession in 1837 to the 1950s, which was the most sexually repressive period in recent English history – a period when the sanctions against pre-marital sex were particularly punitive, when the clitoris got forgotten, when the very essence of femininity was a denial of the woman's sexuality.

Today's custom of cohabitation, to be followed by marriage at the point at which the couple decide they want children, has analogies with the betrothal system that pre-dated the Victorian system of courtship. Betrothed couples lived together and were sexually intimate but the contract was not regarded as binding until they got married, with the proviso that the man would support the child if the woman got pregnant.[11] Cohabitation, like betrothal, is a profoundly rational custom: both give the couple a trial period together before they take the irrevocable step of having children. Both institutions also allow women a lot of independence. The betrothed woman kept her name and single legal status, and today a cohabiting woman will probably have her own bank account and her own circle of friends – signs of separateness which she may give up on marriage.

The changing role of dancing in courtship also looks back to the way things used to be. Club culture restores to dancing its atavistic function. 'When we go to clubs, it tends to be all the girls,' Natalie told me, 'and all we want to do is just dance and have a good time. We don't talk to anyone else except the barman.' For the past hundred years or so, dancing has had a narrowly sexual purpose as a form of regulated physical contact between men and women who otherwise were rarely permitted to touch. But today, as in the more distant past and in other cultures, dancing isn't only a route to sexual pairing, it's also an end in itself. It's about a sense of oneness with the group which may or may not be enhanced by street drugs and is sometimes almost transcendent. 'There was such an intense, communal feeling of happiness, it was overwhelming. Everyone facing each other, smiling, singing, hands in the air.'[12]

The young couple who get into bed together but don't have intercourse are also reverting to an older pattern. In sixteenth- and seventeenth-century England and Wales, bundling or night-visiting was commonly practised by courting couples: this is what those folksongs in which men come tapping at women's windows are all about. The man would come to his sweetheart's window after her parents had gone to sleep and she might choose to let him in and invite him into her bed. Historian John Gillis writes, 'We know from accounts of bundling practice that a certain degree of fondling and kissing was permitted', but couples must have taken care for the woman not to get pregnant while they were still unsure about each other.[13] This situation, where two people who are attracted to one another share a bed in privacy but try to avoid pregnancy, implies a particular kind of sexual activity – orgasmic but not penetrative – a pattern that tends to suit women well.

And it's a distinct change in sexual etiquette today that a

woman's agreement to share a bed with a man doesn't essentially mean she's assenting to intercourse. This move makes sense: it's safer, protecting from infection as well as pregnancy, and it often means more pleasure for the woman. But in the absence of clear guidelines, it's also potentially problematic. In the 1960s and 1970s, there was a generally recognized code: if she went back to his place late at night, and certainly if she got into bed with him, she was saying yes to penetration. Where some of us, but not all, no longer act by that code, everything depends on clear communication, and on that communication being listened to; in particular, men have to understand that for women intercourse has a different meaning to other sexual acts, because of its attendant risks. A number of cases in which men have been prosecuted for rape and subsequently acquitted – the cases of David Warren and Ben Emerson, for instance – have hinged on this issue: surely if she shared his bed, undressed, massaged him, had orgasms, slept beside him, she was assenting to intercourse? No, not anymore. Articles critical of the women in cases like these are invariably written by female journalists now in their forties and fifties, who followed a very different code when they embarked on their own sexual lives.

Over the past ten years, there's also been something quite new in courtship customs for those in their teens and twenties, something that's never happened before. Today women are looking at men. Looking is the first move in a more egalitarian courtship sequence for women: before you ask you have to choose – and in order to choose you have to look. Most women in this age group may not be asking – but they're certainly looking.

Suddenly we're surrounded by images of beautiful men. Gorgeous male bodies are used to sell ice-cream and aftershave. The unreconstructed male has lost his appeal: it's no longer the essence of masculinity to smell of sweat and be covered in coal dust. Young men are dressing stylishly, growing their hair, even waxing their chests. Sex education videos like *The Lover's Guide* include scenes that show off the man's body as well as the woman's – and women sometimes confess to watching those aroused male bodies with the educational soundtrack turned down. And then, of course, there are always the Chippendales, and Adonis, and all the other sexy floor shows that women flock to see.

In some innovative publications today, this new female looking is taken one stage further and the male image is deliberately presented as part of a new courtship ritual. First there was the magazine *Alaska Men*, an attempt to get around the acute woman shortage in Alaska: women across America wrote in to pursue relationships with men they liked the look of. Sony Magazines' *Boyfriend Catalog*, which has photos of teenage boys from Tokyo and Osaka and details of their weight, height, hobbies and blood group (the Japanese equivalent of star sign) was first published in March 1995: all 170,000 copies sold. Here, *Marie-Claire*'s 'Man of the Month' featured one man at a time with a photo and a few details: women who wanted to go out with him wrote in, he chose one of them, and their evening together was described in the magazine. In September 1995, *Cosmopolitan* introduced their Eligible Men Service. 'Each month, we'll feature four single men, all looking for love.' The photos are grouped together on one page: to find out about the men's occupations, 'relationship history' and 'idea of relationship bliss', you have to turn over. A male way of going about things – with looking as primary – is structured into the way the men are presented; you've decided who you like the look of before you know anything about them. There's an air of not quite being serious, and sometimes a lot of laughter, about all these ventures: but they're unquestionably the first step in a new female courtship sequence.

As people get older, courtship becomes more secret. A majority of people over thirty are in long-term relationships, so much courtship over that age will be adulterous. When a friend starts to talk about 'needing something for me', 'searching for something', or even 'having a mid-life crisis', you know you are going to hear an adultery story. There is no knowing how many people have affairs. Research will probably underestimate the numbers involved, because some people are going to keep this secret part of their lives hidden even from sex researchers. A recent ICM survey found one in five people admitting to having an affair while in a steady relationship – and it seems reasonable to assume that this is a conservative estimate.[14]

In her book, *Adultery*, Annette Lawson writes, 'If the social institution of marriage is changing, adultery, as its underside – as another but hidden institution, deviant, like the Mafia, the rules of which are secret – must also change.'[15] And what of the courtships by which adultery is arranged? Do the sexual negotiations in these deviant relationships mirror those in socially approved relationships, or do they have their own rules?

There are ways in which adultery is formally different from the classic courtship story. The love-into-marriage narrative is linear: the courtship gradually intensifies, with more intimacy, more sex, more disclosure, and with marriage or cohabitation as its climax. But the adultery story has a different structure. Unless it leads to the break-up of the marriages and the lovers marry one another – in which case it reverts to the shape of classic courtship – the adulterous relationship has no momentum: it isn't 'going anywhere'. This is reflected in our fictions. David Lean's 1940s' film, *Brief Encounter*, and Harold Pinter's play, *Betrayal*, are two of the most wonderful adultery stories of the last half-century. Both start with the end of the affair, and *Betrayal* moves backwards in time throughout, so the moment of high drama at the end of the play is the beginning of the relationship – the disclosure of attraction.

There may also be differences in courtship behaviour where the intention is to form a secret relationship. There are some kinds of sexual strategy – playing games, blowing hot and cold, playing hard to get – in which we may create deliberate obstacles to heighten tension. It's plausible that there will be less of this behaviour when people have adultery in mind, given that obstacles are built into affairs – practical restrictions like separations, and psychological impediments like guilt and emotional conflict. So in some ways the courtships by which adulterous relationships are negotiated may be a little different. But research suggests that, in general, adultery is arranged much like any other form of sexual relationship. The rules about who initiates, who pays, who waits for the phone to ring, are much the same.

The high rate of adultery is part of a wider picture: for a host of reasons – including the availability of contraception, women's greater financial independence, and the fact that we live so long – our relationship structures are becoming increasingly fluid, with a new tendency toward serial monogamy. And because men tend to pair up with younger women, there is now a huge number of women in their forties and fifties who find themselves back on the dating scene. If they're looking for another lasting relationship, they may have a sense that time is running out. Geraldine, who is forty-five and just separated, said, 'My sister told me, "You'd better get a move on." My solicitor said just the same – and I know what they mean. I know I've got about four years – I'll keep my looks for four years . . .' Often women in Geraldine's situation find it hard to meet available men – or they may work with men they like but struggle to know how to transform a companionate relationship into a sexual one if the man isn't making any moves. These women, more than any others, are acutely aware of the advantages of making the moves themselves. They're also ideally placed to take the initiative because they're experienced enough to know they can survive rejection. But, even among this group, it's rare to meet women who ask men out.

COURTSHIP STORIES: What a man's still gotta do

Courtship is the narrative part of our sexual behaviour. With its clear goal and many potential impediments, it lends itself to story-telling. In a sense this book is about stories – the stories that shape our sexual interactions. Courtship stories are about what it means to be male or female, about money, about danger, about heroism, about guilt and punishment, about waiting around.

Our stories have a complicated relationship to the events of our lives and how we experience those events. They shape what we feel; they may also shape what we do. They are a rich source of morality and help us to make predictions about experience. But they can also be fallacious, because the very act of ordering our experience into a story necessarily involves simplifications and distortions.

There are different genres of courtship story. First, there are the stories we tell ourselves about what happens to us. Often these private stories concern our closeness to or deviation from the traditional scripts. Hannah says no to sex on a first date because she believes that if couples make love too soon the relationship is less likely to last. Here, she's using a story as a guide to her own behaviour. Gaby believes she lost a man she loved because she made herself too available: her story provides Gaby with an explanation for what went wrong, and also prescribes how she should behave in future.

Then there are private stories that enter the public world. These are invariably formulaic: personal experience is shaped into predictable patterns. Some radio shows invite people to write in with their own love stories. Classic FM for instance has 'Classic Romance, sponsored by Black Magic chocolates'. Here the climax to the narrative is invariably the couple's realization that they're in love – a realization that only comes after many weeks of looking into one another's eyes to the accompaniment of music from the popular classical repertoire: 'As we listened to "The Lark Ascending" in the beautiful setting at Kenwood we knew we were deeply in love . . .'.

On ITV's 'Blind Date', the public and private spheres are entangled in a thoroughly post-modernist way. Though these are real people having a real relationship, the viewers share in the narrative tension. We guess who'll be chosen, we're there at the moment of revelation, we speculate on what will happen – and we're there, too, when they come back and say how it all went, to see how the actual narrative matches up to our imagined one. The programme is set up on principles of scrupulous equality: a man chooses one of three women, and a woman one of three men. But when the couple return from their date, the real world breaks through the egalitarian veneer, and the carefully scripted innuendo of the earlier dialogue – 'If I were a beer and you pulled me, I'd certainly make your legs wobble' – is replaced by the clichés of our unequal courtship rituals – 'He respected me', 'I told him I had a stop button', or, from a man, 'I came away with nothing'.

And then there are the stories that are purely public and shared – our novels and films. These public stories reflect collective preoccupations – but they also shape those preoccupations. And our public stories tend to take the same line as many of the people I interviewed: they may question male initiative but in the end they always sanction it. The plot dénouements – like the things that people *do*, as opposed to what they *say* they do – reaffirm men in their traditional role.

Recently, some of our favourite films have explored male sexual initiative in the context of a renewed interest in the erotic and narrative possibilities of lengthy courtship. *Dangerous Liaisons*, *The Piano*, *Pretty Woman* and *Four Weddings and a Funeral* are all love stories that investigate the possibilities and limits of male sexual power. These films show where we are now – what is open to question and what is taken as read.

To make a story of courtship, it has to be protracted – and within the traditional script that will depend on the woman's continuing lack of compliance: she has to be difficult to woo. One way to achieve this is to set the story in the past. *Dangerous Liaisons* takes place in eighteenth-century France, where the grotesque physical displays of the period – the pushed-up breasts, powdered hair, hips in cages – mirror the artifice of the manners; both appearance and behaviour involve a fabulous exaggeration of notions of sexual difference. The plot centres on two seductions. The Marquise de Merteuil begs her friend the Vicomte to seduce and corrupt Cécile, the convent-educated innocent her former lover wants to marry; this is seduction as an act of revenge. The Vicomte then sets out to seduce a pious married woman – Michelle Pfeiffer as Madame de Tourvel, seething with delicately suppressed sexuality. The sadistic thrill comes from the clash between the male and female agendas; for the Vicomte, seduction is an elaborate game, but for the women who are the objects of his sexual interest, it's a deadly serious thing.

Jane Campion's film *The Piano* is also set in the past. Ada, the mute heroine, enters into a sexual bargain with George Baines, her taciturn neighbour: in order to buy her beloved piano back, she'll do just what he says. He tells her to take off her stockings, then her dress to reveal her marvellously authentic whalebone petticoat, then all her clothes. It's a formalization of a traditional courtship process that proceeds in stages dictated by the man, in which he gradually undresses and exposes her and learns her secrets; she's there to be revealed and it's his initiative that makes that happen. This is a film that strives for authenticity, not just in its relishing of the textures of the period – the lisle stockings with holes in, the greasy unwashed hair – but also in its recognition of the potential cruelty inherent in the gender roles of the time.

21

As with *Dangerous Liaisons*, the film's erotic charge comes from its sadism: it's the eroticism of male control. Once the bargain has been agreed, the man has all the power. The sadism is only tolerable because we know the outcome – that she'll come to desire him, too. A lot of women loved it.

Where protracted courtship has a contemporary setting, the goal of courtship can't simply be the sex. Today people make love too early in the process to allow space for much of a story. To make a narrative of it, the significance of making love has to be changed: there has to be a different consummation.

Pretty Woman gives the courtship theme a clever twist, restoring the kiss to its climactic place in the narrative. This is a Mills and Boon story from a decade or two ago: 'and then he kissed her . . .'. Julia Roberts is a hooker whom Richard Gere pays to spend a week with him. She's fallen for him; will he fall for her? As she's a prostitute they have lots of sex anyway, but kissing is defined as more intimate than sex – something she doesn't let her clients do. It's only when she lets him kiss her that their relationship changes and becomes something more than a business arrangement.

Four Weddings and a Funeral is also about a courtship that proceeds beyond sex. Superficially, the film might seem to challenge gender stereotypes. Charles is a type of the new hesitant masculinity, all fluttering self-deprecation, and his story is a female one – the story of a search for a spouse, while Carrie is quite sexually assertive. But it's his definition that matters: though they've made love twice, it's only when he asks her to have a relationship with him that the courtship is completed. It all looks quite fresh and contemporary – but it's really highly traditional. Men define what a relationship is about, men make the arrangements, and women are blameless whatever they do, so long as they remain indirect – however much pain they may cause by their failure to be clear about what they want. Carrie behaves very badly, and her sin is a failure of initiative: when her marriage breaks up, she doesn't get in touch with Charles, though she knows he adores her: she simply turns up at his wedding.

In each of these films, the end of the courtship process isn't sex but a re-definition. In *Pretty Woman* and *Four Weddings and a Funeral*, a private sexual arrangement becomes a publicly recognized love affair. In *The Piano* and *Dangerous Liaisons*, the courtship ends with the person who entered coldly into a sexual arrangement or contract falling in love. So the Vicomte, who seduced the virtuous Madame de Tourvel for the sheer pleasure of making her unvirtuous, falls in love with her, and in *The Piano*, Ada, as in all the best patriarchal fairytales, falls in love with her oppressor.

These films all supply intriguing glosses to the traditional narrative movement. Yet for all their variety, they only deviate within the conventional parameters. They explore different kinds of male sexual power: the cynical and sadistic power of the seducer, the financial power of the man who uses a prostitute, the erotically explicit control of the man who strikes a sexual bargain that allows him to make all the moves, and, in *Four Weddings*, the highly tentative and self-conscious instrumentality of Charles the New Man, who finds it such a struggle to do what a man's gotta do. In all these love stories, it's still the man who sets the terms of the bargain, makes the arrangements, defines, pursues, seduces. We're playing around with the script, we're self-conscious about it – but we aren't yet going beyond it.

The seeds of change are there – in public and in private. Our favourite public love stories – the films we all go to see – are questioning the traditional roles, yet they rarely transcend them. And when people talk about their own courtship behaviour, they emphasize their deviations from the classic script, as though hungry for things to be different. But mostly it's still men who make the initial moves.

Yet, of course, there *are* women who initiate and there always have been. Who are these women and what can we learn from them?

CHAPTER 2
WOMEN WHO DO

'When Gilgamesh had put on the crown, glorious Ishtar lifted her eyes, seeing the beauty of Gilgamesh. She said, "Come to me, Gilgamesh, and be my bridegroom; grant me seed of your body, let me be your bride and you shall be my husband . . ."'

(Epic of Gilgamesh, 3000 BC)

A WOMAN writes erotic letters to a man. In a sexual initiative rare even between the most intimate partners, she shares her highly transgressive fantasies.

She says her imagination runs riot. She hopes he has the same unusual dreams as her. Sometimes, she says, she scares herself with what she really wants. She finds his inner violence a turn-on. She wants to know all about him, to learn his inner secrets.

She urges him to greater and greater intimacies, to an exposure of the depths of his psyche, of the most secret parts of himself. She wants to feel overwhelmed by him, so she's completely in his power. She urges him to show less control. In fact, she says, she wouldn't be scared if he'd committed acts of extreme violence. The revelation that he has this potential is something she longs for. 'In certain ways,' she writes, 'I wish you had because it would make things easier for me . . . That's the kind of man I want . . . .'

The woman was the policewoman known as 'Lizzie James'. The man was Colin Stagg, who was under suspicion for the murder of Rachel Nickell on Wimbledon Common. The sexual letters were an elaborate entrapment technique devised by a forensic psychologist.[1]

'Lizzie James's' use of a sexuality that has been invented for her in an attempt to elicit a confession from a man suspected of a sex crime is an extreme example of a time-honoured use of female initiative, where women make the first move in order to get men to confess to crimes or to give up their secrets. Mata Hari, the Belgian spy executed by the Germans in the First World War, was perhaps the most celebrated exponent of the art. During the Cold War, both sides recruited women who specialized in seduction and blackmail. Today, in Russia, there are the 'swallows' – well-educated women fluent in foreign languages who are trained by the Russian security services to set honey-traps for foreign businessmen.[2]

This initiative has absolutely nothing to do with the woman's pleasure. She is initiating as part of her work, and for decidedly ulterior and covert motives.

These women make good fiction, because of the tension generated by our uncertainty about them. They are stock characters in thrillers and spy stories. They are sexually exciting and they always mean trouble. When, in John Grisham's *The Firm*, Mitch, the clever but naive lawyer, encounters a beautiful woman with a twisted ankle on a beach in the dark, a woman who unbuttons her blouse and tenderly pulls his hand towards her, we know there will be trouble ahead. Sure enough, someone is busily clicking away with a long-range lens. Eve Kendall, the blonde agent in Hitchcock's *North by Northwest*, only has to start making direct sexual suggestions to Roger Thornhill and we know she's up to no good – though in the end, like most of the fictional entrappers, she falls in love with the man she's seeking to ensnare: perhaps we couldn't quite tolerate the idea that this highly appealing woman might have ulterior motives for going through her seduction routine.

The last few years have seen the emergence of a new group of initiating women with secret motives for their seductions. According to a recent *Sunday Times* article, these women can be found hanging out in New York bars and cafés.

Sofia is dressing for work. She has 'shimmied into a figure-hugging, moss-green power suit that accentuates her peachy skin and has tucked her cleavage into a low-cut silk teddy.'[3] She goes into a bar, picks out a man, sits down beside him and crosses her legs seductively and starts chatting him up. He loves it and makes a date with her. What he doesn't know is that she is a decoy from the Check-a-Mate agency: his wife has paid $65 an hour to have a 'fidelity check' done on him.

This is women's work. Eighty per cent of the agency's clients are women checking up on their partners, so most of the decoys are female. Given that there's apparently only a one in ten chance that your man will resist a Sofia-style overture, that $65 could surely be better spent.

Unsurprisingly, given her choice of work, Sofia is deeply contemptuous of men. Her appearance speaks of seduction – but her talk is full of contempt and hatred. To her, men are 'scumbags'. The contrast between her appearance and behaviour – that seductively feminine persona – and her covert purposes and perceptions makes her deeply alarming.

Women like Sofia – who initiate to show men up in all their weakness, to take some act of delicious revenge, to punish men for some crime or misdemeanour, or just to have a good laugh at men's expense – have always been around in comic fictions. In *Twelfth Night*, the pompous steward Malvolio is the butt of a cruel joke. Maria, the serving-maid, writes him a love letter purporting to be from the beautiful Olivia and leaves it for him to find: he promptly appears in yellow cross-garters as specified in the letter and everyone falls about. And in the *Tales from the Thousand and One Nights*, there are a number of comic stories of women who make the first move.[4] Al-Haddar, the Barber's Second Brother, is seduced by a beautiful and wealthy young woman who plies him with wine, then takes off all her clothes. She urges him to undress, too, and to chase her through the house. She entices him into a darkened room where he falls through a trap door into the market of the leather merchants who laugh at him, beat him up and take him to the Governor of Baghdad to be publicly disgraced.

The women's strategies in these stories are predicated on beliefs about male sexual weakness. The men succumb to the women's overtures because they're such dupes: they're so easy to pull. The laugh is on men for their willingness to be persuaded that such marvellous dazzling women – so far out of their class – might actually want them. As Sofia says, 'Men think with the wrong head.'

ALTRUISTIC WOMEN: Kissing the frog

Another classic story-line concerns a female sexual initiative that is essentially altruistic. The motive here is perhaps too noble to be described as ulterior – but these women do have something in common with women who seduce for laughs or to show men up, in that their motives for making a move are hidden, and have nothing to do with their own pleasure. In these stories, women take sexual initiatives to save somebody.

One of the most widely found folk or fairytale themes is the 'animal groom', in which a woman is married to an animal or monster. Here a kiss or act of love initiated by a woman effects a magical metamorphosis. In 'Hans My Hedgehog', 'The Frog Prince' and 'Beauty and the Beast', the heroine kisses or shares her bed with some physically unprepossessing creature, often in response to a request from her father – perhaps in order to set her father free, or to fulfil a pledge made by him. She does it with a sense of repulsion but is pleasantly surprised how it all turns out: the frog becomes a prince and the beast beautiful.

Psychoanalyst Bruno Bettelheim reads a deeper meaning into these stories. For Bettelheim, the animal represents children's feelings about adult sexuality and adult genitals – the frog, which blows itself out when excited, is a particularly vivid symbol – and the transformation of frog, hedgehog or beast into prince is a metaphor for a psychosexual transformation that must be accomplished if sexual maturity is to be achieved. The story shows that, in order to enjoy sex, 'the female has to overcome her view of sex as loathsome and animal-like', so that what was once repellent becomes desirable.[5] In the story, the woman – usually a pubescent girl – initiates without any hope or expectation of pleasure, and has a delightful surprise. Here is one female initiative that has a happy ending – though it wasn't embarked on with that intent and the woman's motives are purely altruistic.

Feminist writer Robin Norwood, in her self-help book, *Women Who Love Too Much*, has a different take on these stories.[6] She sees them as terribly misleading lessons for women, with their implicit promise that women can save and reform unlovely men through the power of their sexual love. She suggests that whenever a woman says, 'I thought I could save him', she's been taken in by the patriarchal propaganda that urges us to love addicted or disturbed or needy men – that urges Beauty to 'stand by' the Beast. Intriguingly, the suspicion that there's some dreadful patriarchal kernel to these stories seems to be shared by today's canny little girls, who find stories like 'The Frog Prince' unacceptably wimpish and favour the Babette Cole version in which the princess's kiss works the other way round, and the unappealing prince that the princess doesn't want to marry is turned into a frog.

Here then is our first category of initiating women. These sexual initiatives are purposeful and direct, but the motive has nothing to do with the woman's own pleasure: she is doing her job, serving her country, setting her father free, exposing a man's weakness, saving someone, doing her bit for the

Russian industrial complex. And, except in the fairytale where her move breaks the spell that bound him or kept him beastly, the men who succumb to the women's advances come to regret it; they find themselves recruited as spies, in prison, blackmailed, rejected by their women, or made a laughing stock.

BAD WOMEN: Watering the tree of strife

Njal's Saga is a labyrinthine Icelandic epic that dates from the thirteenth century. It tells the story of Njal and Gunnar and Gunnar's wife, Hallgerd. As Hallgerd grows into womanhood, she becomes very lovely, with long legs and long silken hair that veils her body and, at first, only Hrut her uncle sees through her: 'The child is beautiful enough,' he says, 'and many will suffer for her beauty; but I cannot imagine how thief's eyes have come into our kin.'[7]

Hallgerd exemplifies a peculiarly female form of wickedness; she acts covertly, she's a stirrer. A whispered word from Hallgerd, and storehouses go up in flames, minor slights are brutally avenged, and men come home with their axes covered in blood. Her sexual power, that has men falling over themselves to do what she wants, is part of a wider pattern of wickedness: she 'waters the tree of strife'. The bad sexual woman goes back a long way.

Fairytales are a particularly rich source of bad sexual women. Feminist commentators on fairytales have noted that the powerful instigating women in the stories we know best are without exception wicked. In Perrault or Grimm, good women are passive, sometimes so passive they're fast asleep or comatose in glass coffins. The women who get things going are always bad.

For today's children, these vibrant and alarming presences are most vividly evoked by Disney films. Who are the truly terrifying characters in the Disney films we saw as children – and which today's children watch so avidly? Marina Warner comments that children find the masculine beasts in fairytales thrilling rather than scary – and certainly children above about three can be rather fond of the Beast in Disney's *Beauty and the Beast*, with his shaggy mane, lolloping gait and poignant air of self-pity. But the wicked women in Disney are something else. Some are directly based on fairytale, others are more recently invented but have fairytale resonances – and all of them send small children scuttling behind the sofa. In *The Sleeping Beauty* there's the Wicked Fairy, and in *101 Dalmatians* Cruella de Vil, who steals puppies to make into fur coats. *The Rescuers* has Medusa, who sends little Penny down a mine shaft in a bucket to hunt for a diamond. And in Disney's first film, *Snow White*, there's the Wicked Queen, whose baroque savagery makes her the most alarming of all Disney's creations.

These women are the very embodiment of that 'return to glamour' which fashion journalists periodically attempt to foist on the reluctant woman in the street. They dress as vamps. They wear black and red, the sexual colours. Cruella de Vil and Medusa have spiky heels and spaghetti-thin shoulder straps, and the medieval-style villainesses have blood-red lips and fingernails and far too much mascara. For these women, desirability is everything; their aim above all is to go on looking good. This is why they send little girls down mines to look for jewels, or demand that the hearts of pretty teenagers be brought to them in caskets, or trap loveable puppies to turn into fur coats, or put nubile princesses out of the competition for a hundred years. These projects derive their urgency from the fact that these women are ageing and can't bear it; they seek to hang on to their central role on the sexual stage at a time in the life-cycle when they should be handing over to a younger, more innocent generation. In seeking to present themselves as sexual women when they should be mothers, they go against the natural order. Their concern with appearance is also a sadistic agenda – in that the feelings, safety and even lives of others are sacrificed to the women's superficial pleasures.

One of the perennially puzzling questions about women who do take sexual initiatives for their own pleasure is why, in our books and films and stories, they are always always bad. Part of the answer may lie here, with Cruella de Vil or the Wicked Queen – in the fact that some of the wickedest sexual women are in stories for children.

The wickedness of the Disney villainesses is very specific. It's about being horrid to the weakest and most appealing creatures – small cuddly animals and the nicest little girls. It's about competing sexually with the Princess when you're old enough to be Queen Mother. It's the precise opposite of mothering. For the child, this absence of mothering behaviour is the very essence of female badness. And the story makes clear that it's the woman's sexuality that drives her to behave in this unnatural way. So from the child's viewpoint, there's a profound opposition between nurturant and sexual behaviour in his or her mother.

Freud devoted much attention to children's horror of the primal scene – the sight of their parents having intercourse. In *PsychoDarwinism*, Christopher Badcock puts forward a plausible sociobiological explanation for this.[8] He argues that the child doesn't want her parents to have sex because she doesn't want them to reproduce anymore. Another brother or sister takes something away from her: she wants to keep everything for herself – the breast milk, the food, the parental care. And because it's the mother who provides most of the nurturing, it's the mother's sexuality rather than the father's that is particularly problematic for the child. A father can spread his seed around without taking anything away from his own offspring – but a mother's sex drive inevitably pulls her away from her child.

Some feminist writers such as childbirth guru Sheila Kitz-inger have suggested that the absolute division between the maternal and the sexual in women's lives represents a triumph of patriarchal values.[9] According to this view, patriarchy has taught us to overlook the voluptuous beauty of the pregnant body, lied about the orgasmic delights of giving birth, and tried to deny the powerful sexuality of mothers. Motherhood and sexuality, runs the argument, don't have to be split and polarized as they are in our society.

This has never made sense to me. The conflict certainly isn't experienced by women themselves as something that's externally imposed: it's felt at a very deep level. When a woman is most wrapped up in her children – when those children are dependent babies – she tends to feel little interest in sex, and the rebirth of her libido as her children become less dependent always involves some distancing from her children. Perhaps she pushes them away a little, or perhaps she's just acknowledging their need for independence. Either way, she may experience this as a re-assertion of her own 'selfishness' and her children will probably see it that way too. This re-discovery of herself as a sexual being may also pull a woman away from her present family towards a new partner, with all the disruption for the child that such a move entails. No wonder children don't want their mothers to be sexual.

This opposition between mothering and sexual initiating is one of the fundamental principles of sexual behaviour in the natural world. There are some species in which courtship roles are reversed: the female initiates and the male responds.[10] And in all these cases where the female makes the first move in courtship, the male does most of the childcare: he guards the eggs and the young as well, as in some species of birds, or, like some fish, he carries the eggs with him, brooding them in the mouth. Sea-horses reverse roles in a startlingly complete way. The female has a sort of penis, a 'prehensile ovipositor', which she uses to inject eggs into the male's body where they develop: and the female sea-horse actively courts the male. In the 1920s, a biologist observed a courtship in the *Crypturellus variegatus*, a species of bird in which the male alone incubates the egg and raises the young. He wrote that when the two sexes saw one another, the female 'gave utterance to a veritable ecstasy of calling' – while the male gave only 'a restrained, philosophical exhibition of emotion'.[11]

This broad pattern can also be traced out in human courtship. Just as, in the natural world, female animals which don't rear the young are more likely to initiate so, too, in human society, it is those women who aren't looking to bear and rear children as a result of the courtship who are most likely to make the first move.

Maybe the badness of female sexual initiators seems so natural because it hooks into a genuine conflict in the female psyche. Maybe the fairytale villainesses hint at dilemmas that are built into the female sexual life-cycle.

BAD WOMEN TODAY: Get down to business

But this notion of a perennial conflict between our sexuality and our feelings for our children – and specifically between sexual initiating and mothering behaviour – is only part of the story. There must also be something peculiar to our own time about the appeal of wicked female initiators for, recently, in our most popular public fictions, there's been a positive efflorescence of wicked women who make the first move. The bad sexual woman whose story goes back to Sumer is still doing her stuff down at the multiplex – being a bitch, wickedly scheming, having great sex and, in the end, getting her just deserts. The tremendous commercial success of the films in which these women feature suggests they have something special to say to us today.

In stories for children, the sexual initiative-taking of the bad woman can only be hinted at. In films for adults, we're left in no doubt as to what she does.

Meredith Johnson in *Disclosure* attempts to seduce Tom Sanders in her office. She grabs him when he's making a phone call, snatches the phone away and presses herself against him. 'Get down to business,' she says. In *Presumed Innocent*, Carolyn Polhemus pulls Rusty Sabich by his tie into a dark office: 'You're going to be so good,' she says as she meaningfully removes her earrings. In *The Last Seduction*, Brigit sticks her hand down the trousers of the man she's just met in a bar. When she first meets Nick, Catherine Tremell in *Basic Instinct* says, 'Have you ever fucked on cocaine, Nick? It's nice . . .': she also famously flashes her pubic hair at a group of policemen – which is about as direct as an indirect initiative can get. Alex in *Fatal Attraction* doesn't make the first move: she is asked to dinner by Dan. But she does signal her interest in an affair by saying, 'I can be very discreet'. And then, when he doesn't ring after their weekend together, she takes a whole range of follow-up initiatives that might be more typical of men – she rings him at work, rings him at home, buys opera tickets, turns up at his office. Later her initiatives become still less conventional.

These women have all entered the public world on their own terms. They power-dress, they carry briefcases, they understand financial markets and make lots of money. They are also all bad. It isn't just a question of breaking a few rules and wearing fuck-me shoes. These aren't just Gutsy Girls who Get Ahead. They are seriously wicked. Catherine Tremell is a serial murderess. Carolyn Polhemus takes bribes, and loses interest in Rusty when she finds he's less ambitious than she'd like. When Meredith Johnson's attempt to have sex with Tom backfires, she takes out a sexual harassment suit against him, and the attempt at seduction turns out to have an ulterior motive – to frame him and have him fired for a mistake she'd made. Alex abducts Dan's child, has a close affinity with Cruella de Vil in her propensity for doing horrible things to cuddly animals – the emotional climax of the film is her boiling of the pet rabbit – and turns up in Dan's bathroom with a carving knife. And Brigit, by far the most stylish of the bunch, makes off with the money from her husband's drug deal, kills off a few philandering partners along the way, and then – in a neat inversion of notions of women's vulnerability to male violence – murders her husband with her Mace spray.

The role sex plays in these stories is the mirror image of its role in the traditional woman's romance. In Mills and Boon, the heroine doesn't always enjoy sex – she may well have her first orgasm in bed with the hero – but her whole life is about love, and love is the motor and climax of the plot. In the bad woman stories, it's the other way round: the women enjoy sex effortlessly – they certainly don't need hours of delicate fingerwork – but it isn't the main event. Catherine Tremell may be 'the fuck of the century', but what really turns her on is writing books and sticking ice-picks into people. Often a sexual encounter is about something else, a means to an end – as it was for the women with ulterior motives at the start of this chapter. Through sex, the women in these films further their career ambitions, get material for their next book, or find someone to take the rap for their crimes. They are *using* the men.

When these stories are aimed at women, they're funny. We laugh – and we want her to win. The story taps into that part of every woman that makes her grin when she says 'Lorena Bobbitt'. *The Last Seduction* is a woman's film. And we identify with Brigit: we long to smoke with her kind of style, to speak with that husky rasp, to be so coolly unburdened by conscience. And Brigit gets away with it triumphantly in the end: the final shot in the film shows her reclining in her stretch limo as she languidly burns the last piece of evidence incriminating her.

But when the story is aimed at men, it is horror, and the woman is punished. *Fatal Attraction* is a male fantasy – and here the initiating woman meets a bloody death.

These stories are powerful: they shape our thinking. *Fatal Attraction*, in particular, has been a stunningly successful piece of modern myth-making. It's as fantastic as *101 Dalmatians* – but people talk about it as though it were real. Sara told me, 'Quite honestly I think women who ask men out are punished. It's like *Fatal Attraction* – I think that's what happens.' Geoff said, 'If you have an affair, you need to be sure you can trust the girl – you don't want to end up like *Fatal Attraction*'. Sara and Geoff don't question the film's veracity; Alex seems plausible to them. As Adrian Lyne, the film's director, apparently remarked, 'Everybody knows a girl like Alex.'[12]

The notion that Alexes are everywhere involves two distortions of thinking – an over-reaction to women's new assertiveness, and an over-valuation of sexuality as the key to personality.

There's often a ludicrous over-reaction to small gains for women. As Susan Brownmiller comments, '"The women are taking over" is a refrain many working women hear from their male colleagues – after one or two women are promoted at their company, but while top management is still solidly male. In newsrooms, white male reporters routinely complain that only women and minorities can get jobs – often at publications where women's and minorities' numbers are actually shrinking . . .'[13] So, too, the fact that women are asserting themselves a bit more sexually gives rise to fantasies that the world is full of glossy and alarming women who help themselves to the sex they want without regard for the destructive consequences.

In every system of oppression, what is kept down is fantasized about and feared. Studies of colonization have looked at the way the qualities of the oppressed group or race, especially their sexuality and aggression, are exaggerated and then feared: hence, for instance, notions about the super-potency of black men. So, in the fantasies that underlie these films,

the kind of sexual initiative that women might be taking –
asking for the touches they want, perhaps – becomes a shocking or destructive sexual assertion: Meredith sexually harassing Tom, Brigit putting her hand down a man's trousers in a
public place.

The second distortion that drives these fantasies is the over-
valuation of sexual behaviour as a true litmus test of personality – especially for women. In the films, the women's sexual
behaviour is part of a gestalt. Their assertiveness in bed is
one manifestation of their assertiveness in every area of their
lives. The woman who makes the first move in her sexual
relationships puts herself first in other areas too, and the
woman who disregards the traditional sexual script is deficient
in other traditional female qualities. Like Hallgerd in the old
Icelandic saga with her 'thief's eyes', she takes things that
rightfully belong to others.

Sex is sometimes seen as the key to personality for men as
well. Hence the demands for the resignations of adulterous
politicians: if they cheat on their wives, runs the argument,
they surely can't be trusted to govern the country well. But
it's also recognized that for men sex isn't the whole story.
Oskar Schindler, for instance, is venerated as one of the great
altruists of the twentieth century, for the hundreds of lives
he saved during the Holocaust. He treated women badly: he
was openly unfaithful to his wife, seduced his secretaries, and
doubtless created a lot of misery all round. He fascinates us
as a flawed human being who was also capable of startling
love and courage.

But a woman's sexuality is never seen as a thing apart. It's
impossible to imagine a female Oskar Schindler – a woman
who was thoughtless and promiscuous in her sexual life, but
also revered for doing great good.

The bad woman script takes it as axiomatic that a woman's
sexual assertiveness is part of a wider assertiveness or even
aggressiveness in her psychological make-up. But this is a

distortion. A woman's courtship behaviour doesn't essentially correlate with the rest of her personality. When I talked to women about their courtship styles, I simply didn't find that the more assertive women were more likely to ask men out.

Certainly there may be connections between a woman's willingness to take direct initiatives and other aspects of her *sexuality*. Among the women I talked to, the few women who sometimes made the first move tended to be good at asking for what they wanted in bed, turned on by visual sexual imagery, and attracted to younger, less affluent, less powerful men. And women with a very indirect style at the start of courtship tended to be attracted to powerful or older men, to be turned on by masochistic fantasies and to find it hard to ask for what they wanted in bed. Indirect women were also more likely than women who sometimes made the first move to have had sex forced on them at some time.

But there were no consistencies at all with the women's behaviour at work or in other parts of their lives – no connections between how they'd rate on sexual assertiveness and the rest of their personality and functioning. I met women with high-status careers and an air of great self-assurance who had the most reticent and evasive courtship styles – and quiet women with conventional views and unremarkable jobs who were married to men they'd asked out.

Female sexual initiatives are not part of a gestalt – and the fact that a woman makes the first move doesn't reveal anything about other aspects of her personality. And it certainly doesn't mean she is more likely to assert herself to accomplish evil ends.

The bad sexual woman may be great entertainment – but there's no psychological truth in her. Adrian Lyne is wrong. None of us knows any girls like Alex.

BEAUTIFUL PREDATORS: She took me to her faery grot

There is a sub-class of bad sexual women who are scarcely women at all – women who, in a more profound way than Sofia the man-trapper or 'Lizzie James', are not what they seem.

These women are exquisite. They are quintessentially feminine, scarcely made of solid flesh, almost translucent, with the perfect facial features of beautiful children – yet the enchanting surface is pure illusion.

The romantic poets – Keats, for instance – adored the beautiful predator.

> *I met a Lady in the meads*
> *Full beautiful, a faery's child,*
> *Her hair was long, her foot was light,*
> *And her eyes were wild.*
> *She took me to her faery grot*
> *And there she wept and sighed full sore . . .* [14]

She takes the initiative; she takes him back to her place. There she weeps and sighs, moving the man with some hint of sorrow beyond words – but it's all just part of her seduction technique. She leaves him spent and desolate, enslaved or vampirized amid a barren landscape – 'The sedge is withered from the lake.'

Lady Arabella March in Bram Stoker's psychotic last novel, *The Lair of the White Worm*, is another beautiful predator. [15] In Ken Russell's film version, luscious Amanda Donohoe entices a marvelling young man back to her house, where she strips to her black suspenders, grows a splendid set of fangs and kills him with a venomous bite. Bob Dylan also seems to know about these women and their beauty, their initiatives and their supernatural erasures and thefts: his

Melinda 'invites you up into her room' – but then she 'takes your voice and leaves you howling at the moon'.

One of the most delectable predators can be found in Angela Carter's short story, 'The Lady in the House of Love'. Some of Keats's themes re-surface in Carter's thoroughly camp post-modernist telling. This Lady hides her lust for blood behind an air of exquisite vulnerability. She is so delicate she is almost transparent, her hair 'falls down as straight as if it were soaking wet', she has 'the fragility of the skeleton of a moth', her nails and teeth are 'as fine and white as spikes of spun sugar . . .', and she seems weighed down with some hidden sorrow: 'A certain desolate stillness of her eyes indicates that she is inconsolable . . . When she takes them by the hand and leads them to her bedroom, they can scarcely believe their luck.'[16] Later the unvampirized parts are buried under her roses, which grow obscenely lush. She is saved from her undead torment by a man on a bicycle who, totally oblivious to all the clues, sees only a nice girl who needs looking after, and undoes the enchantment by sucking the blood from a cut on her hand.

The predator has feminine qualities to excess – she is almost too beautiful, too fragile, too difficult to console. The one thing that doesn't fit is her taking of initiatives. The men should have suspected: why would so lovely a creature need to make the moves? She takes him back to her place, she invites him into her bed – but the consummation is not at all what he had in mind.

These stories hint at archetypal fears about women's sexual attractiveness. Evolutionary psychologists have argued that the biological purpose of female beauty is to publicize good genes and good health and so to suggest that this woman is a good reproductive bet; apparently, for instance, symmetry of feature, which is one of our criteria of beauty, is only found in an organism that has been well-nourished while developing.[17] If this is what female beauty is for, then the male fear must be that this is all illusion. (As indeed it often is – given women's struggles to re-make themselves with all the money and skill at their disposal.) So in Keats's poem the landscape is barren and withered; for all those signifiers of health and youth – the woman's childlikeness and loveliness – there is no fertility here.

In these stories, essential feminine qualities are subverted. The female fragility which evolutionary psychologists suggest appeals to men because it suggests youth and implies that the woman is not carrying another man's child is in fact a hint that all is not well: here, she is so thin because her unnatural appetites need appeasing. And the nameless sorrow with which she moves the man, stressing her vulnerability, allowing him to take on the role of protector – as strong women still do around men they desire – is just one of her courtship ploys.

The very imagery of vampirism itself – or of the Knight left 'so haggard and so woebegone' – suggests the capacity of female beauty to drain the male body. Camille Paglia writes of the temporary impotence that follows desire and its consummation, 'That women can drain and paralyze is part of the latent vampirism in female physiology.'[18] And on the psychological level, this imagery of greedy women who drink the man's lifeblood perhaps hints at the male fear that women want just that little bit more than men are willing to give.

Among the romantic poets Coleridge, in particular, seems to have been preoccupied with women's capacity to 'drain and paralyze'. In his notebooks he describes dreams in which he was pursued by ghastly female figures who attempted to mutilate or abuse him.

. . . was followed up and down by a frightful pale woman, who, I thought, wanted to kiss me, and had the property of giving me a shameful Disease by breathing in the face.
. . . the most frightful Dream of a Woman whose features were blended with darkness catching hold of my right eye and attempting to pull it out.[19]

Coleridge's dreams of 'frightful' women are reminiscent of delusions sometimes experienced by men suffering from psychotic illness, when feelings of arousal are associated with the delusional presence of a woman – and the man's response is felt as something dragged out of him, as an assault. The fantasy of the succubus, the medieval female demon who arouses men in the night against their will, probably had its origins in such delusions.

The purest expression of these fears of unnatural initiating women in Coleridge's work can be found in his unfinished poem, 'Christabel', which Camille Paglia describes as 'blatant lesbian pornography'.[20]

Geraldine is a beautiful witch or vampire, dressed in white silk, 'surpassingly fair' – the original lipstick lesbian, perhaps. She's literally glamorous (glamour means magic or spell), and Christabel, the sweet and guileless heroine of the poem, is completely taken in by her enchanting surface. Christabel finds Geraldine moaning in the moonlight outside her castle, invites her in, and unwisely lets her share her bed. Geraldine undresses – revealing an unspecified witch-like deformity – 'a sight to dream of, not to tell . . .' and some vague and terrible sexual assault takes place.

Like the other voluptuous predators, Geraldine has a sob story – in her case, a tale of gang rape:

> *Five warriors seized me yestermorn,*
> *Me, even me, a maid forlorn,*
> *They choked my cries with force and fright,*
> *And tied me on a palfrey white.*

But as with everything else about her, this is a fabrication: Geraldine herself is the rapist.

Geraldine has certain masculine qualities which are underlined for the reader of the poem and which are clues to her unnatural purposes, but which innocent Christabel doesn't recognize. She looks rather than being looked at – always a cross-sex sign; she has a penetrating gaze – 'her large fair eye 'gan glitter bright'; but sometimes her eyes shrink as small as a snake's. And she is in total control: she tells Christabel to undress and get into bed, pretends to pray, then gets in too and pulls her to her.

> *O Geraldine! one hour was thine*
> *Thou'st had thy will!*

It's always men who 'have their will' of women: this is a way of describing sex that belongs exclusively to male experience.

The voluptuous predator connects with both the bad sexual woman and the man-trapper. Like Alex and Brigit, she is wicked. Like Mata Hari and Sofia the decoy, she has ulterior motives, sometimes of the most extreme kind: she wants blood. Above all, she is not what she seems. Her unfeminine sexual initiatives point to her unnaturalness. But the object of her sexual attentions, dazed by her loveliness, is blind to all the clues.

LIBERTINE WHORES: Those scandalous stages of my life

> 'My maiden name was Frances Hill. I was born at a small
> village near Liverpool in Lancashire, of parents extremely poor
> and, I piously believe, extremely honest . . .'[21]

These words, from the first page of John Cleland's *Memoirs of a Woman of Pleasure* of 1748, inaugurated a new literary genre all about women who initiate and enjoy it. John Cleland's two-volume story was a blockbuster of its time. This first prostitute confession was followed by a host of others, especially in France. Today's pornography has its origins here. 'Pornography' actually means 'the writing of prostitutes'.

In these books, the heroine briefly describes her childhood and adolescence, then comes to her main subject matter, her training and progress as a prostitute, depicted in a series of sexual encounters which are always graphically described, and in the case of *Fanny Hill*, highly colourful: John Cleland invariably describes genitals as roseate, rubied or vermilion. Unlike earlier English prostitute biographies, such as Hogarth's *A Harlot's Progress*, which ended in misery and death, the story ends happily with the prostitute's worldly success and contented retirement.

The heroine of these stories is always sensible, clever and sensuous. She makes a lot of money. In the French versions, she's often a proponent of the anti-religious philosophy of the time. And she loves her work.

She is, of course, entirely a male creation. The first-person narrative is a confidence trick; it creates the illusion of a female subjectivity that is entirely absent. Though the woman appears to be speaking for herself, she tells us nothing about female sexuality. The use of the first person is an erotic device; as writer Lynn Hunt puts it, 'The reader is provided with the vicarious pleasure of an encounter – be it only textual – with a prostitute.'[22] Her sexual initiatives are contained within the male imagination: they express male desires. This is what makes her initiatives so very acceptable.

The ultimate libertine whore was created by the Marquis de Sade. Juliette is the heroine of his pornographic novel of 1792, *Juliette ou les Prosperités de la Vice*, the companion volume to his *Justine ou les Malheurs de la Vertu*. Juliette and Justine are sisters and polar opposites. Juliette is the archetypal whore, Justine the perfect virtuous courtesan. Juliette enjoys sex, Justine is abused. Juliette is knowing, Justine is innocent and guileless, her innocence a constant incitement to the sadism of others. Juliette is brunette, Justine is blonde: Angela Carter has Juliette as the original bold brunette – like Barbara Stanwyck or Joan Crawford, and Justine as one of the many put-upon blondes down to Monroe, whose 'dazzling fair skins are of such a delicate texture that they look as if they will bruise at a touch, carrying the exciting stigmata of sexual violence for a long time'.[23] Juliette makes lots of money, Justine has to plead to be given shelter – invariably with dire consequences. And Juliette *initiates*; she is the subject of her sexual encounters: while Justine is passive, used, done-to. Even among prostitutes, it seems, there are madonnas and whores.

Juliette the sexual initiator has some of the qualities of Fanny Hill or her French counterparts in books like *Margot la Ravaudeuse*: she's affluent, clever, materialistic and knowing. But unlike Fanny she is also very wicked. She seduces her father, is impregnated by him, murders him and subsequently aborts his child. She enjoys orgies in churches, poisoning, robbery, murder, castration, necrophilia. As Camille Paglia warns – don't read de Sade before lunch.

Juliette is the most striking and influential example, but there are many other initiating women in de Sade's stories. Madame de Clairvil, the Princess Borghese, Catherine the Great of Russia and Charlotte of Naples all have something in common with the bad sexual woman: they lack maternal qualities, their goals are money and power, they enjoy sex but it isn't an end in itself. Yet these fabulous female initiators go way beyond the bad-woman script. With their cruelty, vast sexual appetites and schemes for world domination, they have a close affinity with the ogresses in the roughly contemporaneous French fairytale tradition – like the prince's mother in Perrault's version of 'The Sleeping Beauty', who was 'of the ogre race' and liked eating the fresh meat of little children[24].

The female initiators in de Sade's pantheon are also literally phallic, in that they have masculinized physical attributes and like to reverse roles. They have obstructed vaginas, or enlarged clitorises: they use dildos and are enthusiastic about buggery – which was a capital crime in France at the time. In the phantasmagorical world that de Sade's characters inhabit, metaphor becomes reality. Here, the idea that the woman who takes sexual initiatives must have some male attributes is given concrete expression, in that she penetrates.

In reality, women rarely penetrate for pleasure: the dildo-wielding lesbian is a myth. But there is one group of women who regularly penetrate with objects – women who abuse children.[25] Such abuse involves the expression of cruel or violent impulses, and this equation of female penetration with cruelty is apt, because this is what most interests de Sade about sex – the way it can be used to control, exploit and dominate. De Sade seems to have little interest in gender, in the relationships between men and women: what really fascinates him is the relationship between master and slave.

Pornography today has lots of initiating women. Juliette is the prototype of one kind of pornographic heroine – though since de Sade's time she's been very much watered down – just as her sister Juliette is the prototype of the 'heroine' or victim of the masochistic scenario.

But all this female initiating is contained in structures that are by and for men: men pay, men say what they want, men write the stories. Or if women write the stories it's to please their men – like 'Pauline Reage' who wrote *The Story of O* for her lover, or Anaïs Nin who wrote purely for money for an anonymous collector of erotica, and whose erotic style was by her own admission 'derived from a reading of men's works'.[26]

Pornography is one context in which even extreme female initiatives meet with a lot of male approval – because the larger arena is male pleasure. It's interesting to reflect that today's pornography originates with a male fantasy about prostitution – a fantasy about women who obey male desires, however extreme, to the letter, and in so doing experience pleasure. No wonder women find pornography so problematic. We're cut off from it at source. For, whatever the fantasy, prostitution in reality has absolutely nothing to do with a woman's own sexual self-expression. The prostitute is yet another female initiator who isn't doing it for her own pleasure.

FAT FUNNY WOMEN: Come up sometime and see me

In the most celebrated come-on in cinematic history, Mae West, well past forty, all huge round shoulders, cleavage and diamonds, approaches a young and impassive Cary Grant, whom she believes to be a Salvation Army officer. 'I always did like a man in a uniform, and that one fits you grand. Why don't you come up sometime and see me? I'm home every evening.'

Mae West does all the male things. She looks with lust, she expresses approval of what she sees, she makes the arrangements. She defines what happens; she even does it in a typically male form of humour – in the celebrated one-liners that she wrote herself and that invariably express sexual appetite: 'It's better to be looked over than to be overlooked', or 'When I'm good I'm very very good, but when I'm bad I'm better.'

Angela Carter has suggested that Mae West's sexuality could only be tolerated on the screen because she didn't become a star until she'd reached virtually menopausal age. 'This allowed her some of the anarchic freedom of the female impersonator, pantomime dame, who is licensed to make sexual innuendos because his masculinity renders them a form of male aggression upon the woman he impersonates . . . She made of her own predatoriness a joke that concealed its power, while simultaneously exploiting it.'[27]

Mae West is larger than life. And her successors today are the fat funny women like Dawn French, Jo Brand and Vanessa Feltz, who also make a joke of their libidinousness while simultaneously exploiting it. Dawn French tells us that fat is sexy; Jo Brand jokes about tampons and oral sex; Vanessa Felz writes salacious articles for *She*, and a tape of her writings is called *What are these strawberries doing on my nipples?* All three project a public persona that is explicitly about sexual appetite.

Why should big women, at least in their public and comic personas, be free to express sexual interest directly? There's the obvious equation between appetite for food and appetite for sex – but are there deeper or more subtle explanations?

Fat has certain culture-specific qualities. Today we see female fat as unappealing, but in this we're quite different from most other cultures. In some African societies, women are fattened up for marriage. In the Finnish saga, *The Kalevala*, a girl is urged by her mother to eat up to make herself beautiful:

> *One year eat melted butter:*
> *you'll grow plumper than others;*
> *the next year eat pork:*
> *you'll grow sleeker than others;*
> *a third year eat cream pancakes:*
> *you'll grow fairer than others* . . . .[28]

Fat women are, in fact, physiologically more feminine than thin women, because they have higher levels of female hormones. But paradoxically, because of the public preference for thin women, we see fat as a denial of certain female qualities. Femininity is about reducing yourself; fat is about substance and taking up space, about a kind of power – which may be seen as male. And to be fat is to have permission to do masculine things. Conventional beauty imposes restrictions and implies a behaviour code: girls learn this at adolescence – drop your eyes, keep your knees together, don't be too available. But fat may confer the kind of licence that post-menopausal women have in some societies – like Bali, where Margaret Mead found that women of child-bearing age were expected to behave modestly, but older women could use obscene language as freely as any man.[29]

A need for initiative also results from the common perception of fat women as unattractive. More men are turned on
by female fat than would publicly own up to it, given fat's
extreme unfashionability. But that is never acknowledged,
and in their public personas these women aren't there to be
looked at. They have to express their sexuality through what
they do – or what they say they do – rather than through
what they look like. They have to bypass the normal mechan-
isms. Fat puts you outside the sexual game. The fat woman
can't wait for the man to come on to her; she has to go and
get what she wants for herself.

The fat funny woman is quite different from the women
we've considered so far – the women with ulterior motives;
the bad women, the predators, the prostitutes. The fat funny
woman has her own sexual pleasure – and that alone – in
mind. She introduces another principle of female initiating.

Imagine the most orthodox paradigm of a sexual relationship. A heterosexual couple: she's young and pretty; he's a
little older, taller, richer and higher status than her; they're
entering into a sexual relationship with a view to marriage
and reproduction. That's the stereotype. And the further we
move away from that stereotypical coupling, the more likely
we are to find female initiatives. The fat woman doesn't fit
the stereotype because of her unconventional appearance.
And whenever women are unconventional in other ways –
perhaps in their ages, perhaps in their sexual objectives –
they also become more likely to make the first move.

OLDER WOMEN: Here's to you, Mrs Robinson

The Graduate was made in 1967. It tells the story of the
seduction of naive Benjamin by his family's forty-year-old
neighbour, Mrs Robinson. The affair comes to an end when
Benjamin falls in love with Mrs Robinson's daughter, Elaine.

Mrs Robinson takes every initiative. She makes the suggestions, touches first, sends him off to book the hotel room, takes off her own clothes. In other ways, too, she behaves like a stereotypical man: she's the one who just wants sex and doesn't want to talk.

The gender dynamics of the film haven't worn nearly as well as the Simon and Garfunkel soundtrack. Today, in a social climate in which women consider themselves attractive well into their forties and fifties, we like Mrs Robinson a great deal more than once we did. Her brittle sexuality fascinates, and there's something sad about her transformation from feisty seducer into vindictive old hag. By contrast, Benjamin's relationship with Elaine seems pallid and asexual, though we're clearly meant to approve of it.

But even though it all looks very different from the way it looked when it was made, *The Graduate* remains an intriguing film. In spite of the two decades of sexual liberation that have elapsed since it first came out, it's still one of the most striking examples of female sexual initiating on celluloid. Compared to Mrs Robinson, Alex in *Fatal Attraction* is quite the Girl Guide – at least until she starts going crazy.

Here is another kind of woman who initiates – in our stories, and in reality: the woman who initiates sex with a much younger man. This pairing is another illustration of the principle that women are more likely to make the first move in unconventional relationships. Usually she does it to please the man. One model is the golden-hearted whore who gives a young man his first sexual experience: like the woman with armpits that smell of smoke who seduces José Arcadio in *One Hundred Years of Solitude*: 'She had lost the strength of her thighs, the firmness of her breasts, her habit of tenderness, but she kept the madness of her heart intact.'[30] Mrs Robinson, though, isn't in the least like this. What was once shocking and is now interesting about her is that her motives aren't remotely pedagogic. She does it all for her own pleasure.

Because of this clash between the two versions of the

seductive older woman – the warm altruistic sexual teacher, and the hard self-seeking aging seductress – when we come across cases of women having sex with boys, we don't know what to think. Child protection workers struggle to know how to respond to accounts of sexual contact between older women and under-age boys. Such cases give rise to heated debate. What frame of reference to use? Is it abuse – or love and mutual pleasure?

A male social worker told me, 'This lad was about thirteen, and the woman was around thirty. There was a lot of hinting and denying but nothing that amounted to a disclosure – but it was clear as daylight what was going on. My colleague was keen to see it as abuse – and was arguing by analogy that you should treat it as though it was a man with a thirteen-year-old girl. I felt intellectually that the argument had some force, but I couldn't get worked up about it. There was no issue that he was being coerced into it. There was a very inconclusive child protection conference and it was registered as "grave concern" rather than abuse.' But the older man who has sex with an under-age girl will always be seen as an abuser.

From time to time, cases of female teachers having sex with pupils hit the headlines. There's confusion in our reaction to these news stories. We don't know how to judge what has happened.

Jane Watts at forty-two had sex with a thirteen-year-old pupil whom she'd first met when she was his teacher at primary school. The newspaper reports when the case came to court in 1994 used a language of relationship: she 'seduced' him.[31] They'd have used a quite different language if it had been a forty-two-year-old male teacher and a thirteen-year-old girl.

Tina, one of the women I interviewed, had a story like this to tell. As a young teacher, she'd been strongly attracted to a sixteen-year-old boy in her class. 'I wormed and wheedled and went out of my way to be near him and with him,' she said, 'and I asked him out and I took him out. He was desperately shy. I finally got him out, I thought, God, I've put this boy in a situation that he doesn't really want to be in for the time being – so I kind of left it – there was no need to be in contact because I was causing the contact – and then I used to get messages from his sister saying, "Oh, Kyle said, give him a ring for a game of tennis if you ever feel like it." But I never did – I moved on to someone else and the excitement had faded into the past.'

Is she a loving teacher or a scheming seductress? She doesn't know what to think of herself. She's in love and wants to be with him: she worries he'll feel abused. Kyle, too, is ambivalent. He seems shy and out of his depth. But then he sends messages hinting he might still be interested.

This theme of older women initiating with younger men will crop up again and again in this book. In our stories, older women do sometimes seduce younger men – but not very often because as a culture we don't have much interest in older women as subjects of fiction. In the real world, though, being older than the man she wants is the kind of unconventionality that most frequently encourages a woman to make the first move.

Tina decided not to pursue the relationship with Kyle, but is now living with a man twelve years younger than her, a relationship she initiated.

LITTLE GIRLS: I got sommat to show you

One of the most delectable female initiators is a little girl. 'She was yellow and dusty with buttercups and seemed to be purring in the gloom; her hair was as rich as a wild bee's nest and her eyes were full of stings . . .'[32] This is Rosie Burdock, who gives her name to Laurie Lee's autobiography *Cider with Rosie*, first published in 1959, and celebrated for its explicitness about childhood sexuality.

Rosie is a girl around puberty, her age unspecified – ten or eleven, perhaps, to the narrator's thirteen. In this encounter, he has the female role. She's the one who plots and plans, asks, persists, tells him how he feels, makes it happen; he's the one who says no when he means yes, acquiesces in her schemes, is swept away, has a sexual awakening.

> 'I got sommat to show you.'
> 'You push off,' I said.
> I felt dry and dripping, icy hot. Her eyes glinted, and I stood rooted.
> 'You thirsty?' she said.
> 'I ain't, so there.'
> 'You be,' she said. 'C'mon.'

She takes him to the secret place she's found under the waggon, gets him drunk on cider, and makes her move. 'Then Rosie, with a remorseless strength, pulled me down from my tottering perch, pulled me down, down into her wide green smile and the deep subaqueous grass.'[33]

Many of us have vivid memories of childhood sex play with other children of our own age. Perhaps we undressed and looked, or shared a self-stimulation technique involving blankets or rope-climbing we'd just discovered, or played Doctors and Nurses, or did 'what grown ups do'. Sometimes there was a sexual thrill, sometimes it was purely play – and it wasn't abusive, because there was no bullying or power imbalance. And girls suggest and start off these activities just as often as boys; girls also think up sexual games, explore, express curiosity, look and show.

This kind of initiating female behaviour fades at puberty – or perhaps becomes channelled into transient lesbian expression, in that mutual caressing of breasts with a best friend that many women who now feel thoroughly heterosexual recall from adolescence. Rosie probably wouldn't have made such audacious moves with a lad she fancied a year or two later. With sexual maturity, the adult rules about male/ female relationships assert themselves and, while they're learning how they're expected to behave, girls tend to be especially traditional – hence the rigidity of the double standard for girls in their early teens. Once the potential is there for conventional heterosexual pairings between almost sexually mature teenagers, girls act by the rules: no more wide green smiles and deep subaqueous grass.

Unless the object of a girl's affections is a musician in her favourite band – in which case those rules may be flagrantly disregarded. Groupie behaviour can be seen as an extreme form of childhood sex play. The feeling itself may be deeply serious – a girl with a crush, just like a mature adult in the throes of sexual obsession, will think about almost nothing else – but there's no hope of a response. The best that the boldest and most persistent rock chick could hope for is a one-night stand and a chance to steal his cigarette lighter to show off to her friends. This is a sexual behaviour that's 'outside': it's not about pair-bonding. And in this context a girl or woman may play extravagantly, taking outrageous initiatives – sending him her knickers, insinuating herself past the security men and hiding under his bed, or like 'Cynthia Plastercaster', making intimate casts of her favourite rock stars as a lasting memento of her passions.

PERVERSE WOMEN: I really fancy you and Josh

The older woman and the little girl are unconventional subjects for sexual stories because we don't think of them as having any sexuality. But women who fit the classic sex object mould may also initiate if they want an unusual kind of sex.

The most baroque perversity in our stories is sex with animals – a kind of copulation that's necessarily sterile, or in the wilder reaches of the imagination gives birth to monsters –

and that can be read as a quest for extreme sexual experience. Titania wakes on her flowery bank to fall in love with Bottom in his donkey's head. In Greek myth Pasiphaë conceives a passion for Poseidon's white bull and hides herself in a carving of a beautiful cow in order to be penetrated by him. Catherine the Great, the nymphomaniac Russian empress, was rumoured to have died while attempting to have sex with a horse.

These women all initiate. In real life, too, where women have perverse sexual purposes, they're more likely to make the first move.

Anna remembered, 'Cindy just came up to me one night and said, "I really fancy you and Josh, I'd like to go to bed with you both, would that be alright?" I thought, Good grief. Then I thought, Mind you, it sounds quite sexy, I quite like the idea of slightly way-out things – so I told Josh and he said yes and off we went to bed.'

Among my interviewees, sexual arrangements involving two women and one man were always initiated by a woman, and negotiated between the women involved. This makes sense because it reduces competition between the women. Here Cindy initiates from outside the couple. But if it's one of the couple who asks another woman in, again it makes sense for the woman to make the arrangements. If the man made the move, the two women might be in competition, but when the woman does the asking, the second woman is there for her.

This sexual arrangement may seem wonderfully decadent in fantasy. But, in reality, female-initiated threesomes some-times have an agenda that isn't primarily sexual. The three-some can be an attempt to domesticate or make safe a disruptive lesbian desire in a married woman, or a way of defusing sexual jealousy between two women who've slept with the same man. These strategies tend not to work, or only to work in the most temporary way. Three is an uncomfortable number, and such an arrangement can never satisfy the deepest needs we bring to our sexual relationships. (As W.H. Auden put it, 'Not universal love, but to be loved alone'.[34]) It's rare for a threesome to meet more than once. But here women are clearly initiating for their own pleasure, though that pleasure may only be of the most transitory kind.

Group sex situations may also be set up by women, or involve bold female moves. And one reason why a woman might be keen to initiate this kind of sexual activity is that it enables her to have sex with another woman without calling her own sexual identity into question. This was clearly one of the attractions of group sex for Ginny, who said, 'It was with my boyfriend Dave and my best friend Claudette and her bloke and another bloke. We were really quite drunk. Claudette was very flirtatious, we were both flirtatious women, and we were enjoying turning the men on, and we got into playing Strip Jack Naked. We were peeling our clothes off playing this card game and ended up totally naked and there was music playing, and Claudette and I got up and started dancing with each other, very much trying to turn the men on, and enjoying being exhibitionists. It was Dave who came up and put us together physically and Claudette and I just did what was expected really and carried on. The thing that was doing a lot for me was thinking the men were being turned on by it.'

Here the lesbian love-making is carefully placed within a heterosexual frame. Ginny stresses that for her the turn-on was the element of voyeurism and display, rather than the chance to make love to her closest friend.

Hanif Kureishi's autobiographical novel, *The Buddha of Suburbia*, has a female initiator who sets up group sex, but this time with no lesbian element. Marlene is married to Pyke, the trendy theatre director. Her lust for Karim, the narrator, is the ostensible trigger for group sex involving the two couples – Marlene and Pyke, and Karim and his girlfriend, Eleanor.

57

Marlene is a comic figure, a little too old to be attractive: '. . . as my mother would have said, she was no spring chicken.' She initiates with Karim: '"Shall we have a kiss?" she said, after a while, stroking my face lightly.' She has boundless sexual enthusiasm. 'When we broke apart and I gulped back more champagne she raised her arms in a sudden dramatic gesture, like someone celebrating an athletics victory, and pulled off her dress.' But towards the end of the session her libidinousness becomes pathetic as she gets drunk. Even her sexual skills are for laughs. 'When she wanted to stop my moving inside her she merely flexed her cunt muscles and I was secured for life.'[35]

In the end, as so often in male fictions, conventional and male-centred sexual values assert themselves. The group sex ends with the disruption of both relationships involved. At first Marlene seems rather splendid – but she's revealed as a woman past her sell-by date. Her initiatives are comic, and she loses out in the end. It's Pyke rather than Marlene who gets what he wants.

So who are the women who make the first move? Bad women, predators, prostitutes, and women with ulterior motives. Fat women, older women, little girls, and women who want three-somes or group sex.

Meredith Johnson, the Wicked Queen, Mrs Robinson and Mae West may entertain us delightfully. But they're also pro-foundly influential and their influence is of the most retro-grade kind.

They teach us that women only make the first move if they are exceptional, or want something exceptional, and that this isn't something an ordinary woman might do with an ordinary man she likes. And they teach us that men are right to be wary of women who ask them out. As Kevin said, when I asked him how he'd feel about being approached by a woman, 'I'd just always worry there'd be something behind it, or you'd be being pissed about in some way.' No wonder.

Above all, they seem to be showing us that women shouldn't do this if it's true love that they're after. What women who make the first move in our stories never ever get – except in the metamorphosing climaxes of fairytales – is love that lasts.

CHAPTER 3
WOMEN'S FEARS

'I told him I was a nice girl.'

(Woman on 'Blind Date')

HERE'S some typical advice to the girl between about ten and fifteen who's fallen in love and is wondering what to do about it.

'Summer's too short to wait around for him to make the first move, so take a deep breath and do it . . . . "D'you wanna go to the beach with me on Saturday" fixes the place and date and makes your intention clear so that you both know where you stand . . . . [Or you could try] the cheeky approach: "If you don't come to the beach with me this Saturday I'll tell all your mates that you wear knitted underpants".'[1]
'All the signs are there – yes, he probably *does* feel the same way . . . Next time you're both standing there smiling at one another – give him a kiss! That should sort things out.'[2]
'*Do* plan some things to say. You don't need to write a script, just have a few suggested date locations up your sleeve. *Do* be persistent. When his Mum says he's out, he probably is out. (Unless she says it, like, all the time!) *Do* call him. Just do it.'[3]

The magazines in which this advice can be found – *It's Bliss*, *Fast Forward*, *Just 17* – have a very young readership. The girls who buy these magazines are on the cusp between childhood and sexual maturity, poised on the edge of the world of

60

adult relationships – curious, excited, perhaps a little hesitant. Many of them aren't yet going out with boys. Where they do have boyfriends, their relationships may have all the deep seriousness of first love – but they're unlikely to lead to lasting pair-bonding.

The magazines reflect the 'in-between' status of the girls who read them. Sex advice columns, often vibrantly frank, jostle with pictures of polar-bear cubs. The mix of sexual sophistication with the artefacts of pubescent girl culture – Simba rucksacks, pop-star icons, pets, butterfly barrettes – gives these magazines a rather touching charm. And in this half-play, half-serious world of snogs, dreamy boyfs and Russian hamsters – a world that's still close to that 'little girl' one in which girls take outrageous initiatives – making the first move is actively encouraged. Girls are urged to ring him, ask him out, get a life. Take a deep breath and say it – summer's too short. If you want to know if he likes you, give him a kiss. Ring him, just do it. We seem to have entered the broad sunny uplands of female sexual assertiveness already.

Advice for young women who've left the hamster stage behind is quite different, though. Sexually mature women for whom sexual relationships might be about reproduction are urged to take quite another approach.

'Great Date – but will he call again?' asks an article in *Company*.[4] The sub-heading urges, 'Forget waiting by the phone – make that second date happen.' The illustration shows a buoyant-looking woman in a slinky red dress. The promise of both illustration and sub-heading is that this will be all about female assertiveness.

The writer reflects, 'I've called men up. I've even asked a few out on dates . . . I've since discovered how great it can be if you give a man the space to make a move on you. It's a wonderful confidence boost for you when he does ring. Calling him first can deprive you of that pleasure . . . .' What looked at first glance like a paean to female sexual initiatives

turns out on closer inspection to be a manifesto for the courtship backlash – the story of a woman who used to act uncon-
ventionally and who reverts with a sense of relief to the
traditional way of doing things and finds it rewarding.

The writer bases her advice on a concept of men's true
nature. 'Why can't we just come out and say what we really
mean? Something along the lines of, "Listen, I really enjoyed
myself tonight. Let's do it again. How about next Wednesday?"
Why? Because we all know how most men would react to
such a request. What you mean is, you'd like to see him again;
but what he thinks you mean is, "I am after commitment, not
a casual fling, so if you're not the marrying kind, you're wast-
ing my time."'

So what to do? She has a solution: to fib a bit.

'So if, like me, you can't stand shampooing your hair with
the water off in case the damned phone rings after a great
date, get real. He wants to call you? Don't give him your
number. Madness? No. Ask him for his. That's what I did
when I first went out with Jack. I told him the telephone
line wasn't yet connected at my new flat and, because I was
temping, he couldn't call me at work either – but I'd be happy
to call him. It worked. For once, I didn't have to stare at the
phone and will it to ring.'

An article in *Cosmopolitan* is called 'The lure of the sexually
aggressive woman'.[5] The illustration shows a woman with
tousled hair and underwear embroidered with flowers glee-
fully hitting a prostrate man with a pillow. This is female
sexual aggression as sexual display: like the flowery underwear, it adds to her appeal. But the text itself is full of qualifi-
cations. Every description of what an assertive woman might
do is followed by a warning.

'The sexually aggressive woman . . . propositions men as
easily as most of us play coy, never hesitates to tell her partner
what she needs. If he can't handle her directness, she dis-
misses him, reasoning that she's better off with a man who

lets her take the lead. Not all such women are acting out of healthy desire. Some are motivated by a deep-rooted hostility towards men.'

We're warned that not only may sexual assertiveness be pathological, it may also be deeply unattractive – and even lead to sexual dysfunction in the man. 'Few men will take orders from a drill sergeant. Telling him to "give it to me like a man" . . . may immediately kill desire . . . Angry demands may even result in your partner suffering from impotence or premature ejaculation.'

Above all, *Cosmo* Woman is warned not to be too assertive at the start of the relationship. The writer's parting shot is about timing: the risks of female sexual 'aggressiveness' are greatest at the beginning of the relationship. 'It's true that some men are scared off by women who like to take charge; other men may welcome an assertive stance – but only after they're well past the initial stages of courtship. And since nobody likes rejection, you're probably better off playing by the old rules of seduction – at least until your romance develops . . . . Just remember that it's best to hold off until he trusts you. When you are sure that he feels safe, unleash the tigress!'

Both these articles ooze ambivalence. Their ostensible subject matter is female sexual assertiveness: that's the promise of the titles and the illustrations. But the writers have a problem. They like the idea of women asserting themselves – but they're also worried that the woman who makes the first move will drive the man she wants away. They struggle to reconcile their enthusiasm for female initiatives with their beliefs about the nature of men – as creatures who hate to be told what to do, flee from commitment, are scared by women who come on too strong, and only want casual flings.

The solution both writers offer? Be devious.

The *Company* writer's suggestion is to tell a little lie. Women are advised astonishingly often to lie in the early stages of courtship: advice columns in women's magazines frequently urge us to lie to new lovers about how old we are and how many men we've slept with. This advice connects with a long tradition of female sexual pretence – faking orgasms, pretending to be a virgin when you're not, or – its contemporary version – pretending not to be a virgin when you are. Different theories are brought to bear on the later stages of relationships. We're always being told that successful marriages are all about openness and honesty: the Relate buzzwords are trust, sharing and communication. But here we're only on the second date, and covert stratagems are called for. And the highly complicated way of taking the initiative that's advocated is to pretend our phones don't work to take away from him the option of ringing us so we have to ring him . . . .

For the *Cosmopolitan* writer, too, the answer is to act covertly, and to conceal your true sexual nature – 'the tigress' – till you're sure he feels safe. Family therapists sometimes use paradoxical injunctions, where they try to upset rigid and pathological behaviour patterns by giving clients instructions that contain a contradiction: for instance, a client who can't control her anger might be told to lose her temper at a specified time each day. Something rather similar and equally complicated is happening here – when women are told only to act on impulse with great caution.

We've moved a long way from the clear injunctions and cheerful egalitarianism of the pre-teen and teen magazines. In their later teens and twenties, it seems, women enter a sexual world where female initiatives are much more fraught and have all sorts of complicated meanings – insecurity, repressed hostility, a pathological need to control – and where there are huge discrepancies between male and female interests. In this world women may want one thing and men quite another, and women are urged, for their own good, to be cautious and cunning: to be devious when they yearn to be direct, to fib about their phones.

Articles in women's magazines help to set the love agenda of the culture, and shape the stories women tell one another about their relationships. But of course it's two-way traffic: these articles also reflect that culture. And advice to women in magazines, however contradictory or retrograde, does at least accurately mirror the uncertainty and ambivalence that many women feel.

Women react to the idea of female initiatives quite differently from men. 'I wouldn't do it, it's just a thing I've got', they say, or 'You think if you look too keen they'll go off you', or 'It's a nice idea – but I really can't see it working', or 'I just think there are all sorts of things in man/woman relationships which sorry to say are true'. Where do all these fears and worries come from?

FEMALE SHAME: Why true love still waits

Charlotte met a man at a party. 'He was in love with me for the night,' she said. 'He was everso gorgeous, and he was going to Scotland the next day, and he gave me his address and said, "You must write" – and I did write, and I got this letter back which was clearly saying, "I had this fantasy about you for one night but I'm not interested." It was a mistake to hurl myself – I felt I'd crossed some boundary and I shouldn't have done.'

Charlotte's letter was actually a response to a male initiative. By writing to him she didn't really cross a boundary. But she thinks even this was going too far, and what she feels is a time-honoured form of sexual shame that's clearly marked 'Women Only'.

'Shame', says psychotherapist Susie Orbach, 'acts as an internal censor, checking our thoughts and desires; sometimes protecting us from transgression, but more often constraining desire. The desire often can't even be examined because it is fused with a shame that acts as a prohibition,

telling us that it is wrong to want.'[6] And there are good histori-
cal reasons for this vestigial shame about 'hurling yourself'
that tells us that it is wrong to want. It's a hangover from a
time not so long ago when a woman's sexual reputation was
a practical and financial issue with far-reaching implications.

The system of patrilineal inheritance that is the foundation
of any patriarchal system depends on the chastity of women:
men have to be sure that their children are indeed their own.
The very essence of patriarchy is the notion of sex outside
marriage as a property violation. And under patriarchal
regimes the risks of unchastity have far outweighed the pleasures of sex outside or before marriage for women. Women
have suffered appalling punishments for being unchaste: ston-
ing, clitoridectomy, institutionalization, the loss of their children. Within living memory, unmarried women who fell
pregnant were thrown out of the family home and set to scrub
floors in grim Church Army hostels.[7] When the punishments
for a minor sexual misdemeanour were so draconian, it's no
surprise that women drastically suppressed their delight in
sexual expression: it simply wasn't worth it.

The system of male dominance may be dying, but the thinking that went with it lingers on. The traditional sexual code
is still around – but not in its original brutal form. What we
have today is a slim-line fat-free version.

We know we won't be carted off to institutions for delin-
quent women if we act on our desires – but we may still
feel there's a price to be paid for the pursuit of sexual
pleasure.

We don't think it's wrong for women to have sex outside a
committed relationship, but we may still feel shame about
certain kinds of sex – like one-night stands where afterwards
the man doesn't phone.

We don't believe you'd be wise to wait till the ring is on
your finger: today only born-again virgins from the True Love
Waits movement believe you should put off sex till marriage.

But we do suspect that relationships last longer if you don't have sex the first time you go out. (Research shows that this belief is false: the Boston Dating Couples Study found that relationships where people made love the first night were just as likely as others to last.[8])

We don't consider it sinful for women to sleep with lots of men, but we do suspect that women who pursue pleasure too avidly will mess up their chances of having lasting love affairs, like those fictional bad women who flash their pubic hair at policemen or have sex in lifts with decent married men, and who come to no good in the end. It's as though there's an either/or quality about the sexual persona we project – whore or madonna, sleeping around or long-term committed relationships.

We no longer maintain that nice women don't enjoy sex – yet much of the discussion about date rape is based on a concept of the female body as something that needs defending, of the penis as a dangerous weapon, of intercourse as something he wants to take and she doesn't want to give, and of sexual negotiation as a struggle between two parties with opposing interests, a struggle around a possession – the woman's sexuality. All of this is highly reminiscent of the old discourse about virginity.

We no longer believe that a woman who loses her virginity outside marriage is 'ruined', but we do believe that coercive sex usually causes permanent psychological 'damage' – today's version of 'ruin'. Of course, rape can and often does have devastating psychological consequences; but the idea that this damage is inevitable, is quite different to that caused by other kinds of assault, and cannot be repaired, does surely relate back to an antiquated sexual code.

And we know that men aren't put off by women who initiate sex within an established relationship, who suggest innovative sexual practices they'd like to try, or who sometimes like the man to lie back while they do everything – yet we still believe men are turned off by women who take the lead at the very start of relationships.

Among the women I talked to, the ones who held most strongly to this slimline version of the old sexual code were girls in their early and mid teens. Paradoxically, it's among the girls in the age group most often advised in their magazines to take direct initiatives that the double standard has most force.[9] Co-existent with the wholesome upfront egalitarian vision of *It's Bliss* – Take a deep breath and do it – there's another darker, older and desperately unequal sexual universe.

GIRLS AND THEIR REPUTATIONS: Inside she's a Skoda

Chloe is thirteen. She's a thoughtful, cerebral girl, sometimes dazzlingly articulate. When I talked to her, she'd just started going out with her first boyfriend.

I asked her if girls ask boys out. 'Yeah, they do,' she said, 'but the type of girls that ask boys out, they're thought of by other girls as tarts. The girls that get really nice boys and have nice relationships at about fifteen are the girls that didn't run after boys and aren't sort of tarty, because the boys can respect them.

'There's a girl in my class called Lauren. We went to this concert at the boys' school, and she took down her hair, combed it while she was sitting there, folded her waistband over, pulled her shirt out, tucked her socks down. All the boys were looking at her thinking, "What's she doing?" She's very pretty and the boys would all say to themselves, "I don't like her really, she's a bit of a show-off", but to their mates they'd say, "Oh isn't she nice?" She's got a bad reputation with the boys, and now she's never going to get a clear reputation – not after running after them like that. There was a comment that went round the school, I heard it from some boys, "Oh, Lauren: on the outside she's a Porsche but inside she's a Skoda . . . ."'

Roxanne is a street-wise sixteen year old. There's a poignant air about her: friends have described her as looking rather like a hungry puppy dog, with a pleading look in her eyes. When I asked her if she'd ever asked a boy out, she said she thought she'd be able to – but she'd never actually done it.

Roxanne already seems to know quite a lot about the darker side of sexual relationships. 'Some men would just have sex with you and then that's it,' she said, 'just want you for the sex and not want to get to know you, and I think because women find it easy to be intimate with each other and want to be intimate with men, that it's quite hurtful when someone just wants sex. It's different when the woman just wants sex and the man just wants sex, 'cos that's just a quickie, but when the man sort of does it to you, you think, "What's going on here?" – I'm being used by this person 'cos they don't want to know, they obviously don't care whether I feel good about having sex, whether the sex is good for me or whether it hurts me, physically or emotionally . . .'

Natalie is a nineteen-year-old law student. An elegant young woman with a very contained manner, she sees herself as highly traditional in her courtship behaviour, and likes it that way. 'I'd never make a first move,' she said. 'None of my friends do, none of us have ever.'

When I asked her why she felt so strongly about this, she explained, 'I can't stand the idea of someone knowing that I like them when they don't return it. A lot of times my friend's said to a lad, "Oh Natalie does like you, she thinks you're alright," and they'll say, "She doesn't *act* like it," and they think I'm really cold towards them. When I was in secondary school, a couple of boys started spreading stories about me and mud like that does stick, it turned out I had this reputation, and I had this string of unsuccessful relationships, and I couldn't help thinking it was because of that, that they thought that was all I was good for. Now whenever there's someone I like, I act like I don't want to know. I have to know that he likes me just that little bit more than I like him, because that way I don't get hurt as much.

'I tend to be really offhand. Someone asked for my number the other night, and I was really bitchy actually, I just said, "Yeah, look it up", and walked off. I wouldn't have minded going out for a drink, but I think I really really did put him off.'

When Chloe, Roxanne and Natalie talk about courtship, they speak a highly traditional language – a language of being used, of mud that sticks, of girls who act sort of tarty, of playing hard to get to protect yourself from being hurt. These girls all have staunchly feminist mothers: they learnt at their mother's knee that a woman without a man is like a fish without a bicycle, and *The Female Eunuch* and *The Women's Room* were on their shelves at home. But they talk about their relationships as though all that feminist theorizing never happened. I'm saddened to hear these glittering girls still talking like this.

The sexual world they describe is all about reputations. When Chloe's pretty friend Lauren hitches up her skirt and unpins her hair at the concert at the boys' school, she is risking her reputation: and once she's got a bad reputation, it'll stick. It's like that Victorian concept of the unchaste woman as 'damaged goods': in this sexual world, what's done cannot be undone. When the boys in the Fourth Form start spreading stories about Natalie, she worries that her relationships don't last because boys think sex is all she's good for. So she learns to behave in ways that she doesn't like. She calls herself cold, bitchy, and offhand, she's very off-putting and then regrets it, but still feels a compulsion to abide by the old script because your reputation matters more than whether you get what you want.

In much of this, it's the boys who are doing the defining. It's boys who give Natalie a bad name, who reckon that inside Lauren is cheap, however classy her bodywork. But the girls are acquiescing in the definitions, somehow unable to challenge them.

Female sexual shame is the spectre at the feast for girls today. Shame lurks between the lines of these accounts. Roxanne's phrase, 'I'm being used' comes from the new revised version of the traditional sexual language. We're no longer 'soiled' by sexual relationships outside marriage – but if a woman has a sexual encounter without emotional connection, or where her agenda is different from his, or that doesn't lead anywhere, or that she simply regrets, rather than say, 'I didn't enjoy it', or, 'That was a mistake', she may say, 'I was used.'

In this sexual culture, it's not easy to get it right. There's only a narrow strip of ground between being approachable and being 'slaggy'. And the things you do to protect yourself from being used – act bitchy, be really cold – are so easily overdone.

Natalie played *too* hard to get with the man in the club who asked for her number: 'Yeah, look it up . . .' This happened the weekend before I met her. As we talked, her phone rang. She jumped up hoping it was him: it wasn't, of course. But if, like Chloe's friend Lauren, you signal sexual interest in too overt a fashion – flash your legs around, let your hair down – that also means that in the long run you won't get what you want because boys will think that's all you're good for. This sexual culture greatly limits the moves a girl can make. Be too hard to get and he won't ring; be too available, and you won't get a 'nice' relationship.

But we ought to note that most of the behaviours discussed here – like Lauren's indirect signalling, or Natalie's dilemma about whether to give her phone number when asked – actually fall within the parameters of the traditional script. There are no direct initiatives here at all except from some of the girls that Chloe knows, and they are the ones with the 'bad reputations', the girls who are 'thought of as tarts'.

THE SCARLET LETTER: Tales of pleasure and punishment

As you get older, it gets better. This world of such stark double standards doesn't last. Chloe and Natalie believe that once you've got a 'bad reputation' you're stuck with it – but the whole issue becomes less urgent for women past the teenage years. Women in their twenties don't worry about their sexual reputations in this way. The classic worries of the twenties are about sexual performance – Do I come quickly enough? Can he tell when I come? Yet that vestigial belief that the pursuit of sexual pleasure may be punished does persist in certain fears that women have.

The great adultery stories of the last century, those fabulous tales of high drama, yearning and unbearable pain, told how women who acted on their desires met very unpleasant ends – Emma Bovary messily with the arsenic, Anna Karenina under the train,[10] Eustacia Vye from *The Return of the Native* in the flood-swollen stream. The heroines of these novels aren't condemned or judged by the men who tell their stories. Tolstoy said he fell in love with Anna as he wrote her story. Flaubert said, 'Emma Bovary – c'est moi' – and out of his empathy he painted a portrait of extraordinary psychological precision, as when Emma remembers the iced champagne at the ball at La Vaubyessard and longs for another life: 'Piously she folded away in the chest of drawers her lovely ballgown and even her satin slippers, with their soles yellowed from the beeswax on the dance-floor. Her heart was just like that: contact with the rich had left it smeared with something that would never fade away.'[11] That quality of yearning for 'something more' that is the essence of Emma's discontent is echoed in some of the real-life accounts of adultery that women in the 1980s told researcher Annette Lawson. 'The sense of yearning conveyed by these stories,' says Lawson, 'is supported by the most common responses women gave about the feelings they had as they first contemplated a liaison: "I felt compelled by

my emotions to have an affair . . . Life felt very empty . . .'"[12]
But the behaviour of Anna and Emma is so far outside the
accepted parameters of their time that their lives became
untenable – and the arsenic or the traintracks beckoned.
These stories show that this is inevitable: this is the unavoid-
able inner logic of the story of the woman who puts her own
pleasure above her social responsibilities.

In our own century, the punishments for sexually aberrant
women have gradually eased. The 1940s film *Brief Encounter*
is about the unconsummated passion between Alec and Laura
– a doctor and a housewife – who meet accidentally in the
refreshment room at Milford Junction. The couple behave
with a highly erotogenic restraint that makes a great story but
that completely baffled Trevor Howard, who played Alec –
and who apparently took the film's director, David Lean, on
one side and said, 'But doesn't he want to fuck her?' The film
pays homage to *Anna Karenina*: the soundtrack is full of trains,
and when the relationship ends, Laura thinks of throwing
herself under one, though she doesn't actually do it. In this
film, though, there's another kind of price that has to be paid.
After spending a day with the man she loves, though never
makes love to, she rushes home to find her little boy has been
knocked down by a car – and reads his injury very directly
as punishment for her forbidden longings.

When I talked to a group of women with young children
about the effects of motherhood on their sexuality, they told
me one reason they wouldn't have affairs was the risk of
losing their children.[13] This seems surprising. It's highly
unlikely that these women would indeed lose their children
if their marriages broke up. Fifty years ago, maybe, but not
today. This belief is a throwback: deep down women still feel
that the price to be paid for the pursuit of sexual pleasure is
the loss of your children.

There's a moving exploration of this theme in Sue Miller's
novel, *The Good Mother*.[14] Anna, who is separated from her

husband, has a passionate affair with Leo. Anna's daughter Molly sees Leo in the shower and asks to touch his penis – and he unwisely lets her, because he believes Anna would want him to be open about sexuality with her daughter. Anna's ex-husband fights for custody of Molly on the grounds of sex abuse. Anna loses her child. The sexual affair inevitably dies. Anna is left with nothing.

Because today an affair by itself wouldn't mean the mother losing custody, there has to be some other intervening factor – here, Leo's crass if well-intentioned behaviour. But the story derives its power from the stock plot, in which a woman is punished for pursuing sexual pleasure by the loss of her child: the emotional logic of this feels irrefutable – even though it doesn't happen anymore. That split between the whore and the madonna is deeply ingrained in us still.

Anna rings Leo at the start of their relationship, but only after being invited to do so. In Kate Saunders's World War One saga, *Night Shall Overtake Us*, there's a woman who initiates much more directly.[15] Eleanor falls for Lorenzo, who is swarthy, clever and intense, and has the sexiest scars. And it's Eleanor who makes the first moves. She kisses him on the lips – though he doesn't respond; she goes to see him and tells him how she feels, very exceptional behaviour for the time. Through the rest of the story, she is dreadfully punished. She falls pregnant, Lorenzo marries her but is cruel, he neglects her, he beats her, her child is deaf: finally Eleanor dies of Spanish flu. And all these terrible things except her death follow logically from her initiative. None of them would have happened if she hadn't gone to see him.

These books aren't prescriptive, of course. These sophisticated writers, who are both fascinated by the possibilities of female sexual pleasure, don't think for a moment that this is what *ought* to happen. Sue Miller and Kate Saunders have chosen these plots for their stories because they work, they convince us to suspend our disbelief: and they work because we accept that there's something inexorable that determines these kinds of tragic outcomes when women pursue their own pleasure too avidly – and especially when women initiate. As Sara, one of my interviewees, put it, 'I think women are punished for making the first move: obviously women *should* be able to do that, but the game is so set.'

Even the most outspoken advocates of female sexual autonomy have had difficulty shaking off the story in which women are punished for sexual assertion. In *Fear of Flying*, Erica Jong created one of the most sexually free heroines of second wave feminism, outrageous Isadora Wing, who travels across two continents in search of the perfect 'zipless fuck' – in which zippers fall away like rose-petals – and who feels that sex with her husband is 'as bland as Velveeta cheese: filling, fattening even, but no thrill to the taste buds, no bittersweet edge, no danger', and who longs for 'an overripe Camembert, a rare goat cheese: luscious, creamy, cloven-hooved'.[16] Erica Jong said of her book, 'I spent six months writing and rewriting the ending . . . I kept thinking "She's got to die, she's got to die", and I came to understand that I had internalized the patriarchal paradigm, and that while I finally broke with it, something in me wanted to fulfil it.'[17]

COMPETITION BETWEEN WOMEN:
An out-of-date Barbie doll

'When I was at university,' said Amanda, 'I used to get off with people very easily. I had to leave the women's hall I was living in because the Christians said that I was a slag. I could hear them talking about me at breakfast. Especially 'cos I got off with this guy who had a lot of piercings and they all saw him come up the corridor and they'd be closing their doors. After that, when I used to get myself a coffee from the kitchen they'd stop talking. So I left the hall, even though I had to pay a £100 fine.'

A woman may worry that she will deter the man she wants if she takes the initiative. She may have a nagging suspicion that if she acts on her desires she will be punished, and something precious will be lost or taken away. But she may also fear that she will be condemned by other women.

Of course women can be hugely encouraging of other women's sexual assertions. Women have a great talent for friendship, and most of us have close female friends whom we love dearly, and on whom we rely for advice about our relationships with men. Sometimes that advice is very specific. In the glory days of the women's movement in the 1970s, many women went to consciousness-raising groups where they told triumphant tales of first orgasms and borrowed other women's vibrators in a warm atmosphere of sisterly supportiveness. But there's a lot more to us than earth-motherly altruism, and inevitably there will be undercurrents of sexual competitiveness in some of our friendships. Many of us find this a highly uncomfortable issue. We love to cling to a Care Bear concept of womanhood – a concept that's been given its theoretical underpinnings by linguist Deborah Tannen[18] and psychologist Carol Gilligan,[19] who have suggested that women have different speech patterns, organizational styles and value systems to men – and the difference is that women are more nurturant, altruistic and co-operative.

Yet, though we may be less overtly violent than men, studies show that we aren't in fact more altruistic,[20] and of course we do have our share of aggressive and competitive impulses. And there are all sorts of ways, often covert, in which we may try to police the sexuality of other women, and seek to control the expressions of one another's sexuality, wherever they may be along the continuum from indirect – leather pencil skirts – to direct – 'Come up sometime and see me'.

Women not infrequently criticize one another's appearance or clothes – and when we criticize another woman's appearance we're invariably saying something about her sexuality, usually that her sexual signals are too blatant. Amy said, 'I saw a woman at a bus stop recently, just like the kind of thing you see in a magazine. I thought: You silly woman, don't you realize what you're signalling, I'm sure you're not wanting what you look as though you're wanting . . . .'

In particular, one woman may criticize another for going on being too sexual for too long – like Germaine Greer who, in her book, *The Change*, launches a sustained attack on her friend Flora for trying to look sexy in middle-age. 'She projects a deliberately unsubtle image of availability; her hair is dyed a crude shade of yellow; she wears either tight short skirts with slits in the back or trousers, invariably with high heels, usually of the strappiest kind, a gold chain round her ankle. Some part of her peek-a-boo brassière is usually visible . . . When I suggested once that she could end up beaten to death on a vacant lot, she looked at me in despair and said, "Don't you see? I don't care."'[21]

These two female admonitions come complete with over-the-top warnings about the dire punishments for this too-overt or age-inappropriate signalling – for looking like a woman in a magazine, for wearing strappy sandals when you're past it: rape, or an untimely death.

In women's reactions to sexual betrayal, such attitudes to the sexuality of other women are distilled out in a concentrated form. When I talked to Tina, she was very upset because of the break up of her seven year cohabitation. She expressed her feelings forcibly, as any of us might. 'This little tramp that he's been with – I now learn that he's living in her house – well, not her house, it's a council house, she doesn't work, she's a parasite. She's a horrible little thing, she's like an out-of-date Barbie doll with long dark hair with tons of grey growing through it – horrible, common. There's nothing to be jealous of. But, nevertheless, there must be some attraction because he left me and went with her . . . .'

Here are the stereotypical themes of female denigration of the 'other woman', presented with excruciating directness. She's common, she's overtly sexual, and she's gone on being sexual too long – 'long dark hair with tons of grey'. Her sexual attractiveness is only superficial – but the man can't see through it.

But it's the actions at the other end of the continuum – the direct initiatives – which are most likely to be condemned or discouraged. Women who share with others their plots and plans to take direct initiatives may be warned of the risks. Alice was planning to ring up a man she fancied desperately and to ask him out. She wanted support, so she chose to consult a friend whom she knew to be very assertive. 'I can remember saying, "What shall I do? Shall I ring him?" and her saying, "Oh no, don't do that". Me saying, "His number's disconnected, perhaps I should go and see him." "Oh dear no, you mustn't do that."'

There's a familiar pattern of female conversation in which one woman urges another to resist temptation, to keep working at her marriage, to pay no heed to a man's weasel words, to wait for the man to make the moves. It can all sound rather like Victoria Wood's 'Ministry of Warnings'. There's a general tendency when we're asked for advice to go for the conservative line and urge the other person to keep things the same, not to stray from the path, not to take any risks: that way, we feel we're not laying ourselves open to blame. But is something else operating here too?

According to evolutionary psychologists, all our sexual behaviour has a genetic imperative: our aim above all is to get the best genes for our offspring. There is much that women may find irritating about evolutionary psychology: in Mother Nature's great scheme of things as delineated by the evolutionary psychologists, roles are strictly divided between the sexes, and no prizes for guessing which sex gets the money, the power and the urge to sleep around – and which gets the dressing-up. Yet the genetic viewpoint can give a fresh insight into puzzling aspects of our sexual behaviour. And I wonder what an evolutionary psychologist might make of women's warnings to one another about the risks of female initiatives. He or she might see something going on here that's quite different from an altruistic concern to protect the other woman from rejection. A psychologist arguing from a genetic perspective might well claim that when women discourage others from initiating they're actually attempting to regulate the sexuality of other women and control access to the available men.

Competition is built in to any system of sexual reproduction. The biological baseline is that we're all in competition for the best genes, and that inexorable fact is worked out in our lives through our feelings of sexual jealousy and competitiveness – feelings that will sometimes be very painful, as they were for Tina when she spoke to me. Sometimes it might be to women's advantage to acknowledge this more openly. The trouble with female competitiveness is that so often it's covert. Like the Christians in the corridor, who used a moral justification for their condemnation of Amanda with her many maverick men, we may hide our feelings of sexual competition behind something else. Often we disguise our sexual jealousies by couching our criticisms of other women in a traditional sexual code – according to which the woman who has disappointing sex that the *man* initiated is 'used', and the woman who has disappointing sex that *she* initiated is 'punished'. When we talk in this way, we're helping to keep a system going that disadvantages us all in the end.

WOMEN'S CAUTIONARY TALES: Acting really slaggy

Warnings about the risks of being overtly sexual, and above all about making the first move, have their purest expression in a genre of story that women tell one another. It's a story about another woman, a third party who isn't there to tell it her way. Several women told me these stories to explain why they wouldn't ask men out. They launched into them with relish, then backtracked a bit, softening the hard edges of the story by stressing how very sweet this woman was.

Chrissie said, 'There's a woman we know, she's quite a goer with men, we call her Lorna Loose-legs. She's divorced, she's thirty-six, she's ever such a nice lady, she's beginning to get to the stage where she doesn't want to be left on the shelf. She'll chat up anybody, she'll go straight up to men if she fancies them, she goes home with them most of the time – and the next day she takes their phone number and they take hers and then they don't ring her – so she phones them, and often they haven't rung because they don't really want to.

'She does give herself this sort of image, which she doesn't need to, because she's such a nice pretty girl anyway. I often wonder why she gets herself into those situations – where men aren't coming on to her because she's so obvious. She goes straight for them, doesn't really give them any breathing space. She has quite a few relationships, but they're all with men who've got girlfriends and just pop round to see her when they've got a night off, and she doesn't really see it like that, she sees it as more.'

Natalie said, 'There was this girl, Jackie – she was a really sweet girl – but promiscuous wasn't the word for it. We used to hear all sorts of stories. There was one bloke who just came round every Thursday night from Nottingham and slept with her and left, and she was quite happy with that. She'd say, "Oh I can't sleep unless I have sex first." One time just before me and Brett split up, she was really, really flirty with Brett,

we were out dancing, and Brett was on the dance floor opposite me, and I looked across and there was this girl with her
legs either side of him, bending back doing all this shimmying,
and I was laughing so much, because she didn't realize how
awful she looked. And in the end she got what she wanted,
and that was it, and he's not spoken to her since. I disagree
with that. If she was happy with it, and that was what she
genuinely wanted out of life, I'd think, fair enough. But you
can see she's such a child inside this body which acts really
slaggy. Inside she doesn't want to be like that – and that makes
me pity her and I just think she's stupid.'

In these stories, the sexually assertive girl does get her man
– but not to keep. Just as, in our films and stories, women
who initiate may get fantastic sex but won't get relationships,
so, in these private stories too, the girl who 'acts really slaggy'
doesn't get love that lasts.

The underpinning of the story is a belief about the true
nature of female sexuality. What women want is the lasting
love of a good man. Sex that doesn't lead anywhere goes
against woman's essential nature. Even though Lorna and
Jackie might claim they're happy with these men who share
their beds and then go back to Nottingham, the women who
tell the stories know they aren't happy inside.

In these stories, it's always 'her' – not 'you' or 'me'. If Lorna
and Jackie told their own stories, they might have a different
angle on what happened. They might talk about pleasure.
They might say they loved making love with these men but
didn't really want them cluttering up their flats. But what the
woman who tells the story sees is another woman giving sex
and getting nothing in exchange.

The stories of Jackie and Lorna Loose-legs are normalizing
and prescriptive: they show how relationships should work,
they keep the world in place. Like the fictional forms to which
they're closely related – fables or fairytales, which were also
traditionally told by women, or Hilaire Belloc's cautionary

tales, like 'Matilda who told lies and was burnt to death' – these stories have harsh morals. They show that initiating in sexual relationships – 'going straight for them', even acting 'really slaggy' – may get you your man in the short-term, but this isn't the way to a female happy ending as defined by the teller of the tale: 'He's not spoken to her since.' The moral is this: if you initiate you'll attract the wrong men, men who don't really care – or men who might care, but not for you. These men are all out for one thing, and when they've had it, they don't even bother to phone.

When a sweetly elusive woman gets off with a man who makes all the moves, the ending may be just the same as it usually is in these stories – a woman who isn't happy inside, and a phone that stubbornly refuses to ring. But here the storyteller seeks to show that it's specifically the woman's direct initiative – her failure to play by the rules and to follow the conventional script – that leads to the unhappy ending.

The antithesis between the good girl who plays by the rules and gets her man, and the bad girl who takes initiatives and just gets sex, is sometimes told as the story of a pair of sisters. In folk tales there are three brothers: in the sexual narrative, there are often two sisters, who embody that sexual polarity that bedevils our thinking about women – slag/frigid, whore/madonna.

In her book *Sisters*, an exploration of the significance of sisterhood in women's lives, Brigid McConville writes, 'It is quite remarkable, in talking about teenage experiences, how often the word "tarty" is used – by both older and younger sisters.'[22] Such a judgment may even give a woman her life-script, as one sister shapes her own sexual identity in reaction to the other – in what Brigid McConville calls 'the dialectical dance of sisterhood'. One sister settles down and has babies and makes her own playdough: the other wears lots of makeup and has lots of men. The labels can last a lifetime.

Pairs of sisters – one overtly sexual, one good or modest or restrained – crop up everywhere. The original pairing can be found in Sade – Justine the virginal blonde, whose innocence invites the most terrible violations, and Juliette the wicked, self-serving, sexual brunette. Stephen Soderbergh's film, *sex, lies and videotape*, is about a rather similar pair of sisters. Cynthia has a touch of the bad sexual woman about her. She is louche and sexually voracious, her skirt is amazingly short, and she makes the first move with men. Ann is the fresh-faced innocent one, who worries about world problems and doesn't have orgasms. Ann's husband is having an affair with Cynthia – but in the end it's Ann who finds true love. For all its highly contemporary playing about with the relationship between reality and the video image, the film tells the old story about two sisters – one who hurls herself and loses out in the end, and one who is innocent, and who suffers and then is rewarded. The success of the film suggests this is a story we still love to hear.

Now try a different story.

On the mean streets of Jane Tennison's latest murder investigation, it's a cold dark lonely evening. Helen Mirren's Detective Chief Inspector – every forty-something woman's favourite heroine – is shopping for microwave meals-for-one after a day's hard graft. She goes back to her car, and on a sudden impulse phones Patrick Schofield, the sexy forensic psychiatrist she's met on a previous case. She gets his answerphone. She leaves a message that starts off confidently, suggesting they meet up, and then peters out into embarrassment. She switches off her phone and mutters, 'You idiot'.

For all her glamour, Jane Tennison is quite different from the alluring psychopaths of the bad woman narrative, who never do anything embarrassing, who never kick themselves. She's someone we can identify with, handling the phone call badly, feeling a fool – as many a man has done in a similar situation – and surviving. And in the end, against all the logic of the stories we've heard and told so often, she gets her man.

We have so many fears – the fear of being used, of being thought cheap, of missing out on long-term relationships, of featuring in someone else's story about women who are really slaggy. These fears run deep into the subsoil of our sexual culture, and we're not going to root them out overnight.

But it can help to recognize where they come from. The stories that give shape to our fears – stories about how you get punished if you hurl yourself at men, or how you don't get the right kind of man if you make the first move – may be told by women, but they don't serve women's interests. They're all about limiting female initiative and keeping women down. They originally served a system that sought to keep women chaste so that men could be sure that any offspring were their own.

Above all, they're not true. They're a poor guide to how the world works. And we need to nail the beliefs that spring from the language of sexual shame for the lies they are. Like Erica Jong, we need to rewrite the endings of our stories.

The woman who sleeps with a man the first night she goes out with him is just as likely to form lasting relationships as the woman who likes a long period of 'getting to know you'. A girl who gets a 'bad reputation' in the Fourth Form at school isn't stuck with it for life. Women who have lots of sexual partners are no less likely to have happy lasting relationships than their more restrained sisters. Women who have affairs may sometimes cause a lot of havoc – but generally they don't feel a need to fling themselves under the goods train as it lumbers through Nizhny station.

And what about women who ask men out? Anything can happen. Perhaps they'll have a good time: perhaps they'll be rejected. Sometimes they'll have troubled or painful relationships: sometimes their initiatives will lead to lifelong loving partnerships.

Of course there are things to be afraid of. Asking men out

means embarrassment, risk-taking, and maybe regretting what you've done. It can mean putting the phone down and muttering, 'You idiot'. And it does involve more rejection: that's simple arithmetic, because the more moves you make, the greater the chance that some of them won't be welcomed. But it may also mean, as Jane Tennison happily found out, a higher chance of getting the man you really want – the one you've chosen.

CHAPTER 4
MEN'S DOUBTS

'Gilgamesh opened his mouth and answered glorious Ishtar. "I would give you wine to drink fit for a queen. I would pour out barley to stuff your granary; but as for making you my wife – that I will not. How would it go with me? Your lovers have found you like a brazier which smoulders in the cold, a backdoor which keeps out neither squall of wind nor storm, a castle which crushes the garrison, pitch that blackens the bearer, a water-skin that chafes the carrier, a stone which falls from the parapet, a battering-ram turned back from the enemy, a sandal that trips the wearer. Which of your lovers did you ever love for ever? What shepherd of yours has pleased you for all time?"'

(Epic of Gilgamesh)

THE very essence of women's fears is what men will think of them. So what do men themselves say about women asking them out?

They say they'd love it. They think it would be brilliant. They yearn for it to happen – like Dennis, who said, 'There's a lot of people I see I'd love to speak to, but I'm scared. It would be so nice for a girl to make a move.' Or Luke, who told me, 'I've *longed* for this to happen. Asking women out was something I found extraordinarily difficult, because I was so full of a feeling that I'd be rejected'.

Dennis's and Luke's reasons are typical. Men say they're fed up with having to take the initiative, scared of being

rejected, tired of always having to be the ones who do the work. If you get it wrong, they say, you feel undesirable or ugly, a total fool. 'If you get turned down,' said Malcolm, 'you feel really stupid. Really, really stupid. I feel some men enjoy the uncertainty – it just reduces me to paroxysms of anxiety of the most unpleasant kind – it petrifies me . . . .' Or, as Keith put it, 'You have to come out into the open, and once you've done that you're forever exposed in your relationship with that person'. And even if she says yes, the uncertainty about how you're perceived persists, because you don't know whether she's said yes because she likes you or because she had nothing else to do on Saturday night.

All the men I talked to recognized the costs in the traditional male role. None of them said that they thought female initiating was a bad idea or that they wouldn't welcome it.

Obviously these men knew I was writing a book on the subject, which might have shaped what they said. But that isn't the only explanation for their enthusiasm. Anyone who asks this question will get the same answer. Men always and everywhere insist that they'd love women to make the first move.

Shere Hite, for instance, found just the same. Almost every man who responded to her questionnaire said he was always the one who made the initial advance – and they all resented this. By asking who made the first move, she seems to have tapped a deep well of male anger and bitterness. She writes, 'Almost every man resented or felt uncomfortable about this fact . . . often expressing a strong emotional reaction'.

The men who filled in her questionnaires wrote movingly about rejection:

'I make the initial sexual advance, but I don't like to. If the other person doesn't want to have sex with me, I get angry. I get tears in my eyes but I hide them.'

'If I get rejected I feel like a total fool. I feel like apologizing to the woman and slinking off to a corner like the lecherous scum she must think I am.'[1]

Sometimes there's a lot of irritation with women – for their passivity and their refusal to do this work. One man wrote, 'I usually make the initial sexual advance – the initial advance and every other advance after that – and I'm damned tired of it. *I* make the first phone call, *I* make the first date, *I* kiss *her*, *I* touch *her*, and *I* fuck *her*. It's no wonder we grow up to think of women as objects, because that's exactly what many women act like. They operate under the assumption that they have something we want – why don't they ever act like we have something they want? When am I going to be treated like a sexual object? I'd love it.'[2]

For many men, the most painful rejection is if they've suggested sex and the woman says no. (There's a significant gender difference here. Men tend to feel most vulnerable just before sex, while for women the most anxious time comes afterwards – which is why women find that morning-after call one of their most difficult initiatives.) For men, being turned down for sex comes top of their list of painful rejections. But being rejected when they've asked a woman out comes a close second.

Men sometimes feel that rejection hurts more than it should. So effective is our construction of masculinity that a man may assume it isn't as bad for other men, whereas for him the pain needs explaining. A number of the men I talked to went back to childhood experiences to account for this, locating their fear of rejection in some formative experience with a little girl who wouldn't take their proffered lollipop, who icily snubbed them. These early rejections are recalled in excruciating detail.

'When I was nine,' said Patrick, 'I really liked this girl who lived down the road. I was thinking, I really like her, how can I impress her? – which was mainly by playing music very loud and doing silly things like cycling very close to her Dad's car. These things made no impression on her whatsoever, so I said something to the effect, "Shall we go off together to be on our own?" And she said point blank – "No, you're a horrible little boy", and I remember thinking, That wasn't a very pleasant experience, I didn't do things right there. I thought maybe it was the way I cycled round her Dad's car – I'm sure it wasn't . . . .'

To try and impress the girl he likes, Patrick at nine does what little boys do best, rushing around and making lots of noise – braggadocio on a bicycle. When this doesn't work, he worries he overdid it – took up too *much* space, made too *much* noise. You can easily envisage the utter disdain of the little girl, who watches this display impassively and then delivers her judgment with its damning subtext: How could you have dared to imagine that I might think *you* were attractive?

TRUE CONFESSIONS: At least the lads won't sneer

Men's enthusiasm for female initiatives, and the openness with which they'll talk about how bad rejection feels, are apparent in the public world, too. In books and magazines today, men are coming out about the difficulties of making the first move – especially when writing for a female readership, because it's something that women love to hear.

Here for example is Michael Bywater, writing in *Cosmopolitan*:

Secret thoughts of party people:
Man 1. 'Oh my God, what a babe, God I wish I had the nerve to go over and talk to her, but someone that gorgeous is bound to be attached.'
Man 2. 'Will you look at her? Wow! I'd go over and talk to her, except she'd never be interested in me. She'd just sneer. I'm not rich enough, haven't got a Porsche, hair's beginning to thin

a bit, not so you'd notice but I notice, and what could I say that she hasn't heard a thousand times already. No, I'll just drift over and talk to the lads about sport, I suppose, and the office. At least the lads won't sneer . . . .'[3]

Here, traditional masculinity is conceived as a charade enacted by struggling performers who aren't always quite up to it. An ironic blokeishness offers a safe haven from the world of women with their allure, their coolly appraising glances, their disparaging judgments.

Our ideas about what constitutes masculinity are changing fast. With our new sophistication about gender, old-style machismo starts to look a bit like the behaviour of the knights in John Boorman's film, *Excalibur* – who clatter around in massive iron suits, looking awkward and clumsy and funny, yet somehow touchingly heroic too.

Accounts like Michael Bywater's are a sub-genre of the male confession, in which men reveal how hard masculinity is to achieve and how they don't feel as rugged and masterful as men are meant to feel. Books like Nick Hornby's *Fever Pitch* and *High Fidelity*, or Blake Morrison's *When Did You Last See Your Father?* offer a self-conscious presentation of masculinity as unheroic: 'I have measured out my life in Arsenal fixtures,' writes Nick Hornby.[4] Disarming the reader with deliberate self-deprecation and domestic detail has previously been a largely female preserve. The popularity of 'lad literature' points to a huge shift in our perceptions of masculinity. Today it's not just acceptable to talk about how hard it is to be male: it's fashionable and attractive and highly lucrative.

Gender theorist Warren Farrell is also vividly aware of just how painful it is for men to have to do all this male stuff. In his book, *The Myth of Male Power*, he urges women to help men out by making the moves themselves. He writes, 'The adult feminist – as opposed to the adolescent feminist – will encourage women to share the expectation of risking the first kiss on the lips, the first caress on the genitals. Only the adolescent feminist fails to place as much emphasis on resocializing women to take direct initiatives and resorts instead to encouraging women to sue the men who do it badly and marry the men who do it right ... .'[5] Here, 'Come up sometime and see me' becomes the adult feminist's defining moment. For Warren Farrell, women's reluctance to make the first move suggests a lack of substance to their feminism. If women were serious about equality, this is the bit of behaviour they would change.

Male confessions are also in vogue in private conversations. They furnish some of the best chat-up lines. Most of us have at some time been charmed by men who use stories about their own botched attempts at machismo – usually located, like Patrick's, comfortably in the past – as a way of showing sexual interest. These ploys usually work beautifully.

This then is the theory. When men talk about actual experiences of their own initiatives – what they've done and how hard it was – and imagined experiences of female initiatives – the things that they'd like to happen and that aren't happening to them – they seem to be longing for change.

It looks so simple. On the one hand, all these men who are fed up with the demands of the male role, who'd love women to initiate: on the other, all the women who'd love a bit more choice and control. What's stopping us?

ACTUAL FEMALE INITIATIVES: Some sort of walking dildo

I asked Rob if a woman had ever made the first move with him.

He said, 'This woman rang me up and asked me to go to bed with her. It was somebody I knew, and I suspected she had a thing about me, and she got very pissed, and started phoning me up one night and hassling me to go round. I said,

"Thanks, but no thanks". It was pretty awful, particularly as she is not somebody I particularly like anyway, and also . . . somebody who's obviously not in control of what they're doing is not a terribly attractive prospect. She'd just split up with her boyfriend and she thought I might be willing to go round and do the . . . It was horrible, it was repulsive. She knew I wasn't going out with anyone, she presumed I'd be absolutely desperate for someone, in fact she said that. It was horrible, really horrible. She said, "You know we're both desperate", and I thought, Thanks a bunch, you speak for yourself! It was just horrible – it would have been like being used as some sort of walking dildo.'

Luke had also had a woman make the first move. 'This girl Cynthia made a dead set at me at a party. She clung to me like glue throughout the evening. I slept with her in the end because I said something like, "I'm not in a fit state to have a relationship with somebody," and she said, "Well, that's what I want, a completely uninvolved relationship", at which point I think my sexual urges got the better of me. It was pretty gruesome from every point of view. Bad relationship, bad sex, bad conscience afterwards. I didn't really like her, I thought she was silly.'

When I asked Greg if a woman had ever made the first move with him, he looked troubled. He said, 'This woman came to my house and asked me out. It was somebody I'd known and liked very much as a friend, somebody who I knew wasn't very confident, and I'd actually said things like, "I like that outfit" – somebody I was wondering about, and I was still very much not sure, and she asked me out and we went out for a while, and I began to realize she was a very nice person, but it wasn't right.

'I was surprised when she asked me. Maybe I'd been too encouraging when I hadn't really intended to be like that. I'm probably somebody who likes quite a lot of ambiguity in things. Maybe she just assumed because I said these things it could only mean one thing and it didn't necessarily mean that at that time.'

Dennis told me, 'A guy can often know that a girl really likes him – but sometimes you don't fancy her. Me, personally – it puts me off a bit. I know a lot of guys love it, but I don't like it at all. It annoys me because if you know a girl likes you but you don't fancy them, you'll never have a friendship with them – there's always going to be that tension – she's going to be upset, or you're going to be distant. It can spoil a friendship – if one of you backs off, the other gets disappointed. I've had that situation recently – I was quite friendly with this girl, and another friend told me this girl really, really fancied me, and it completely spoiled the relationship – in fact we've since lost touch.

'Some women – it just puts me right off them. They're just there all the time, touching and being so one-track-minded. It's kind of aggressive, it's horrible. I've always wondered – are they coming at you for looks or are they coming at you for emotions? It's strange. Initially it makes you feel good because you're getting the attention, but after a while you think, Oh God, this is terrible.

'I hate a girl who's really touching me a lot. You meet a lot of people, they're touching you, cuddling you. You think, Oh, back off. If I really like them it's nice, but if I'm not yet quite organized in my head as to whether I want to take it any further, I hate them moving too quickly on touch.'

How familiar all this sounds. A friend comes on to you and you don't like them in that way – and it's sad because it ruins the friendship. You're nice to someone you know, then they ask you out, and you think, I didn't mean that. You're touched too soon by someone you're not sure you fancy and you don't like it, you feel intruded on. Someone's persistent all evening, never leaves your side, trying to get you into bed; you give in for a quiet life, and later regret it. An acquaintance who's had too much to drink makes a crude sexual suggestion. You wonder if you're just being pursued for your looks or if they really like you. Someone seems so one-track-minded when you're just not interested. You feel you're wanted just for sex . . . .

Women know this psychosexual landscape like the backs of their hands. Most of us will have been in all these situations and felt all these feelings. Most women would say 'That's how it is'. What's different here is the feeling tone. When they talk about being approached by women they didn't want, Dennis, Luke, Rob and Greg use strong words – horrible, repulsive, gruesome, terrible – and highly visceral imagery – the girl who clings like glue, the walking dildo. Women, of course, may also be irritated by sexual suggestions from men they don't like – but they generally reserve language of this intensity for acts of sexual violence.

These men aren't unreconstructed chauvinists: they're clever, sensitive men who want to have equal relationships with women. And they were all very keen on the idea of female initiatives in theory. Luke said he'd longed for it to happen. Dennis thought it would be great because he was sometimes too shy to approach the women he liked. Rob presented himself as very much in sympathy with the feminist agenda, and saw female initiatives as a welcome part of a changing pattern of gender relationships. Yet in the moments they describe, something else seems to take over – something that goes much deeper than their politics or expressed wishes. When these men said, How brilliant if women took the initiative, it seems they didn't expect it to be like this.

Shere Hite noted this contradiction too. She found men wildly enthusiastic about female initiatives in theory: but men who'd actually been in a situation where the woman made the first move had 'very mixed and negative feelings about it' – and these were often the *same* men who said they'd yearned for women to make the first advance. Some of those cultural images we've already explored – the prostitute, the woman

with ulterior motives, the woman who initiates for laughs –
seem to lurk behind their accounts.

'It turns me off to have the woman be the aggressor
(initially, anyway). I can't stand being "hustled" by a hooker
or a female I'm not attracted to.'

'It's strange, about having a woman make a pass at me – I
haven't gotten rid of the cliché that she might be a prostitute.'

'I feel I've lost control of the situation. I also get very confused. Is she serious, or just joking?'

'My initial reaction to any sexually aggressive woman is to
move away.'[6]

It's crucial to explore this yawning chasm between male
fantasy and male reality. It's this above all that women seek
to understand. If men say they love the idea but sometimes
hate it in reality, they'll be giving women mixed messages.
Men tell us: We'd love you to take initiatives. Women try it
– and sometimes we meet with reactions like Luke's or Greg's
or Rob's. It's not just that the man says no – of course men
will say no sometimes: it's the underlying strength of feeling
that the woman responds to – the sense that she has stepped
seriously out of line. No wonder she'll so often go scurrying
back to the comfort and safety of the old formulae.

Of course mixed messages aren't a male prerogative.
Women too ask for contradictory things, especially in these
times of changing gender values. We want men who are sensitive – but also strong and in control. We want men who
can share their feelings – but still make us feel safe. Sometimes we tell them we want them to play a more active part
in childcare, then always go first to the baby when she's
crying.

Mixed messages are inhibiting: they stop us from moving
on. And this particular contradiction between what men say
about female initiatives, and how they may react – the contradiction, for instance, between Rob's enthusiasm for female
autonomy and his feeling that the woman who invites him

into her bed reduces him to a walking dildo – is one that we need to understand in detail.

So what's going on here? Why are men so amazed when someone they don't fancy asks them out? Why do men call women who initiate 'aggressive'? And what do they think these 'aggressive' women are going to do to them?

SEX WITH STRANGERS: He'd thank her, not sue her

There are active initiatives almost any man would probably welcome. To be approached – with some subtlety – by a woman he fancies and was trying to get up the courage to ask; for a woman he's having a relationship with to initiate sex; for a woman he's having a relationship with to suggest he sometimes takes a passive role in bed. This I suspect is the world men imagine when they say they yearn for women to take initiatives – a sexual world in which these things happen more. In this world, female sexual assertions are basically harmless and often delightful, like the assertion of the woman in the soft porn magazine who takes off her clothes without being asked.

What men rarely envisage is the fact that such a world would also mean inconvenient initiatives from women they didn't like. What happened to Dennis, Luke, Greg and Rob that made them over-react is something they found amazing: approaches from women they didn't fancy.

In a revealing passage, Warren Farrell discusses men's bafflement about sexual harassment: 'If a woman at work caressed a man on his rear, he'd thank her, not sue her,' he says.[7] And what if the marvellously lascivious woman who stars in this little vignette had bifocal specs, a greying perm, support tights and a polyester blouse with a bow at the collar? Would the intimate touches be quite so welcome then? I somehow don't think that's quite what he has in mind.

Why don't men envisage advances from women they don't

fancy? This distortion follows directly from the fact that men are used to taking the initiatives. Just as there's a world of male sexual experience that is largely unknown to women – for there are plenty of women who've never once experienced that male nightmare of asking for sex and being rejected – so there's also a world of female sexual experience that's unknown to men. It's a world of unwanted sexual advances and unwanted sex. It encompasses the extremes of rape and abuse and includes too the banal everyday things, the hand on the bus seat that slips under your thigh, the man who rings in response to your ad for a flat and says he could put you up if you come to an arrangement that he's spelling out in graphic detail as you put the phone down. Incidents like these are part of the downside of daily life for young women – a regular irritant, like traffic jams, word-processor crashes, or getting some mascara stuck behind your contact lens.

Women – even in loving long-term relationships – also have quite a lot of sex they don't want: sex they go along with – to be polite, to please him, because they feel they owe it to him, because he'll dump them if they don't. Women do this less today than in the past, but sex that isn't exactly wanted is still part of female sexual experience. By and large, men simply don't have sex they don't want – in the sense that women do.

When I asked the men I interviewed if they'd ever had sex that they didn't want, they replied in almost identical words. Not at the time, they said – but sometimes afterwards. They usually went on to explain that before having sex they always wanted it, but sometimes afterwards they thought, Why did I bother? The feeling that it hadn't quite been worth the effort was most common after one-night stands – though, as Steve pointed out, the definition becomes circular: 'You don't always know it's a one-night stand till after you've had the sex . . .' This is a very different sort of not-wanting to the kind that women describe.

Under the present sexual dispensation, in which sex follows

from male initiatives, being approached by people you don't fancy and having sex you don't want are almost exclusively female experiences. Men and women inhabit parallel but different sexual universes. And this results in a tremendous gap between the genders in sexual perceptions.

For instance, men and women react quite differently to the idea of sex with a stranger. When psychologists Donald Symons and Bruce Ellis asked men and women how they'd feel about making love with an anonymous student of the opposite sex, the men were much more enthusiastic than the women.[8] Other researchers have found this too: it's a consistent gender difference.

Is this evidence for the greater expansiveness of male desire and men's urge to spread their genes around – in contrast to a woman's need for long languorous evenings of candlelight, confiding and pina coladas before she feels lustful? Well, maybe – in part. But women – just like men – do of course have fantasies about ravishing sex with people whose names they never learn. The difference is that when they're asked by a researcher how happy they'd be to have sex with someone they don't know, it isn't the gorgeous stranger with the ponytail glimpsed on the platform at St. Pancras that they envisage – but the man with a short-sleeved shirt and beery breath who made an obscene proposal in the wine-bar last night. Men envisage an attractive stranger, because women who are not desirable are seen as having no sexuality – but women know that most sexual attention from strangers comes from men in whom they have no interest, and whose advances they find unpleasant or intrusive.

This is why women never have sexual fantasies about being prostitutes. In *My Secret Garden*, Nancy Friday remarks that prostitution is one theme she never encountered in women's sexual imaginings.[9] Prostitution is a profoundly unsexy idea for women – because it's about having sex with men who are so unappealing they have to pay for it. But men, who like the idea of sex with strangers, may have fantasies about women having fantasies about prostitution: Bunuel's film *Belle de Jour* is about a woman who acts out a fantasy of becoming a prostitute and meets a gangster with whom she has brilliant sex. This is a uniquely male conceit. No woman, even in her wildest imaginings, would envisage the earth moving for a prostitute.

This fundamental difference in experience also explains why it's so hard for men to understand about sexual harassment. Women may feel, as many of us did during the Anita Hill/Clarence Thomas hearings, that men 'just don't get it'. There seems to be some kernel of the experience which even the most intelligent and empathic of men somehow fail to grasp: they simply can't see why women might experience unwanted advances or casual banter about pubic hairs on cans of coke as so abusive and upsetting. For a man, for whom sexual interactions have always taken place when he feels like it and with women he likes, it takes an enormous imaginative leap to put himself in the position that women are in much of the time.

Female sexual harassment does happen, but it remains very rare. Just occasionally a story surfaces in the press. In September 1994, the *Sun* had 'Train Girl Fired Over Lust Letters' – the story of Janette Hustwitt, a rail guard, who had been sacked after pestering a man for sex.[10] The object of her affections was Richard Gula, a six-foot-tall bachelor who lived with his mum. Janette had sent him 'red-hot notes' and told him she dreamed of seducing him between black satin sheets. It's a very British sex story, a Carry-On romp with a stock cast – the hulking male *ingénue*, the lecherous fat woman – for Janette, pictured with lots of plump thigh on display, is fitted into the stereotype of the big woman with a big sexual appetite, like all those fat women in our comedy shows who advertise their libidinousness.

No man I talked to had been 'pestered' like this. The only

man who said he'd experienced anything approaching sexual harassment was Rob – and then, he assured me, it was of the mildest kind. 'When I first started teaching I used to go into the secretaries' office to get bits of stationery, and they would make the odd remark – "Oh there's that nice young man again". It sometimes made me feel slightly uncomfortable, but that's probably my own self-consciousness about things.'

Sexual appraisal from older women at work, an unwanted sexual advance from a worker of equal status: both may be unpleasant experiences, but neither involves that key element of sexual harassment, the abuse of power. They're also quite exceptional: they aren't part of the sexual landscape that men regularly inhabit. There's so little in men's experience to enable them to put themselves realistically in a woman's situation. As the subjects of sexual initiatives, men are absolute beginners.

COURTSHIP AGGRESSION: It's like feeding animals

When men describe what it's like to be asked out by a woman they don't find attractive, they invariably call the woman 'aggressive'. In Shere Hite's survey, a man calls a woman aggressive simply because she chats him up when he doesn't fancy her.[11] Why do men use this word so readily, and what does it mean?

'Aggression' has a special significance in courtship: it's a way of clearly labelling a behaviour as sexually unattractive. In the natural world, aggression is what happens when courtship goes wrong. Because the moves that precede sex involve intrusions across the other's boundaries and into the other's space, sexual approaches will sometimes trigger the wrong set of behaviours. Wolf spiders, for instance, are particularly cautious and wary during courtship. In order to mate, the male wolf spider has to enter the long dark entrance of the female's compound. He approaches with great caution.

There's a more drastic potential for disaster than in any vagina dentata fantasy. If he rushes her, she gobbles him up.[12]

Both men and women can experience a sexual advance as aggressive. If we don't feel the least *frisson* of sexual interest in the person, then we'll find their attentions intrusive whatever they do. The subtext of countless articles about sexy dressing in women's magazines is that it's delightful to attract men in an indiscriminate way – yet being desired by someone you don't desire is by no means pleasant, and may feel like an attack. In March 1995, Jonathan Schmitz was invited onto a US television chat show to meet someone who had a secret passion for him. He agreed to appear, expecting his secret admirer to be an attractive woman he knew. The person with a passion for him turned out to be another man. Jonathan Schmitz went home, bought a gun and shot his admirer dead.

But even if you're attracted to the person who's making the moves – or if like Dennis, quoted earlier, you're 'not yet organized in your head as to whether you want to take it any further' – you may be put off by what they do if they get it wrong. And in courtship getting it wrong is usually about being too obvious: just as for the wolf spider, it's about moving too quickly, going too far too fast. A consistent theme for both men and women is that we don't like the other person's signals to be too conspicuous. Men don't like makeup that's too blat-ant – heavy foundation or lipstick that goes over the edge of the woman's lips.[13] Women don't like 'cute-flippant' chat-up lines: according to the close relationships researchers, 'I'm sort of shy, but I'd like to get to know you' goes down better than 'Your place or mine?' which may seem intrusive.[14] People's instinctive awareness that it's all about getting the intensity right – too obvious and the other person will be put off, not obvious enough and they won't notice – is one reason why the whole process can be so anxiety-provoking.

As Malcolm put it, 'The essence of these things is casual – it should be terribly light if it's to be brought off. It's like feeding animals – you just discourage your children from walking up to them too rapidly – and the same basic principle applies – that you mustn't do anything that would frighten someone off. You have to ask "Shall we go out to a movie?" without "and then afterwards we can go for a drink and have a fuck" being too boldly underlined as part of the whole deal.'

So moves that are experienced as aggressive will be off-putting for both men and women. But there's a marked difference between the sexes in our perceptions of what constitutes an 'aggressive' courtship move. Being seen as aggressive is courtship death for women. According to the traditional script, women expect, even enjoy, some dominant behaviour in courtship – not too much – from men. But men don't like dominant behaviour in women.[15]

The iconography of female desirability could be seen as a way of publicizing the woman's lack of aggression. Sexy self-presentation is so often about constriction and fragility. Malnutrition is eroticized. The sexiest clothes are the most physically restrictive: in tight skirts and shoes with spindly heels, you can't kick or run away. There's no sign of Tank Girl with her hard body and combat boots becoming an object of male lust, for all she's so lissom and libidinous. (She has become something of a folk heroine for lesbians though.)

These physical signals have psychological corollaries. The way in which many women's self-presentation in courtship contrasts most markedly with our behaviour in other areas of our lives is that we play ourselves down, make ourselves seem smaller than we are, expose our vulnerability. It's as though in much of our physical signalling and sexual negotiating we're saying, 'It's OK, I don't bite'.

Nothing can change the principle that anything too obvious or intrusive is best avoided in courtship: that's implicit in the nature of flirtation. But what will inevitably change is the definition of 'aggression'. What is perceived as intrusive depends on the norms. Because our traditional gender roles

require us to play down our aggression more than men, assertive courtship behaviour in women is highlighted, by contrast.
The woman who asks a man out, even if she manages to do
it in a way that's 'terribly light', is going way beyond her script.
It looks extreme: it may look 'aggressive'.

But as women claim new territory for themselves, definitions change. Forty years ago, an advisor in a woman's
magazine berated a woman for being aggressive on a date.
The behaviour in question? She had opened the car door herself.[16] In the whole new world that we're working towards,
the notion that it's exceptional and therefore 'aggressive' to
ask a man out may soon sound equally silly.

THE ROBBER BRIDE: Chasing away his erection

Men over-react because they never expected it to be someone
they didn't fancy, and they over-react because they experience a woman's sexual advances as 'aggressive'. But there's
another issue lurking here too, a fear that goes deeper and is
less clearly articulated than the fear of harassment.

Today more men seem to be having problems with impotence. This is the most common category of problem in the
letters received by the Kinsey Institute.[17] In fact, it's unlikely
that more men have trouble with impotence than in the past:
it's probably not that the numbers of men with this problem
have increased, but that more of them go for help. People
today are less embarrassed than they once were about asking
for advice when they're having sexual difficulties – and more
aware that such advice is available. But some sex therapists
have connected this apparent increase in erectile problems
with women's new assertiveness.

Sex therapist Andrew Stanway writes: 'A shy man married
to a powerful woman may be so intimidated by her that he
cannot function properly sexually or puts off doing so either
to protect himself or punish his wife.'[18] In a book based on

Masters and Johnson, Fred Belliveau and Lin Richter describe dominant women who 'overwhelm their husbands until they rebel by ducking behind the curtain of secondary impotence as a way of avoiding the female onslaught'.[19] In the *Cosmopolitan* article quoted in Chapter Three, women were warned that 'telling him to "give it to me like a man" may immediately kill desire', and making too many 'angry demands' in bed might result in your partner suffering from impotence or premature ejaculation. And Marj Thorburn, head of Psychosexual Therapy at Relate, puts it like this: 'We see men now presenting with the dysfunction of disorder of desire – and that's something very new, that's only happened in the last four or five years. And combine that with the increased presentation of erectile failure in men, perhaps we're seeing something of interest that we need to take notice of, because it may represent a reflection of what's happening between men and women generally, in terms of the shift in relationships over time . . . .'[20]

Our explanations for sexual dysfunction are a litmus test of our current preoccupations. For instance, the woman who didn't have orgasms was once seen as inhibited or inadequately adjusted to her female role and called 'frigid' – but since feminist ideas gained wide currency, the problem has been blamed on selfish or insensitive male lovers.

Explanations for male sexual dysfunctions will also reflect a society's current concerns. In his *Sexual Development of the Male*, published in the 1950s, Kinsey occasionally betrays the prejudices of his time in a delectably direct way. He has no doubts about the true cause of impotence: it's all to do with class. 'Few males achieve any real freedom in their sexual relations even with their wives,' he pronounces. 'Few males realize how badly inhibited they are in these matters. In extreme cases these inhibitions may result in impotence for the male: and most cases of impotence are to be found among upper level, educated males.'[21]

For Kinsey, impotence was connected to notions of upper-class effeteness, and the Rousseauesque conceit that too much education cut men off from the primitive roots of their sexuality. Today, the explanation can be found in the new female sexual self-confidence. The assertive woman who 'intimidates' the man so that 'he cannot function properly' is another incarnation of the bad sexual woman: not only does she boil his little girl's pet rabbit and get him fired to cover up her own ineptitude with CD-ROM drives, she may steal his erection into the bargain.

Blaming male impotence on female initiative is one example of a general trend within psychology, in which any challenge to the principle of male dominance is pathologized. The balance of power between the genders supplies explanations for all sorts of psychological problems in addition to sexual dysfunction. For instance, family therapists will often attempt to help problem families by encouraging the father to assert his authority more forcefully. As psychiatrist Robin Skynner puts it, 'Almost all the families I've seen in child psychiatry, where the child was brought as a problem, were mother-dominated ... Research on the healthiest families shows that the power in the family is shared between the parents. But in all but those healthiest families, if one of them is to be the boss, it does seem more often to work better if it's the father rather than the mother'.[22] Breaking with convention is tolerated until something goes wrong, but once there's a problem, the woman's dominance is re-defined as pathological and the purpose of therapy will be to restore the old way of doing things – in effect to restore male authority. So with impotence: female assertiveness becomes a convenient scapegoat for a problem of sexual dysfunction that in fact has quite other origins. The causes of impotence are almost invariably physiological.

Anna said, 'I initiated sex with Josh. I was sleeping in his bed. He and the other men were totally drunk and had all passed out. Then in the middle of the night this figure climbed into bed with me, and I thought, Great! At last we can get some sex going! We were quite passionate and I tried to straddle him, and he immediately lost his erection, and we tried a bit more – I was the one that definitely took an initiative there, and in fact, afterwards, I discovered Josh had some problems with impotence, and with me he'd felt he was getting going again – then I went and took one initiative and it completely freaked him out. I think he felt I had just chased his erection away. We'd gone out a few times by then and I'd found it very difficult to get him into bed and was having a problem understanding that. So then I had to pretend I didn't notice when we were being very passionate, and I had to be very delicate and then one day it just happened.'

Timing is always an issue in sex. When one person initiates – even when there's mutual desire – there's always the risk that the other doesn't feel like it. And if one partner has sexual problems, there's an inevitable danger that the other partner's initiative will reinforce that feeling of failure. Anything that makes us self-conscious or distracts us from the sequence of arousal may inhibit us sexually: this is true too for a woman learning to reach orgasm. So here Anna initiates at the wrong time – when Josh is too drunk anyway for sex: it doesn't work out and he blames her. The myth of the assertive woman who chases away the man's erection supplies a simple story that seems to explain what happened. But it's only a very small part of the explanation.

WELCOME FEMALE INITIATIVES:
She came and took me to bed

'When I was a student,' said Dominic, 'I had a very stormy relationship with a married woman who seduced me. I was nineteen – Erika was in her late twenties with three children. A group of us who'd stayed up at Oxford over the long vac used to go round to her house in the evenings. One night as I was going she came out to the doorstep and gave me a passionate kiss which I wasn't expecting. A few weeks later I was sitting reading in my room in Magdalen College when she came and took me to bed – which I was very pleased about.

'There were things that I found difficult though. She always wanted me to say I loved her, but I knew I didn't. I could never say it when I was in bed making love to her because I just didn't. There was absolutely no point in her divorcing her husband for me. In the end we had a great row in the course of which she threw all my shortcomings at me.'

Kevin said, 'I went to this party – and this rather plump girl came up and we just started nattering, and she was ever so sweet, and I ended up kissing her – then we went back to her house, and down to the prom at dawn. It was rather romantic. Absolutely no planning went into that at all, it just sort of happened. Next day she came round and had a coffee. Then she went off on holiday, and I said I'd give her a ring, but gradually I began to feel it was an obligation rather than something I wanted to do. I suspect what she did of not being very deliberate – she had all the sophistication of a fifteen year old.'

Tony said, 'Suzy was a waitress in the restaurant where I was working as a bus boy. One night she'd gone out with her friends. They came back to the restaurant at about one o'clock, she was drunk, she sat down very close to me, she kept going "Oh you're nice . . ." in a sort of slurred voice. I was really tired and it was really late, one o'clock in the morning, it seemed the best thing to do was to go home and forget all about it. But a couple of days later, we got together. Because she'd said what she'd said, I knew she liked me. I didn't have to do anything then, you could just be with someone.'

Here are three female initiatives that were all welcomed by the men. For Kevin, the woman's initiative led to a pleasingly romantic evening. For Dominic it led to a stormy and sexually-charged affair. And Tony and Suzy now have two little boys, a cat and a mortgage.

Kevin is the unwitting subject of a female initiative. In what he says, there are lots of hints that the sweet plump girl did most of the work: We just started nattering/absolutely no planning went into that/it just sort of happened .... It's usually the woman who says these things. Dominic, though, is left in no doubt as to what Erika has in mind; it's transparently clear what she's about, from her first surprising kiss to her inspirational arrival at his college room to take him to bed. In Tony's story, Suzy is the one who comes and sits close and says she likes him. She doesn't make any arrangements, but this is a very direct initiative – to come out from behind your cover and say how you feel.

The men are unsure about these female initiatives – as, of course, women often are about men's moves. Dominic's relationship with Erika is thoroughly operatic. There are dreadful rows, passionate sex scenes, and an excruciating finale. Tony is uncertain at first. When Suzy tells him how she feels, he goes off into the night. But the next day he comes back. And Kevin enjoys the evening but decides not to pursue the relationship.

Kevin's story raises the issue of follow-up initiatives. When a woman has made the first move, what happens next? A study by Kathryn Kelley, Elaine Pilchowicz and Donn Byrne may throw some light on this.[23]

When they set out to explore the gulf between fantasy and reality in men's responses to being asked out, these psychologists found that most of the men in their study – like most of the men I talked to – had been asked out at least once by a woman, and most of them had accepted. (Given how many times most men will have approached women, this is of course a very small proportion of initiatives.) But almost all these female-initiated relationships – eighty-seven per cent –

had ended by the time the couple had been together three times. Though the psychologists don't raise the issue, this makes me wonder whether something happens around the third date – a transfer of initiative. Researchers who've studied men's and women's courtship scripts don't usually look beyond the first two dates, presumably because at that point the script becomes less rigid. Today, one would expect even the most traditional couples to be involved in joint planning of dates by the third time they meet – with the woman perhaps cooking him a meal, or getting the concert tickets. It follows that men who are asked out by women also have to take back some initiative at this point. If the woman has started the thing off, and the man doesn't then join in with making arrangements, the relationship will stall. For instance, Rowena had asked a man out and he'd accepted. 'But he was funny about it,' she said. 'Every time we went out, he'd say, "Well, where do *you* want to go?" – but sort of aggressively.' Somehow, Rowena's boyfriend was unable or unwilling to take back any initiative himself.

In Kevin's case too, his ambivalence gets the better of him. But Tony and Dominic both soon decide that they want what the woman is offering. And there are striking similarities between these two relationships where the couple connected. Tony and Dominic are both considerably younger than the women who approach them: Tony is seven years younger than Suzy and Dominic about ten years younger than Erika. We've already seen that whenever the woman is older than the man, female initiatives become more likely. In our stories, the older woman is Mrs Robinson, the hard self-serving seductress, or Pilar Tenera, the golden-hearted whore who generously gives the young man his first delightful experience of sex. In real life, she'll be Suzy or Erika – an ordinary woman in love, for whom the fact that she's older than him tilts the balance of power a little in her favour.

For Erika and Suzy there's also a status difference which

may give them courage. Dominic is a student, while Erika is a married woman with money, a big house, a place in the community. Suzy is a waitress but Tony is a bus boy who collects the dirty dishes, well below her in the restaurant hierarchy – and when I talked to Suzy she underlined this status difference, which she recalled with relish. 'It was brilliant, that restaurant!' she said. 'It was totally female dominated. It was owned by a woman and run by a woman. The men were the musicians and washer-uppers and bar-staff. They were absolute minions really. No one bothered what they thought!'

If women use relatively crude markers to do with their own power, or the man's lack of it, when deciding whether to make a move, then visual cues will also play a part in this decision-making. Women may conclude, more or less unconsciously, that men who don't give out strong dominance signals in the way they look or move are more likely to welcome a female initiative. If women do respond to visual cues in this way, you might predict that women will be more likely to initiate with men who are boyish, androgynous, or slight in build. A man with a disarming grin and a fringe that falls into his eyes, or expressive and slightly camp gestures, or a taste for stylish shirts in flamboyant colours, may get asked out more than a man who embodies the stereotypical physical machismo of the lumberjack, roughneck or American footballer. Certainly, no one would mistake Dominic or Tony or Kevin for the kind of man who earns his living drilling for oil or felling timber.

The ambivalence that men have expressed in this chapter may seem discouraging. Yet this ambivalence is absolutely predictable. Female initiating at the start of sexual relationships represents a huge change in our behaviour, which is bound to make people feel insecure. All our cultural models are of women who are up to no good, or out to get a good laugh at men's expense, or into serial killing. And in some sex therapy lore, the initiating woman takes the particularly disturbing form of the robber bride who steals the man's erection. No wonder men are sometimes alarmed when a woman actually makes a move with them.

But men's enthusiasm at a theoretical level has to be encouraging. The first step towards changing something is in the imagination. Men who like the idea in theory are opening themselves up to liking it in practice next month or next year. In what men say about what should happen or what they'd like to happen, we can see how things will be in ten years' time. And many men do recognize – even if largely at a theoretical level – that they too could benefit from a more equal sharing of initiative at the start of courtship. Just as for women, the unfamiliar pleasure is the pleasure Emma in Chapter One told me about – 'It's such a good feeling to go out with someone you've chosen' – so for men, the complementary pleasure is knowing you've been chosen. When men take the initiatives, they may not always be sure if they're wanted for themselves – or if she just said yes because she simply couldn't wait to see *Il Postino*. But men who've been asked know that they're wanted. As Tony remarked, after he'd gone off into the night, uncertain, thinking he'd just forget about it, and then come back: 'Because she'd said what she'd said, I knew she liked me.'

CHAPTER 5
MYTHOLOGIES

'A whole range of images poeticises, kitschifies,
departicularises intercourse, such as wind beating down corn,
rain driving against bending trees, towers falling . . . . The
moment they succumb to this anonymity . . . they cease to be
the lovers who have met to assuage desire in a reciprocal pact
of tenderness, and they engage at once in a spurious charade
of maleness and femaleness.'

(Angela Carter, *The Sadeian Woman*)

IT all began in the twelfth century in Languedoc – or so the
literary critics tell us. We've learnt that many of our ideas
about what constitutes romantic love were first expressed
and explored in the songs of the trouvères and troubadours
in medieval Provence, in the code of courtly love.[1]

According to the conventions of courtly love, the lover
served his lady in much the same way that a feudal vassal
served his lord. The lady was remote and unattainable, and
the lover was devoted and abject, obeying her every wish,
silently accepting her rebukes. Love was a despairing and
tragic feeling – and the woman who was the inspiration for
all this exquisite and urgent emotion was always somebody
else's wife. These ideas were also expressed in the stories in
the roughly contemporaneous Arthurian cycle, in those tales
of doomed adulterous love, Tristan and Isolde, or Launcelot
and Guinevere, which, though darker and more intense, arise
from a similar sensibility.

Courtly love was strictly for the upper classes. It was also totally male-centred – concerned only with men's needs and desires.[2] The lady who is so yearned for is a mere cipher. Because she's untouchable and essentially unknown, she's a perfect receptacle for male fantasy.

Romantic love wasn't invented in the Middle Ages, of course. All cultures have love songs, love potions and love charms, and tales of lovers' quarrels, elopements and suicides. The author of the *Kama Sutra*, who lived in India some time between the first and the sixth century AD, describes romantic love, and Confucian tales from seventh-century China tell of the conflict experienced by men and women who've fallen in love with someone who doesn't meet with their parents' approval.[3] But many of our specific beliefs about romantic love over the past few centuries can certainly be traced back to that moment in medieval Provence. The special kind of romantic love that was elaborated then has been the background to European literature, and to much of our thinking about sexual relationships, for the past eight hundred years.

In *Creative Mythology*, Joseph Campbell writes that in the poetry of the troubadours and the story of Tristan and Isolde, 'love is born of the eyes, in the world of day, in a moment of aesthetic arrest, but opens within to a mystery of night'.[4] This sexual sensibility that he traces out in twelfth-century literature is one that we still feel at ease with today. Many of our own ideas about love are contained in these poems and songs: love at first sight; passion as irreconcilable with marriage; adultery as inherently toxic; sexual love as an ennobling emotion that justifies transgressions.

Today, as for Dante or the troubadours, the essence of romance is falling in love with a stranger across a crowded room, in that 'moment of aesthetic arrest'. Desire begins with looking, and is startling, mysterious and overwhelming.

The most sexually passionate relationships are still seen as a poor basis for lasting partnerships. Women's magazine editors love articles about great sex with unsuitable men: 'If he's wrong for me, how come the sex is so good?'[5] In fact research suggests that the belief that companionate relationships are the best basis for marriage may not be valid: a high level of 'erotic love' – a physically passionate relationship with a lot of intimate disclosure – seems to be the best predictor of relationship stability.[6]

Extra-marital affairs are still viewed as potentially tragic. Adultery researcher Annette Lawson argues that the legend of Tristan and Isolde's tragic and illicit love shapes our thinking about extra-marital sex even today, and this is why adultery is seen as inevitably toxic and destructive[7] – in spite of the evidence that eighty per cent of people who have affairs stay with their original partners.[8]

And the idea that romantic love justifies transgressions still underpins the thinking of young teenage girls. Sociologists Celia Cowrie and Sue Lees have found that girls invariably base their decisions on whether to sleep with their boyfriends, not on whether they'd like to or think they might enjoy it, but on whether they're 'in love'.[9]

Why do we still find old mythologies, like those medieval notions about romantic love, so beguiling? Do they reflect psycho-sexual truths? Or are they, as Angela Carter suggests, merely 'spurious charades of maleness and femaleness'?

MALE MYTHOLOGIES: You have to make the moment

Geoff is twenty six. He's tall, dark, clean cut. He spoke with relish about how he approached women.

'It's a challenge, isn't it? Men love a challenge. She would keep you guessing – she would throw out the vibes, but at the same time take other vibes back – so you would never know.

'I love that in relationships, I really love the first half-hour. It probably sounds old-fashioned – but, I love it. I prefer the chase – you meet someone, have a bit of eye contact, bump into them and have a quick conversation, meet them again, the whole thing develops slowly, it's like a game. And usually, the people you get to know quickly are the ones you back off from – 'cos you think, there's nothing to get to know there.

'I suppose you look for interest in a woman. And there are so many types of women and each type needs a different approach. You get the girls who are very attractive, who look bubbly and good fun, and you'd want to make them laugh. You've got other girls who look sort of deep, and you'd play more to their intelligence. And then you have the girls that are really talkative, and you'd agree with everything they say. Like a salesman speaks to the customer the way the customer likes to be spoken to.

'I've had four major relationships in my life, and the ones that have lasted are the ones I've had to chase. Unfortunately it's been the same story – I've chased, and then once I felt I was in complete control of the situation, I'd start to get bored. It's probably a fault of mine. You've chased to get something, you've got it, then you hope for another chase, so you start looking for something else. That sounds really sad!'

Keith is a psychologist in his late thirties. He gives the impression of thinking deeply before he speaks. When I asked how he went about asking women out, he said, 'You've certainly got to form the intention to do it with the same degree of deliberation you would to buy a pound of plums from the greengrocer's. It's not going to happen just because the idea pops into your mind.

'There was a very profound belief in my family that things would happen if they were right to happen. Rather like what Michael Portillo would call the dependency culture – that there ought to be someone to provide things. It's an outlook I now associate with people who are the recipients of a lot of local government and NHS services – that services ought to be laid on for them.

'Then at some point I suddenly realized I bloody well had to do it, you couldn't expect it to kind of happen. I grasped the basic fact that it was no use waiting for it to fall into place. And like all these things, you grasp it imperfectly – I just go on and on having to find that out, that you can't wait till the moment is right, that you make the moment. You can't necessarily will the moment you're in to be the right moment for what you want to do, but you bloody well have to line things up so that the moment arrives. You can't just hope it'll turn up like a kind of psychic giro from the DSS to provide you with whatever you need.

'When I was twenty, I took a year off college and I hitch-hiked to Greece. It was very much to do with autonomy and proving myself – because it was frightening, not knowing where you're going to sleep – and managing with just your rucksack and not much money. I wanted to live on my own and look after myself. It made me feel immensely better. It sounds idiotic, but I'm sure I was more confident approaching women after I'd done it – knowing you could do something grown-up. Which is funny, because now it seems a rather adolescent thing to do.

'There's this belief from my upbringing that if you just wait around things will sort themselves out – which I just have to struggle against all the time.'

Keith grew up in a family with an unusually 'feminine' ideology: just wait around and it'll happen. But because that doesn't get him what he wants, he moves to a more tradition-ally male position. He comes to recognize that it's up to him to shape his experience – to line things up, to make the moment.

None of this comes naturally to Keith. There's a sense of struggle about it. First there's an intellectual recognition that this is what he needs to do to achieve his goals: then he deliberately learns the behaviour – setting himself the task of hitching to Greece to prove that he can manage on his own. And the behaviour is reinforced – because it gets him the women he wants. He adopts the traditional male mythology because he finds it works.

For Geoff, by contrast, traditional male behaviour feels instinctive. He doesn't have to travel halfway across Europe, armed only with a sleeping bag and a water bottle, to learn it. More than any other man I talked to, Geoff loved the chase. His account of what he enjoys about courtship is full of the imagery of pursuit – overcoming obstacles, having a goal and working towards it, winning the woman.

In theory, Geoff was totally in favour of women asking men out – and recognized the active part they played in the process of courtship. He said women would often come up and talk to him and touch him. But in his thrill-of-the-chase narrative, in his account of the interactions that really excite him, he is the active one. The best bit is the very beginning. He loves the state of uncertainty created by the woman's mixed and ambiguous signals; her mysteriousness and withholding are essential to this scenario. Here, women are the goal, the quarry and the object of study: 'There are so many types of women.'

The underlying image is of a man striving to achieve mastery: he wants 'complete control'. But he recognizes that there's a flaw implicit in his approach; once his object is achieved, the thrill dissipates, and off he goes again, looking for new beginnings.

In spite of their very different personalities and upbringings, Geoff and Keith have both ended up with much the same formulation – making the moment, achieving control, planning, pursuing. Getting off with women is all about doing.

HEROES: There where they saw it to be thickest

In all our old courtship stories, tasks have to be performed, journeys undertaken, dragons slain, battles fought – by men. In one kind of narrative, the courtship quest, the tasks and the need for daring are implicit in the situation that faces the hero, often because he has to travel vast distances and overcome obstacles to win the woman. In the Welsh story-cycle, *The Mabinogion*, for instance, the Roman emperor Maxen dreams of a beautiful girl sitting on a chair of red gold, and sets off on an epic journey to find her.[10] In another story type, the tasks and obstacles are externally imposed – often by the woman's father or guardian. In the Book of Genesis, Jacob tends Laban's flocks for seven years in the hope of winning Laban's daughter Rachel – but Laban then demands a further seven years' work before he'll hand her over.

All this male activity gives the woman who is being courted a lot of information. The man's successful performance of the tasks shows that he's serious and will stick around, attests to his intelligence and good genes, and proves that he'll be able to protect her and her children physically, a crucial male attribute in the many societies in which disputes have been solved by fighting.

Warren Farrell has imaginatively suggested that there are parallels between today's sexual harassment legislation in the US and the tasks and obstacles in the old courtship narratives. He's come up with the baroque theory that men's fear of being sued re-introduces an element of danger to the sexual quest – 'allowing her to select for men who care enough to put their career at risk; who have enough finesse to initiate without becoming a jerk and enough guts to initiate despite a potential lawsuit.'[11]

The courtship model in which the man has to seek her out dangerously or prove himself is one that most women would now find thoroughly suspect. A story-line in which the woman is the goal of the quest and the engine of the plot – like Helen launching a thousand ships – renders the woman essentially passive. Today the mythology of the male sexual quest or chase has its corollary in the male culture of sex as conquest – scoring, collecting notches on the bedpost. To women, it immediately suggests unappealing young men holidaying in Torremolinos, playing the numbers game. The notion of women as objects is not that far removed from the extreme objectification involved in rape. When active man pursues passive woman for sex and women are viewed as passive objects rather than active agents, the scene is set for sexual aggression. Rapists see women or children as sexual objects without feelings, which is why treatment programmes for perpetrators of sexual violence focus on the development of empathy – so the aggressor begins to understand that his victim is more than just a body.

The male mythology of the courtship quest is perhaps most blatantly in evidence today in the accounts of conception given in every biology textbook. The usual story features a plucky little sperm which heroically undertakes a difficult journey and eventually succeeds in penetrating the egg – an egg that has been shed by the ovary, swept away down the fallopian tube and is now hanging around, waiting for things to happen. Sometimes the sperm is envisaged as harpooning the egg, or attacking it with jackhammer and pickaxe.

Professor Emily Martin of Johns Hopkins University has recently suggested that this imagery simply doesn't match up to the biological reality.[12] Sperm are altogether less thrusting, dynamic and enterprising than used to be believed. In fact, they dither: the movement of a sperm's tail propels the head sideways with a force ten times stronger than its forward movement. And the ovum plays an equally active role in fertilization: the ovum's adhesive surface holds the sperm in place until the genetic material contained in its head can be taken in. Here the male courtship mythology is getting in the way of our understanding.

The sexual quest is part of a wider mythology about men – man as the hero, purposeful, struggling against some kind of opposition, seeking out adventure, like the knights in the thirteenth-century *Queste del Saint Graal*: 'And now each one went the way upon which he had decided, and they set out into the forest at one point and another, there where they saw it to be thickest'.[13] Heroism – this deliberate, even reckless, seeking out of the most challenging, demanding thing – has until now been a male prerogative. Adventure means something different for women. When Yvonne Roberts calls her novel, *Every Woman Deserves An Adventure*, we know she's promising us a picaresque tale of sexual encounters, rather than a Fiona Fflyte-Campbell style trans-continental trek.[14]

Implicit in the notion of aspiration is the possibility of failure or falling. Male stories are also about hubris, about pride and downfall, about reaching too high and falling too far and losing everything: Faust, Satan in *Paradise Lost*, banished to hell for his pride, Icarus the original high-flyer venturing too near the sun.

Psychological testing has come up with a startling illustration of this male theme of the catastrophic fall, and its obvious analogy with the experience of ejaculation. In thematic apperception tests, men and women are presented with certain pictures and asked to tell stories about what is happening in the pictures. There are striking gender differences in the stories we choose to tell – suggesting that there may be elements in the traditional mythologies which do connect with our physical differences. When women are shown a picture of a man and a woman swinging on a trapeze, they usually tell a story that moves from 'deprivation' to 'enhancement'. At the start of the typical female story, the couple will have problems – perhaps they're arguing, or she can't conceive, or their act isn't going well: but they manage to resolve their difficulties and it all ends happily. But when men tell a story based on the same picture, the narrative movement is usually from 'enhancement' to 'deprivation'. After a triumphant display on the trapeze, they both fall to their deaths – or he drops her.[15]

MEN'S STORIES TODAY: Stepping off the cliff

In men's sexual behaviour and beliefs today, we can still trace out the shape of the old stories – for instance, in the belief that women can be won by male achievements, in the recurrent theme of risk in men's sexual stories, and in the motif of the unattainable object, seen and lusted after but never approached.

In the male mythology, sex is the motive of and reward for much human enterprise. And male ambition is still fired by the thought of all the women a man believes he'll attract with his success or earn with his money.

Women also start out believing they'll be loved for their successes. Little girls have fantasies about winning silver cups and being acclaimed by audiences of thousands – but they give up this dream at adolescence. Or today, perhaps, in a culture of greater female aspiration, they manage to hold onto the dream of success, but still give up their childhood belief that people will love them for it. A clever girl will play down her ambitions when with a boy she likes: successful women gratuitously introduce a few of their vulnerabilities into the conversation when they start to flirt. But men take it as read that career success will make them more attractive. Men brag and exaggerate their achievements in courtship conversations. Geoff and Keith, the men we heard from earlier, both deliberately introduced their achievements into the conversation as part of their seduction technique. Geoff sometimes lied to get a woman into bed, laying claim to career success he hadn't had. Keith preferred a more subtle approach: he felt that his work with disturbed children might add to his sexual appeal if 'left lying around at the back of the conversation'.

Risk – deliberately sought out, even relished – is also a big theme in men's stories. In her book, *Adultery*, Annette Lawson describes how she interviewed a doctor who loved rock-climbing – and who seemed to seek out risk in his sexual life too, breaking several taboos at once by having sex with a patient in her bedroom while her husband was downstairs.[16] One of the men I interviewed seemed to come from the same mould. Dominic was also a doctor with a passion for rock-climbing. He'd married at twenty-one, and he and his wife had seemed to have an exemplary relationship – happy, stable, companionable. Then in his mid-forties, he'd suddenly developed an intense sexual attraction to another woman. This was love at first sight – in that 'moment of aesthetic arrest' that Joseph Campbell describes. Dominic had struggled with his feelings and finally decided not to consummate his passion. And for him, as for Annette Lawson's doctor, there was a direct equation between rock-climbing and the risks of illicit sex – which he brought in to explain, in his very English way, why he hadn't made love to the woman he'd wanted so much. 'It would have been rather like stepping off a cliff,' he said. 'Exhilarating to start with, and rather painful at the bottom.'

This theme of risk and the potential for disaster implicit in risk-taking is explored by Josephine Hart in her novel *Damage*. Stephen is a successful politician, happily married, in his fifties, who falls obsessively in love with his son's fiancée, Anna. By giving in to his desire, he wilfully destroys his own life and other people's: his son dies, his wife leaves him, Anna walks out, his career is ruined. The imagery of the death reiterates the theme of the story – the death is by falling. But it is Stephen's son who dies in place of him, falling over the banisters as he backs away after he comes on the couple making love. The wrong person has died – and Stephen's wife rages at the injustice of this. '"When you knew you were lost . . . you should have killed yourself . . . .Why oh why didn't you kill yourself? You knew how to do it . . ."'[17]

In fact statistically women are more at risk than men of

losing everything through sex – more likely to lose their jobs if they have sexual relationships at work, more likely to wreck their marriages if they have affairs and their partners find out.[18] The female story of desire and loss is different though. In the great female adultery stories, the woman's tragedy is about what's done to her – it's usually a man's initiative that sets the story in motion. But the man's tragedy is brought about by the flaw in his character. In the *Damage* scenario, the man is totally responsible: he makes a deliberate move – and loses everything. He isn't 'ruined' by the actions of somebody else: he deliberately steps off the cliff. Whatever takes place, he started it himself.

Ted has been married twice and also had a cohabitation of several years. He talks about his sexual life absolutely as something that he has engineered and is responsible for. He told me, 'The two women I really wanted were Fran and Caroline, and in each case massive chaos ensued – trauma, people getting hurt – and so it's actually been very deliberate in both cases. At the time it was the dominant thing that you wanted to do, and then decided I suppose that the risks and the problems were worth it.' Our traditional distribution of roles puts the burden of responsibility onto the man because he initiates. Ted instigated the events that led to the breaking and making of relationships in his life, and he takes full responsibility for that. He can't claim – as women often do – that it just 'happened': it wasn't me, it's not my fault. He can't imply – as women often do – that he was an innocent bystander at the events of his own sexual story. Given that few relationships start between two people when neither of them is involved with anyone else, the potential for damage is implicit in our sexual negotiations. It is perhaps a real psychological strength in the male mythology of sexual conquest that it includes a recognition that harm may be done. There may be a fight, people will get hurt, and someone has to take the blame.

When men tell their sexual stories they may also reveal a profound romanticism that has its origins in the traditional mythology. The hard-to-attain and inaccessible woman who is the goal of all this male activity is readily idealized – because for a long time she doesn't have to reveal much of herself. She can be fantasized about because she isn't known. Hence men's tendency to be more romantic than women. Men fall in love more quickly than women, are more likely to idolize the object of their desires, and hold more beliefs that can be traced back to the code of courtly love. In one study, men and women were asked to say how much they agreed or disagreed with statements like: 'Romantic love often comes only once in a lifetime', 'Somewhere there is an ideal mate for most people', 'Love happens swiftly, without warning', and 'Love at first sight is often the deepest and most enduring form of love'. The men held significantly more romantic beliefs than the women.[19]

Unattainable women, and women who were loved and lost, haunt men's life stories. Both represent a failure of male initiative – the unattainable woman because he didn't dare approach her, and the woman who was loved and lost because what he did just wasn't good enough. In her research on male sexuality, Shere Hite found that the men who responded to her questionnaire often said they hadn't married the women they really loved – or at least, with a retrospective romanticization of the relationship, believed they had really loved.[20] Such a lost love may give shape to the subsequent life story: 'Everything I've done since we broke up has been for her . . .' is usually a motif in a male narrative. She's the only woman for him, and he's still trying to prove himself to her even when he's lost her. This activity without hope is a sad mirror-image of the purposeful activity that's directed at winning a woman in the future.

Novelist Nick Hornby knows all about this obsession with a woman who long ago moved on. In *High Fidelity*, Rob, the narrator, describes how he felt when his girlfriend – dramatic, different, exotic Charlie – left him for one of the sophisticated men on her design course. 'I lost the plot for a while then. And I lost the subplot, the script, the soundtrack, the intermission, my popcorn, the credits and the exit sign . . . Everything happened so fast. I had kind of hoped that my adulthood would be long and meaty and instructive, but it all took place in those two years; sometimes it seems as though everything and everyone that has happened to me since were just minor distractions. Some people never got over the sixties, or the war, or the night their band supported Dr Feelgood at the Hope and Anchor, and spend the rest of their days walking backwards; I never really got over Charlie. That was when the important stuff, the stuff that defines me, went on.'[21]

FEMALE MYTHOLOGIES: The princess in the tower

What are the female stories that counter all this male activity, risk and romanticism? And how are they enacted in our courtship behaviour today?

In our mythologies of difference, the woman's passivity is sometimes so exaggerated and intensified that she's actually entranced. Some of our most exquisite narratives of the winning of love have the woman in a coma or sleep that's near to death – Perrault's Sleeping Beauty in her beleaguered castle, Brunhilde on her rock, Snow White in the glass coffin.

The film *Working Girl* has a contemporary re-working of this motif. The imagery of this film subverts its ostensible plot. It purports to be about a woman assertively making her way in the adult world of work, but Tess, the aspirational secretary, has the cute manner and lisping voice of a little girl, and in her love life she acts like the comatose heroines of the old stories: her affair with Jack begins when she passes out in his arms from a mix of alcohol and tranquillizers.

Sleep implies an awakening. And the psychosexual underpinning of these stories is the theory that women need to be woken up to sexual pleasure. It's commonly assumed that women have their first experience of sexual pleasure in a teenage encounter with a skilled lover after a period of sexual latency. The female 'sexual awakening' is a cliché of biographical writing. In her biography of Daphne du Maurier, Margaret Forster writes, 'Geoffrey held her hand and she felt, for the first time, a physical thrill which she identified immediately as quite different from any feeling she had had before . . . . Her sexual awakening – and that is what it was – left her more dissatisfied with life than ever . . . .'[22]

But there is no psychosexual truth here. It's boys, rather than girls, who experience a sexual awakening in adolescence: according to Kinsey's researches, teenage girls only experience a mild increase in sexual interest.[23] And first intercourse for women, far from being an awakening, may be much less satisfying for women than earlier sexual explorations on their own: many women have their first orgasms as a result of solitary sexual explorations in childhood. But the old mythologies linger on – even sometimes in sex counselling, when doctors advise women that they need to 'relax' in order to come. A recent sex manual by Danish sexologist Dr Lasse Hessel, which describes and illustrates positions promising to bring women to orgasm from G-spot stimulation, contains a particularly outrageous expression of the Sleeping Beauty conceptualization of female sexuality. Dr Hessel comments of the 'relaxation' stage after sex: 'to a woman this phase is often the most pleasurable.'[24] According to this Danish sex expert, even during sex it's the sleepy bit that the woman likes best.

In many of the old stories, too, there is a barrier that must be broken through – a wall, circle of fire, hedge of thorns. A psychoanalyst might see the barrier as the woman's virginity – with the conquest of the hymen as the hero's culminating task. But the barrier also has other meanings. Exploring this imagery, I've become aware of my own ambivalence about this imaginative architecture. The tower which the woman inhabits in the story is restrictive, a place of confinement, but it's also a place of safety – like the calm enclosed space we need in order to give birth or breastfeed happily, or like the women-only college where we can concentrate peacefully on our work.

As Marina Warner has put it, exploring these multiple meanings of the woman in her tower, 'The tower encloses something, it's a symbol of enclosure, that's why the Virgin Mary is called a tower of ivory – she's pure, but at the same time she can give birth; she's called an enclosed garden, she flowers, but she's walled – it's her womb, the magic womb that produces the Saviour . . . . The tower's a symbol of her virginity, so she's called the Tower of David, the tower of ivory, or the spring shut-up, the fountain sealed. These are all images of impregnability, of fastnesses, and in that sense of her miraculous virginity which was both closed and fertile at the same time.'[25]

The imagery is beguiling. These walls are ambiguous. They protect even while they restrict. They nourish and nurture. They hold a secret.

What is the woman doing in these beautiful but restrictive, safe but confining spaces? Usually she's waiting. Women in traditional courtship stories do a lot of waiting. Sometimes she's waiting for a lover who'll eventually come to her, and who'll transport her from a state of near-death languor into sexual ecstasy. Sometimes she's waiting for a lover who isn't going to come back, and waiting shades over into abandonment, as it does for Ariadne on Naxos, the classical type of the abandoned woman, or for Madam Butterfly, or for John Fowles's French Lieutenant's Woman, who stands looking out to sea in a highly covetable cloak, and whose waiting has a post-modernist tinge: she's made the whole thing up, and the lover she's watching for never existed.

Tennyson's *Marianna at the Moated Grange* is one of the ultimate waiting women.[26] Here, Tennyson re-works the situation of abandoned Marianna in Shakespeare's *Measure for Measure* in a marvellously extravagant way. Marianna waits and weeps in her dreamy house, in the gloomy shadow of the poplar, surrounded by all the detritus of despair and bad housekeeping – broken sheds and rusted nails and flowerpots thickly encrusted with blackest moss. '"He cometh not," she said.' And, of course, he doesn't.

Let's see how these courtship stories are enacted in women's lives today.

TELEPHONES: The painful part of the game

All this waiting has a precise contemporary equivalent. Once hanging around in her tower or moated grange, today she's 'hanging on the telephone', waiting for his call.

Dorothy Parker wrote a six-page story about a woman waiting for the telephone to ring. 'Please, God, let him telephone me now. Dear God, let him call me now. I won't ask anything else of You, truly I won't. It isn't very much to ask. It would be so little to You, God, such a little little thing. Only let him telephone now. Please, God. Please, please, please . . . . If I didn't think about it, maybe the telephone might ring. Sometimes it does that. If I could think of something else. If I could think of something else. Maybe if I counted five hundred by fives, it might ring by that time. I'd count slowly. I won't cheat . . . .'[27]

She may be waiting to see if he's going to ask her out, waiting to see if he's going to ask her out again, or, like the woman in Dorothy Parker's story, waiting for that morning-after call to know if he's still interested after the first time they've made love.

All the women I interviewed had been in this situation at some time in their sexual histories, especially when teenagers, and all of them hated it. Even women who'd been quite ebullient about their skill at the traditional indirect moves tended to sober up when they got to this bit.

'Oh God, I can't bear it. You sit there looking at it, your stomach churns.'

'I used to *pray* for them to burst into life, with some men. I'd spend a whole weekend looking at the damn thing. I never want my daughters to go through that.'

'Waiting for the phone is one of the worst things in the world. That's the painful part of the game.'

In her book, *The New Other Woman*, Laurel Richardson explored the situation of young single executive women in the US who were having affairs with married men. The women entered into these relationships feeling assertive and autonomous, convinced they could have affairs on their own terms. But they ended up falling in love and staying in, 'waiting for the phone to ring'.[28]

That phrase – 'waiting for the phone to ring' – immediately conveys the women's powerlessness in their love affairs. We often use this phrase as a symbol of, or shorthand for, female helplessness. Telephones invariably feature in the morality tales women tell one another: as we saw in Chapter Three, cautionary stories about women who take direct sexual initiatives and how they are punished often conclude, 'And he never even phoned her . . .'. Occasionally a woman will subvert the power the phone has over her. Silent phone calls made to unnerve an ex-lover or a lover's wife seem to be a predominantly female form of persecution. We recognize the covert aggression in this: our previously boundless adoration of Di did diminish a little when we heard about the series of silent phone calls made to a male friend from her apartment. But mostly women feel powerless in relation to phones. Given a list of sexual initiatives to grade in order of difficulty, women almost invariably told me that one of the hardest things would be to ring him up the day after making love for the first time.

This was the only initiative that some women rated as harder than asking him out the first time.

This bit of modern technology has invaded our unconscious life. Telephones haunt our dreams, along with the age-old symbols like snakes and fire and the sea. Psychotherapist Clarissa Pinkola Estes says that the malfunctioning telephone call is the subject of one of the nightmares we most commonly dream.[29] The phone won't work, or the numbers on the keypad are out of order, or the wires have been cut – like Sylvia Plath's black telephone off at the root: 'the voices just can't worm through'.[30]

During courtship, we'll be very much aware of these fears of being cut off or of not getting through, because of the way sexual love triggers feelings of attachment and fears of abandonment. When the phone stubbornly refuses to ring, a strong and sensible woman can start to think like an abandoned child, feeling first loss, then rage with the person who's made her feel so bad. As Dorothy Parker's woman puts it, in a fleeting moment of insight: 'This is silly. It's silly to go wishing people were dead just because they don't call you up the very minute they said they would . . .'.[31] Male mythologies that are all about activity and scoring and winning the woman protect much more effectively than the female mythologies against the fear of loss that is the downside of desire.

But there are also practical reasons why telephones cause such angst. The telephone requires somebody to take an initiative. On the telephone you can't do any of the things that women do to try and influence things while keeping to the traditional script. You can't just happen to be around – coincidentally wearing your tightest trousers – or make an ambiguous move.

While men make the calls and women wait for them — as many of us still do — the telephone exaggerates our courtship roles in a retrograde way. No wonder women tend to laugh ruefully when they talk about this, recognizing that waiting for his calls is highly anachronistic behaviour. It's about as far from any notion of female autonomy as you can get.

MAGIC: One way to fish for your boy

Lucy, aged fifteen, has her own way of trying to influence the telephone. 'Whenever I think someone's going to ring, they never do – but if I don't, they do. My friends kind of sit by the phone, and it never goes. I try not to think about it – so that it does.'

This is magical thinking. Lucy has developed a superstitious ritual to try and make it happen: like a child avoiding the cracks in the paving stones or touching every third lamp-post, she tries not to think about it – so it will ring.

Magic is one kind of instrumentality that women have always had in courtship, one way in which waiting women have tried to influence things. Medieval clerics for instance often warned against women's use of potions and spells to excite or quell love – aphrodisiacs or impotence spells, and magic woven into cloth.[32] And in the old love stories, the makers and users of magic are always women. Mostly an older woman makes the magic – often a potion – and a young woman uses it. Isolde's mother concocts the love potion that is intended for Mark and Isolde's wedding night – but drunk with such dire but poetic consequences by Tristan and Isolde. In Hans Andersen's terrible tale, *The Little Mermaid* – which no girl of an impressionable age should be allowed anywhere near – the Sea Witch makes the potion that takes away the Little Mermaid's voice and gives her the beautiful human legs that will make her attractive to the Prince – though every step is like walking on knives.

And today, what do women do when they fall in love? Like Lucy, we may develop magical rituals. Sometimes the rituals are ways of making the phone ring. Sometimes they make use of synchronicity: If I go there again, do that again, perhaps it will 'happen' again. Or we may develop superstitions about particular clothes. We have lucky moon-and-star earrings or a yellow halter-neck T-shirt that always seems to work. Occasionally there will be some slight element of rationality in this: Suzy, the owner of the yellow T-shirt, did add, 'Mind you, there wasn't very much of it.' But mostly it's pure magical thinking. Some women may go further: they'll visit fortune tellers, or ring *She*'s 'I-Ching Line', or consult *Options*' 'Russian Runes', or get a friend of a New Age bent to read the tarot. And all but the most sceptical women when in love will consult their horoscopes.

The ever fatter horoscope supplements that come with the women's magazines in January bear witness to women's insatiable appetite for magical predictions. And women consult horoscopes about their love lives, not their economic aspirations or career trajectories. The priorities are always the same. 'Horoscope Special: Love, Sex, Power' says the cover of *Cosmopolitan* for January 1996. 'Your Stars for 1996: Love Sex Work Money' says *Elle*, widening the possibilities out just a little.

We turn to the irrational when we feel out of control of our lives. In society as a whole, there's most interest in the paranormal at times of political unrest and economic uncertainty. Men in occupations that put them at risk, like miners or sailors, may be highly superstitious, as may gamblers or athletes or others who don't have much control over the outcome of their endeavours. And men also visit fortune tellers. Men I've known have consulted psychics when they've been given a diagnosis of serious illness or were facing some terrible reversal of fortune – such as the prospect of going to prison for a crime committed by someone else. But women turn to the paranormal primarily for help with their sex lives. Women go to fortune tellers to talk about their love affairs: Prophet Samuel, a Tottenham psychic, has said that on an average day, twenty-two of the thirty people who consult him will be women who want to make a man come on to them or come back to them. And the reason for women's fascination with magic and the irrational in all its forms is surely that we feel we have so little control during courtship because according to the traditional script we have a much more limited repertoire of possible behaviours than men. There are so few direct ways in which we can shape what happens.

Sometimes in women's magazines this female fascination with the paranormal collides with self-help culture to produce a kind of do-it-yourself love magic. A recent piece in *Cosmopolitan*, based on the work of 'internationally acclaimed personal development consultant', Jasminder Kaur Love, recommended the following formula for attracting your perfect partner: make a 'wish list' – a list of the qualities you're looking for in a man: shout your wish list out to the accompaniment of loud music: keep quiet for twenty-eight days about what you're doing – 'If you let the cat out of the bag you'll get severe interference on the signal you've sent out and you won't get results' – then wait hopefully for your perfect partner to appear.[33]

Here the magic spell is couched in psychological language. We're told for instance that this is 'really just one step up from positive thinking'. The teen magazine, *Just Seventeen*, went further with their 'Be Your Own Cupid Kit'.[34] This supplement was all about indirect ways, based on evolutionary psychology, to attract the boy you fancy, like wearing musky scents because they're closest to human pheromones and putting on lots of blusher because a high colour suggests you're healthy and therefore a desirable mate. There was nothing about being direct and picking up the phone. It concluded, 'You've tried flirting, you've tried science, and you've even tried our fail-safe attention-getting methods to get your boy. Still no joy? Fear not, 'cos there's one more way to fish for your boy – our final suggestion is the use of the "Ancient Arts".' And this guide to the wax-candle spell, moon magic, footprint magic and chanting was taken seriously enough to come with a warning: 'White witches always say that you should be careful what you wish for, 'cos it might just come true . . . . What this really means is that if you attract a person and he turns out to be totally wrong for you, then you may just end up living in misery . . . . The best way to avoid such scenarios is to imagine that you are drawing "the best possible relationship" towards you, rather than a specific person . . . .'

Magical formulae don't seem out of place in articles on how to attract men because there are close analogies between magic and what women do in courtship. The practice of magic is about an indirect relationship between what is done and what happens. There is, for instance, what Sir James Frazer in his compendium of magical practices, *The Golden Bough*, calls homeopathic or imitative magic.[35] To kill an enemy by imitative magic, rather than stick a knife in him, you'd burn a wax image containing his nail parings. Perhaps women's fascination with magic relates to this isomorphism. The woman who follows the classic courtship script, who glances in the direction of a man she likes and runs her hand slowly through her hair – something she'd love him to do to her – is rather like the magician in a traditional society, in her attempt to influence what happens by indirect means and imitative magic.

Magic was a word women often used when they talked to me about how they negotiated their sexual relationships. 'If you start to break it all down, it sounds calculating, there's less magic. You'd rather not think it through.' 'I love that magic moment, when it just clicks and you know it's going to happen.' 'If we lay down too many rules won't it take the magic away?' There's a sense here of courtship for women as something that doesn't quite happen by human agency, will and choice – something irrational, mysterious, something you have no control over. How different from the men who spoke at the start of this chapter: Geoff, who loved to chase till he felt 'in complete control', or Keith, who approached the woman he wanted as deliberately as if he were going to buy a pound of plums.

Our discourse about female desirability often has a subtext of witchery. Many of the words used to suggest female sexual attractiveness have their origins in magic – bewitching, beguiling, enchanting, glamorous, alluring. And products sold to women to make us more desirable are frequently promoted as 'magic'. 'Amarige, a Magical Feeling'. 'The Enchanted Evening collection by Estée Lauder – magical make-up colours and fragrances for the party season . . . .' Here magic is the metaphor used to suggest the indirect effect that these lipsticks or perfumes will have on the man who is desired. What happens between spraying on the perfume and being desired by the right man is a magical process – not susceptible to reason, or your own direct efforts. You put on the perfume, and wait for it to happen.

Scent for men is marketed quite differently. In an advertisement for Paco Rabanne aftershave, a man with a very direct stare looks out of the page: we may not quite feel comfortable meeting his gaze. And the slogan is the clearest possible message that what 'happens' depends on his agency: 'If you want to be remembered, it's up to you.' Here there is no intervening process between his putting on of the aftershave and its effects on the outside world. There is no magic. It's up to you.

KEEPING WOMEN DOWN: A special kind of domination

These mythologies of initiating, desiring and dominant men and waiting, desirable and elusive women are extraordinarily persistent. Why do we still find them so seductive and appealing? What functions do they serve for us today?

These, it seems to me, are the three possibilities. Courtship mythologies that exaggerate gender differences may serve to keep women in their place. Or they may persist because men find them arousing. Or perhaps it's their meaning for women which is the source of their appeal.

First, there is what we might call the orthodox feminist explanation – because it's predicated on the notion of a social order designed to maximize male power. Do our courtship mythologies serve to keep women down?

When a man and a woman lie in bed together, the man will almost invariably lie on his back and the woman will lie on her side with her head resting on his shoulder. Musing on this, sociologist Irving Goffman wrote, 'Cross-sex affectional gestures choreograph protector and protected, embracer and embraced, comforter and comforted, supporter and supported, extender of affection and recipient thereof; and it is defined as only natural that the male encompass and the female be encompassed . . . . And this can only remind us that male domination is of a very special kind, a domination that can be carried into the gentlest, most loving moment without apparently causing strain.'[36]

Goffman explores male dominance as something that's habitual, that feels natural, and that men and women both collude in without consciously intending it. And even today, the imaginative context of heterosexuality is still that kind of easy intimate male dominance that he describes. Men and women replicate a pattern of male dominance and female submission in their choice of partner. By and large women choose men who are older, higher status, higher-earning than we are – though this is changing a bit: and most strikingly we choose men who are *taller* than ourselves. (If he's shorter than her on 'Blind Date', it's a non-starter, a joke, and in the video of the date she'll be shown bossing him around and slinging him into the pool.) Our ineradicable preference for pairings where the man is taller than the woman hints at the fantasies of protection and domination that still govern our sexual choices.

To say men have more power than women in courtship is not to say that they *feel* empowered. At the start of courtship, both people are likely to feel that the other one has all the power. Whenever I started to talk about this with men, they would always immediately assert – often quite forcefully – that the male role in courtship doesn't feel powerful. But it is undeniable that the male role gives the man more room for manoeuvre and more control than the woman, and that this – like the man being taller than the woman – feels natural to us. This is the kind of dominance that 'can be carried into the gentlest, most loving moment without apparently causing strain.'

It may be easier to see how this power imbalance works by looking back. Today we have the vestiges of a system which was in full and pernicious flower in the 1950s – when it was unfeminine for a woman to get out of a car without assistance. The courtship rules then in operation were plainly about limiting the woman's access to the public world. Writer Beth Bailey comments, 'For a woman to ask a man for a date was inexcusably aggressive, and he could justifiably, according to some authorities, simply cut her off in mid-sentence and walk away. By charging women who did not defer to them . . . with masculinity (and thus with being unattractive and undatable) men could make women's submissiveness (femininity) a pre-requisite for participating in the dating system'.[37]

Today, there undoubtedly are some men who use this power in a deliberate way. Laura Martin, in her book on avoiding rape, *A Life Without Fear*, explores a pathological extreme of this:[38] she suggests that if you're uncertain about a man you're going out with, you should test his need for control by choosing the wine or deciding where you will sit: if this makes him angry, you should get out fast. (See also Chapter Nine.) Such men are dangerous exceptions, of course. It would be a distortion to suggest that most men who follow part, or all of the traditional script, do so to establish their dominance and keep the woman down. All the men I talked to would have been justifiably appalled by such an accusation. But the fact remains that the effect of the traditional script is to allow a kind of male control – just as a woman's decision not to wear high heels when going out with a man who's only half an inch taller than herself allows a kind of male control.

If male initiative in courtship is at some level about asserting male power, if it is indeed a vestige of traditional habits of thought – with which women collude of course – then the start of the relationship is the ideal time to establish this pattern. The first moves in any relationship are the defining ones, laying down interactional rules that can be hard to change later. It can be fascinating to look at our first meetings with people who later become significant in our lives and see how our later relationship is sketched out. These early interactions, or the interactions during which a friendship shifts into something potentially sexual, also establish the fantasies that underlie the relationship and give it its emotional flavour.

As Milan Kundera puts it, in *The Book of Laughter and Forgetting*, 'Every love relationship is based on unwritten conventions rashly agreed upon by the lovers during the first weeks of their love. On the one hand, they are living a sort of dream; on the other, without realizing it, they are drawing up the fine print of their contracts like the most hard-nosed of lawyers. O lovers! Be wary during those perilous first days! If you serve the other party breakfast in bed, you will be obliged to continue same in perpetuity or face charges of animosity and treason!'[39]

This theory then offers one explanation as to why it's during those perilous first days of a love affair that we behave in the most conventional way – the way that gives the man most of the overt control.

TURNING MEN ON: Resistances to satisfaction

So to the second possible explanation for the persistence of these mythologies. Is there a physical imperative here? Does the inevitable deferring of gratification implicit in the sexual chase or quest heighten male sexual arousal? Does it persist because men find women who have to be pursued more exciting?

Freud certainly thought so. 'Pleasure in marriage,' he wrote, 'does not bring full satisfaction ... It can easily be shown that the psychical value of erotic needs is reduced as soon as their satisfaction becomes easy. An obstacle is required in order to heighten libido; and where natural resistances to satisfaction have not been sufficient men have at all times erected conventional ones so as to be able to enjoy love.'[40]

Behavioural psychology offers a certain amount of support for Freud's theory that 'resistances to satisfaction' increase desire. Scientists who've attempted to shape the behaviour of laboratory rats by giving them rewards have found that the rat that learns quickest is not the rat on a fixed ratio schedule – the rat that gets most rewards – but the one on a variable ratio schedule – the one whose rewards are unpredictable, who sometimes gets rewarded and sometimes doesn't.[41] Like the rats, if we think we might get something we want but we can't rely on it, we may want it more and work that much harder to get it. So maybe the woman who puts the man on a variable ratio schedule – blowing hot and cold – increases his desire.

Some men I talked to felt there was something in this – and not only men like Geoff at the start of this chapter who explicitly loved the chase. Ted said, 'It's obvious really – you'll value something more if you've had to work for it.' Steve said, 'If the relationship is on the rocks, she can keep it going longer than it would by being a bit inaccessible.' But other men, faced by too many 'resistances to satisfaction', will simply give up.

Reticence and reserve can be sexy, of course, especially in societies where there are a lot of prohibitions on sexual behaviour, because in such societies reticence won't be read as lack of lust. The film, *The Age of Innocence*, set in upper-class New York society in the late nineteenth century, had Michelle Pfeiffer as Countess Olenska playing hard to get amid the luscious place-settings, creating a great sense of sexual tension while giving absolutely nothing away. The intensification of desire by the use of restraint may seem almost perverse to our hedonistic culture, but it can generate a highly-charged eroticism from the smallest gesture. The film's erotic climax is the moment when Daniel Day-Lewis unbuttons her glove.

But obstacles quite patently can't be a universal need for male sexual arousal. For instance, this theme seems quite tangential to gay male culture. Men who love men seem to largely dispense with 'resistances to satisfaction'. There are the occasional stories of the unattainable beautiful boy – Tadzio in *Death in Venice*, enchanting and untouchable in his blue-and-white bathing suit[42] – but much gay culture involves initiatives of extreme directness and clear signalling about preferred sexual practices.

Even if traditional scripts do have a sexual pay-off for some heterosexual men – men like Geoff, for whom the chase is such a major source of pleasure and excitement – there may be a price to be paid in terms of female sexual arousal. The woman whose elusiveness is deliberate, and who teases and evades in order to turn him on, will be doing this at a cost to her own arousal – because she can't be spontaneous. Of course, men aren't totally spontaneous either: beliefs about the overwhelming impulsiveness of male sexual desire are clearly a distortion – or, as Helen Zahavi has remarked, there would be more rapes in Dixons on Saturday mornings. But scripts that are all about male pursuit, male spontaneity and male initiative, and female responsiveness, female veto and female control do undoubtedly curtail female sexual expression more than male. Sex is best if you have it when you feel like it – but according to the traditional script, only the man acts on impulse.

TURNING WOMEN ON: Someone big and tall and fiery

So to the third possibility: that women like this charade – that male dominance and male instrumentality turn women on, and persist because women are choosing men who demonstrate those qualities.

There's an interesting paradox here. Women are very ambivalent about big strong men. As Annette Lawson writes in her study of adultery, 'Women want simultaneously to be magically transported and to determine their own fate. Throughout my book, women speak of these two desires'.[43] We're going through a period of transition: it's scarcely surprising that we should be pulled between these contradictory desires.

The fantasy of male control is a common turn-on for women. In most female fantasy, both public and private, male dominance persists as an arousing idea, in those familiar themes of erotic violence, bruised lips, 'sweet, savage love,' being overwhelmed or swept away. The strongest, most autonomous women admit to these fantasies, women who are happily married to loving gentle partners who get up to the children in the night and make wonderful spaghetti carbonara – women like Liz, who said, 'I have a fantasy about a man who's just terribly male, someone big and tall and fiery. There'll probably be a sort of predatory aspect to him, in terms of wanting to get you into bed. I've often been very attracted to musicians – I suppose I always think they must have wonderful hands! And there's this predatory quality about musicians too – this passion for their instrument, to possess it, and I want to be possessed like that, with that kind of passion.' Or as Amanda put it, 'All my fantasies revolve around a man taking control, taking initiatives, and saying, Do this, do that, and almost being a bit domineering. Once I said, "I think we should try something different", and Joe said, "What?" and I said, "I don't know", and he got really cross, he said, "I even have to decide what we're going to buy in Sainsbury's . . .". I think it would be nice to have someone say, "Come on darling, let's do this . . .". But he never does.'

Yet, though the fantasy of male control is a turn-on for many women, the reality is that reducing male control in bed tends to increase female pleasure.

Whether a woman has orgasms reliably, for instance, seems to depend on whether she feels in control and can concentrate on herself and ask for the kind of stimulation she needs. In her self-help book for women who don't have orgasms, Rachel Swift writes, 'When I began devising this plan I realized an important truth about myself: I had only really begun to enjoy sex when I'd realized that the man did not have to be sexually dominant. In other words, the more control I gained in the bedroom, the closer it brought me to satisfying sex, to overcoming this pernicious barrier.'[44]

During intercourse itself, the most pleasurable position for many women is the dominant position. Any sex therapist is likely to suggest to a woman who's not enjoying intercourse that she tries going on top, because it gives her more control over the rhythm of love-making.

It makes sense too for the woman to be the one who initiates sex. A woman's interest in sex can vary a lot through her monthly cycle. For now, women may express this by indirect initiatives – by getting out their sequined tops and sexy little skirts, for instance. Desmond Morris writes, in a rather baffled way, 'A recent research project that measured the amount of bare flesh displayed by females dancing in nightclubs made

a remarkable discovery. It emerged that the females unconsciously increased the amount of flesh exposed by their costumes at precisely the times when they were ovulating . . . .
They themselves had not calculated that they were ovulating
and had no idea that they were varying their displays according to their physiological condition'.[45] Only a man could claim
that this was 'unconscious'. Quite obviously the women were
dressing more seductively because they felt sexier in the days
leading up to ovulation – as many of us do – and were keener
to get off with someone than at other times. But how much
better if women took advantage of their sexiest times by initiating directly, rather than just 'increasing the amount of flesh
exposed by their costumes'.

In all sorts of ways, then, male dominance can detract from
women's pleasure. A woman may choose a man who exercises
a lot of control in courtship because of the promise that he'll
be like that in bed – but when they do get into bed together,
she may find that dominant male sexual behaviour doesn't
give her the satisfaction in reality it promises in fantasy.

But maybe even the fantasies are starting to change. Maybe
dominant male behaviour is losing its appeal to women even
at the start of courtship. Some US psychologists asked, 'Do
Nice Guys Really Finish Last?'[46] They found that women rated
a man as more sexually attractive if he was warm, altruistic,
wanted to know what his partner thought, and really listened
to what she had to say. A smidgin of traditional male
behaviour didn't go amiss: women liked a bit of dominance –
but only in men who were also agreeable and altruistic. Dominant men who weren't 'nice' got very low ratings for sexual
attractiveness.

So what function is served by these 'spurious charades of
maleness and femaleness'? Perhaps they persist because they
keep women in their place by enabling men to take control
right at the beginning, when it matters: yet most men will

deny that they experience the male role in courtship as power-ful, and insist that they wouldn't want that kind of power anyway. Perhaps they turn men on – but only some men, some of the time. Perhaps they turn women on – yet it seems to be the fantasy rather than the reality of male sexual domi-nance that's arousing.

The antithetical roles we enact in traditional courtship – hunting men, waiting women – look increasingly anachronis-tic. There's nothing inherent in human sexuality that requires male dominance and male initiative. We may find the familiar scripts reassuring, even arousing, but the polarization of our courtship behaviour disadvantages us all, both men and women. It's time to do something new.

Alice said, 'I met Tim at a party and we talked all evening. I gave him my phone number and then after three weeks when he didn't phone, I phoned him. I was very nervous phoning up and saying, "Hello, you won't remember me". We talked for a while and he said he'd ring me the next week but he didn't. I rang again, but his phone was disconnected, so I went all the way from West Finchley to Colliers Wood to see him. In fact he'd been ill with the flu, that was why no one had seen him.

'I think it was because I'd recently broken up with someone I'd lived with for seven years. I was into doing new things – I thought, Haven't done that one before, I'll have a go . . . .'

Alice's account brings together a lot of the themes from the old male courtship stories. She steels herself to do something that feels difficult, in order to achieve a goal she very much wants. She sets herself a challenge, risks rejection, persists when there are setbacks, overcomes obstacles. She even goes on an epic journey, travelling right across London to see the man she wants. And with her courage and persistence she wins him. She and Tim now live happily together in a cottage in Kent.

For women contemplating this kind of action, the language,

the psychology and the mythology are there, ready and waiting. It's just that they've never belonged to women. It's time
to steal them and make them our own.

But if we're going to initiate, we'll also have to give something up. Taking on the male mythology means giving up
some of our comfort, leaving the walled safety of the places
where women have always sat and waited. It means putting
away the magical predictions and picking up the phone.

CHAPTER 6
LOOKS AND SMILES

'The most curious part of the thing was, that the trees and
the other things round them never changed their place at all:
however fast they went, they never seemed to pass anything.
"I wonder if all the things move along with us?" thought
poor puzzled Alice. And the Queen seemed to guess her
thoughts, for she cried, "Faster! Don't try to talk!"'

(Lewis Carroll, *Alice in Wonderland*)

IN summer 1994, our newspapers were full of Bienvenida
Buck, a beautiful blonde with a penchant for exuberant hats,
who was having an affair with the First Lord of the Admir-
alty. At the time she was married to Tony Buck, a peer in his
seventies. A *Sunday Times* report described Bienvenida's first
encounter with her future husband, as seen through another
woman's eyes. 'This weekend Countess Artsrunich recalled
that evening: "Bienvenida was very tartily dressed in black
stockings, a short black dress and with long bleached hair
falling over her shoulders. She was introduced as the hostess,
but it was obvious she didn't have a clue what that involved.
Tony Buck was bewitched. It was obvious to everyone else
that she was just going for people with a title, whether they
were married or not. She must be given credit for her
ambition, but not for very much else."'[1]

In 600 BC Sappho said much the same, though rather more
elegantly.

I hear that Andromeda
that hayseed in her finery
has set a torch to your heart
and she without even
the art of lifting her
skirt over her ankles . . .[2]

The complaints are just like Countess Artsrunich's. Andromeda is tarty and common. She lacks finesse and she overdresses.

In real life, of course, the woman who follows the traditional script is rarely as passive as the entranced heroines of the old stories. She certainly won't be going on epic journeys, taking risks or fighting dragons – but she may be signalling furiously. And women from Sappho to Countess Artsrunich have always been acutely aware of other women's sexual signalling – and often very disparaging about it.

To ask a woman if she's ever asked a man out is invariably to be told about this system of indirect if sometimes blatant signalling – the kind that we do with long bleached hair and a short black dress. You will be told that well, no, she hasn't asked anyone out exactly, but she does feel she has some control over the process, because she shows him how she feels in other ways. Many women were at pains to point out that their indirect language was very clear. Sometimes women claimed they actually initiated sexual relationships in this way.

I want to look at this system of signalling that women have always used, rather than initiate directly. What precisely do we do? What's wrong with what we do? What might we gain by being more direct?

SOPHIE: I didn't want to look obvious

Sophie has long dark hair, a lot of glamorous jackets, and a high status job in business. But in spite of appearances, she's certainly not in the Meredith Johnson mould.

Here is Sophie being indirect:

'There was a guy at college I liked. He had a bike with a blue milk-crate on the front of it that he'd nicked, and I used to follow his bike round. When I saw which library he was studying in, I'd run into the loo and put on my makeup and chew my lips so the blood came to them and then saunter past – Hi!

'Then there was Ross. I'd met Ross at a party and had a crush on him, and somehow his friend Simon met me too and had a crush on me – so I went out with Simon because I knew I'd see Ross more. Simon's parents had this beautiful house in Putney, and he phoned me in the summer holidays and said, "Would you like to come to lunch?" and then he said Ross would be there too, and I thought, That's God being nice to me, I must have done something good. And we sat out in this garden in Putney at this teak table, and there was Ross this golden boy at the end.

'I was in a really hyped-up state – you know when you're in the middle of an obsession – and we went into the city and I decided to have my hair cut and meet them – and I had all my hair shaved off round the back – I don't know why – and I met them at some tube station – and I put my head down and said to Ross, "Feel my head" – and that was the first moment . . . you know when you can feel somebody's touching you in a way that means more.

'I went back to Birmingham and I knew that Ross was back there, but he lived with Simon – so I phoned up and said, "Is Simon there, please?" It was Ross's voice, he said, "No, I'm afraid he's not", I went, "Oh – could you just tell him Sophie rang, please?" and Ross went, "*Sophie!*" I said, "Oh hi, I was just going to phone up Simon to know if he wanted to come out this evening," so Ross said, "Well, I'm going out this evening with some friends, d'you want to come?" and I said, "Well, I was going to ask Simon if he wanted to come out with a group of my friends", 'cos I didn't want to look obvious . . . . And he said, "Where were you going to go?" and I knew he always went to the Albert, so I said the Albert. It was the summer holidays and I hardly had any friends at Birmingham, I had to phone round my friends. "You've got to come out to the Albert and *pretend* . . ." – so I got about five friends together all sitting round in a pub they didn't like.

'And it was that evening that we first slept together.'

Sophie exploits the traditional system for all it's worth. This is about as far as women can go, while staying within the parameters of the traditional script.

She's at once audacious and feminine, very indirect and very knowing, in her following of bicycles, her studied casualness, her chewing of her lips in the library loo. And in her interaction with Ross, nothing is what it seems. She leads his friend on when it's really Ross she wants. She pretends she's ringing his friend when it's Ross she wants to talk to. When he's there, her golden boy, in the summer garden, she reads it as a magical reward: I must have done something good. Even when he asks her directly – 'I'm going out, d'you want to come?' – she remains indirect – 'I was going out with my friends'. She lets Ross make the arrangements but she sets the scene and supplies the extras – five friends who have to sit round looking relaxed in their least favourite pub. She aims to give an impression of just being friendly – with a sub-text of 'Look how popular I am' – yet of course she does want him at some level to pick up her sexual interest in him. It's all very feminine – covert and hidden, but calculated. No wonder there's a male nightmare about seductive women who conceal the most ulterior motives behind a delectably feminine façade.

Yet in some of what she does, Sophie hides her motives even from herself. She goes to the hairdresser and has her head shaved, she 'doesn't know why'. Then, in a delicious piece of self-exposure, she lowers her naked head for Ross to caress. In a single gesture, she reveals herself, she gives him permission to touch her, and she sets up a kind of touch that most women love: he strokes her head.

Sophie is dazzling. But her story also shows just how uneasy most women are with the element of calculation in the female role in courtship. Her actions show how much she wanted Ross, how determined she was to get him, how hard she worked: her account would surely flatter him. But she's embarrassed about it. In the end she did tell him how she'd gone about it – but not till they'd been living together for seven years.

There are some hairdressers in Chapter Eight who readily talk about their indirect ploys, but most women I know don't talk about these things. Often we'll hide our plots and plans from our friends. Sometimes it's as though we're even hiding them from ourselves, like Sophie when she has her radical haircut. We'll certainly hide them from the man in question – maybe for years, maybe for ever. And the more feminist our aspirations, the more embarrassed we'll probably be about all this covert strategizing.

In a wider sense, too, we may feel there's something a little suspect about these devious ploys. Psychological studies show that indirect behaviours are rated by both men and women as less healthy than direct behaviours.[3] Yet the classic script gives women no choice but to be indirect and manipulative. What does it mean for women's self-esteem that what we do to achieve this most crucial of objectives – to get into bed with or into a relationship with someone we love – is so often underhand and secretive?

But we may also be reluctant to talk about or even think about our courtship moves because we believe they *shouldn't* be deliberate. It's a common female belief that in an ideal world sexual relationships would 'just happen' in a seamless and spontaneous and natural way – like the flowers growing or the moon rising. We may feel that by attempting to 'make it happen' we're distorting the process – 'taking the magic away'.

There is, of course, one situation in which a woman has to initiate: a lesbian relationship. Yet, even here women long for empathy and seamlessness. The romantic lesbian fantasy seems to be of relationships which just happen, in which women simply merge in a sweetly spontaneous clinch. *An Emergence of Green* by Katherine Forrest is a romance from Silver Moon Books, the lesbian equivalent of Mills and Boon. The story describes the developing attraction between Carolyn and Val. Until page 147 there are lots of ambiguous touches, which aren't clearly initiated and might be friendly or affectionate rather than sexual: 'Val's big hand was unexpectedly soft; and Carolyn was aware as she dozed of its warm protectiveness, the cushionlike flesh of the fingertips'.[4] Even when the two of them finally embark on a sequence of touching that ends in orgasm, again it's not explicitly sexual at first: 'Carolyn said softly, "I am cold. I should've worn something warmer." Without hesitation and without thought Val turned and took her into her arms, held her to warm her . . . . Carolyn uttered an indecipherable sound.'[5] In opposition to all this merging, fusion and mutuality, male sexual approaches are described as 'invasion' – 'There would be no invasion that night.'[6] You might hypothesize that one source of appeal in lesbian sex would be the opportunity it offers women to explore the active side of their sexuality and to take initiatives. Yet even in lesbian fantasy we find this persistent theme of empathic sex that no one has to initiate. This is plainly an idea that women find deeply alluring.

Agony aunt Irma Kurtz also enjoys this dream of empathic sexual negotiation. In her book, *Irma Kurtz's*

Ten-point Plan For An Untroubled Life, she writes about the kind of courtship in which our desires are transmitted by a kind of telepathy without the need to *do* anything.

'A woman writes, "Dear Irma, I am falling in love with my co-worker. He doesn't know. We are really good friends and there are times I think he might feel the same way about me. I'm afraid to spoil our friendship. Do I have to leave my job?" I reply, "Desire makes heat and it shows first in the eyes. Look him in the eye, think heat, feel heat, transmit heat, and if he doesn't get the message, he's probably a dud . . .". A while ago I met a woman from Boston who made her living going round America giving courses in flirtation – a bit like teaching breathing, I would have hoped . . . . But practically every postbag brings in letters from women sexually attracted to men who see themselves as friends, no more, no less. But, for crying out loud, unless the guy is married, or she is, or he is gay, or he is seriously depraved, what is she waiting for? Are we losing our ancient gifts to such a degree that we no longer know ways to show sexual interest more subtle than to throw the guy to the ground and grab his crotch?'[7]

This way of thinking about courtship places the blame squarely on the man if our messages aren't read correctly. We've inherited ancient gifts, it's all instinctive and easy as breathing – and if the man doesn't feel the heat, there's something wrong with him.

It seems to me, though, that courtship isn't quite like breathing: it's more like learning to walk. It's a series of skills that we have to learn – and, as with all behavioural skills, some people master them much more easily than others. Let's look at the steps we take as we move towards intimacy – and, in particular, let's look at the woman's moves.

WOMEN MAKING IT HAPPEN: The electric moment

'It's a kind of one step forwards one step backwards dance,' said Clara. 'I love it, the thrill, the touch, the whole pattern. It's one of the best things there is . . . .' Anthropologist Helen Fisher divides this 'one step forwards one step backwards dance' into five stages – attention-getting, recognition, talk, touch, and body synchrony.[8] Each stage has a distinct escalation point, where the couple either move forward to the next stage – or the interaction stalls and one or other withdraws. And, according to the classic script, a lot of this early stuff is woman's work – setting the scene, signalling with your eyes, keeping it going, touching first, filling in the silences.

The woman's moves at the start of the process have been painstakingly analysed by Monica Moore, a psychologist who has studied the behaviour of people pairing off in singles bars in the US.[9] She identifies fifty-two categories of 'female solicitation behaviours' – things women do to get male attention. Here, for instance, is one of a number of female glances she describes, a type two glance or short darting glance. 'The woman directed her gaze at the man, then quickly away (within three seconds). The target axis of the horizontal rotation of the head was approximately twenty-five to forty-five degrees. This behaviour was usually repeated in bouts, with three glances the average number per bout . . . .' She also observed and classified other kinds of behaviour: the head toss, the skirt hike, the lip lick, the lip pout, the hair flip – and the neck presentation: 'The woman tilted her head sideways to an angle of approximately forty-five degrees. This resulted in the ear almost touching the ipsilateral shoulder, thereby exposing the opposite side of the neck. Occasionally the woman stroked the exposed neck area with her fingers'. This stroking of her neck is one of those sexual gestures in which, in a kind of imitative or homeopathic magic, the woman does to herself what she'd like him to be doing to her.

To make quite sure that these were courtship behaviours, Monica Moore also watched women in other contexts. The average number of flirting acts per woman per hour was 70.6 in a singles bar, 18.6 in a snack bar and 9.6 in a library. It dropped to an all-time low – 4.7 – in a women's meeting: women who love women, it would seem, use a different visual language.

The singles bar crystallizes out this behaviour. It's an 'open field', in which people don't have prior connections or reasons for interacting, and everything depends on non-verbal signals.[10] In a 'closed field' – say an office – the sequence would be more variable, and the attention-getting wouldn't have to be concentrated into a few seconds. The semantics of the office affair are a little different: 'Conversations meant to be overheard and slightly unnecessary memos,' said Clara, who was in the first careless rapture of an office affair when she spoke to me. But many of the moves would of course be the same.

If it's male attention you're after, it pays to be good at these things. A finely-honed talent for flirting seems to be much more important than what you look like. The more of these solicitation behaviours a woman displayed the more often she was approached – regardless of how attractive she was. Reading Monica Moore, you inevitably find yourself wondering if life would have taken a different course if you'd really mastered the neck presentation.

Monica Moore's observations are borne out by anthropologists, who suggest that certain female solicitation behaviours are shared by all cultures – or at least all cultures where men and women are permitted to look at one another. Anthropologist Irenaus Eibl-Eibesfeldt identified what he called a universal pattern in female flirting. 'First, the woman smiles at her admirer and lifts her eyebrows in a swift, jerky motion as she opens her eyes wide to gaze at him. Then she drops her eyelids, tilts her head down and to the side, and looks away. Frequently she also covers her face with her hands, giggling nervously as she retreats behind her palms.[11] Here, as so often in women's traditional courtship behaviour, there's a mix of submissiveness and directness, a kind of affected shyness.

We also share certain cues with animals. Male animals use dominance gestures when they court, and men also express dominance: they exaggerate their body movements, swagger, use up more space. Women toss their heads and fiddle with or flip their hair: animals too use their heads in flirting – female mud turtles extend and retract their heads, female albatrosses toss their heads.

It's a matter of personal style how flamboyantly or elliptically we signal. Tina had had an affair with an attractive young teacher at her school. The other girls called him 'Mr Swoon': Tina wanted him and vowed she'd get him. She was fifteen at the time. I asked her what she'd done. 'I bounced bra-less in my games kit on a trampoline outside the window of his teaching room,' she said.

Melissa took a different approach. 'I would always cultivate a rather mystical and distant air,' she said, 'and deliberately emphasize being unavailable, because men like to chase what's unavailable. I used to wear a big floppy black hat all the time, coming over one eye. I suppose it was sexy in the sense that it suggested mystery and unavailability. And I'd talk about religion and Gorecki – deep and meaningful and slightly mysterious things . . . .

'I remember a friend saying to me, "Of course it's alright for you – you just have to stand there and look vacant and mysterious and they all come running". And I thought, That's funny – I always felt like a wallflower. And once someone at university said, "Where's Melissa?" And this woman said, "Oh just look for the group of men and you'll find her in the middle of them!" So that was how I was seen, although it didn't feel like that at all.'

Melissa's behaviour looks very different from Tina's. One woman goes for the in-your-face appeal of the stripper, the other for the seductiveness of the woman who smoulders behind a veil. Melissa's big floppy hat is clearly used as a form of veiling, and veiling has a double meaning – it's about modesty but it's also about allure. It's another example of the ambiguity of female courtship behaviour with its mix of signals: what seems modest may also be done coyly, with provocative intent, because what is hidden arouses curiosity and draws the eye.

It's clear from what Melissa says that indirect initiatives, however effective, do not necessarily make women feel powerful. She knows from what other people say that she's seen as a man-eater: she feels like a wallflower. Women don't always own and feel empowered by their skill at the early moves of courtship – perhaps because our talent for attracting men in general is irrelevant if we don't get the man we want. I spoke to several women who'd obviously been very good at attracting men, yet never felt confident in their skill: like Clara, they'd always felt like 'the fat girl bulging in a pink dress that stood by the wall'.

The next stage is the 'recognition phase' – where eye meets eye and the couple move into talking range. Helen Fisher says, 'In Western culture, where eye contact between the sexes is permitted, men and women often stare intently at a potential mate for about two to three seconds during which their pupils may dilate – a sign of extreme interest. Then the starer drops his or her eyelids and looks away.'[12] In one of their more pleasing coinages, anthropologists call this meeting of eyes 'the copulatory gaze'.

Because pupil dilation is an involuntary reflex, it's a reliable index of sexual attraction. We instinctively respond to it – though of course we aren't consciously aware of it. And much of our imagery for falling in love is about the eyes and looking, both as the place where passion is 'engendered', and as the means by which we communicate that passion. In *A Midsummer Night's Dream*, Oberon's magic liquor dropped in people's eyes causes instant infatuation with the most unsuitable subjects. In the film, *Brief Encounter*, the passion that draws two passing strangers together begins when she gets some grit in her eye, and he comes over to help her and they stare into each other's eyes.

A stare, if not 'copulatory', signals dominance. If you want to learn to assert yourself, say all the self-help books, you should dare to stare into other people's eyes. Looking is powerful. Forbidding women to look – to meet men's eyes, and to look at men's bodies for pleasure – has, in the past, been a way of reinforcing women's subordination. In the pornographic *Story of O*, the female sex slaves at the Castle of Roissy always have to keep their eyes lowered; they're punished in various painful and imaginative ways if they dare to meet men's eyes.[13] There are fairytales too in which women are punished for visual curiosity. In *Hans My Hedgehog*, one of the loveliest of the 'animal groom' stories, a woman is forcibly married to a monster in the form of a hedgehog. She wakes in the middle of the night to see him peel off his coat of quills and emerge as a beautiful naked man. The tender eroticism of this story derives from its presentation of male nakedness as a moment of discovery and delight for the woman, with the inaccessible masculine body and psyche as a coat of spines, and the peeling off of that spiky skin as a ravishing image for self-disclosure and self-revelation. Inevitably though, trouble ensues. This looking is forbidden – and the couple have to endure many trials before they are reconciled.

Attitudes towards looking by women are rapidly changing. Increasingly we're looking at men's bodies – and we're also meeting men's eyes. No surprise, then, that the way we use our eyes in courtship is changing. Today we use much more deliberate eye contact than our mothers did. We don't go in for so many of those coy smiles, where women rapidly drop their eyes, and we hold men's gaze for longer.

Next comes talk. This is the negotiation point at which the sequence is most likely to break down. As Tom put it, 'Sometimes conversation goes well and has a certain kind of mutual charm to it, and other times it's like pulling teeth.' The information we give through non-verbal signalling, including appearance, is limited and tenuous compared with what we give away when we talk. When we're wondering whether to kiss, get into bed with or marry someone, we're hugely influenced by their class, education, intelligence and opinions – which are all rapidly revealed in conversation. The principle of 'assortative mating' dictates that we pair up with people who are like us; it's through talk that we explore these connections. The effects can be extraordinarily direct. Women with strong political convictions – particularly, for some mysterious reason, those with leftist sympathies – will describe how they stop fancying somebody point blank if they don't like the way he votes.

Through talk, we also hint at our intentions, often in code. For instance, 'My wife/husband doesn't understand me . . .' has conventionally been the way to signal availability for and interest in a secret liaison. Clara recalled, 'It was before we'd kissed, before anything was clear. He said he'd been married for such and such a time and in that time he'd had quite a few affairs, and that made an enormous impact on me – I felt I was free to have one as well. I suppose he'd sussed out intuitively things that might be impediments to his pass to me, and one was that I might think I was going to get pregnant, so he told me he'd had a vasectomy, and the other was that I might think I was breaking up his marriage. If he hadn't said he'd had affairs before, I wouldn't have had an affair with him.'

In all these moves of the one step forwards, one step backwards dance, and the little decisions about what we say and
do, we also sketch out certain power relations. According to
the traditional script, women disclose more in early courtship
conversations. This female disclosure is a conversational
equivalent, perhaps, of the man undressing the woman – the
sort of revelation and exposure that was the theme of the
film, *The Piano*, where Ada took off her garments one by one
on George Baines's orders, as part of a sexual bargain. As
Sophie put it, 'You start revealing things; when you start talking about relationships you know you're onto a winner – and
then if you start talking about sex, it's very flirtatious.' Certainly it's flirtatious, but it can also be disempowering if it
isn't mutual – if he doesn't reveal himself too.

Today though, there's an increasing tendency for men to
reveal themselves in courtship conversations. Psychologist
John Nicholson wrote in 1980, 'Revealing too much about
yourself seems to be found a particularly unattractive characteristic in men, whereas women are more often damned for
being too discreet about themselves.'[14] He goes on to give
some stringent advice to the man who misguidedly feels the
urge to pour it all out when talking to women: Don't. This
seems dated. It's implausible that women would react so
unfavourably to men's self-disclosures today. In fact, women
love men to talk about themselves, and shrewd men make
the most of this. Men told me that when they were trying to
get off with women they would deliberately talk about emotional issues because they knew women liked this kind of
conversation. Over the past few years there's been a feminiz-
ation of courtship conversation: women now set the agenda,
and people who are pairing off tend to talk about the things
that *women* like to talk about. Later in the relationship, women
may recall those lovely confiding sessions and wonder where
they went.

But though there will now probably be disclosures on both

sides, many women do still adopt a submissive role in what they say. What women often choose to disclose is their vulnerability – even their incompetence. Natalie and Kim are two highly competent women working in the law – but for both, this demonstration of ineptness was a regular part of their courtship repertoire. Natalie said, 'I'm studying law – and as soon as people find out I say, "Oh I'm the crap one in the group" – 'cos I know a lot of people just think straightaway I'll always have my nose in a book and never have any time for having fun.' Kim said, 'I wouldn't say, "I've done this brilliant thing . . . ." Now, I'd say, "I'm a terrible lawyer, I'm awful. I really admire the way you . . . ." And when I was at college, it would have been, "I just don't seem to be able to get to grips with T. S. Eliot, you've really got this brilliant way of . . ." When really I didn't believe it, really I thought I was very good at T. S. Eliot.'

For many of us, this playing down of our abilities seems to happen automatically during courtship. But it's anachronistic – at odds with our behaviour in other areas of our lives – and it may be counter-productive, because men don't always find it attractive. Tom said, 'A woman who's interested will look at you very intently, take great interest in what you say even if you're a bit pissed and not making much sense, and probably act in a slightly subordinate way. What you feel is that you're being looked up at. And she'd say rather less than you do – kind of deferring. It isn't something I like terribly because I don't like women who subordinate themselves. None of the women I'd regard as relationships I really valued did that.'

Sometimes this projection of our vulnerability develops into a request for help – which Monica Moore calls an 'aid solicitation'. It's a charade of course; in courtship women put themselves across as much more helpless and needy than they are. Diane said, 'I never consciously thought, How can I make myself look weak and vulnerable? I just found myself doing it. I can remember on one occasion coughing in the car park and seeing Mark walk past, and I went cough, cough, cough, more and more, and I thought, What's the matter with me? And he came over and said, "Are you alright?"'

It's likely that these displays of helplessness and neediness, reminiscent of the nameless sorrows of the beautiful predators in Chapter Two who 'wept and sighed full sore', have a clear evolutionary purpose. If female sexual selection is all about looking for men who'll be good fathers to our children, then with our childlike or vulnerable behaviour we may be testing out men's parenting potential and selecting for men who are nurturing and who respond to 'aid solicitations' with help and support rather than irritation. Strong women who manage offices or run intensive care units may be deeply troubled by these helpless and childlike elements in their own courtship behaviour. But there's a cure that's highly effective. Once couples have children themselves, they never buy each other cuddly toys or make up pet names for each other or do any of the other things that so embarrass us when we observe them in others, and that are probably best understood as rehearsals for parenting. And once a woman becomes a mother, she's unlikely to collapse into an appealingly quivering heap at the prospect of changing a plug – at least in her relationship with the father of her child.

The fourth of Helen Fisher's five stages is touch. First there are 'intention cues', little truncated gestures, embracing movements that stop short of touch – leaning forward, resting one's arm towards the other's on the table. Then comes touch itself – usually on the shoulder, forearm or wrist.

People are very aware of this touch. They know who tends to touch first, and men often say they like the woman to do it, that it can be invasive if the man touches too soon. Both men and women remember who touched first in a particular relationship – though they may interpret it differently.

Julia put her arm round Don in the pub after a union meeting they'd both attended. Recalling the moment, he said, 'You touched me, and I responded to that.' But she denied any sexual intent: 'You'd told me about your divorce and I just wanted to put my arm round you and show you I understood . . . .' Even in our interpretations of what we do, men are direct and women indirect. Here Julia seeks to hang onto the ambiguity years after the event: she insists it was just a nice friendly comforting hug. But Don interprets it as a sexual touch, and dates their sexual relationship from this point.

Sometimes, though, women do own the sexual intent in the first time they touch – and refer to this touch to show that they make the first move. But in fact this female touch is part of the conventional script: in the singles bar studies, for instance, the woman usually touches first. Where men initiate almost everything, this is one move that women can make. Warren Farrell suggests that the hallmark of a direct initiative is 'an ego on the line'; there must be a real risk of rejection.[15] By his criterion this touch doesn't qualify. It has to seem indirect and friendly. It's quite different from a kiss on the mouth or an invitation to dinner.

Men muse a great deal on these female touches and how to interpret them. Rob said, 'You walk somebody to their door and they give you a chaste little peck on the cheek. Then you walk off down the street and you think, "Now, hang on, what the hell did that mean?"' Tony said, 'Even if someone's just a friend, if you're just walking along and they put their arm round you, it's a bond. The man tends to feel quite good about that, even though it's not always a sexual thing – but it's saying, "OK, we can be intimate so far – you can invade my space." It depends how people touch you. If someone touches you softly on your face, that's quite intimate, so you probably think, Well, I can invade your space a bit more.'

The first unambiguously sexual touch, the kiss on the lips, is still a male prerogative. It's incredibly rare for women to initiate this. And when women talk about how we try to 'make it happen' indirectly, it's as though we're pushing against the restrictions of our role, using our passivity in as active a way as possible. If the woman is yearning for the man to make this move and he's reticent, she may set the scene rather like all those comatose heroines in the old stories, by lying back, kneeling down, turning away, not moving, not talking.

Diane said, 'I had my back to him and I was fiddling with a dry leaf, I was kind of vulnerable, turned away, and he either would come and touch me or he wouldn't, and if he did, then it would be the electric moment. And he did and half an hour later we were in bed.'

Amanda said, 'With Joe I remember saying, "D'you want to play a game of backgammon?" and he obviously couldn't play and I was so bored, and I laid back on the floor and I went, "*Oh* I'm so *tired*", and I thought, If he doesn't pick this sign up I'm just going to give up on him altogether.'

Clara said, 'It was about twenty past four, the kids were coming back, and I thought, Shit, I've given him lots of opportunities. I've gone ninety-nine per cent of the way, he's only got to make the gesture and he hasn't done, and as he was ready to go I was kneeling on the carpet, I made myself kind of low, looked up at him, Here's a low head, touch me, sort of thing. And he put his hand on my head and if he hadn't then he'd have been really kind of crazy. And he did, and he kissed me, and that marked the end of the courtship, a kiss and it was clear. I would never say, "Can I kiss you?" or have kissed him – as soon jump into the Niagara Falls . . . .'

As Clara points out, the courtship process according to one definition ends here, where the sexual intent is clearly revealed and shared.

The last of Helen Fisher's five stages is body synchrony, where the couple start to move in tandem, briefly at first, then gradually mirroring one another more and more. This presages the synchrony of sex. It's a mutual thing: no one initiates it. Dancing, which in many cultures has a crucial role in courtship, is a formalization of this process: it ritualizes the responsive and mirroring movements of couples who are very attracted.

Research studies show that people who are intimate adapt to one another's rhythms when they're together, gesturing, talking, breathing, in time. When we feel deeply in tune with another person we may be sharing their rhythm at a micro-level: electroencephalographs show that even our brain waves get 'in sync'. And the body synchrony that is the outward manifestation of this does seem to be a reliable sign of intimacy. The psychologists who've studied singles bar behaviour say that once a man and a woman start mirroring one another consistently, you can confidently predict that they'll leave the bar together.

EXTREMELY BLOODY AMBIGUOUS:
Reading women's signals

How clear is this indirect language, the language of the hair flip and the aid solicitation and the coy smile?

I asked Melissa, who has a classically feminine courtship style. She said, 'I think most people are very adept at signalling the kind of relationship they want, and other people are very good at picking up those signals. I think you're quite capable of conveying to a man that you're interested, but only in a long-term relationship with children – I think the rules of the game are as subtle as that. There are unspoken things that go on between men and women where men and women know what the rules are – and I've never been in a situation where boundaries were crossed because I think I've always given the right messages. I don't think it's possible to get it wrong unless you're mentally ill. I think messages are very clear unless you mean to go across them.'

But Malcolm saw it differently. He said, 'Women's signals are extremely bloody ambiguous and you never know quite where you are. There are women who don't give out strong signals who you nevertheless get off with – it doesn't follow that because you're not getting a real come-on that you should give up and go home. Checking out whether a woman's interested, you're up against vast differences in personal style – from women who adopt a rather intimate and confiding manner with any reasonably personable man they come across, to some who are fairly inhibited even with people they like rather a lot. It's unbelievably hard to tell.'

These accounts are representative of men and women's positions. Most men feel like Malcolm: you never quite know where you are. But most women agree with Melissa – they think their cues are as clear as day, and men are simply being obtuse if they don't pick them up . . . .

Why are women so sure? Firstly, because it's empowering to believe your signals are easy to read. It gives you some control even within the limits of the traditional script. It makes the whole process seem less random.

But there's another reason too for our certainty. Research shows that women are better than men at interpreting non-verbal cues in every social situation. So when we attempt to communicate with our eyes, hands, hair and smiles, we're using a language that we speak and read more fluently than men. In particular, men tend to misinterpret friendliness as seductive behaviour. One study investigated the hypothesis that friendliness from a member of the opposite sex might be misperceived as a sign of sexual interest. A man and a woman had a five-minute conversation while a hidden man and woman observed. Male actors and observers all gave the female actors higher ratings for 'promiscuity' and 'seductiveness' than did female actors and observers.[16]

But what of the woman whose intent *is* sexual – who's deliberately hiking her skirt, tossing her head and stroking her hair? As with those other categories of women's work – housework and secretarial work – what women do during courtship is easily overlooked. Much of the time, it seems, men aren't consciously aware of what women are doing – though of course they often respond.

Biologist Timothy Perper claims that of the singles bar pick-ups he has observed, women initiated two-thirds with their 'subtle non-verbal cues'.[17] I'd question this: in systems terms, there's an issue of where you punctuate the interaction – how you slice the behaviour up in order to observe it – and it seems to me that women only send out those subtle non-verbal cues to men who are already looking at them. But whatever the punctuation, what is not open to dispute is that women are doing a lot of work at this stage. Then towards the end of the sequence of attention-getting, gazing, talk and touch I've described here, there's a shift: it's now the man who's doing all the work – he puts his arm round her, kisses her, starts to seduce her. When the man takes over, it's the end of the ambiguity.

When Perper asked men to describe the pickup sequence, all but three left out the initial parts, where the woman is sending out up to fifty-two varieties of non-verbal cue – but all spoke at length about what they themselves had done. At least within the highly compressed enactments in singles bars, the men don't seem to know what the women are doing: the women's work is invisible.

I asked men how they could tell if a woman was interested.

Rob said, 'It's partly body language, partly to do with keep-ing the conversation going when you get those little hiatuses – you can tell that there's a kind of prompting going on. Or perhaps they go and get a drink and come back, and you think, She doesn't have to come back.' Geoff said, 'I think it comes down to eye contact and the physical side of it – they move closer.' Tom said, 'If you move close and they move away, you're not going to get anywhere.'

Faced by the 'extremely bloody ambiguous' nature of women's signals, trying to read this non-verbal language, men home in on the least subtle cue – the gross motor signal – as the best indication of a woman's sexual interest in them. She doesn't move away.

No wonder there are so many jokes about men who just don't get it. In Sue Townsend's novel, *Adrian Mole: The Wilderness Years*, for instance, Bianca, who has great legs and an upper second degree in Hydraulic Engineering, offers to mend Adrian's shower. 'She hung about after she'd fixed the shower and talked about how lonely she is and how she longs to have a regular boyfriend. She asked me if I have a regular girlfriend. I replied in the negative. I sat in the armchair under the window and she lay on my bed in what an old-fashioned kind of man could have interpreted as a provocative pose. I wanted to join her on the bed, but I wasn't sure how she would react. Would she welcome me with open arms and legs? Or would she run downstairs screaming and ask Christian to call the police? Women are a complete mystery to me. One minute they are flapping their eyelashes, the next they are calling you a sexist pig. While I tried to work it out a silence fell between us, so I started to talk about the revisions I am making to my book. After about twenty minutes, she fell into a deep sleep . . .'.[18]

This disparity – women thinking you have to be mentally ill to misread their signals, and men thinking, Now, hang on, what the hell did that mean? – is potentially fraught because not just at the start but throughout the courtship process, every move the man makes depends on reading it right – on knowing whether she'll welcome him with open arms and legs or call the police.

Tony, one of the men I interviewed, has a beautifully clear sense of courtship as a process. Like the psychologists and anthropologists, he divides courtship into distinct stages, each with an escalation point at which a risk has to be taken, a boundary crossed. And like Geoff, Tom and Rob, he comes back to physical closeness as the most reliable signal that his move would be welcomed.

'You don't think, I really like you, I'll kiss you – 'cos they might react pretty badly – so how d'you know when it's alright to kiss someone? You don't. It's another line, isn't it? You can get close to them, your heads get close – and it gets to a certain point, and you can think, well, either they'd have backed away or perhaps they do want to kiss. There's no one particular sign to say, "It's alright to kiss me", or for you to say to someone, "OK, you can kiss me."'

I asked Suzy, his partner, who in her experience tends to kiss first in relationships. 'The first kiss? Doesn't it just happen?' she said.

APPEARANCE AS A SEXUAL SIGNAL:
Faster, don't try to talk!

But to limit a woman's signalling to the five-point plan – solicitation behaviours, recognition, talk, touch and body synchrony – is of course to overlook a huge part of the female script. It leaves out the things she does before ever she gets to the bar, the things she really works at. The singles bar studies suggest that the woman's gestures and gaze are the most important elements in attraction, more instrumental than appearance. Flirty women get more attention than pretty women. But if she's to get him near enough to talk and touch and synchronize, first she has to make him notice her. And advice to women on how to get your man is focused above all on that moment: it's about self-presentation, about getting him to look at you.

Women's magazines are our main source of advice about appearance as courtship display. The agenda of women's magazines is the getting and keeping of relationships with men. There will be articles and agony columns on what you should say or do to get and keep your man: but the meta-message is always that it's appearance that matters most. A few articles on sexual communication cannot compare with the impact of page after page of gorgeous anorexics in marvellous clothes. And the magazines constantly stress that the whole point of looking like this is to turn men on. 'Sexy' and its synonyms are clichés of fashion journalism.

'The siren suit. Stretch fabric, severe tailoring – the new shape suit focuses tightly on the body . . . .'[19]

'Shapely, slick and sexy sums up the new mood of fashion as spring sees the return of grown-up clothes for real women . . . .'[20]

'The look is rich bitch rebel – the sizzling hot, smouldering essence of Sixties and Seventies swank rock glamour, and sex, sex, sex. She's the modern "It" girl and she's wearing Gucci . . . .'[21]

The message is unequivocal. Women's clothes are for attracting men – making them look, turning them on. Sexy appearance is the most crucial of female indirect initiatives. In the pages of fashion magazines to look sexy becomes almost a moral imperative. And this isn't the throwaway sexiness of a pretty woman with slept-in hair who's grabbed her boyfriend's shirt. Here, sexiness is all about a glamorous high-fashion labour-intensive look – the glossy makeup and two-inch heels of the Disney villainess. This is what it means to be desirable.

Over the past decade, there's been ever more stress on women's looks, with supermodels as the new female icons. Supermodels are everywhere, putting their name to novels and falling off their shoes to great acclaim. You can even buy Supermodel sticker-books with peel-off frocks in Sainsbury's: the catwalk is right up there with the Tropical Rainforest and the Haunted House as a favourite fantasy scenario for pre-schoolers. The whole point of the supermodel is her ravishing appearance: at least actresses or film stars do something – but the idolization of the fashion model involves a further narrowing down of the meaning of female attractiveness, because the supermodel is there to be photographed: her arena is the still image.

Yet during the decade of the supermodel, there's also been an apparently paradoxical tendency in some fashion writing to play down or deny the signalling function of female appearance. The latest line about appearance is that the Madonna-style post-feminist can look sexy and that's fine, because she's not doing it just to attract men, she's doing it for herself. She's expressing her sexuality, she's not bothered by political correctness, she can take her kit off and still be powerful . . . . *Cosmopolitan* assures us, 'Bra-burning in the Sixties may have been a symbol of freedom for women but, in reality, it wasn't that easy. For many it was all a bit of a let-down, in body as well as soul. Today's bra-buying boom and the clamour for great fitting and glamorous underwear is synonymous with woman's well-developed confidence and more upfront attitude in the Nineties.'[22] Or, as the cartoon has it: 'Post-feminism – keep your bra and burn your brain'.

A ten-year-old girl I know tells wonderful stories about a shameless sexual heroine called Clorinda, who wears spiky heels and shiny lipstick and who sexually abuses cute-looking boys in the park. Clorinda is the very essence of the Madonna-style post-feminist. The self-contained sexual heroine who features in the more erudite fashion columns properly belongs here, in these ten-year-old imaginings, in this world of pre-pubescent fantasy, at a time of life when girls are still innocent of the structural inequalities that trammel our most intimate relationships.

Of course dressing-up can be fun. But the central role of appearance in female sexual identity still disempowers women in so many ways. Appearance preoccupies us when we should be thinking of other things. Our preoccupation uses up masses of female energy. It makes us miserable and envious. It's hugely expensive. It means that ageing holds more terrors for women than for men because older women can feel they have lost a central part of their sexual identity. And sometimes it hurts. Anorexia is being diagnosed in six year olds,[23] women are dying after liposuction, some fashion models have a daily calorie consumption roughly equivalent to a famine victim's, and it is hard to think of a better example of sadism as properly defined than the solicitous careful cruelty of the plastic surgeon who repeatedly improves his wife on the operating table.[24]

The idea that looks are power is about as plausible as the old notion that the Mecca Miss World competition was all about personality. Given the meanings of female clothing, dressing up is the very antithesis of power. The sexier you look, the more you're disempowered. As image consultant Mary Spillane puts it, when warning professional women against turning up to corporate dinners in skimpy clothing – 'If you show too much you'll blow your chances . . . the more skin you show the more power you lose'.[25] In January 1995, an edition of the ITV programme 'The Time, The Place' on the subject of men's fashion was taken off the air when some black activists in the audience staged a protest because a black male model was dressed in a skirt: they claimed this was demeaning to black men. For these protesters, merely to put on a female garment signified vulnerability and submission.

The argument that glamour is empowering also falls apart when we look at the life stories of many of our icons of female perfection – which are so often punctuated with suicide attempts. Diana has cut herself and thrown herself down the stairs. Brigitte Bardot took an overdose and cut her wrists. Marilyn Monroe killed herself. Daniela Rocca, who starred in *Divorce Italian Style*, was for a brief spell in the Sixties the darling of Italian cinema. When she was deserted by Pietro Germi, her lover and the director of the film that made her, she slashed her wrists and languished for twenty years in mental hospitals.

Women are in a double bind. We strive to be desired for what we look like: we're convinced that's where our happiness lies. Yet there's something inherently problematic about being desired entirely for our looks – because we feel that these bodies that we've worked so hard to perfect are a product, not quite ourselves. As we'll see in Chapter Eight, there's a close analogy to the way men feel about being loved for their money.

And, at present, the pressure to look good is actually getting worse. Sexual selection is about scarcity and competition. It doesn't matter what you look like – as long as you look better than the rest. This is what Matt Ridley calls the Red Queen principle, after Lewis Carroll's Red Queen who had to keep running to stay in the same place.[26] And today, with images of ravishing women constantly before us, and the technological means to achieve an ever closer approximation to perfection available, we're having to run faster. Computer enhancement of the photographic image means that the icons of female beauty in the magazines have bigger pupils, longer legs, fuller lips, even than *themselves*. Clever editing means that women in sex scenes in films are often composites – and no one woman is going to look as good in bed as the two doubles who helped Sharon Stone with the sex scenes in *Basic Instinct*, each presumably with her best bits on display. And cosmetic surgery is becoming almost compulsory in the US: all affluent Americans have immaculate teeth – and even veteran feminist Gloria Steinem has her smile plumped up with collagen.

In 1990, US writer Naomi Wolf shot to fame with her incisive critique of *The Beauty Myth*.[27] What happened then can be read as an ironic little fable about the impossibility of opposing women's preoccupation with appearance. Naomi Wolf is a beautiful woman, beautifully photographed – and somewhere along the line she metamorphosed from a polemical feminist into the leading exponent of a new brand of cerebral chic. The image completely cancels out the message. She tells women that beauty is a tyranny – that the beauty myth disempowers and oppresses us. I agree. But there's nothing that makes me quite so dissatisfied with my own appearance as a quick glance at Naomi Wolf's dustjackets.

Why should women's looks matter so much? Why can't we simply give up this preoccupation?

An evolutionary psychologist might argue that that's how it's always been, and that's how it's meant to be. There's a genetic argument that runs like this. The state of a woman's body is much more important to reproductive success than a man's: she carries the baby inside for nine months and then has to feed it, and she also has to be young to be fertile. So signifiers of female youth and health will always be important. Men are drawn to beautiful faces because of their symmetry: a symmetrical organism is one that hasn't been subjected to adverse conditions while growing. Large breasts suggest – spuriously as it happens – that she'll be good at suckling his child. And Caucasian gentlemen prefer blondes because blonde hair means youth: only very young women have naturally fair hair.[28] According to this argument, women's looks will always be more important than men's – while the most attractive men will be those with big salaries, big desks and big BMWs to demonstrate their ability to provide – or perhaps to hint by analogy at their size and potency.

These arguments about the biological importance of women's looks are always put forward by men, concerned thoughtful male evolutionary psychologists who explain regretfully that that's how it is, and how it will have to stay – like Matt Ridley: 'It is a cruel, despotic fashion, one that enforces its pitiless logic at the expense of many a brilliant, kind and accomplished woman who happens to be plain . . .'.[29]

But is this 'pitiless logic' really inescapable? Is this really how it has to be? Must appearance necessarily remain women's most crucial sexual signal?

The scientific principle of parsimony dictates we should always look for the very simplest explanation for an observed phenomenon. So what is the simplest explanation for the way the 'Beauty Myth' persists, however often it is exposed? Why does female appearance remain such an urgent concern, in spite of all the changes in women's role, all the things we've achieved, and even though we know it's costly – in time, money, self-esteem?

The answer is surely that this hasn't changed because the bit of interaction where female appearance matters most hasn't changed – the first few moves in courtship. He still asks her out. And while she remains dependent on indirect initiatives, her appearance will continue to be a huge preoccupation. She uses her looks to 'make it happen' – to get him to make his move. She has to make him look at her, and she has to make him think of sex when he looks at her.

While appearance plays such a crucial role in courtship for women, there's no way we're going to give up our obsession with what we look like. Women who choose to ignore the conventions of attractiveness have too much to lose. The rewards of looking good are obvious: you get a bigger choice of men. And because more men approach you, there's a greater chance they might include the one you really want. But appearance would surely lose some of its urgency for women if she could approach him directly – if she could ask him out.

It's right at the start of relationships that looks matter most. As relationships develop other things come to matter more – whether the other person is sexy or clever or kind. If she asks him out, he might be delighted to find she's all those things, though she'd never have caught his eye across a crowded room.

AMBIGUITIES: A miniskirt on a feminist

Anorexia in little girls. The devaluation of older women. The hard work. The casualties. The general grumbling discontent with ourselves so many of us feel. Lots of reasons to want to free women from this compelling need to attract the male gaze. But what about courtship itself? What problems does this system of female signalling pose for both men and women?

First, indirect signals are *ambiguous*. As we've seen, women believe their signals are crystal clear – but men don't know how to read those signals. 'Extremely bloody ambiguous, and you never know quite where you are.' And, if men aren't sure about the meanings of looks and smiles and aid solicitations, they're still more bemused about the meanings of clothes.

'A miniskirt on a feminist is a signal whose ambiguity and inconsistency is quite deliberate,' wrote Philip Norman, in a tirade about Germaine Greer's appearance on the 'Late Show' in a short skirt.[30] There's an implicit nostalgia here for a time before feminism when sexy clothing signalled something straightforward. But the nostalgia is spurious. Such a time never existed. Any indirect initiative is of its nature ambiguous. And ambiguity is built into sexy female clothing, whether the woman inside the clothes is a famous feminist theorist or a classic mistress with an underwear collection to rival a Martin Amis heroine and a pretty little flat in Chelsea. It's never quite clear what a woman means. Just as she might be flicking her hair back to attract a man she wants or because it's fallen in her eyes, so she might have chosen that dress which fits like a bandage because she wants to lure a particular man into bed – or because her magazine says it's in fashion, or her friend's got one like it, or her other nice dress is in the laundry basket.

Clothing poses particular problems, because the language of fashion is so fluid. The meanings of clothes are shifting, devious; this is why fashion so fascinates – but it also makes it a tricky way to get a specific message across. What was worn seriously on the S/M scene in the Eighties may now apparently be worn with 'irony'. Yet how exactly do you convey the fact that your leather bustier or skintight vinyl trousers are ironic to the man who finds them a turn-on?

Indirect initiatives are also *indiscriminate*. A woman may

cross her legs and hike her skirt to attract a man she likes. Half the men in the room will probably notice – but the one she wants may be looking at someone else.

I asked Kirsty whether she put more effort into her appearance when she was in love. 'When I fell for Jake,' she said, 'I lost two stone in weight. I was up every morning at six o'clock having baths, using little bits of moisturizer which I don't have normally, suddenly preening my nails – and I think you get a kind of glow, it's like a drug, your breasts become a little larger and your body becomes more sensual and you feel that people treat you differently. You wander round with these bright eyes and these big breasts and this kind of clean smile. When I've been in that state, I've always had men asking me out. This went on for ages and ages, before I got off with Jake.'

Kirsty glows, suffused with love amphetamines. She puts more effort into her appearance and looks luscious. Lots of men are attracted. Lots of men ask her out. But for weeks she fails to get a response from the one she really wants.

Clothes in particular are totally indiscriminate in their signalling: they're there for all to see. They use up a lot of visual space compared to solicitation behaviours, and can't be switched off because you've got to walk past a posse of men coming out of a pub. Even if there's no ambiguity in a woman's intention, and she's chosen this dress deliberately and with care because she wants sex, she sure as hell doesn't want sex with just anyone: in fact, it's highly unlikely she wants sex with anyone at all other than the man she's got her eye on. Yet non-verbal signals don't give her much scope for conveying that – and sexy clothing gives her no scope at all. Like the moth broadcasting its pheromones, sexy female clothing signals to everyone for yards around.

One result is that she may get a lot of attention from the wrong man. This may be intrusive or alarming. Dressing sexily is by no means always pleasant. We've asserted that you never get raped or sexually harassed because of what you're wearing, in order to place the moral responsibility for sexual violence where it rightfully belongs, but this assertion flies in the face of what we experience: that to dress to attract a man you want will also increase the amount of unwanted sexual attention you receive. This is the reason for the discrepancy between the fantasy and the reality of wearing overtly sexy clothes. A woman may buy a wet-look satin dress in the belief that she'll get a pleasing sexual *frisson* from wearing it – as you do if someone you like keeps looking at you with interest. But when she goes out in it, she feels uncomfortable and tugs the hemline down – as you do if someone you *don't* like keeps looking at you with interest.

But there's another kind of wrong man, too. He's the one she didn't really have her eye on, but who happens along and seems as though he will do. Attention from this man isn't alarming or intrusive: in fact it's reasonably pleasant. It's just not quite what she had in mind. Charlotte, who described her courtship strategy as 'being in the right place at the right time in the right clothes', put it like this. 'I think the worst trouble my style got me into was sometimes I didn't get the people I really wanted – because of not being direct enough. I'd perhaps make do with someone who was slightly easier to impress.' A woman may settle for second best, because, in spite of all that furious signalling with hair flips and purple lycra and lip-pencil, the man she really fancied never looked her way, and, within the limits of the traditional script, there was nothing else she could do, no other strategy open to her. The man who is 'slightly easier to impress' features in a lot of women's sexual stories. Sometimes she'll even find herself walking up the aisle with him.

Courtship is a delicate negotiation and there will always be ambiguities, as we play around with possibilities in that one step forward, one step backward dance.

Tony, the man I interviewed who had such a fine-tuned sense of courtship process, remarked, 'If someone comes up and says, "I really like you", that would probably put you off a bit – you'd think, It's like you've gone through four or five stages, you know nothing about me, and you've said you really like me. If you haven't gone through the stages it takes away some of the pleasure. Otherwise you'd just go up to someone and say, "I like you, I'd like to spend the rest of my life with you", or "I'd like to see more of your body, take your clothes off".'

Like Tony we may enjoy the ambiguities: we may also feel they are obligatory. But our present courtship script, which assigns the moves so rigidly to either one gender or the other, surely puts unnecessary obstacles in our way.

CHAPTER 7

DO WOMEN SAY NO AND MEAN YES?

Elizabeth: John – grant me this. You have a faulty
  understanding of young girls. There is a promise made
  in any bed –
Proctor: What promise?
Elizabeth: Spoke or silent, a promise is surely made.

                       (Arthur Miller, *The Crucible*)

'**H**AVE you ever been with a man who wanted to engage in sexual intercourse and you wanted to also, but for some reason you indicated you didn't want to, although you had every intention to and were willing to engage in sexual intercourse? In other words, you indicated "No" and you meant "Yes"?'

This was the question that psychologists Charlene Muehlenhard and Lisa Hollabaugh asked 610 college women, in an infamous study carried out in 1988.[1] Thirty-nine per cent of the women answered in the affirmative: they'd indicated no to sexual intercourse when they meant yes. And of the women who'd said no and meant yes, thirty-two per cent had done it only once, forty-five per cent two to five times, nineteen per cent six to twenty times, and three per cent more than twenty times. The study was repeated in Russia and Japan, with broadly similar results. Muehlenhard and Hollabaugh call this behaviour 'token resistance'. There were two explanations for their token resistance cited by virtually all the women: they didn't want to seem promiscuous, and they weren't entirely sure about their partner's feelings.

This study worried psychologists R. Lance Shotland and Barbara Hunter a great deal.[2] So they set up a further study in an attempt to establish more precisely what token resistance involved. They found that much the same proportion of women as in Muehlenhard and Hollabaugh's study agreed with the statement that they'd wanted to have sex, but for some reason indicated they didn't want to: again, one in three women had done this at least once. They then looked more closely at the evening on which the woman had said no and meant yes, to establish the precise sequence of events. They found that many of the women didn't mean yes at the same time that they said no – but they changed their minds in the course of the date. They started by saying and meaning no, then got turned on, and meant yes – but they'd never made it verbally explicit that their intentions had changed. For the man who is trying to understand this behaviour, though, this remains a very puzzling communication.

In both studies, most women (two out of three) had never engaged in token resistance: of those who had, most had done it only five, or less than five, times. The fact remains that saying no and meaning yes – or saying and meaning no, then changing your mind and meaning yes, but not actually *saying* yes – is something women say they do, on a massive scale. For one out of three women at least some of the time, no doesn't exactly mean no.

Many of us will recognize this behaviour: we've been aware of our friends or sisters doing it or we've even done it ourselves. Token resistance is a troubling consequence of women's reliance on indirect initiatives. Because a woman's signals are indirect, she can convey one thing with her body and say the opposite, or signal something and then deny she meant it, or express wanting and not wanting at the same time. She can say no and mean yes.

Of course, no always means no where the man is using threats or force. This obvious fact needs underlining – because the awareness that most of us have that women's signals can be ambiguous and complicated has sometimes been grossly misused by the defence or the judiciary in sexual violence cases. In a rape trial in 1982, a judge told the jury: 'Women who say no, do not always mean no. It is not just a question of how she says it, how she shows it and makes it clear. If she doesn't want it she only has to keep her legs shut and she would not get it without force and then there would be the marks of force being used.'[3] Here the recognition that women's sexual communications may be contradictory becomes a mitigation for sexual violence in any situation where the woman is too paralysed with fear to fight physically. No wonder advocates of fair treatment for women have had to reiterate constantly that 'No means No'.

But does it really make sense to generalize from rape to sex? It's certainly fashionable to do so. Many contemporary feminist theorists have traced out a continuum between the ordinary and the extreme, and then gone on to claim that events at different places on the continuum are much the same. So the definition of rape is broadened out to include sex that makes the woman feel bad – or even all sex in a society where men still have most of the power. 'I call it rape whenever a woman feels violated', says Catherine MacKinnon.[4] 'Romance is rape embellished with meaningful looks,' says Andrea Dworkin.[5]

I believe these very broad definitions of sexual violence can be confusing and even dangerous. It's surely significant that rape survivors take a quite different line. Women who've been raped make an absolute distinction between sex and sexual violence. As one rape survivor has put it, 'Rape is as different from sex as a punch in the mouth is from a kiss'.[6] That distinction surely holds, too, for the interaction that precedes the rape. In one situation a man is using threats or violence to

impose his will on the woman: in the other, two people who
are attracted to one another are doing that 'one step forward,
one step backward dance' that we looked at in the last chapter,
as they negotiate the timing of a sexual relationship they both
want.

So does no always mean no in a normal dating relationship?
Muehlenhard and Hollabaugh's disturbing study seems to suggest that it isn't that simple. In certain special circumstances
in the initial stages of sexual relationships, it seems, women
do sometimes say no when they mean yes.

What are these 'no's and 'yes's about?

COMPLICATED 'NO'S: I'll agree in ten minutes

Here are the responses of three women I interviewed to the
question, 'Have you ever said no when you've meant yes?'

Chrissie said, 'I think I've said no when I've wanted to
say yes, and been annoyed afterwards. I think you basically
wonder whether this is going to go anywhere – I don't like
flings, I like people to like me and want to have a lasting
relationship, so if I know somebody's just doing it for a quick
one, that tends to stop me. It's the fear they'd just be using
me.'

Emily said, 'I did with one man. I knew him quite well but
hadn't seen him for ages – and that night we felt very attracted
– but I knew it would just be a one-night stand because he
lived in Ireland. And at first I did say no but I really wanted
to go to bed with him. I think I meant something like, Go on
trying to persuade me, and I'll agree in ten minutes. It was
like there was more negotiating to be done – a feeling I
couldn't give in that easily.'

Josette said, 'There was a man I went out with at school –
he was absolutely gorgeous. But he pushed the pace with sex
with me, and I just wasn't ready for him. I was sixteen, I just
wasn't very sure and I couldn't handle it. There was lots of

touching and kissing, and I guess he got so turned on and felt it was his right to carry on further, and I wasn't having it. In the end we got up and went home and he was so furious he dumped me. He didn't call me again.

"I still feel very disgruntled about that – I think, I wish I had slept with him, then perhaps it wouldn't have finished in that abrupt way. Considering how I felt about sex less than a year later, it was so silly to have stopped at that point.

"I suspect actually – even though I was being incredibly adamant with my "no"s – what I meant was, "Yes, we'll do it next time". I think I was being very adamant in order to demonstrate to him that I was a nice girl, and then next time I'm sure I would have done. I think my no meant yes ultimately but not on that occasion.'

In the classic Mills and Boon scenario, which derives its erotic charge from a masochistic rape fantasy, her body says yes and her mind says no, he overrides her expressed wishes, and it's all a big turn-on. But life isn't like that. In real life, sex that's coercive, rushed or only half-willingly entered into is always always bad sex – as all women know.

None of these women wanted that. None of them wanted the man to override their wishes and go ahead and have sex without any further negotiation. But when Chrissie and Emily and Josette said no they were attempting – and sometimes failing – to communicate something rather more complicated. These 'no's were qualified. They did mean no – but with reservations. No – unless you can convince me you want a serious relationship. No – but we'll do it next time. No – but don't stop trying to persuade me.

For Chrissie and Emily and Josette, this is one stage in a process. In each case it's the first sex in a relationship. The Muehlenhard and Hollabaugh study doesn't differentiate between first sex and later sex[7] – but Shotland and Hunter did find that 'token resistance' was usually something that happened before the couple first got into bed together.[8]

Seventy per cent of the women who had said no and meant yes hadn't yet had sex with the man. In any new relationship, there's a 'loss of virginity' which has its own rules and meanings, and which is negotiated differently to subsequent sex. This is the moment for token resistance and complicated 'no's.

The reasons Chrissie, Josette and Emily give for their behaviour are all similar, and very like the reasons given by ninety-eight per cent of the women who'd done this in Muehlenhard and Hollabaugh's study – not wanting to be used, not wanting to seem fast, showing that I was a nice girl. These are all issues that are around when a woman first considers whether and when to sleep with a man. The very start of a relationship is a time when fantasies flourish. It's when we have a lot of desire and very little information – when, in writer Janet Malcolm's words, 'we must grope around for each other through a dense thicket of absent others'.[9] This is when we enact those spurious charades of maleness and femaleness, as we slot each other into categories and refer back to our simple stories to make sense of what happens. 'He'll lose interest once he's got me into bed just like Jack did.' 'She's another of those women who'll want to change me and keep straightening my tie.' As we get to know one another our simple stories get elaborated, or replaced by more complex and subtle approximations to the reality. In particular, those ideas about sexual shame loosen their hold on us. Worries about being fast or being used recede once the couple have made love, if the relationship continues.

Contradictory signals aren't unique to women, of course. At any one moment in time a man's communications will probably be quite clear, since he has to say or show what he wants by his unambiguous touches, invitations to dinner and direct attempts to get the woman into bed. But across a time-span men may be just as contradictory as women.

The other striking common denominator of these stories is the youth of the women. Chrissie is now in her early twenties,

Emily and Josette are both recalling incidents from their teens, and the research studies all involve women at college – who'd be between eighteen and twenty-three.

We can now add a little more precision to the suggestion that women sometimes say no when they mean yes. When young women are thinking of making love with a new partner for the first time, by saying no they may sometimes be communicating something more complicated.

JESSICA: Unavailable till the last minute

One woman talked about doing this often. Jessica is now married with young children. She's an assertive, ambitious woman who's had anti-pornography articles published in political journals and is a great advocate of women's causes. But she's also an expert at the coy glance, the neck presentation and the hairflip, a skilled player of the old courtship games, someone who raises being hard to get to an art form.

'Saying no when you mean yes is recognizably part of a game. I've done it quite often. It was all part of my style, to be unavailable till the last minute – so once you were, the game was over. There are signposts with men – whether you inherit them from the collective unconscious or your mother or whatever – there are guidelines and signposts you seem to know – he lets on he's interested, and then you sort of go, "Well, I might be interested or I might not . . . ." And then him saying, "Come on then", and you saying, "*No!*" . . . . I found myself doing it, but I knew I was doing it – it was conscious, but natural too.

'I think I did lead men on, but that was part of the game and they accepted that and they quite liked it too. In terms of what men call women, I'd have been a frigid prick-teaser. I was a bit madam-ish, and liked to keep them well away. I'm not particularly proud of myself, the way I did it.

'With one man, I did it far too much, and in the end he

absolutely hated me. He asked me to marry him and I laughed at him – he was really, really angry after that. I remember being very shocked when he slept with my two best friends – but that was to get back at me because I wouldn't.

'I think it's natural and right that women are very wary about which man they accept, because the implications are so much more dire for them. You don't want to give in to any old man who will then reject you and call you a slag because he won't look after you and the baby. So I think there's a lot invested in testing a man out, testing his commitment out, before you actually sleep with him. And that still stands today.'

Jessica's courtship style seems to come straight out of a John Fowles novel: you can just imagine her staring soulfully out to sea in a billowing black cloak. For Jessica, this kind of behaviour – evasive, contradictory, enigmatic – feels absolutely natural. It's something she started doing in an almost instinctive way. But she can also offer a comprehensive intellectual justification for the way she behaves.

Firstly, she acts like this because she's testing him out. For fertile women there is always more risk in sexual intercourse than there is for men: there is no evading that fact. Contraception simply isn't foolproof. A recent report from the Royal College of Obstetrics and Gynaecology estimated that one in three pregnancies is unplanned, and in seventy per cent of these unplanned pregnancies, the couple were using contraception.[10] And there are certain common female psychological structures that follow from our child-bearing potential. Wanting to hold on to the man after sex, even after lousy sex; feeling fragile the morning after and needing to know he still likes you; being choosy; finding casual relationships pointless or unappealing; and wanting to test him out before getting into bed with him. Her 'Well, I might be interested and I might not . . .' tests his persistence, and by implication his willingness to stick around once they've started having sex.

Many female courtship behaviours make sense as a form of testing-out. Most obviously, as Jessica suggests, we test male commitment and willingness to provide. But there's another kind of testing-out going on here too, though Jessica isn't explicit about this. The system which prescribes that the man should initiate and the woman respond hinges on the man's respect for the woman's veto. Perhaps one purpose of 'no's that we don't quite feel is to check that we have some control. When women are with a new man whom they haven't yet had intercourse with, they'll often push his hand away or say no to some activity – however much they want him. With our 'no's are we checking whether he respects our limits? Perhaps only once we've said no to something do we feel safe to say yes, wholeheartedly.

Steve felt that for a woman to say no might give her eventual yes more validity – because then he knows she means it. 'Some women don't ever say no to anything. It's kind of like pushing at an open door. You're not sure if it's open because it's meant to be open or just because it's been left open. There's a kind of discomfort about the situation, even when it's pleasant.' When the man makes all the direct moves, and nothing is explicitly discussed, how can he be sure she really consents? Because this time she doesn't say no.

This testing-out could also be seen as part of the worry work. Worrying is traditionally part of the woman's script. It's usually the woman who thinks: How will this affect our relationship?; who insists on the condom; who murmurs, 'But you're married . . .'. She may feel that only once all her fears and worries have been expressed and explored can she let herself go. There's a medieval allegorical poem, *The Romance of the Rose*, in which different facets of the personalities of the protagonists in the courtship drama are personified: and the Lady who is the object of the Lover's devotion is guarded in her rose garden by the allegorical figures of Shame, Fear and Danger – who in some sense are parts of herself.[11] For many women today, Shame, Fear and Danger are still hanging around at the start of their relationships – and sometimes we seem to need to acknowledge their presence: 'You don't want to give in to any old man who will then reject you and call you a slag . . .'.

Her no that means 'No, but I might still be interested . . .', 'No, but maybe next time . . .', is also about controlling the timing. When the man initiates and the woman has the power of veto, the timing of first sex depends on the woman. As one of the men I interviewed reflected, somewhat ruefully, 'In the end it's always the woman who decides.' The man's traditional script is about hurrying things along, making sex happen sooner. The male love poem is usually about the man's struggle to impose his own timing on the woman, and he'll often wheel on the heavy artillery – death and decay and the fact that she won't be beautiful for ever – in order to strengthen his case with his hard-to-get sweetheart. Elizabethan love poetry is full of these urgings and warnings, like Shakespeare's caution that she won't be quite so pretty when forty winters have besieged her brow, or Marvell's highly persuasive admonition to his coy mistress:

> *The grave's a fine and private place*
> *But none I think do there embrace . . . .*[12]

The woman's script is to put him off till she's sure – of her feelings, his feelings, whether he'll stick around if she gets the nine month blues and be there to hold the baby.

Of course there's no monopoly on either of these antithetical aspects of desire. Men also feel the fear and women the urgency, and, as we saw in the last chapter, many a woman has yearned to push things forward with a hesitant man: 'If he doesn't make a move soon, I'm going to give him up . . .'. But the traditional script polarizes these impulses: the woman expresses the one and the man the other.

Jessica is looking back several years to her early twenties

when she describes this behaviour. As we've seen, the double standard, which judges female sexual activity more harshly than male, operates most powerfully for young women.[13] When women over twenty-five talk about playing hard to get, they usually locate it firmly in the past. But women of any age at the start of a new relationship may insist 'No, not now' as a way of saying 'I don't normally do this sort of thing – I don't hurl myself at every halfway attractive male'. Her 'No, not now' is also a message about this man's desirability, when she does 'give in' to sex: that this is a man she is willing to transgress for.

For Jessica, saying no when you mean yes is a behaviour that has a profound emotional logic and is rich in meaning. But some women have never felt the need to do any of the things that Jessica describes, even at the very start of their sex lives. These women may find all this a foreign country. We tend to over-generalize from our own individual sexual style: we assume that everyone else does much the same. I once submitted an article on playing hard to get to a women's magazine. One editor didn't like it. 'Women don't do that anymore,' she said. Another editor was more enthusiastic. 'Great,' she said. 'I do that all the time.'

PLAYING BY THE RULES: I'm not particularly proud

The Rules is a pretty little book decorated with silver hearts. The authors, Ellen Fein and Sherrie Schneider, promise 'time-tested secrets for capturing the heart of Mr Right'. Here are some of the Rules:

Rule 2: Don't talk to a man first (and don't ask him to dance).
Rule 3: Don't stare at men or talk too much.
Rule 4: Don't meet him halfway or go dutch on a date.
Rule 5: Don't call him and rarely return his calls.
Rule 6: Always end phone calls first . . .

> *Rule 12*: Stop dating him if he doesn't buy you a romantic gift
> for your birthday or Valentine's Day . . .
> *Rule 14*: No more than casual kissing on the first date.[14]

This book was actually published in 1995 – a year when a
woman became Chief Constable of the Lancashire Police
Force, and Calvin Klein advertised his new unisex fragrance
with images of sexy slouching androgynes. But the only hint
that it doesn't date from 1955 comes with Rule 31: 'Don't
discuss the Rules with your therapist'.

With its Grandma-knew-best theme – and the book actually
starts with a little anecdote about 'Melanie's grandmother'
who made men wait nervously in her parents' front room in
Michigan, and who had 'more marriage proposals than shoes'
– *The Rules* is part of a courtship backlash strand in relationship advice that's been particularly apparent over the past
two or three years. In courtship backlash articles, women
describe how after briefly flirting with egalitarian courtship
behaviour, they've gone back to the old ways and been richly
rewarded. For instance, in *Cosmopolitan*'s 1995 opinion piece,
'Why I don't call men', Anya Schiffrin asserted, 'Unlike our
mothers, we no longer have to wait for the man we fancy to
make the first move. Instead, we blithely pick up the phone
and dial . . . But I still maintain: *don't do it* . . . When they don't
call you, it is because *they have decided not to*.'[15] The nostalgic
way the piece was presented made the sense of retrogression
explicit. It was subheaded 'why women with style don't touch
the dial', and illustrated with a picture of a woman in 1950s
swimwear.

Articles like 'Why I don't call men' and books like *The Rules*
take us back to the codes that governed women's courtship
behaviour when phones had dials and a polka-dot bikini that
almost came up to your waist was the very sexiest thing. The
woman who follows the Rules will veil her interest, play hard
to get, refuse him sex and keep a timer by the phone so she

never talks to him for longer than ten minutes. It's an extreme and self-conscious version of the kind of ultra-traditional behaviour that Jessica described. But courtship backlash pieces always include an assurance that we aren't giving up our aspirations to equality by behaving like this – we're just protecting ourselves from getting hurt.

Is there anything wrong with this? Yes, quite a lot, according to psychological research.

When Jessica talked about the way she played by the old rules, she said, 'I'm not particularly proud of myself, the way I did it.' And this is the first problem that you create for yourself when you say no when you mean yes, or go in for any of the other traditional withholding female behaviours: they make you feel bad about yourself. This is one reason why reading *The Rules* is so deeply depressing. Generally, we reward and admire generous, warm and spontaneous behaviour; we dislike mean, cool or withholding behaviour. In fact, 'warmth' is the interpersonal quality that is most important to us. If people are given a description of a person which includes the epithet 'cool', they will immediately decide they don't like the imagined person, however appealing the person's other attributes may be. In traditional courtship, women are compelled to display personal qualities which in general we don't admire. We have to be indirect – but generally we value directness in human behaviour. We have to be reticent and elusive – but in general we value spontaneity and warmth. Women may choose to act like this because they believe it will get them what they want, but they won't feel good about themselves for doing it. Natalie, a nineteen year old, who never made the first move and even refused to give her phone number to a man she liked, described her own behaviour as bitchy, frigid and off-hand.

When I was interviewing women, I asked them all to tell me about the most sexually assertive thing they'd ever done. It was a lovely question to ask. Here are some of their responses.

'It's great to have power over a person, to know you can make someone feel really good and feel a lot of pleasure by being dominant over them. It's like getting a kick out of it, it's a high in a way, like drugs or something.'

'I can remember having sex in the loo of a train. It was my idea – we both liked slightly titillating situations. I can remember drawing into Euston station having orgasms – that was quite sexy.'

'There was a guy and we'd been good friends for a long time and I fancied him. We were quite drunk and it was a beautiful day – and I said, "I do love you, you know," and put my head down on him and lay on him, and he said, "I've always loved you." Nothing much happened, we just kissed, and it's since petered out into a normal friendship – but at that moment, it was a very strong sexual tension, it was so strong it felt like there was a light surrounding us . . . .'

Though these responses were so varied, the feeling tone was always the same. As the women described the risky or forbidden or generous things they'd said or done in a moment of daring or delight, they glowed with pleasure – whether they were recalling something deeply romantic and loving, or remembering an erotic scenario that might have come out of a soft-porn video. It's unimaginable that a woman would glow with pride and achievement as she said, 'I never returned his calls, I never accepted a Saturday-night date later than Wednesday, I always ended phone calls first . . .', even if the couple finally got together.

But *are* they more likely to get together in the end if she keeps a timer by the phone? Not necessarily. This is the second problem about token resistant behaviour: far from hooking men, it may put them off. We believe men like it because *some* men do – men like Geoff in Chapter Five, who felt that the relationships he'd most valued were the ones he'd had to chase. Because these men fit so neatly into our male mythology of courtship, we over-generalize from them; we believe all men are like that. Beliefs rooted in long-established mythologies need only the tiniest bits of evidence to hold them in place. If it works for one man, we take it as proof that it works for all. When it doesn't work for another man, we discount that fact because it doesn't fit. Yet a lot of men will simply give up if faced by a woman who masks her feelings, always finishes the date first and follows the advice to 'avoid staring romantically into his eyes' on a first date. Men invariably say that eye-contact is one of the main cues they use to tell if a woman is interested.

Tom, the kind of man who would be put off, felt that even if he managed to get a woman who behaved so elusively into bed, the effort and uncertainty of it all might detract from his enjoyment. 'You're so worn out and wound up after an evening of that, that you don't enjoy the sex nearly as much as if you had it earlier in the evening before you got knackered. It's terribly nice if a woman makes a clear statement about how she feels – not just a murmured endearment, but something that's more definite and considered. You're in this miasma of peeking from behind net curtains – even if you're in some kind of physical relationship with somebody –'cos the courtship doesn't stop once you've had a fuck, does it?'

Rob felt that enigmatic and withholding behaviour might work for a while, for some men – but for himself he couldn't be bothered with it. He said, 'I think you might deceive yourself into thinking that because somebody was hard to get it therefore might be more interesting in the long run – but you'd probably be sadly disappointed. I'd just give up. If somebody evinced no interest, I'd just think, To hell with it.'

A basic tenet of hard to get behaviour is putting off first sex. Ellen Fein and Sherrie Schneider are very keen on this: 'We know this is not an easy Rule to follow, particularly when you're out with some really cute man and he's driving fast in his sports car and kissing you at every red light. He's a great kisser and you wonder what else he's good at . . . . If you're

getting too excited, end the date quickly so you don't do anything you'll regret.'[16] It's a common female belief that putting
off sex leads to more lasting relationships. Women's magazines often run articles about postponing sex till you really
trust one another, so that when you finally have it it's deep
and meaningful. Yet when you listen to people's sexual histories, you so often find that in those relationships that lead
to lasting loving partnerships, couples made love the first
night they met or ten minutes after they confessed how they
felt. Not always, of course: but often. As we've seen, research
studies have found that couples who have sex the first time
they go out are just as likely as others to stay together.[17]
Postponing sex because you think it will increase the chances
of lasting commitment is one of our slimline fat-free versions
of the old sexual code – and it's based on a false premise. In
the 1950s, when, according to the fantasies current today,
stable families lived exemplary lives behind their privet
hedges and no one got divorced, couples generally didn't have
sex till they were engaged: but the one doesn't follow from
the other – sexual restraint in the early stages doesn't make
relationships more long-lasting.

The third problem about following *The Rules* is the potential
effect of withholding behaviour on female desire. Playing hard
to get is the antithesis of spontaneity – it's all about self-
control, about hiding your enthusiasm. Not looking into his
eyes. Not talking to him for too long on the phone. Putting
off making love – however much you long to do it now.

Even when you do finally let him get you into bed, you're
still advised to keep your wishes and feelings under wraps.
'The theories of Masters and Johnson (who are now divorced)
are not to be ignored, but please wait a good amount of time
before you begin holding lengthy seminars about your needs
during sex . . . .'[18] Research has made a clear link between
sexual assertiveness and sexual satisfaction for women:[19]
assertive women enjoy sex more than shy women – and

women who are naturally shy can have a much better time in bed by behaving as though they are assertive and learning to ask for what they want when they want it. Yet the authors of *The Rules* advise that even the most direct and self-confident women should be retiring and oblique.

So to the final problem about playing hard to get: when do you stop? How do you change a relationship in which you never accept a Saturday-night date later than Wednesday into the kind of sexual relationship we most value and generally aspire to today – which is egalitarian and emotionally intimate, with a lot of mutual disclosure? Just as men who are hooked on the thrill of the chase have a problem with long-term relationships – because once you've got what you've been chasing the excitement dissipates – so for women there's an implicit flaw in making mystery your main sales pitch. This is recognized even by Jessica, who was so good at justifying her elusiveness. She conceded, 'The relationships that have really lasted have been friendships rather than that overtly sexual courting – because you can't keep up the mystery bit for long, can you, once you really get to know people'.

Token resistant behaviours may make us feel bad about ourselves, deter a lot of men, reduce our capacity for pleasure, and form a bad basis for a lasting relationship. But what they may achieve is to select for a particular kind of man. Saying no and meaning next time, or later, or maybe, sifts out men who are persistent from men who may be sexually or intellectually exciting but are less self-confident or assertive. At one point, Ellen Fein and Sherrie Schneider are devastatingly explicit about this. 'The kind of men who once nauseated you because they were open books, called too much, wrote mushy cards, and told their friends and parents about you long before you said anything to your friends and parents, you now find attractive and desirable.'[20]

Persistence, of course, doesn't have to be proof of devotion.

It could just mean that he's not very sensitive to non-verbal cues. This is the man whom the authors of *The Rules* call 'Mr Right'.

BEN: I wasn't going to be thwarted

But the biggest problem about this behaviour is that women who play hard to get and say no when they mean yes are colluding in a courtship culture in which our wishes may be disregarded or overridden. A man who's experienced one woman's token resistance may assume another woman's resistance is token when it isn't, or may read her maybe as yes when that isn't really what she meant.

'When I went to see my sister at college,' said Ben, 'I hadn't slept with anyone for two years, and I was beginning to get really quite desperate about it and wondering whether I'd ever do it again. My sister had this American friend who appeared in this shirt which just came down to the tops of her thighs – she obviously had something on her bottom but you couldn't see what it was, and she just behaved in a very flirtatious manner for ages on end. She paid a lot of attention to me, she looked at me a lot, she carried on going round in this night-gear at eleven o'clock in the morning, she just wasn't wearing quite enough clothes really: that was one of the things that I felt, she was just wearing less clothes than people do in daytime.

'I don't think she wanted to sleep with me at all, but when it came to it . . . . She put up all sorts of objections like her room-mate would find out, and she hadn't got her diaphragm in her room – but I had a condom. I suppose she was implying she just didn't want to do it, but I wasn't going to be thwarted really by anything other than physical resistance . . . No, that's not true, if she'd said, "No, I'm going" – well, she could have gone, I wasn't stopping her. But it was almost like the way she gave in was conceding that she'd probably committed herself to it without quite intending to, by being so flirtatious – as if she accepted that, yeah, she'd obliged herself to do it really. It was just such an imperative for me to sleep with somebody somehow – I wasn't actually going to rape somebody, but it's as close as I got really – if I'd been more of a gentleman I'd have said, Why don't you trot off?

'It was nice for me, and I think it was probably neither here nor there for her – she didn't seem particularly bothered by it. She disappeared fairly quickly once it was over.

'She was behaving throughout the day in a way that was quite calculated to arouse a man – she wasn't just being friendly or chatting. I don't think it was very terrible to follow through – she took off her own clothes, for goodness sake.'

Is Ben culpable? He has sex with the girl in the shirt – and it seems quite possible that she doesn't want it. Yet, given the range of female behaviours that the classic script encompasses – indirect initiatives, token resistance, complicated 'no's – what he does is completely comprehensible.

The story shows how badly things can go wrong for women when we rely on indirect signalling, with its implicit ambiguity. Everything about the girl in the shirt is ambiguous. Was she flirting or did she have a very open transatlantic manner? Did she think he was attractive or was she going out of her way to be pleasant to her friend's brother? Was her indirect reluctance – I haven't got my diaphragm, my room-mate'll find out – based on real reluctance, or was she just doing the worry work? Did the indirect signal of her clothing mean she wanted to have sex with someone – or was it just that she couldn't be bothered to change? Men so often grossly over-interpret the meanings of women's clothing – Why is she wearing that? What does it mean? What is she after? – as women over-interpret the meanings of men's phone calls – Why hasn't he rung? Why did he ring me just then? Why did he ring off so quickly? Here, Ben reads her clothing as a clear signal: sub-text – If you'd seen it you'd have understood. But maybe it wasn't a signal at all: maybe her jeans were in the laundry.

We don't know – because Ben doesn't know – what she really thinks and what she really wants. Her non-verbal communications are full of contradictions – but she says neither yes nor no. He chooses to read the lack of a direct no as permission, even though he has his doubts.

How can such situations be avoided? Research suggests that women have to learn to say what we want: and we have to do it early on in the process. We won't always have to do this. But it's an approach that every woman should have in her repertoire for those occasions when she suspects his agenda is different from hers.

Charlene Muehlenhard and Sandy Andrews made a video of a couple going on a date.[21] The woman did a lot of things that have been shown to increase men's ratings of how much a woman wants sex and how justifiable it would be for a man to have sex with her against her will – their equivalent of the suggestive shirt in Ben's account: she asked him out, wore a low-cut top and tight trousers, drank alcohol and went to the man's flat. The researchers made two versions of the tape. In one, she said what she wanted directly and early in the evening: 'I hope you don't misinterpret my going to your apartment on the first date, but seriously, I don't want to do anything more than kiss tonight.' In the other version, she said no only once he'd already made a move.

In the first version, where she told him what her limits were early in the evening, men rated her as less likely to want to 'pet' or have sexual intercourse, they rated her as 'leading the man on' less, and they tended to rate it as less justifiable for the man to engage in 'petting' after she said no. The men said they liked this approach – and felt they would like a woman who took it. They knew where they were with her; they didn't have to guess.

Of course this kind of clarity isn't always called for: many happy sexual relationships are negotiated with looks and touches – and no-one ever has to say 'I hope you don't misinterpret my going to your apartment . . .'. But the directness of the woman on the video is one possible strategy in situations where there might be confusion. Such an approach probably won't protect a woman from a man who's potentially violent, but it might help in a situation like the one that Ben describes. It might prevent a lot of bad sex.

COURTSHIP LIES: There's a promise made in any bed

Token resistance is one of many delicate distortions of self-presentation that have always been part of courtship. When we're sexually attracted to someone, we may lie, hide something, or present a particular side of ourselves. It's partly because of these distortions and evasions that we call courtship a game – and of course they aren't a female prerogative. But the man's distortions are different. According to the traditional script, he brags, exaggerates his feelings, overstates his enthusiasm, in order to get her into bed – while she stresses her vulnerability, conceals her feelings, plays hard to get, in order to test him out and get him to stick around.

Geoff said, 'You portray this image when you first meet someone, and you carry on portraying that image – and you usually find that the image you've portrayed when you first meet a girl isn't what you're like. I put myself across as this quiet, sentimental, emotional, nice guy – I'm not that quiet!

'The classic example of telling a fib or a lie to attract someone is if you meet a girl, and you think the girl might be interested in a one-night stand, and so you work towards the one-night stand because you won't see them again. You might tell them anything, just to impress them. Then after a while things change a bit and you think, This person's really quite nice, and you hate yourself for saying things. I think you can get over it, if you're honest about it, but the longer you let it go the worse it gets. I've met girls where I've said, "Listen, what I said last night is a load of bullshit, what I actually do is such and such", and it's taken a lot of courage to say that.'

One category of courtship lying concerns the kind of relationship we want. Courtship has two possible aims: sex, or a sexual relationship. People may say or imply they're after the one when they're really after the other. Two people may be working to different agendas, but they may hide this from one another, as in the film *Dangerous Liaisons*, where the Vicomte de Valmont's seduction of Madame de Tourvel has different meanings for him and for her. He approaches her because it gives him a sadistic thrill to entice her from the path of virtue: she surrenders to him because she's stirred by deep emotions. Where our agendas are very different, courtship becomes a battle of wits in which we try to work out one another's true intentions. This may be acted out around saying 'I love you'. His 'I love you' which he doesn't quite mean is the mirror image of her saying no and meaning yes. He exaggerates his interest to get her into bed: she plays down hers to test out his commitment.

Keith said, 'There are times when you signal only half-commitment because you don't want to take on a big obligation. You talk about whether you want commitment or not – or just make your move in a way that's more to do with "I really fancy you" than "I love you". That's not something I would say lightly, and not just because I'm full of sincerity. If you say "I love you" when you're seducing somebody, then you're implying that you'll stay with them and be faithful – it's this thing about not wanting to be seen to have broken a promise.'

During the Cold War, playwright Sacha Andersen was a respected leader of East Germany's artistic dissident movement, admired by many in the West. But in the Alice-in-Wonderland world that East Germany became after the Wall came down, where nothing was as it had once seemed, he was exposed as one of the Stasi's top informers. Reinhilde, his girlfriend, at first stood by him when his duplicity was revealed – but eventually came to feel her position to be untenable and left. Her reason for leaving was the fear that the love affair might be built on a falsehood. 'If I can't believe anything you say,' she said, 'how can I believe you when you say you love me?'

Yet these words are so often said untruthfully – even by those who are generally direct in their dealings with others. In our sexual relationships we may express some of the deepest, most real parts of ourselves: but we are also all secret agents.

CHAPTER 8
MONEY

'Acrisius had no sons, but only this one daughter Danae, and
when he asked an oracle how to produce a male heir, was
told: "You will have no sons, and your grandson must kill
you." To forestall this fate, Acrisius imprisoned Danae in a
dungeon with brazen doors, guarded by savage dogs; but
despite these precautions, Zeus came upon her in a shower
of gold, and she bore him a son named Perseus.'

(Robert Graves, *The Greek Myths*, Vol. 2)

WHEN a woman starts earning serious money, something
changes. A study of two-career couples found that once
women were earning at least sixty per cent as much as
their partners, they became much more likely to take the lead
in bed.[1] What is the nature of this relationship between money
and sexual initiative? Are women with money more willing
to ask men out?

Whenever an explicit link is made between money and
sex, we react with outrage. A bishop's suggestion that tax
allowances might encourage people to marry is greeted with
scepticism, US writer Ginie Polo Sayles's workshops on 'How
To Marry The Rich' with horror. We want to believe we marry
for richer, for poorer – for love, not money: 'Better a dinner
of herbs where love is . . .'. Money and love are antithetical:
money contaminates love.

Yet financial imagery pervades our understanding of sexuality. When we think about sexual relationships, we think of

value, profit and loss, investment, and what is owed. Cheap, free, spent, ruined – all have sexual meanings. Sex without commitment is free love. Just after ejaculation a man is 'spent'. A woman who had sex when she shouldn't was once ruined; now she is merely cheap. Those women who started initiating sex when they earned sixty per cent as much as their husbands show that the way we use these words is more than metaphor, and that the financial language of sex expresses psychosexual and economic realities.

So are affluent women more likely to make the first move? To answer this question we need to look at the sexual meanings of money for both men and women.

A LITTLE LIZARD: The role of money in courtship

In the natural world, the male who wants sex will offer food to the female. The male common tern gives his chosen mate a fish, the male roadrunner offers a little lizard. When a black-tipped hangfly catches an aphid or housefly on the forest floor, a gland in his abdomen exudes attractive secretions which encourage any female who happens to be passing to stop off, eat and mate. Through these courtship behaviours, the male is making the female a promise. He's showing that he can provide for her, and promising to provide for her offspring.[2]

Among all peoples, too, men give women presents before making love. Often the present is food or drink – a fish, beer or sweets: sometimes he'll give her something with a less direct symbolic meaning like tobacco or beads. In our own society, the traditional trappings of sexual relationships have been things the man buys – drinks, meals, and gifts of jewellery, perfume and flowers. When we think of romance, we think of red roses, dinner by candlelight, Chanel no. 5, champagne, a diamond solitaire. The essence of romance is male expenditure. Women, unlike females in the natural world, do give gifts to their lovers – but in every culture it's far more common for men to give gifts to women than the other way round. And the meaning of the roses or ring remains the same as the meaning of the lizard for the roadrunner: the gift is a proof that he's serious, and a promise that he can provide.

In human society, male providing is particularly important. Human children are dependent for years and need a massive investment of care, which has always limited and still limits the mother's capacity to collect resources – to grow grain, rear livestock, sack cities, or make a killing on the stock exchange. Because paternal provision has always been so crucial in human parenting, the material is at the very heart of the human marriage contract. So often it has been money rather than passion that has shaped courtship and dictated its pace and pattern. In the eighteenth century, the marriage rate among rural working people dependent on weekly or even hourly wages correlated very closely with the price of bread: when it was high, few married, and illegitimacy rates soared.[3] In the late 1940s, with housing shortages and no credit available, engagements of four or five years were common, as the man saved up for the down payment on the mortgage and all the trappings of post-war domesticity – the walnut sideboard, Ideal boiler and three-piece suite.

But, this model of men with money providing for women with none is simplistic – because sometimes the woman will have money of her own. For families with money, marriage has always been about the accumulation of wealth. So Imran Khan undertakes to marry 'a nice Pakistani girl', but chooses Jemima Goldsmith, who is not only delectably beautiful but unimaginably wealthy. Imran chose for himself – but in all cultures and throughout history, rich parents have often prescribed whom their children shall marry. In Victorian times, for instance, the marriage choices of the children of the wealthy were rigorously controlled by debutante balls, where people only met suitable marriage partners. But for labouring people dependent on wages, with no means to endow their children, there was no such incentive to limit their children's choices.[4] The children of the poor chose for themselves and were more likely to marry for love.

In special circumstances, this still applies: Prince Charles didn't quite have a free hand in his choice of partner. At least in this sense, having money in the family has given not more freedom but less. Hence the appeal of the fairytale in which the princess rejects all the carefully selected suitors, and gives her hand to the gardener's boy: it's moving because it's about choosing on erotic rather than mercenary criteria – a luxury that has rarely been enjoyed by rich daughters. In the stories, though, the gardener's boy usually turns out to be a prince in disguise – according to the fairytale principle that you get given back, in a glorious denouement, what you thought you'd given up.

But even when the rich marry the rich on their parents' instructions, the principle of male provision still underpins these choices. The tendency is still for women to marry up – to marry men with more money – and for men to marry down.

These then are the deeper meanings of courtship giving. Through the money he spends on her, the man offers the woman a promise, symbol and illustration of his capacity to provide. And whenever a man and a woman approach one another with sexual intent, however brief the sexual connection they have in mind, these meanings are still around. They may only want an isolated night of casual passion, but if he pays for her vodka-and-orange and her dinner, the spending arrangements sketch out a relationship in which he provides for her and her children.

But today there are challenges to the traditional economic meanings of courtship. Relationship patterns are changing. Children are not such a clear goal as once they were, because more women are choosing to do other things with their lives. Men's capacity to care for their families financially is under threat from short-term contracts and unemployment. More men are staying home to care for the children, and more women becoming the main breadwinner. Many women have their own money and can provide for themselves. Many men have none.

How have these changes shaped the sexual meanings of money? Who pays today?

GOOD TIMES: Courtship spending today

I asked Natalie, nineteen, who paid when she went out with men.

'Not me – *God*!' she said. 'Although I would take my wallet with me on a first date, I wouldn't expect to have to get it out of my pocket. If they're prepared to spend all that money on you, they're not going to do it just for the good of their health, are they? It must mean they like you. And the more money a person has, the more good times you can have 'cos you can be out every night instead of saying, "Oh no we'll stay in and watch telly 'cos we haven't got any money. Wait till the end of the month darling".

'I do like being bought things – I've got a bedroom upstairs full of perfume. If they turn up with roses for you, that's really nice. I think if I was in a relationship and I was never given a present ever . . . well, I think I'd dump him. I couldn't care less actually if it was a flower picked out of the garden, it's just a gesture, isn't it?

'It's weird with me. I like to be paid for, I like to be driven – but I would hate it if somebody tried to tell me what to do . . . .'

Under the courtship system which is now disintegrating, money was central to the definition of a date. A date happened when a couple went to the pictures or the Palais and spent money. And this spending was the man's prerogative. It wasn't a date unless he paid.

Etiquette books from the 1940s and 1950s are disparaging about 'going dutch'. The expression apparently comes from 'dutch treat', a derogatory term for a false treat where the guests ended up paying their own way.[5] Girls were warned that if dutch dating was absolutely necessary, the girl should give money to her date in private so that it at least *looked* as though he were paying for her.

Today this system is breaking down. But a new system has yet to emerge. We're playing a new game, but we're not quite sure of the rules. So, as you'd expect in a period of transition, there's little consistency about how people behave. The patterns vary from one subculture to another: students and stockbrokers may behave quite differently. Patterns also vary through the course of individual life-histories. There may even be variation in the course of a single evening, when we find ourselves following a number of contradictory courtship scripts, like one woman who claimed she often made the first move, but still expected the man to drive and pay. And as you'd also predict in a time of change, our uncertainty creates a lot of anxiety.

Natalie has one solution to the confusion – to stick rigidly to the old script. In her reasons for wanting to be paid for, pragmatism and symbolism merge. She likes to go out with men with money because you can have a good time. She glows with pleasure as she says how she loves to be given sensuous presents like perfume. But she also enjoys the symbolism of the love token, the gift that's just a gesture, the flower picked from the garden. Most of all she wants the sense of being 'valued' that comes from having money spent on her. It proves he's serious, it shows that she matters. The idea that what is spent on you shows how much you are worth isn't unique to courtship, of course: a business contact would judge how she was valued by the lavishness of the restaurant where she was entertained. But in a time of transitory passions and forgettable beds, this meaning of money may have a particular urgency for women looking for something a little more sustaining than Isadora Wing's zipless fuck.

According to numerous surveys, US college students generally share Natalie's conservatism about courtship spending. Most men and women expect the man to pay – especially on the first date. And men with a lot of dating experience stress that a man should always check he has enough money in his wallet before he goes out with a woman.[6]

For Natalie and the friends she goes clubbing with – who also all want to be paid for – these attitudes to money are part of a wider expectation. They keep to the old script in every detail: they'd never ask a man out.

Chloe at thirteen has just started going out with boys. 'If the boy asked you out,' she said, 'then he should pay or you should split the cost. And if a boy turned up on a date, after asking you out, and said, "Ooh sorry I haven't got any money, can you pay for me?" you'd do it the first time, but not after that. If they kept making you pay for them it's obvious they're just using you to get to the cinema a few times.

'If he's willing to pay, at my age it means they're using their *pocket money* on you. Wow, they must like you! So that's a really good sign.'

Chloe is a little more egalitarian than Natalie. Here, there are two possibilities: he pays, or you split. But it isn't on for the girl to pay for both.

For Chloe, as for Natalie, paying is an index of interest and seriousness. It's how you know he likes you – and beware the boy who's using you as a cinema ticket. This is a male meaning of 'being used': being wanted just for your money.

Chloe also talked about presents. 'First a boy sends you a Valentine's card,' she said, 'and you probably haven't sent him one 'cos you're too nervous to see if he would or not. Then you maybe go on a few dates and get to know him, and when his birthday comes you might give him a card, and when it's your birthday he might give you a present, and you just go higher each time . . . . But if a girl gave something bigger than a boy gave her, that would be *awful*.'

Chloe likes clarity and order. Her careful hierarchy of giving is structured by a clear sense of propriety. It's embarrassing if the girl gives more than the boy. It's rather 'fast', like asking him out, having sex too soon or leaving too many buttons undone. This is the double standard encoded in presents and greeting cards. Even in our giving, she feels, we should let him make the first move.

Chloe and Natalie both know just where they stand. But some of the older people I talked to had a quite different pattern: they'd changed from one script to another at some point in their lives. These were people now in their thirties, forties or fifties who'd started dating under the old dispensation. Then they'd gone through those profound rites of passage of our culture – divorce and higher education. They'd left empty marriages, hungry for something more, or done Open University sociology courses, or entered higher education as mature students and read Simone de Beauvoir, and they'd 'found themselves', 'grown', 'become different people'. There was a 'before' and an 'after' in their sexual stories – and that absolute division in their self-perception was reflected in the pattern of who pays.

Ted had left his first marriage after doing an Open University course. 'The sort of people I met in my teens and early twenties would have been rather different to the ones I met later,' he said. 'After my first marriage I changed completely in ideological outlook – so the people you meet change completely. After that, we'd usually split the bill: it would have been understood rather than negotiated.'

People like Ted who pointed to a change in their expectations about who should pay always saw this as an outward sign of a deep inward shift in their perceptions of gender relationships. As Rob, thirty-five, said, 'I can't imagine going out with someone who wouldn't pay for themselves. It would say a lot about the kind of relationship they were expecting – that they anticipated some kind of dependence.' For Rob, the woman who 'lets' him pay conjures up a whole world of patriarchal practices, a world in which women get bought expensive engagement rings, marry in white tulle, take their husbands' names and expect to be cared for financially – a world he wants no part in. But even here, among the people who hold most passionately to feminist ideology, the change is to split the bill; women still aren't paying for men at the start of courtship.

Men and women with these beliefs about money may deviate from the traditional script in other ways too. Both Ted and Rob had had significant relationships that had been initiated by women.

If patterns of spending vary with age and ideology, we might also expect them to be different in secret relationships. This is one of the issues Annette Lawson raises in her book *Adultery*.[7] Do secret relationships simply mirror open relationships – or do they subvert the recognized way of going about things? In fact she finds that illicit love affairs are highly conventional economically – with the man doing most of the paying.

But there is one intriguing difference between spending patterns in open and secret relationships. Adultery doesn't cost a lot: in fact sixteen per cent of the people Annette Lawson talked to said their liaisons cost nothing. This is no surprise. Given that many married couples share responsibility for paying the bills, secret relationships that involve conspicuous consumption risk rapidly becoming less secret – if, for instance, the money a man spends on his lover shows up on his Visa bill: and unexplained gifts could lead to no end of trouble, like the cuff-links with entwined initials that Camilla gave Charles. But perhaps there are also other reasons more profound than the fear of being found out for the lack of spending in adulterous relationships.

Adultery isn't about parenting. As we've already seen, research suggests that eighty per cent of people who have affairs stay married[8]: those adulterous relationships which lead to a new marriage and a new family are the exception rather than the rule. And if the deeper meaning of courtship spending is a promise that the man will provide for the couple's children, it follows that gifts and expenditure will be less significant in illicit affairs. The traditional meanings will still be around – but in much more vestigial form than in pairings where marriage and a family might be the destined goals.

A study from the 1960s shows this in a wonderfully pure form. The men interviewed by sociologist Morton Hunt for his study of adultery in the US said they had to 'spend part of the family income' on their mistresses for their extra-marital sex to amount to infidelity.[9] Their sexual behaviour felt illicit only when it meant taking money away from their families. The sexual transgression was defined solely in terms of the financial one.

Women who expect to be paid for, or men and women who share: these seem to be the possibilities, in both open and secret relationships. With courtship spending as with other courtship initiatives, we've moved away from the scripts of the 1940s and 1950s, but we're still a long way from equality. At the start of sexual relationships, women still don't treat men.

Why are the old patterns so persistent? Let's look more closely at the sexual meanings of men's money – first for women and then for men.

WARM-NATURED DIRECTOR SEEKS VULNERABLE
LADY: What men's money means to women

'When I was an adolescent,' said Malcolm, 'I felt the system was unfair, I felt the woman ought to pay. But, as a political campaign, not spending money on the women you're trying to get off with is a particularly futile form of opposition. And I found that the more I just did the most conventional quasi-chauvinistic thing of buying stuff and flattery and paying for things, the more successful I was. So women who say it doesn't matter and it's all sexist crap – that's fine, but where were they till I started doing it, that's what I want to know.'

If many men still pay, it might be because, like Malcolm, they find that women like it. Are women still looking for good providers? Do rich men turn us on?

Psychologist David Buss studied thirty-seven people in thirty-three countries.[10] Everywhere he found the same. Men say they want women who are beautiful. Women say they want men with goods, property and money.

Nearer home, there's plenty more evidence that women are looking for partners who can provide. The marriage bureau, Dateline, keeps records of the response to the advertisements they publish. A survey of the most successful advertisements in Dateline magazine reveals a striking sex difference.[11] The men whom lots of women want drop broad hints about how much money they have. To call yourself 'wealthy' is too direct and a turn-off – like saying you're 'fat' or 'fun-loving'. But advertisements that hint at high-status jobs, luxurious life-styles and homes in the best part of town get hundreds of replies. 'Six-feet-tall, slim presentable man . . . I'm divorced, financially secure in my own home in central London, happy in my rewarding and interesting management career, and enjoying a relaxed lifestyle . . .'. 'Warm-natured director, div-orced . . . well read, well travelled, beautiful house/garden in

South London . . . .' This is money as sexual display and as promise of provision.

But the women whose advertisements are most successful, in addition to the obligatory 'attractive', underline their vulnerability, especially their financial vulnerability. 'Very lonely auxiliary nurse, thirty-one, full of love, shy, romantic, SOH, anxiously hoping for a letter from you . . .'. 'Kentish lady . . . writer, artist, nature lover, country girl, homemaker, vulnerable, penniless, looking for love, home, security . . . .'

The women's financial neediness is part of a courtship display, along with their shyness, loneliness or anxiety. Women assume that these vulnerabilities will be attractive to men, and the massive response to their advertisements proves them right. The men who write in are responding to the women's financial neediness as something that complements their own affluence – as an emptiness they can fill.

Here, men offer abundance – height, achievements, affluence – and women offer scarcity. The vulnerable penniless Kentish lady is an emotional and financial version of Jodie Kidd, a female minimalism pared down to the bone. Excess is never part of women's courtship display. Women may flaunt their bodies – but never their achievements, wealth or success. A woman who wants love would never come swaggering along like Aladdin in Disney's film, with a grand procession full of elephants and camels and dancing boys.

In the courtship script at its most traditional, this is precisely spelt out. One of the gender differences that's eroticized in women's romances is that he has money and she has none. Advice from Mills and Boon to aspiring writers stipulates that the hero should be more affluent than the heroine.[12] The hero's money is part of a gestalt that's all about power. In the fantasies of being 'swept away' or even raped which give the stories their erotic charge, the male attributes that are highlighted are all signifiers of dominance in the world and metaphors for dominance in bed – his hard body, steely penetrating stare, big bank balance and superabundant cash flow.

Rich men as the sole focus for women's erotic yearnings: this might seem a one-dimensional view of female sexuality. After all, rough trade is a well-established category of female erotic interest. Women are always falling in love with builders who come to refit their kitchens or eyeing up half-stripped men working on the road. But though such men do feature in women's sexual fantasies, they are usually transient presences in women's lives. Money is a persistent theme in women's real-life sexual choices – especially when they are looking for someone to live with or marry.

And the erotic appeal of money is by no means confined to women who relish stories about the sweetness of submission to rugged men with bulging wallets. A survey found that US women who make more money than most pay more attention than most to the wealth of potential spouses, not less. Apparently even 'leaders of the feminist movement' want 'still more powerful men'.[13] And women who want to have power in the future may also choose wealthy men – like Baroness Thatcher, who married a millionaire.

The older we get, the sexier we tend to find men's money. *Options* magazine is aimed at women in the twenty-five to thirty-five age group – and a survey on 'The Perfect Man' found huge numbers of *Options* readers fantasizing about male affluence.[14] The women who responded mostly wanted their perfect man to earn more than them, often a lot more: thirty-five per cent wanted him to earn at least £50,000 more than them – only ten per cent wanted him to earn the same. Fifty-two per cent said they'd feel comfortable with him paying for everything, and only nineteen per cent wanted to go halves on everything.

In *Second Chances*, their study of divorce, Judith Wallerstein and Sandra Blakeslee looked at the choices people made the second time round.[15] They found that, while men tended to

choose women who liked sex more than their previous partners, women chose men who were better providers than their
first husbands.

I found this held for the women I talked to: they described
how they'd become more attracted to men with money as
they'd got older – especially once they'd had children. Money
may not matter till we are mothers, but once we have children, it makes a huge difference to our choices. Any woman
who's up to her elbows in small plastic animals and left-over
bits of bacon sandwich is likely to be open to the fantasy
allure of the very rich man. Before children, money means
luxuries – cardigans in cashmere, holidays in Provence. Afterwards, it means services – someone to clean the cooker or
hold the baby. In particular, you need money to be able to
work outside the home with pre-school children, especially
if, like ninety-two per cent of women, you want to work part-
time. Before you can get back to the office, you have to buy
the childcare.

Younger women tend to be more romantic about money –
or the lack of it. 'I certainly wouldn't go out with someone
because they gave me lots of things or because they had
money,' said Roxanne, just sixteen. 'I couldn't do that to
myself, 'cos that would be cheating on myself as well as them.
I am a material girl, 'cos everyone is, but I'm not so materialist
that I need people to buy me things to show that they love
me, because you just know if someone loves you, you just
know it.'

'Can't buy me love,' protests Roxanne. But as we get older
we sing a different song. Naomi is forty-one, happily married
but on a tight budget: she's a part-time nurse, her husband
runs an alternative bookshop and they have three young
children.

'At my grandfather's funeral there was a multi-millionaire,'
she said. 'And I looked at him in the church and I thought,
Mmm, that's a really good-looking bloke, I really fancy him.

I did have a little fantasy about being swept off my feet by a multi-millionaire – and I guess that's something that's only come to me recently because money didn't use to mean anything to me at all. I used to be very scathing about money – but, since having children, I've realized just how wonderful it would be.'

This shift in Naomi's attitude to money is a cognitive change – an intellectual recognition that money matters. But it's experienced at an emotional and sexual level: for half an hour or so, the multi-millionaire turns her on. The money is eroticized, as in that strange and extravagant tale of the impregnation of Danae, where the lover comes in a shower of gold.

Kim too had noticed a shift in her feelings about money. 'I haven't been attracted to rich men in the past,' she said, 'but now it's different, 'cos I'm thinking of having kids and don't necessarily want to carry on working full time. So at the moment I'd do anything to marry somebody really rich. Paul and I went through a bad patch a few months ago – and I was thinking whether there were any of my unmarried friends I could go out with – in my normal manipulative way – making lists!

'There's a man I was friends with at university. Bruce isn't at all materialistic, he's now a part-time social worker in London – and I thought, Maybe I could go out with Bruce – and then I thought, I'd have to work full time – and I thought, Would it really irritate me? 'Cos I've always thought what he does is really good, I've always said, "I think it's brilliant that you don't mind being short of money but you do what you want". But suddenly I thought that it might irritate me that I was going out to work from nine to five doing a job I didn't particularly enjoy. He would just say, "Don't do it . . .". But then you want to live in a nice place for your kids.'

HOUSES OF VIRGINS: What men's money means to men

Women's attraction to men with full granaries or big Volvos is only half the picture. What is the sexual meaning of money – their own money – to men?

'If women didn't exist, all the money in the world would have no meaning,' said Aristotle Onassis. Or, as J. Paul Getty Sr put it, 'A lasting relationship with a woman is only possible if you're a business failure.'[16] This promise of money for men – that money buys sex – is expressed directly through the institution of prostitution, and more indirectly in courtship and marriage patterns, because money gives even an ugly man the wherewithal to seduce beautiful women. Onassis's own money, of course, bought him the western world's number one female icon.

The distinction between power and money that we make today has only been valid since the Renaissance. Further back, the two were synonymous. A man's power – his ability to get other people to do his bidding – depended on his wealth – with a little help from violence. And there was a time in human history when the principle that money buys women was acted out on a mind-boggling scale.

Matt Ridley calls this 'the polygamous moment'. Sketching out early history in broad strokes, he shows how, with the invention of the plough and the domestication of cattle, it became possible for one man to grow much more powerful than the rest by accumulating a surplus of food with which to buy other men's labour. This was the age of the despots: the six independent civilizations of early history – Babylon, Egypt, India, China, the Aztecs and the Incas – were all ruled by one man at a time. The despots wielded unimaginable power and wealth – and used that power and wealth to acquire women. Their histories are catalogues of conquests, atrocities and dazzling sexual excess. The Inca Sun King Atahualpa kept fifteen hundred women in each of many 'houses of virgins' throughout his kingdom. The Aztec ruler Montezuma had four thousand concubines. The Chinese Emperor Fei-ti had ten thousand women in his harem. The Indian emperor Udayama had sixteen thousand consorts guarded by eunuchs in apartments ringed by fire.

The harems weren't only about sexual indulgence. They seem to have functioned as prodigious breeding machines. Wet nurses suckled the babies, so the concubines would start ovulating again soon after giving birth. The Tang Dynasty emperors of China kept records of menstruation and conception in the harem, and only had sex with women who were fertile. The result was a kind of extreme genetic despotism. Most men couldn't reproduce: and many of the citizens of the kingdom would be the king's own children.

Sometimes, in men's assertions about male sexuality, one can detect a nostalgia for this form of sexual organization, as though the harem is the shape that completely untrammelled male sexuality would take. Writer Warren Farrell for instance talks about giving up lots of women as an 'adaptation' – and his strength of feeling gets the better of his syntax. 'A restrained kiss was male adaptation. Or his saying "I'd like to make love" rather than "I'd like to have sex". Or his willingness to give up a lifetime's stimuli of beautiful women in every commercial to commit to sex with one woman exclusively, and less of it than he wants. This is perhaps the most unappreciated adaptation in all human behaviour . . . .'[17]

The memory of the polygamous moment lingers on – though the fantasy is of course about being the despot with the concubines, rather than the ordinary man who under this system was condemned to a life of near-celibacy, and who'd have been put to the sword, along with all his relations, fellow villagers, servants and llamas, if he took a risk on sex with one of the emperor's women. The harem was a sexual arrangement that was profoundly prejudicial to men – because virtually all the women belonged to the king. As Matt

Ridley remarks, it was democracy, not concern for women's situation, that did for the harem: the purpose of anti-polygamy statutes is to protect men.

Only the leaders of religious cults have harems today. David Koresh of the Branch Dravidian sect had one, and so did the Bhagwan. David Berg of The Family had his 'Hookers for Jesus'. Most recently, Revd Chris Brain of the Nine O'Clock Service in Sheffield achieved the rare feat of building up a harem within the Church of England. According to the members of his congregation who have since spoken out, he had a group of seven 'lycra-lovelies' – 'attractive anorexic-looking women all with very similar hairstyles' – who kept house for him and his family, and whom he would take to bed to relax him after a hard day's work. He also apparently had non-penetrative sex with about fifty female members of his congregation, on a variety of pretexts – 'sexual healing', 'experiments in sexual ethics', 'explorations of intimacy' and 'discovering a post-modern definition of sexuality'. One of the women involved gave an insight into harem psychology when she said, 'I felt in some way that he owned my body – I was his to do what he wanted with.'[18]

But even though such arrangements are exceptional today, the old thinking persists in our ambivalent reactions to the sexual misdemeanours of powerful men. Today politicians and other high-profile men whose sexual indiscretions come to light may be forced to resign, but for reasons that are confused and inconsistent. David Mellor had to go after his affair with Antonia da Sancha because of his hypocrisy: there was a widespread feeling that members of the Cabinet should live by the moral principles they were always preaching to the rest of us. Revelations about Rupert Pennant-Rea, the Deputy Governor of the Bank of England, having sex with Mary Ellen Synon on the boardroom carpet were just too embarrassing. It was poor judgment that did for Gary Hart, who withdrew from the Presidential contest after being photographed on a pleasure cruiser with model Donna Rice on his knee days after urging photographers to follow him around. In the case of Prince Charles, some churchmen have expressed religious scruples about having an adulterer as head of the established church – ironically, given that the Church of England was founded by a king with a rather more ostentatiously transgressive marital track-record and with the express purpose of legitimizing his adultery. And sometimes men do get away with it. Paddy Ashdown cleverly chose as his lover a woman who was by no means a bimbo, who behaved with great decorum, and who looked rather like his wife – all attributes likely to make women less critical of the affair. Everyone thoroughly approved.

We're inconsistent because we hold two contradictory ideas about the sexuality of powerful men. On the one hand, we want our leaders to be exemplary – to uphold the marital ideals we all aspire to. On the other, we're not in the least surprised when they don't – because deep down we suspect it's in the nature of powerful men to behave like this. Americans understand, writes the journalist who covered the Gary Hart case, that 'the same kind of drive that propels these guys from the mud to the stars might also endow them with larger-than-life appetites in the bedroom.'[19]

But in fact a man's sex drive is determined, not by his career success or the money in his account, but by the level of one particular hormone in his blood. A study of ninety-two young Greek soldiers showed that the number of orgasms they had per week was directly related to their blood concentration of dihydrotestosterone: 'superstuds' who had lots of orgasms had higher levels.[20] But because we still hark back to the polygamous moment, the idea that money and power give men 'larger-than-life' appetites seems natural to us. This is one of our simple stories about sexuality. When it's the local window-cleaner who has a lot of women, we just tell a different story.

Of course money and power do make a difference – but not

because they give men bigger sexual appetites. The difference money makes is on another level entirely. What affluence does above all is to make men feel more entitled to sex. Money empowers men to initiate.

Money is obviously an aid to seduction: given an equally appealing partner, a woman is likely to find dinner at Quaglino's a sexier experience than a takeaway chow mein. And being able to buy that wonderful dinner may make a man feel more attractive. If he has more money than her, he may feel he has some kind of right to ask her out: he has something to offer.

When I asked men if there had been women they'd fancied and fantasized about but hadn't approached, they all told me about women who were of higher social class and/or had more money than them. I asked what had stopped them from approaching these remote and yearned-for women. They all said the same: they simply assumed she wouldn't be interested in them.

As Sam put it, 'She was a doctor. She was really lovely – South American – with this amazing long dark hair. I fancied her like crazy, but I'd never have asked her out. I just felt without knowing anything about the woman that she moved in different circles from me. I was fairly sure she'd have said no, so it wasn't really worth the risk – and I suspected my wallet wouldn't have stood the heat.'

Here is another way in which initiatives mesh with money. The biggest single obstacle to male initiatives is the man's awareness that she has more power and money than him. If he feels she is out of his class, however much he wants her, he's less likely to make a move.

Dennis was unusual in that he'd been out with a woman who was seriously wealthier than him. 'It was nice at first,' he said. 'I suppose it's good for your ego – this girl is obviously not going out with me for my money! But it became a bit of a problem. I felt it was too much – you lost that sense of power in the relationship. I felt there wasn't a balance in it. She was over the top with it, she'd throw it about a bit. It was kind of false. I ended up hating it.'

Dennis equates money with power – and with less money than her, he feels he loses power. For him this situation is 'false' and out of balance. Financial 'balance' in a sexual relationship is achieved when he has as much or more than her: it's upset when she has more than him. It feels only natural for the man to have more money.

If money buys women, what if the man has no money? Most of the men I talked to volunteered this as a serious problem in courtship. When I asked men over thirty whether dating was more difficult for young people today than when they'd first started going out with women, they always said yes – because young people today have less money.

If his money means a man has some value, some intrinsic worth, something to offer, to lose his money may also be in a profound way to lose his sense of self. Men kill themselves because of debt: women don't. I once worked for nine months counselling people admitted to a casualty ward after attempting suicide, and in all that time never came across a woman who'd tried to kill herself because of money problems. Of course poverty makes everything worse, and for many women who attempt suicide it certainly adds to their troubles, but the primary cause is most often a problem with her part- ner – usually violence – or a sexually abusive childhood that still haunts her. Concepts like shame, ruin, being used, and even self-destruction, cluster around love and its abuse or the lack of it, for women – and around money and the lack of it for men.

The fact that money is a central part of a man's identity, especially his sexual identity, also explains the ruinous effect of unemployment on people's sex lives. In a survey of three thousand unemployed people for Jobsearch UK, two out of five said they made love less often since losing their jobs, more than half said their sex lives had been spoiled, and fourteen per cent said they 'didn't make love at all anymore'.[21]

WERE THERE KISSING OR NO KISSING:
The downside for women

So money buys women. It means he can take her to lavish restaurants, it means he feels entitled to the best women: but it also means something more specific. Money buys sex. This is the downside of the system where the man pays 'for' the woman.

Where gifts are given in exchange for sex, any sexual act by the woman becomes a commodity – something that has an economic value. 'Ruin' for a man used to mean financial ruin, but for a woman it meant she'd had sex when she shouldn't, and there's a close equivalence between the two meanings. A ruined woman was one who had lost her capital assets – her virginity – and had nothing to put on the market.

A song from Shakespeare's *Measure for Measure* deals beautifully with the sexual exchange involved in courtship.

> *Take O take those lips away*
> *That so sweetly were forsworn.*
> *And those eyes, the break of day,*
> *Lights that do mislead the morn,*
> *But my kisses bring again*
> *Seals of love, but seal'd in vain* . . . .

The conceit is of the kiss as one of the artefacts that are exchanged in the courtship economy. Now the singer wants those kisses back.

Yet maybe this notion of kisses as part of the accountancy of courtship is more than just an arcane metaphor. Under the betrothal system in England and Wales in the sixteenth, seventeenth and eighteenth centuries, there were certain legal safeguards against breach of promise: and if one or other had changed their minds, the couple would go before the church courts in an attempt to retrieve their courtship gifts – the rings, loving spoons or locks of hair – that might then be offered to another lover. One of the legal documents that governed these breach of contract suits, *A Treatise of Feme Coverts or the Lady's Law*, contains a fascinating example of the differing valuation of male and female sexual acts. This legal code stipulates that if a man had had a kiss from his betrothed, he could recover at most half his gifts from her, but the woman 'whatsoever she gave, were there kissing or no kissing in the case, she may demand and have all again.'[22] Her kiss has a different value from his. Her kiss enters the courtship economy, but his doesn't. The mutual kiss is something she gives and he takes – his profit, her loss. A sexual act by the woman has a market value – like a ring or coin or piece of lace. In the song from *Measure for Measure*, the idea that her kisses have a value is a lovely literary conceit, but in the *Treatise of Feme Coverts* it's shown to be an economic reality.

Until the present century, the market value of a married woman's sexuality was something that could be worked out quite precisely. Patriarchy has always conceptualized adultery and rape as theft from one man by another. In Dr Johnson's infamous words, 'We hang a thief for stealing sheep, but the unchastity of a woman transfers sheep and farm and all from its rightful owner'. And under English law until the present century, a husband could bring acts of 'criminal conversation' against a wife's lover and gain an adultery payment from him: in effect the lover was compensating the husband for what he'd stolen from him.[23] The sum of money represented an exact valuation of what sex with the woman was worth.

This may all seem like another country, where they do things differently. But the commodification of female sexuality was a linchpin of the dating system that is only gradually

falling apart. Advice columns from the 1940s and 1950s reiterate the idea that a woman's sexuality and sexual acts have a
market value:

'A girl who passes out kisses like candy is putting a pretty
low price-tag on her affections.'[24]

'Kisses, like other good things in life, are valued in proportion to their scarcity.'[25]

'Who wants second-hand goods?'[26]

'Kisses freely given are cheap and valueless.'[27]

'Why should a person buy something he can get for
nothing?'[28]

'The boys find her easy to afford. She doesn't put a high
price-tag on herself . . . .Your clothes can cost a lot, but you'll
look cheap with that toss of the head . . . Reprice your line.
Make yourself scarce and watch your value go up.'[29]

'The engagement ring is no substitute for the wedding ring
. . . Even the most frugal man is capable of forfeiting his
deposit.'[30]

We cannot distance ourselves entirely from this. The sexual
exchange system expounded by agony aunts of the 1940s is
still around. It structures the cautionary tales we heard in
Chapter Three – the stories women tell about those other
women who ask men out, and who give sex and get nothing
but sex in return.

And this value system has a particularly pernicious consequence – which is still with us. If the man has spent enough
money on her, to her 'value', he may feel he's earned sex –
and she may feel she owes him sex.

Keith recalls, 'With Moira I remember signing the cheque
for dinner and being fairly clear what I could expect to get
for it – which was just fine because I was quite pleased to get
it . . . .' Keith and Moira both read the same meaning into the
financial exchange – and they're both happy with it. It can
be a form of signalling by the woman: if she lets him pay
she's assenting to sex.

But there are huge pitfalls in a system where men spend in exchange for sex. It's an interaction that may lead to the negation of female wishes and desires. If *she* feels she 'owes' him sex – and goes along with it, though it isn't really what she wants – there will be little pleasure for her in the sexual encounter. And if *he* feels she 'owes' him sex – even though she doesn't want it – the scene is set for coercion. Where men pay for everything, the risk of rape increases, and both men and women are less likely to condemn the man than if expenses were shared.[31]

But the sexual value system that is set up when the man pays can also distort the dynamics when both the man and woman want to make love. Anna shows how things can go wrong when a financial agenda – an agenda that's all about who owes what to whom – is superimposed on a couple's desire for one another.

'There was someone I went out with when I was at school. He was ten years older than me, and drove an expensive car and took me out to expensive places to eat. We had an awful lot of foreplay, he never tried to push it further than that and I was a bit puzzled – he'd say, "No no no, you're a virgin, I mustn't go any further". I was just very taken aback. One time we'd stripped and had had a lot of foreplay and were getting very passionate, and I just assumed that sex would take place, and I wasn't stopping him, but he wouldn't have sex with me. And then afterwards he used to hold it over me – "I could have had your virginity if I'd wanted". He used to play this funny game with me if I wasn't doing things that he wanted – "I could have had your virginity . . ."

'I just used to tell him it was his own stupid fault. What did he expect – *gratitude?*'

He spends money on her. He's 'earned' sex. But he doesn't help himself to what is owed to him. And because he doesn't cash in his credits, he feels she should be grateful. He holds it over her. He feels she owes him something for his abstinence.

But Anna has a different agenda. She just wants to make love to a man about whom she feels 'very passionate' – and is thoroughly fed up when it doesn't happen.

YOU ALWAYS PAY ANYWAY: The downside for men

In her research for *The Hite Report on Male Sexuality*, Shere Hite set out to explore men's feelings about prostitution. She asked them, 'Have you ever had sex with a prostitute? How did you feel about paying for sex?' She got a response that she hadn't expected. Men told her, 'You always pay anyway'.[32]

Resentment about courtship spending is a theme that runs through male pronouncements about sex. Here, for instance, is Kinsey, writing in the 1950s, and in the course of his tirade, painting a deliciously detailed picture of the social life of wealthy Americans at that time:

'Hundreds of males have insisted that intercourse with a prostitute is cheaper than intercourse with any other girl. The cost of dating a girl, especially at the upper social level, may mount considerably through the weeks and months, even years, that it may take to arrive at first intercourse. There are flowers, candy, "coke dates", dinner engagements, parties, evening entertainments, moving pictures, theatres, nightclubs, dances, picnics, weekend house parties, car rides, longer trips, and all sorts of other expensive entertainment to be paid for, and gifts to be made to the girl on her birthday, at Christmas, and on innumerable other social occasions. Finally, after all this the girl may break off the whole affair as soon as she realizes that the male is interested in intercourse. Before the recent war the average cost of a sexual relation with a prostitute was one to five dollars. This was less than the cost of a single supper date with a girl who was not a prostitute . . .'[33]

For her book, *Secrets About Men*, Barbara de Angelis talked to men about their 'biggest turn-offs'. We learn that men don't like women who wear baggy knickers, talk about former lovers, are excessively clingy, or are very unresponsive in bed. But the biggest turn-off of all was the 'woman who cares only about a man's financial status'. Barbara de Angelis comments, 'I don't think any other topic elicited more angry responses from the men I interviewed'.[34]

Sometimes, as well as the anger, there's laughter – of a rather sardonic kind. A *Sunday Times* trailer for Desmond Morris's BBC programme on courtship in 1994 ran, 'Before you know it, you are exhibiting "tie signs" such as arms round the waist, followed by the pupil enlargement, hot flushes, sweating, panting and increase in heart-rate which are universal reactions to a sheaf of restaurant bills . . . .'[35]

Men are angry for two reasons. One is practical: if women expect to be paid for, it puts pressure on men to earn. The other goes much deeper.

The economic model of courtship arose because men have had to provide for women's offspring. This is the meaning that is echoed throughout the natural world – for instance, when a tern gives his mate a little fish. But it's behaviour which is also open to another interpretation: that men have to pay because they want sex more than women.

The idea here is that the one who gets most pleasure pays. This notion was around, though pleasingly inverted, when Hugh Grant was arrested on Sunset Boulevard for committing a lewd act with a prostitute. There was much puzzlement over why he'd chosen to pay for something that lots of US women would have adored to have given for free: and some women went even further in their protestations – like the woman who turned up outside the courtroom with a placard that said, 'I would have paid *you*, Hugh'.

If we believe that generally payment is in exchange for pleasure, and men pay during courtship because they want sex more than women, we're putting a sexual interpretation on a financial transaction. The assumption is that a sexual dynamic – him wanting and enjoying sex more than her – is being expressed through an economic exchange – him rewarding her for giving him sex. But maybe it also operates the other way round. Maybe the money shapes the sex. Maybe the financial interaction distorts or corrupts the sexual one.

When men do all the financial giving, they may question whether they are wanted for themselves. This was certainly what Shere Hite found when she asked men, 'Did you ever feel a woman was having sex with you because of something you could give her – your prestige, position or economic advantages?' The replies were amazingly bitter.

'After about two years of marriage, I came to realize that my wife had used sex for a home and security. We separated and I made up my mind it would never happen again.'

'In my opinion, my wife makes a so-called professional prostitute look like an amateur!'

'I have felt a woman has had sex with me because of what she thought I could give her – and I resented being like a piece of meat or a land deal – so many dollars per square foot.'

'It does piss me off that women bitch about being used, but at the same time acknowledge that their man is also their meal ticket.'

'In just about every relationship I try to fathom out what the woman thinks I am going to do for her. At this point in my life I am well used to being used.'[36]

Such bitterness is scarcely surprising in a cultural context in which blatant descriptions of sex within a relationship as a means to a material end are still encountered – when for instance a saleswoman at an Ann Summers party describes how to use a basque with lots of fiddly fastenings down the front to get yourself a new dishwasher: let him undo a few buttons, get him turned on, then say he can only undo another if he promises to come up with the goods. It's a scenario that seems to come straight out of the 1950s, when the heroine of a story in the *Ladies Home Journal* explained, 'I'm going to tell you a secret now. It's about girls and how they dress and how they do their hair. Men always think those things are frivolous matters. Nothing could be further from the truth. The girl in the red dress with the plunging neckline may be only shopping for a washing machine as she tangos so sensually on the dance floor. She may know very well that it takes this dress to get that fellow to let her wash those clothes in that washing machine he's going to buy her when they are married . . .'[37] In both these sexual encounters, it's not the man who is wanted, but the household appliances he can buy. The washing machine is the end, and sex is merely the means.

Models of female sexual behaviour which are all about financial reward persist today. The career mistress may be something of a curiosity – but she's still around. She crystallizes a kind of female sexual aspiration that is predicated on the model of sex as a system of exchange.

For Bienvenida Buck, the classic mistress who crashed the English class system with such style in 1994, the purpose of her sexual relationships was twofold – upward mobility and financial gain. In an article in *Woman's Journal*, she wrote 'Materially, the aim is to want for nothing and to have your unique attention rewarded with a yacht, penthouse and a couture wardrobe.'[38] Good sex had nothing to do with it. She told a reporter, 'With these powerful men it was never anything to do with physical enjoyment: you don't feel a physical passion for these men'.

Bienvenida did sometimes complain about her lovers – but never about the sex, because she didn't expect the sex to be particularly pleasant. It was rather her lovers' failure to observe the niceties of romance that she found upsetting: 'All I asked was for them to send me flowers or a little card or something if I am not well.'[39] Here, the lover is assessed on his handling of the material side of courtship. She's in it for the symbols – the flowers, dinners, champagne. These are what really excite her and what she lusts after. The symbols become the thing itself.

US writer Ginie Polo Sayles is another great enthusiast for financially profitable seductions. In her book *How To Marry The Rich*, she sets out her strategies for catching an 'RM' (Rich Man). She suggests you first acquire some 'body-conscious clothing in vibrant colours' and learn to cross your legs seductively, always remembering that 'the higher your leg is crossed on your other thigh, the higher wattage your signal is.'[40] Once you've mastered the necessary skills, you could pose as a journalist and interview a man whose bank balance you've had your eye on, or go and chat up a rich widower you've identified through the obituary columns, or book yourself into a detox clinic where lots of RM hang out. Anyone feeling queasy is reassured: 'You are not the American Red Cross . . .'.

It's a book to read with horrified fascination. Yet in a way this is what women have always done: we've always used secret stratagems to hook men who are good providers. Ginie Polo Sayles's only sin is to spell that out quite shamelessly. And like Bienvenida she knows that the point of all this leg-crossing and perusing of obituary columns isn't the ultimate orgasm. If you want to marry a rich man, she says, forget about great sex: your criteria should be simple – 'money and nice manners'.

So here are some of the sexual meanings of men's money. It may be about self-confidence, potency, entitlement to beautiful women and lots of them, the nerve to initiate – even the right to sex, regardless perhaps of what the woman wants. But it is also, it seems, about resentment, bitterness, 'being like a piece of meat or a land deal', doubting if he is wanted for himself.

RICH AS A TROLL: What women's money means to women

In the film, *La Reine Margot*, based on a novel by Alexandre Dumas about the Huguenot massacres in sixteenth-century France, Isabelle Adjani's audacious queen roams the murky streets of Paris in search of a really good one-night stand. This doesn't seem surprising. She is, after all, the queen; she can do what she wants.

So far we've looked at men's money, and what it means to both men and women. But where it's women who have the power and money, the sexual story, it seems, may have a quite different shape.

In Anglo-Saxon times, according to historian John Gillis, there were two distinct forms of wedding. One form was for young women. They were 'given away' by their families and gifts symbolic of authority such as a sword were given to the husband – who symbolized the power balance in the new relationship with devastating precision by stepping on his new wife's foot. But when widows married again, they favoured a form of 'self-wedding' in which the woman gave herself to the groom, and the joining of the couple was marked by more egalitarian symbols – rings, kisses, the clasping of hands.[41]

Here the young woman subordinates herself in the wedding ritual – but the widow claims equality. This is significant: widowhood is a fascinating status. Before women had much earning power, widows would have been the main group of women with their own money. Historically, the young heiress's money has come with strings: her sexual purity was closely guarded and her husband was chosen for her. But the widow's money was more truly her own. In previous eras of high mortality, too, many widowed women would still have been young and desirable. And the young widow has had a very special status as a symbol of female sexual self-determination.

One of the feistiest women in medieval literature is

Chaucer's Wyf of Bath, who has been widowed not just once but five times. The twin poles of the philosophy by which she has lived her life are her belief in female autonomy and her opposition to chastity – 'God bad for us to wexe and multiplye,' she says. Five centuries before Freud, she asks what women want, and comes up with a clear answer: mastery. In her Prologue she sets out her programme for matrimonial reform, describing her five marriages and showing how everything worked out best when she was in charge. Her Tale is her own version of the Loathly Lady. A knight has to choose if he'd rather have his sweetheart ugly and faithful, or beautiful and sexually free. Wisely he leaves the decision up to her – and she promises to be both fair and true.

The rich widow was a special case because her money was so subversive. The woman who has more money than the man she desires undermines the whole construction of sex as a system of exchange – that system under which the woman's sexuality becomes a commodity, and the man may feel he isn't really wanted for himself. But under patriarchy there were always limits to the widow's sexual independence.

In *Middlemarch*, George Eliot explores the widow's auton-omy and the limits to that autonomy by means of an artificial device – the financial conundrum she sets for her heroine, Dorothea.[42] Dorothea has been left a lot of money by her late husband, the dreary cleric, Casaubon. This money is empowering. As an autonomous widow, she's now in a strong position to take an initiative with Will Ladislaw, the man she loves. Except that Casaubon, jealous of her fondness for Ladi-slaw, has written a special clause into his will, stipulating that she loses the money if she marries him.

Even though Dorothea's money has strings attached, the fact that she has money and Ladislaw has none still changes the conventional sexual balance of power – which is one reason why the story still seems so fresh to us today. This was nicely reflected in the 1994 BBC dramatization of the novel, which was cast to appeal to women. Dorothea with her neat hair and modest make-up wasn't there to be looked at: it was Ladislaw with his smouldering gaze and tumbling curls who was obviously the object of desire.

Today we've moved into a new era. Now some women have money that comes neither from their fathers nor from their deceased husbands – money that they've earned themselves. How does this affect their sexual behaviour?

Research hints at an intriguing relationship between occupation and sexual style. When women move into previously all-male spheres such as law, business or accountancy they become much more like men in sexual profile. They have more partners and more adulterous relationships, and they're less concerned with intimacy and commitment. A study of women working in the financial centres of New York and San Francisco and who were having affairs 'found them taking a fairly cool approach to problems more typical of men – and this approach was followed through in their extramarital lives as well . . .'.[43] It's the *Cosmopolitan* fantasy incarnate – the suave accomplished woman in her Ralph Lauren suit and Manolo Blahnik shoes, equally in control in the boardroom and in bed. But when men move into stereotypically 'feminine' occupational spheres such as social work, their sexual profiles become more like women's.[44] They have fewer sexual partners and fewer affairs, and intimacy and commitment start to matter more. Here, the profile is pure New Man – that elusive paragon who cooks brilliant pasta and gets turned on by intelligence.

Perhaps particular careers attract particular personalities – but Annette Lawson, who carried out the study, questions whether personality differences account for the contrasting sexual patterns, because when people changed jobs they also seemed to change their sexual styles. There might also be circumstantial explanations: for instance, business often involves travelling – and travel has been a great inducement to illicit sexual encounters ever since Tristan and Isolde drank the love potion on board ship.

But the most glaring disparity between the 'male' and 'female' occupational spheres is income. Lawyers and accountants earn a very great deal more than social workers or psychiatric nurses. And I'd suggest that it's this distinction above all that accounts for those striking divergences in sexual style.

You could speculate that money – her own money – might shape a woman's sexuality in all sorts of ways. Commitment may matter less to a woman who can pay her own way, because she doesn't need her lover to stick around to support her. Financially independent and successful women may postpone children or not want children – and so may be happy with one-night stands or relationships that aren't 'going anywhere'. And if she's not looking for a good provider, the woman with money may choose her lovers largely for their sexual attractiveness – rather like the peahen who has no expectations of parental care from the male, who just goes for the genes for gorgeousness.

Money might also tip the balance in a married woman's decision to have an affair. Adultery is a big financial risk for women: a woman's adultery is more likely to end a marriage than a man's, and after divorce women are much worse off than men. A woman with her own money might think the risk worth taking. Annette Lawson says that nearly a third of the women in her study of adultery felt that success at work had 'influenced them towards a liaison'; she found this connection between success and secret affairs to be more marked for women than men.

Some might balk at this vision of monied women hurling themselves at gorgeous but improvident men for adulterous one-night stands. But however we might view this behaviour, what does seem to emerge is a new psychosexual principle: money makes women more sexually independent – more casual, less clingy, more willing to take risks – more like men. And any increase in women's sexual autonomy might also mean more female initiatives at the start of courtship.

In *The Bodyguard*, Whitney Houston is Rachel, a rich rock star who employs strong silent Frank – Kevin Costner – to protect her from a stalker. She's paying him – we're constantly told it's 'good money' – and she makes the first move. She's very 'feminine' – sweet, tentative, coy – in how she goes about it, but she does ask directly.

'Frank, I have this problem. I can't go out for a date because you have to be with me every minute . . . So the only thing I can figure is for you to take me out. That's what I was wondering . . . I mean, what do you think? Only if you want to . . . . This is *so* embarrassing!'

Sadly, as in the cautionary tales in Chapter Three, she gets her man, but not to keep. Those cautionary tales, as we saw, are based on patriarchal principles: they don't tell us how the world works. But is at least this part of the story valid? Are rich women like Rachel more likely to ask men out?

Throughout the natural world, it's the sex that invests least in parental care that initiates. So, as women either become the main bread-winners or choose not to have children, you'd expect more female initiatives.

And if high-earning women have more one-night stands, as Annette Lawson implies, they'll also initiate more. The farther sex moves from the courtship-into-marriage paradigm, the more likely women are to make the first move. I asked an American banker if the women she knew asked men out. Some did, she said. 'But the ones who do have all given up on committed relationships. Perhaps they've been hurt. They're looking for toyboys. If they're just after sex, then yes, they might ask men out.'

Women who aren't looking for providers may be attracted to men who have less money than them – and that too may lead to deviations from the classic dating script. Tina had made the first move, but always with younger, poorer men, and she felt her money was incompatible with the traditional feminine display of vulnerability in courtship. 'When you're the provider and bread-winner and pillar of your children and job, how can you start pretending to be Little Miss Come-and-look-after-me?'

There's also the direct sense in which money is tied up with initiative. In business as in courtship, the assumption is that if you initiate, you pay. If you suggest a drink together, you buy the first round: if you book the restaurant table, you'll be given the bill. The woman with the capacity to pay is also a woman who might make the arrangements – book the table, ask him out.

We've seen how money means sex for men – but not for women. Women don't assume they'll have more pleasure if they get rich: they assume they'll have more pleasure if they get *thin*. For women, still, scarcity rather than abundance feels sexy. But is the meaning of money about to shift for women? As they start to enjoy the autonomy – including sexual autonomy – that money gives, will women start to find their earning power exciting, even libidinous?

In *Fire With Fire*, Naomi Wolf traces out the changes in her own attitude to money after the success of her book, *The Beauty Myth*. She claims to have been quite unnerved by her first enormous royalty cheque: 'The cheque was a phantom presence disrupting my sense of where I stood in the world. It felt defeminizing, like a mark of maleness stigmatizing me . . .' But as she learned to manage her money and to use it well, she started to relish it. She says, 'I began to tell young women something that I had never, ever heard from a woman when I was growing up: it is really fun to use power, to use money to further positive goals.'[45]

Little girls still aren't encouraged to aspire to riches. No-one tells little girls that money matters – with the splendid exception of Pippi Longstocking, the exemplary heroine of Astrid

Lindgren's books from the 1950s. Pippi lives alone with her monkey and her horse, and is scruffy, strong, clever and wealthy, with a suitcase full of gold coins which she uses to buy thirty-six pounds of sweets for poor children. Pippi exults in her money: 'I'm rich as a troll!' she says.[46] I've watched my own daughters devour these stories voraciously – ever hungry for tales of girls who act out their own fantasies of heroism, boldness, insouciance and generosity. Pippi uses her gold coins to do good in the world and to have a good time – possibilities that many women only recognize long after they've made the career decisions that will restrict their own access to money for life.

THE HAIRDRESSERS' TALE:
Women with money and men with none

Women with a lot of money they've earned themselves remain exceptional. But women who have very little money may still reverse the traditional financial patterning of the sexual relationship – if their men have even less. At one end of the economic scale there are Annette Lawson's cool-headed women who work in the financial centres of Los Angeles and New York, with their designer jackets and casual liaisons: at the other, there's another group of women who are also clever, articulate and financially independent, if not quite so lusciously dressed – the Leicester hairdressers.

In a study carried out in the East Midlands in 1986, sociologists Kristine Beuret and Lynn Makings talked to female hairdressers who were dating men who were unemployed.[47] They wanted to see how the women's relatively greater spending power affected their relationships.

They found the women striving to prop up the outward form of a conventional dating relationship, but subverting it from within. The women were very sensitive to the impact of unemployment on their boyfriends, and went to great lengths to protect the men's self-esteem. They'd developed elaborate strategies to imply, both to their boyfriends and to outsiders, that the man was still in charge of the money.

'When I'm out with my mates I drink Bacardi and coke but when I'm with Barry I have lager. He saw me drinking with the girls once and got upset when he saw the shorts, but I said it was Linda's birthday and we were having a treat.'

'I pretend that one of my customers works at Next and gets seconds cheap. I got him a smashing jumper last week, it cost me £39 but I told him it cost £5. He insisted on giving me the fiver too, poor sod. Men have no idea do they?'

Through these economic subterfuges, the women preserved the appearance of male control, while actually taking control themselves, to achieve some goal of their own – holidays in the Canaries, Bacardi to drink, a boyfriend dressed by Next.

Beuret and Makings wanted to know if the women had asked the men out. They hadn't. But their financial strategies and their courtship behaviour were all of a piece. At the start of the relationship, as in their handling of the money, they were covert but deliberate – taking very conscious but indirect initiatives while making it seem that the man was making the move.

'Well I saw him going into the betting shop, next door but one, and I thought, H'm, tasty. So when his sister came in to have a blow-dry I dropped a few hints that I'd be in "Mr C's" Friday night and Bob's your uncle. In he strolls, buys me a drink and so that was it.'

'You can't let on what you're up to, but you've got to give them a bit of a push haven't you.'

These women never claim it 'just happened', and they're quite unembarrassed about saying what they did. And as so often there's a close correspondence between the handling of money and the dynamics of the relationship. Both in the first moves and in the spending of money, the hairdressers are covertly in control.

It is also quite clear what these women were in the relationships for. They talked very directly about physical attraction. 'Sometimes when I'm working,' said one woman, 'I suddenly think about him and I get this feeling in my stomach and I almost have to sit down. It's fantastic . . . .' There were 'strong indications,' say the researchers, 'that sexual attraction, and their own sexual satisfaction, were very highly-valued aspects of the relationship.' But, in spite of all this physical pleasure, they were wary of sharing these men's beds on a more permanent basis. When asked about marriage they were guarded: 'I do love John but I prefer seeing him rather than living with him. I work hard at this job and I want to start my own business . . .'.

These relationships may be cocooned in tradition, but there's a very different creature growing inside, struggling to be born. It looks as though the man is still in control of the traditionally male parts of the relationship – asking her out, and paying – but it's the woman who creates that illusion. And in various profound ways these relationships are untraditional: the women emphasize physical pleasure, and they don't want marriage or cohabitation – at least, not yet. They're there for the sex rather than the money.

Here the old system is still in place, but under strain. The Leicester hairdressers are pushing at the limits of the system, but in very feminine, covert ways. The financial shift presages a profound shift in the balance of power in the relationship – but these women, aware of the devastating meanings of financial impotence for the men they love, do all they can to keep to the outward form of courtship, while changing it from within.

Money and sex have an intimate relationship which is acted out in our lives. Natalie judges a man's commitment by how much he spends on her, Tina initiates but only with men who are less well-off than her, Naomi starts to get turned on by men with money once she has children of her own, and some of the women in Annette Lawson's study feel their career success has motivated them to have affairs. And men may use their money as a form of sexual display, or, like Sam, find a woman's own money the biggest disincentive to asking her out, or, like Keith, feel entitled to sex because they've spent money on the woman, or, like many of the men in Shere Hite's research, feel bitter because they suspect they're only wanted for their money.

Money has a direct effect on female sexual initiative. A woman who earns good money is more likely to make the first move. And if she makes the first move, she will probably also take on some or all of the giving and spending at the start of courtship. Eventually we should move right away from our anachronistic assumption that this behaviour should necessarily be gendered, so that women as well as men take pleasure in giving, as they seem to have done in previous centuries under the betrothal system, when women often gave gifts – like Bridget Rose who gave Edward Arden 'six-pence and a cluster of nettles', explaining that 'as close as these three stick together, so fast should her harte stick to him.'[48]

CHAPTER 9
DANGER

'All the better to eat you with.
The girl burst out laughing: she knew she was nobody's meat.'
(Angela Carter, The Company of Wolves,
The Bloody Chamber)

'I'VE had a situation which was almost rape,' said Amanda. 'It was the closest I've been.

'I was on holiday in Crete, I was about twenty. We were sleeping on a beach, we had no money, and these guys used to buy us a meal. There was this Cretan bloke – he was quite good-looking – and there was a mountain behind our beach, and I said, "I'd love to go up that mountain and see the view." He said, "I'll take you up if you like" – and I just didn't think – so we started to go up this mountain. It was that kind of coarse brambly stuff and I was wearing a Monsoon skirt – it was just all wrong – I was in these sandals with thin little straps! And we got to the top and we sat down and he pinned me down.

'I was really frightened and it got further and further, and in some ways I was consenting, but . . . I didn't know how to get out of it, I didn't know how to change the situation, I certainly didn't say No no no, but I came out of it feeling all those things like having to have a shower, and kind of tarnished, and What have I done? Because it was definitely me, really, I could have got out of it. It was like, I'm on holiday,

I'm going to try and enjoy myself – but on the other hand I just didn't want it to go that far.

'I felt abused. But also a kind of affection for him, which I always feel after I've had sex with anybody. I don't know if it's a biological thing – whether, if you're going to mate with somebody, females are programmed almost to then want to stay with them so they can look after the children, even if it's horrible. So you're torn between this feeling of I've been violated and I'm filthy and I'm horrible and yuk – and the other feeling of "Will you be coming round to the beach this evening . . . .?"'

Many of us have stories like Amanda's to tell, stories of bad sex, miscommunication, and feeling 'tarnished'. The woman in the story is usually young – in her teens or early twenties. Often these stories are set abroad, because when we're on holiday or working abroad, we're more likely to take risks, to fail to abide by an accepted code, or to misunderstand. In these stories, the expectations and hopes we bring to a situation – 'I'm going to try and enjoy myself', 'I'd love to look at that view' – are about as appropriate to what transpires as a floaty Monsoon skirt to a climb up a Cretan mountain.

You could tell this story as a rape, but Amanda believes that would be wrong: 'I certainly didn't say No no no'. But it's a frightening and distressing experience, as will invariably be the case when the woman doesn't want sex, but somehow doesn't manage to say no – because she's too polite, feels she's already gone too far, or can't see a way out. I found that when women described situations where they didn't want the sex but didn't make that clear – or made it clear much later in the process than would have been ideal – they were usually very forgiving of the man involved, though when discussing similar things that had happened to others they'd rush to man the barricades on behalf of the other women. Most women are by no means the vindictive harridans featured in tired articles on political correctness. Charlotte, for instance, had been staying in a village in Sicily, where she got a lot of delicious attention because she was the only blonde. It all turned sour when a man took her for a walk and tried to make her have sex. She had to hit him and yell to make him let her go. She put it down to a misunderstanding.

Here Amanda unquestionably initiates the sequence of behaviours that ends with the sex she doesn't want. The two of them were attracted: he was 'a good-looking bloke' – and she implicitly acknowledges that she was interested in some sexual activity when she says, 'I didn't want it to go that far'. He's been buying her food – and, as we've seen, the male giving food to the female is one of the most widespread court-ship behaviours, found throughout the animal kingdom. And then she suggests going up the mountain to look at the view. She makes the first move. But the outcome was in no way her intention. 'I just didn't think,' she says. There's a clash of agendas. She chooses to climb the mountain, but she ends up in a place where she doesn't want to be. And as she stumbles through the scrub in her strappy sandals, she starts to feel it's just all wrong.

Studies show that men and women often communicate indirectly when initiating sexual activity.[1] Direct verbal suggestions about sexual contact may be experienced as intrusive. So instead we drop hints, touch experimentally and observe the other person's behaviour, and make inferences as to whether they are interested in sex. And, according to the traditional script, women are more indirect than men – even, as we've seen, to the point of saying the opposite of what they want. So men have to do more inferring than women. Trouble arises because men and women often make different inferences about the same behaviours. The same set of actions can have 'his' and 'hers' meanings – with men much more likely than women to interpret a variety of behaviours as evidence that the other person wants sex. And psychological studies have shown that men read female sexual enthusiasm into the most unpromising situations.

In one of the nicest of these studies, men were given two descriptions of a man and a woman going on a date.[2] In the first scenario, the woman did several things that previous research suggested would signal a lack of sexual interest: she wore a blouse with a bow at the collar, a pleated woollen skirt and penny loafers, she 'never kissed the man voluntarily', and she drank iced tea rather than alcohol. (I'm reminded of a friend who was having a drink with a new man, and who asked for an orange juice – whereupon he enquired if she was a virgin.) When the man in the scenario made sexual advances, the woman said no three times and tried to move away. When men read this account and gave a rating for how much the woman wanted sex, their average rating was almost at the middle of the scale – 4.5 on a scale where 1 meant 'she did not want to at all' and 9 meant 'she wanted to very much'.

In the second scenario, the woman did several things that research shows men read as signs of sexual interest: she wore a miniskirt, drank alcohol and 'voluntarily kissed the man'. Here, the men's average rating for how much she wanted to have sex on a scale from 1 to 9 was 6.7 – even though she said no.

In another study, men were given a description of a date in which the woman began protesting early during foreplay, the man used force to obtain sex, and the woman used force to try to resist.[3] Even here, men's ratings of how much she wanted to have sex were greater than the lowest possible rating.

It's in the context of this well-researched male readiness to see sexual enthusiasm all around that Amanda suggests going up the mountain to look at the view. And her story raises a crucial question about initiating. If men read sexual enthusiasm into the most unpromising situations – how will they read a direct female initiative? If we make the first move, will we expose ourselves to sexual danger?

THE PREDATOR: Why are we so afraid?

You're alone in your home at night. You know there's a prowler outside in the dark. You try to dial 999 but you can't get through. Suddenly you realize the prowler is in the house close to you. You feel his breath or his touch. You wake terrified, heart racing . . . .

Psychotherapist Clarissa Pinkola Estes calls this the 'predator' or 'dark man' dream. She says it's so common that it's unusual for a woman to reach twenty-five without having dreamt it.[4]

The predator dream combines the essential elements of every woman's worst fears – the dark, the stranger, and in her house. In this dream we experience, in compressed and symbolic form, the fears that haunt us in the waking world. And women today are very afraid. High profile crimes, like the murders of Marie Wilks or Celine Figard or Rachel Nickell, get inside us: we think of our children weeping over our dead bodies, we dream of speaking into the emergency phone on the motorway but the ominous footsteps are coming closer and there's no one there at the other end of the line. To protect ourselves from the sexual violence we so fear, we take a lot of precautions. Some of these strategies don't cost us very much: we make sure we have the keys in our hand as we approach our front door at night, we lock the car doors when driving, we don't have our first names put in the phone book. But there's a high price to pay for some of our safety measures. Many of us impose a voluntary purdah on ourselves. Some women avoid multi-storey car parks. Many don't like using public transport at night. And one woman in two in the UK is too scared to drive alone after dark.[5] No wonder we dream the predator dream so often.

This fear – far from being self-evidently justified – is extra-ordinarily interesting. For a start, violence is much less common than people think. A survey found that people on average thought that twenty-six per cent of people had been victims of violent crimes in the previous year: in fact it was two per cent. And the wrong people are afraid. Women and old people are most afraid – but it's men in their late teens and early twenties who are most at risk from violence.[6] In an impassioned article, journalist Philip Norman wrote that he now sees 'any female reading alone on the Hyde Park grass, or descending a dark escalator in the Underground not with a wolf whistle but with an unspoken prayer: please God let her survive!'[7] A quick glance at the murder statistics would show him that it's actually the young *male* on the Hyde Park grass he should be praying for.

We're not only wrong about the most likely victims: we're wrong too about the most likely aggressors. The predator who stalks our dreams is a stranger. Yet the rape at knife point in a dark alley is a very rare crime. Women are far more often raped or killed by men they know.

Why are women so afraid? One obvious reason is that crime reporting distorts the reality. Violent crimes get a lot more media attention if the victim is female. Murders of attractive young women make national headlines; but when a talented seventeen-year-old man on his way to the local fish and chip shop is brutally murdered by a gang of youths, it only makes the local press. The murder of Johanne Masheder in Thailand led to anguished newspaper articles asking why young girls risk their lives on the backpack trail: yet of forty-three Britons murdered abroad in 1995, only eight were women.[8]

The murders of women fascinate more than the murders of men because of one of our culture's most disturbing fan-tasies – the eroticization of an attractive female body that is comatose or even dead. *New York Post* journalist Bill Hoffman was quite explicit about this in his comments on a murder case he covered: 'I remember the morning the case broke, we were listening to the police radio. We heard the words "Central Park, young white teenager, gorgeous and strangled", and it was like TNT was planted under our rear ends – everyone flew out of here like bats out of hell. It was sex, tits and ass, and a strangling – we knew it would sell.'[9]

The imagined eroticism of the comatose or dead female body is still more in evidence in many of our fictions. Our books and films are littered with beautiful corpses. Nicholas Roeg's film *Bad Timing* juxtaposed a woman's struggles on a life-support machine after an overdose with her contortions during orgasm. In the film *Rising Sun*, from the novel by Michael Crichton, the murder of a prostitute, who was supposed to have enjoyed near-strangulation as a sexual technique, was constantly replayed. (Personable women who like being half-strangled as a way of intensifying their orgasms are somewhat over-represented in popular fiction: in real life this is a uniquely male perversion.) Even the nearness of death becomes erotic: a few years ago a book of photographs entitled *Marilyn: The Last Session* was promoted as a Christmas gift. There are of course plenty of dead men in our stories too: but they're never meant to be a turn-on.

This necrophiliac culture seems to support the most paranoid female hypotheses. We could see the fear generated among women as a backlash phenomenon, a deeply conservative impulse to keep us in our place – off the streets, waiting to be asked. And is it a backlash against women's sexual freedom in particular? That's certainly how it feels. We're most afraid when we're aware of ourselves as potentially sexual beings, rather than in other roles. As a social worker, I've worked in inner city teams where half of us had been physically attacked in the course of our work, and never felt afraid. I'm more likely to be nervous walking across a railway bridge after an evening out – where the risk is minimal. A professional role feels empowering – even when in reality it puts you at risk: but a sense of yourself as a sexual object goes hand in hand with a sense of yourself as a potential victim of sexual violence. There was an RAC 'knights of the road' commercial in which a woman ran out of petrol in a seedy part of town. We knew she was a doctor – but she was shown dressed up for an evening out with her boyfriend; if she'd had on her white coat rather than her sexy dress as she waited in her car to be rescued, perhaps we wouldn't have found her fear so convincing.

If we feel most at risk when we're aware of ourselves as women rather than as doctors or lawyers or social workers, this is because we have absorbed the message that it is our sexual freedom – however limited – that so endangers us. The beautiful corpse teaches that women put themselves terribly at risk – just by being there, but especially by being attractive. By implication, she has a further warning for us: that to aspire after further sexual freedoms – to ask men out, initiate, change the courtship script – would also be to increase the risks we run.

THE VAMP NARRATIVE: How Jennifer courted death

The belief that women do put themselves at risk by initiating sex is taken as axiomatic by the police, the judiciary and most of the media. Attitudes to prostitutes provide the purest example of this.

Some feminist writers have made bizarre claims about prostitution. 'Women have to acknowledge and accept the untamed, bold, proud and compassionate spirit of the whore as an aspect of ourselves,' writes Nickie Roberts, author of a history of prostitution.[10] The whore as the celebrant of female sexuality has her antecedents in the male fantasies we looked at in Chapter Two – de Sade's Juliette for instance. This fantasy of bold proud sexual women grates against the realities of prostitution – the young girls, often abused, often on the run from bleak children's homes, to be found in the red-light districts of our cities. But this distortion arises because the prostitute is a sexual initiator – though of course, except in male fantasy, her initiatives have nothing to do with her own pleasure: they're motivated by the need to buy herself her first hot meal of the week, or pay the bill in Tesco's, or keep up the instalments on her nice new sofa. It is also her role as an initiator which is seen as putting her uniquely at risk.

It's undeniable that prostitutes are made highly vulnerable to male violence by the nature of their work – which necessarily involves going somewhere secluded with a stranger. Over the past few years in this country, women working as prostitutes have been among the main victims of serial killers, along with runaways and young gay men.[11] And recently we've been forcibly reminded of the risks that some prostitutes run. There are at the time of writing nineteen unsolved murders of women who have been strangled and dumped, often by main roads, and mostly in the Midlands. Many of these women were working as prostitutes, and often in a particularly high-risk way: Tracey Turner, one of a number of women whose bodies were found in Leicestershire, is believed to have worked at motorway service stations, approaching drivers and offering them sex in their cars.[12]

The kinds of initiatives that prostitutes take are sometimes seen as so dangerous that they become an explanation, almost a justification, for sexual violence. One of the most alarming pronouncements along these lines came from Mr Justice Alliot, when he gave a rapist a jail sentence that was shorter than the recommended minimum because his victim was a prostitute. In passing sentence he said, 'While every woman is entitled to complain about being violated, someone who for years has flaunted their body and sold it cannot complain as loudly as someone who has not.'[13] QC Helena Kennedy comments, 'So entrenched is the idea that prostitutes have it coming to them that, in order to allay speculations and emphasize the seriousness of the risks to real women, the police often feel obliged to stipulate that female victims are not prostitutes.'[14]

It's in part because of the risks run by prostitutes – the group of women most obviously involved in initiating sex – that making the first move is seen as so dangerous. These risks are generalized to include any woman who takes a sexual initiative. As we've seen, there's a hierarchy of female sexual signals, from the indirect – a lycra miniskirt – to the very direct – an invitation to dinner. Behaviours anywhere on this continuum will make press, public and judiciary less sympathetic to a woman's situation if her conduct is examined in court – whether she's there as defendant or victim.

The female defendant who has taken sexual initiatives, or even whose self-presentation includes overt sexual signals, will receive less sympathy, and may not be believed. Because unchaste women are seen as more likely to lie, prosecution lawyers may ask irrelevant questions about a woman's sexual conduct, to imply that she's promiscuous. When Sara Thornton was on trial for the killing of her violent husband, she was asked by the prosecuting QC if she was in the habit of going out without wearing knickers, in an attempt to discredit her.[15] Helena Kennedy says she urges women defendants to avoid any sexual signals that might suggest they don't quite fit the old ideal of sweet submissive womanhood: 'I say, "For God's sake, keep your tattoo under wraps, get yourself an angora sweater".'[16]

But it is in the treatment of victims of sex crimes that these prejudices stand out most starkly. In most rape cases, the issue is not whether intercourse took place, but whether the woman consented, or, to be more precise, whether the male defendant *thought* she consented. This is why a sexual culture in which women don't always say what they want is so dangerous, because the man can argue that he believed the woman was consenting – whatever she said or did. If it's clear that sex happened, and the woman claims it was rape, the defence will seek to prove that she really wanted sex, or seemed to be signalling that she wanted sex. Much will be made of any sexual signals the woman gave or sexual moves she made. If she wore provocative clothing, drank in a bar, or was out on her own, these behaviours will be used to build a picture of a woman who would consent to anyone. For instance, in the 1983 gang rape in Big Dan's Tavern in New Bedford, the crime on which the film *The Accused* was based, the fact that the victim was drinking alone in a bar full of men was used against her.

The conduct of the female victims of sex crimes is judged against a set of rigid moral standards that are no longer applied in everyday life. Even in sex crimes where consent isn't an issue, the victim will lose sympathy if she dressed sexily or went out on her own. A woman who initiated, whether directly or indirectly, will be seen, not as an innocent victim but rather as a vamp, a provocative woman who enticed the man and is therefore to be blamed – because, according to one of the simple stories that still hold sway in the criminal justice system, men are unable to control their sexual urges and it's up to women not to provoke them.

In her book, *Virgin or Vamp*, Helen Benedict looks at the way the female victims of sex crimes are presented in court and in the media. The most startling case she examines is the so-called 'Preppie Murder', the 1986 murder of eighteen-year-old Jennifer Levin in Central Park in New York by her boyfriend Robert Chambers – the case covered by journalist Bob Hoffman, quoted earlier.

Levin had been out with Chambers three times and they'd slept together. The night before her body was found, she'd been in the same bar as Chambers, and at some point she'd gone over to talk to him. At first he didn't seem interested, but then he spent several hours talking to her, and the two of them eventually left the bar at four-thirty in the morning. Her strangled body was later found in Central Park. Chambers had been seen hanging around in the vicinity.

Benedict identifies a number of factors which all serve to classify a woman as a vamp rather than an innocent victim. Levin had most of them. She was killed by someone she knew, there was no weapon, she was of the same race and social class as Chambers, she was young and attractive – and she'd been drinking and flirting in a bar the night before her death. And the story told about Levin in the press was the story of the provocative woman who entices the man, and who therefore has it coming to her.

In an article in *New York* magazine, headlined 'East Side Story', journalist Michael Stone wrote, 'She was high-spirited and popular, and she'd been interested in Chambers for some time. They'd had a few flings, and she'd confided to friends how sexy she thought he was. Levin now told the other girl she wanted her boyfriend, and over the next three hours, friends saw Levin flirting and talking with Chambers at the bar.' Later he suggested that Levin was so sexually pushy she drove Chambers to violence: 'It's possible that Levin triggered Chambers's anger through her persistence'.[17] Other news stories also presented Levin's drinking and flirtatiousness as dangerous and self-destructive. A story in the *Daily News* was headlined, 'How Jennifer Courted Death.' This was also the line taken by the defence. Chambers's lawyer Jack Litman said in his closing statement, 'It was Jennifer who was pursuing Robert for sex . . . that's why we wound up with this terrible tragedy'.[18]

But what did Levin actually do? She went to a bar that she knew well and that was full of her friends. She talked to a man she'd already slept with twice. Later she went to the park with him. She did things we have all done. Yet, according to the vamp narrative used in much of the coverage, to do these things is to 'court death'. As Helen Benedict says, 'According to the moral guidelines that are invariably applied to sex-crime cases, good girls don't do any of the things Levin did that night: They do not stay up late in bars, they do not drink underage, they do not go to Central Park with a boyfriend, they do not talk about, let alone enjoy, sex, and, above all, they do not chase men'.[19]

The vamp narrative is a crystallization of a widely-held prejudice. The woman who takes sexual initiatives is commonly seen to be putting herself in danger, and if she gets into trouble, she may not be believed, or her conduct may be used as a vindication of the assault, or used to condemn her. In sexual attitude surveys, both men and women consider a woman who is raped on a date to be less deserving of sympathy if she asked the man out.[20] This was the very first issue raised by a number of men I talked to: if women ask men out, won't they be putting themselves at risk?

DANCES WITH WOLVES: Is it risky to ask men out?

When I was researching this book, I heard two almost identical hitch-hiking stories. Both were set abroad, and in both, the driver started to say how attractive he found the hitch-hiker, and then put his hand on their knee – at which point the hitch-hiker said they weren't interested and demanded to be dropped off in the nearest town. Ginny, a slender five-feet six, told her story in response to a question about sexual danger. Rob – who is a hefty six-feet two – told his to raise a laugh.

For Ginny, an unwanted sexual advance in an isolated place is always going to be more frightening than it is for Rob. Though the risks may be exaggerated in our minds, women of course are vulnerable, because we are generally smaller and weaker than men, especially in the upper body.

But the belief that we can protect ourselves by emulating the sleep-walking heroines of the female mythologies is about as useful as that persistent belief of children that causes such problems for teachers running 'Stranger Danger' programmes – the belief that you can tell a stranger by his nasty jagged teeth and sneaky expression. Far from keeping ourselves safe, we may actually endanger ourselves if we stick to a passive role and a traditional script.

The belief that women put themselves at risk by initiating assumes that the most dangerous point in sexual relationships is the pick-up. A lot of our fear is focused on that very first bit of interaction, the bit that we're looking at in this book. We imagine that there's most danger in casual sex, in one-night stands, and at the beginning of relationships before the other person is known. This fantasy is explored in *Looking for Mr Goodbar*, the novel by Judith Rossner.[21] Theresa is a teacher of deaf children who wants to explore a hidden part of herself. She goes to singles bars and picks up unsuitable men – and in the end she's murdered by one of them.

But the Mr Goodbar fantasy is misleading: the pick-up is not the most dangerous point. This belief probably arises for two reasons. Firstly, there's our fear of strangers. Secondly, there's our awareness that the pick-up is the moment of great-est *emotional* danger. It's at the very start of a relationship that we feel most vulnerable – and, of course, it's particularly risky for the person who initiated, because of the danger of rejection. Perhaps the confusion arises because we've equated the physical risk with the emotional one.

The truth is that we have most to fear, not from someone we've just got off with, but from people we know. Sexual coercion is unlikely at the start of a relationship; rape is more likely a month into the relationship than on a first date.[22] The risk of physical abuse increases with the length of the relationship, and so does the risk of sexual aggression: most male violence only emerges once the relationship is estab-lished.[23] And a rape attempt by a well-known perpetrator is more dangerous: a man the woman knows well is more likely than an acquaintance to complete a rape and to injure the woman.[24]

Certainly it's worrying that people believe that rape is more likely if the woman asked him out. But it doesn't essentially follow that women who initiate are more likely to be assaulted in reality. And in fact, if we look closely at the research, what starts to emerge is something very different. It seems that, far from endangering ourselves, we may be able to protect ourselves by taking a more assertive role at the start of the relationship. A submissive demeanour and an angora sweater will project the right image in court: but, in real life, they may get you into trouble.

When I was talking to women, I started to build up a speculative sexual profile of women who have a very indirect courtship style. And one thing I kept finding was that indirect women had experienced more coercive sex than sexually assertive women. Psychological studies confirm this impression. These studies suggest that, rather than putting us at risk, behaviour that deviates from the conventional female courtship script can help to keep us safe. Asking a man out is part of a set of new female behaviours – driving yourself, paying for yourself, deciding where you will go, saying what you want and don't want. Doing these things can actually protect us.

Here are the results of some of these studies.

The traditional way of doing things increases the risk of sexual aggression in courtship: if the man initiates the date, pays the expenses, and drives, sexual aggression is more likely to occur.[25]

According to sexual attitude surveys, both men and women believe that sexual aggression is more justified if the man paid for the date.[26]

Women are at greater risk of being sexually assaulted if they are submissive, unsure of themselves, passive, anxious to please, easily intimidated and convinced they could not fight back.[27]

A study of courtship violence found that there was no personality characteristic that distinguished women who'd had one experience of courtship violence from women who hadn't: it was just bad luck. But women who'd been assaulted by men they were going out with on more than one occasion did have a personality profile: they were more likely than other women to allow 'even a slight degree of control by the male' and had experienced more controlling behaviours by men during the dating relationship. These controlling behaviours were: jealousy, monitoring and controlling the woman's activities, using force as discipline, criticism and forced sex. The women who'd had more than one experience of courtship violence had permitted this kind of male control rather than ending the relationship.[28]

Research also shows that men and women with traditional sex-role attitudes are more accepting of coercive sex. Psychologists Rodney Cate and Sally Lloyd comment, 'Sexually-abusive males, as opposed to non-abusive males, tend to hold traditional beliefs about women'.[29] Sally Lloyd also suggests that the risk of courtship violence is increased by sexual scripts that reward the man for sexual assertion and the woman for passivity, and by the romantic notion that the man should sweep the woman off her feet. Nancy Friday has described the fantasy of 'being chosen, being kissed, being led like the walking blind into a dark chamber where, magically, the romantic feeling of surrender is made to happen . . .'.[30] Male sexual violence is the dark side of this longing to be swept away which still permeates female sexual fantasy.

These studies all show that conventional scripts increase the risk of coercive sex. Violence becomes more likely where the man seeks to be dominant and controlling and the woman expects, accepts or welcomes that control. And if she feels that male control is 'natural', the way things usually are or ought to be, she's also less likely to get out if there's trouble.

The orthodox moves establish a male dominance which increases the risk of violence in specific ways. If he pays, he may feel he has earned the right to sex: if he drives, he has her on his own territory, which can have a disinhibiting effect. But these moves also establish a traditional dynamic in a more general sense. They set up an interaction where he is active, she passive, where he is the initiator and she the gatekeeper: where he always goes as far as she will let him. This is some-times called the adversarial approach to courtship.[31]

One of the men I interviewed had given all this a lot of thought. Malcolm doesn't come across as the kind of predatory male women warn their daughters about. But he's reluctantly concluded that for now the adversarial approach is the one that works. He conceptualizes courtship as a struggle between two people who may seem to have opposing interests.

'It's like what you hear from these men who try very hard to be new men – they get pissed off because they don't actually get any women. All these women who talk about how good it is for new men to be new men, they don't exactly flock around. The trouble is while the thing is set up like it is, men who don't take a fair degree of initiative and who assume any lack of enthusiasm or no said, while not taking effective action to remove themselves from the situation, actually means no – they're hardly going to get any sex.

'There have been a couple of times when if somebody wanted to tell the story as a date rape afterwards they could probably have done that. A man shouldn't persist with a woman who's clearly unwilling – but I think if you let things drift in a certain direction and then kind of want to stand on your legal rights, it's neither sensible nor very admirable really. The way in which women, who have been leapt on by men they didn't know or haven't given any come-on to, have been treated in the past has muddied the waters, hasn't it?

'I've never felt that you can work on the principle that the woman's made the decision before you take her out. I think there are some women who are to be seduced by insistence. You've got to make it clear that your will is to do it – I don't mean that you wouldn't stop if they said no – but, until they say something that makes it very clear that they'd rather not proceed any further . . . . I assume that a lot of women would want you to make some move to make yourself clear, they would want to know that it hadn't just happened because you'd absent-mindedly copped off with them when you'd actually been thinking of going home and finishing your volume of Proust.'

Malcolm shows how the potential for sexual danger is built into a dynamic in which men make the moves and women exercise a right of veto. In Malcolm's experience, the male role in courtship is about initiating and persisting until the woman has clearly said no. Though most men, like Malcolm, will stop if she tells him to, the seeds of sexual danger are there: 'You've got to make it clear that your will is to do it . . .'.

What can we learn from all this about keeping safe?

PROTECTING YOURSELF:
Why you should buy the popcorn

Laura Martin's *A Life Without Fear* is a self-help book on how to avoid rape. 'A rapist needs two things to carry out an attack,' she says. 'Opportunity and a victim . . . . Because we know what a rapist needs, we also know what it takes to avoid rape. Rape is not just a matter of chance. Rape is a preventable crime. We must avoid situations that are likely to give a rapist an opportunity to commit the crime, and we must project an attitude that already says, "I am not a victim!".'[32]

She lists what she sees as characteristics of a potential rapist. Her 'Red Flag traits' could be seen as an extreme version of traditional courtship behaviour. For Martin, dangerous men are those who embody the most conventional masculinity:

they follow the classic script to the letter, and are angered by deviations from that script. Among her 'Red Flag traits' are these: 'He must control every situation – where you go, what you eat, what you wear, whom you see. He gets angry if you try to pay for your own meal, drive yourself, plan activities'.[33]

Taking initiatives on the date can be part of a strategy for testing out the man. Our assertions can have a protective function because they identify men with a pathological urge to control. If you're unsure about the man you're going out with, says Martin, you can test how controlling he is by making some of the arrangements yourself. 'See what he does if you order for him at the restaurant, you choose the wine for dinner, you open the doors for him, you choose the movie, buy the popcorn and decide where you will sit.'[34] If the man over-reacts or gets angry at any of these, he may be dangerous. 'Men who are angered by small acts of assertion, such as opening your own door or ordering for yourself, are sending loud, strong signals to you . . . Pick up on these signals, and listen to your inner voice.'[35] This fits with the study, quoted above, which found that a man who later becomes violent will usually have tried to control the woman from the beginning of the relationship, often starting with quite small acts. The corollary is also true. Men who are comfortable with female assertiveness are unlikely to be men who rape.

Here, female initiatives are part of a strategy for testing out a man's urge to control. But the kinds of initiatives we've been discussing may also have a protective function. If you don't know the man you're going out with well, says Martin, you should either drive yourself, or somehow provide your own transport to and from the date: and you should 'communicate with your date honestly and clearly. Tell him up front what you expect or what you don't expect'.[36] In other words, at the first sign of trouble, ditch the traditional script.

*   *   *

Roxanne, world-weary at sixteen, reflected, 'It takes a lot of courage to say no. People think that if you say no the bloke'll stop, but it's not like that, just saying no these days doesn't stop a bloke from doing it. You either have to physically get him off you, or move away from him and show him clearly. I don't think just saying no is enough.' How best to protect ourselves in a culture in which 'just saying no doesn't stop a bloke from doing it'?

In one of our oldest woman-in-danger stories, she's not quite sensible and not quite good: she's out on her own, she refuses to recognize the danger, she talks openly to a stranger, and she deviates from the path – in search of her own pleasure.

'He asked of her whither she was going: the poor child, who did not know how dangerous a thing it is to stay and hear a Wolfe talk, said to him, I am going to see my grandmamma . . . . Well, said the Wolfe, and I'll go and see her too; I'll go this way, and go you that, and we shall see who will be there soonest.

'The Wolfe began to run as fast as he was able, the shortest way; and the little girl went the longest, diverting herself in gathering nuts, running after butterflies, and making nose-gays of all the little flowers she met with. The Wolfe was not long before he came to the grandmother's house; he knocked at the door toc toc. Who's there? Your granddaughter, the Little Red Riding-Hood, said the Wolfe, counterfeiting her voice, who has brought you a custard pye . . .'[37]

It's a cautionary tale – and the self-protection strategy implicit in the seventeenth-century story is precisely that advocated by today's judiciary and much of the media. Stick to the traditional role, be good, be sweet and submissive, be a virgin not a vamp, never chase men, keep to the path on the way through the woods, get an angora sweater. And, above all, don't be like Jennifer Levin: don't cross the bar to speak to him, don't say you want him, don't make the first move.

But research on what actually happens suggests a very

different approach to keeping safe. Pay for yourself. Drive yourself. Project an attitude that already says, 'I am not a victim'. Understand about territory and don't go back to his place unless you trust him. Tell him directly what you want and don't want. Be wary of men who are angered by deviations from the traditional roles. And if you feel threatened, be prepared, like Roxanne, to abandon all your polite good-girl behaviour and shout, scream and fight.

The cautionary tales and warnings about sexual danger that are still largely unquestioned are a poor guide to keeping ourselves safe. We'd do much better to emulate the inviolate heroine of Angela Carter's re-working of the story, who projected that sense of self-assurance that Laura Martin advocates – and knew she was nobody's meat.

CHAPTER 10
HOW TO

WHEN I was 11, a boy called Geoff bought me a blue ice-pole as we waited for the school bus. I liked Geoff and I liked ice-poles – but I told him I didn't want it. He never bought me another. Later I felt sad and wondered why I'd felt I had to say no to him. But it took me years to learn the obvious lesson.

I find it easy to empathize with the women in this book who follow the most retro courtship routines – with Jessica, who said no and meant yes, with Natalie, who told a man who asked for her phone number to look it up, or with Clara, who'd as soon have jumped into the Niagara Falls as initiate the first kiss. When I started out on my love life, I was just like them. I hung around waiting for things to happen, believed in the magical efficacy of a favourite black T-shirt, responded to the stirrings of desire by studying my horoscope and making with the lip-pencil, and projected a deceptively vulnerable persona in conversations with men I liked. I'd often be unable to put what I wanted into words, occasionally I said no and meant maybe, and once, at midnight in a motorway service station with a man I adored, I feigned a coolness and disinterest I certainly didn't feel, in the belief that this would help things along: it failed horribly. I didn't do these things consciously or deliberately: I 'found myself' doing them. Elusive behavioural styles felt absolutely natural – so completely had I absorbed the injunctions of the traditional script.

But eventually I came to understand what I might have

learnt from Geoff at the school gate if I'd had my eyes a little wider open. This way of going about things might meet with lots of social approval – my mother advised it, magazines promoted it, stories in which sweetly shy girls got their man reinforced it – but it wouldn't work for me. One of the most significant discoveries of my early adult life was about the absolute value of clarity and directness in my relationships with men: saying how I felt, deciding precisely when I'd like to get into bed with somebody, knowing what I wanted and being able to ask for it. This kind of self-assertion brought immediate rewards. It's a principle that I've seen enacted time and again since then in the lives of women I've talked to. Everything works out better once we know what we want and have the nerve to ask for it.

And this in the end is the only reason to change the way we behave – above all at the very start of relationships, where the stakes are highest. No woman is going to ask a man out in order to show what a big strong woman she is, or to strike a blow for the sisters, or to make the world a greener and pleasanter place. The kinds of motivations that get women marching to Reclaim the Night, speaking out about sex abuse, or campaigning against pornography, are utterly irrelevant here. Sex is a selfish business: and so is the process by which it is negotiated. A woman will only widen out her repertoire if she thinks this might get her where she'd love to be – in bed or in a relationship with that man with the lived-in face and the louche leather jacket, who holds her gaze a little too long but never makes a move.

Courtship, this narrative part of our sexual behaviour, is one of life's great pleasures, in spite of – or maybe because of – its ephemeral and tentative nature. Our post-sexual liberation culture is perhaps at present re-discovering these pleasures: the recent revival of interest in tales of protracted wooing, in Jane Austen or Edith Wharton, implies a pervasive public ennui with the casualization of sex – of sex without a story. Sometimes women worry that a new script might detract from these pleasures. 'Won't it take the magic away?' said Lesley, fearing perhaps that she might not get her quota of scented summer evenings seething with suppressed eroticism if she made too bold a move. Yet to widen out our repertoire seems in practice to enhance our enjoyment of the courtship ritual. Women who do go out with a man they've looked at, liked and bravely approached revel in their achievement: 'It's such a good feeling to go out with someone you've chosen'.

Feeling good about choosing and being in control at the very start of a relationship is something new for women – and something very significant. Those moments when we negotiate our sexual relationships are rich in meaning: sometimes this is where our future takes shape. Retro courtship styles give women only tangential control over that future. At one end of the spectrum, there's the woman like me in my teens and early twenties, who drifts through her relationships in a kind of dream, like the entranced heroines of the old stories in their castles and moated granges. A woman for whom sex and relationships just happen, and who, if her looks and smiles and sexy clothes don't work, if the man just doesn't get it, has no other strategy open to her. A woman who 'finds herself' in bed, in a relationship or walking up the aisle with someone whom she may never clearly have chosen. (And how many women end up with a man who wasn't their first choice – because they didn't dare approach the man who was?) At the other end of the spectrum there are those women who are learning about the new gratifications that come from being brave and taking risks to win the man they want. These women don't rely on their new velvet hipsters to make it happen; they may have little interest in their horoscopes. Instead they rehearse some cool chat-up lines with their friends and then take active steps to make their yearnings and fantasies a reality.

COMING ON STRONG

The discoveries that many of us have made in our own love relationships are backed up by psychological studies. Coming on strong is good for women: that's what the sex researchers tell us.

Women enjoy intercourse more if they go on top. A pre-orgasmic woman who learns to say what she wants and who stops regarding sex as an arena where the man should always take the lead can transform herself into someone who's reliably orgasmic. Sexual relationships are more satis-factory if it's the woman who initiates, because of the predict-able but dramatic way our capacity to lose ourselves in sexual pleasure – or even to be willing to make the effort – varies through the month with the hormonal cycle. Women get more aroused to fantasies in which the woman initiates sex than we do to the standard pornographic scenarios. The submissive woman who's the subject of sadistic male initiatives may turn women on still – but perhaps only in the absence of alterna-tives: the scene in *Disclosure* in which Meredith grabs Tom and tries to make him have sex was such a turn-on for women that it gave the film a reputation as a hot dating movie. And a comparison between the sex lives of assertive and unassertive women found a correlation between assertiveness and reported sexual satisfaction: bolder women say they have better sex lives.

So too in the first few moves of the sexual game. We can enrich our love lives if we play a more active role in shaping what happens right from the beginning – if we initiate, speak out, book the table, say what we want. It won't always work of course: success isn't guaranteed, any more than it is for men. To ask men out is to raise the stakes. It's to increase your risk of rejection: that's inevitable, it's built in to the arithmetic. But it's also to increase your chances of getting what you want.

But going out with the man she has her eye on isn't the only reward for the woman who asserts herself. Once female initiatives come to be an unquestioned part of our sexual negotiations, we'll be creating a new sexual culture, one with many benefits for both women and men.

The traditional script dictates that women convey their desires indirectly – with hair flips and neck presentations and strappy sandals. This is why appearance matters so much. Over-valuation of female beauty takes a terrible toll on women's self-esteem – for the adolescent girl who used to feel just fine about herself and who now lingers in front of the mirror, enumerating her physical defects: for the woman in mid-life who may fear that, as she loses her youthful looks, she is also losing some essence of her sexuality: for the woman of any age who compares herself to the gorgeous anorexics in the magazines and is filled with self-disgust. But because it's with our looks that we make it happen, we can't simply decide like sane and rational beings that we've got the whole thing out of proportion. It's different for the woman who's prepared to make the moves: her wit and courage and nerve may count for more than her mastery of the art of eyelash curling.

The indirectness of traditional female signalling is problematic in other ways as well. Women think their signals are as clear as day: but men, who are anyway notoriously bad at reading non-verbal signals, find women's cues 'extremely bloody ambiguous, and you never know quite where you are'. And female signalling is also indiscriminate: it signals to everyone in sight. A man you don't like may think you're licking your lips and wearing that sexy T-shirt for him: the one you really want may fail to notice. We have so little control: the traditional script puts us in an essentially passive relationship to our desires. Some of our iconic images of female sexuality celebrate that passivity. When Marilyn stands over the hot air vent, her skirt billowing up round her wonderful thighs and a look of sweet complicity on her face, even her self-exposure – that most submissive of sexual moves – isn't something she chooses, but something that's done to her. A woman's looks may do their work in spite of her – with results that she never intended. Feminists have been writing for years about this eroticization of female passivity and how it demeans and restricts us. Yet the images are with us still: Tama Janowitz's stories about New York in the nineties are full of stylish women who have sex with someone with whom they have no connection so they can live in a nice apartment in a brownstone. We won't really put this world behind us until we start taking control where it matters most, in the first few moves of our sexual negotiations.

Sometimes the indirectness of traditional female flirtation can shade over into contradiction. There are women in this book who've confessed to saying no and meaning maybe. Women's token resistance and complicated 'no's can lead to a lot of bad sex – sex that only happens because women don't communicate clearly, and men don't know how to read women's communications. We're not talking abuse here – just the sort of obscurely unsatisfactory experience that leaves you both with a lingering sense of futility. The clearer communication that goes with a new courtship style should help us avoid such confusions. This doesn't guarantee good sex, of course. Sexual pleasure can't be prescribed for: that's part of its fascination. But being clear you both want it is surely a good place to start from.

More progressive sexual routines might also help protect us from sexual danger – or at the very least alert us to the potential dangerousness of certain men who have a pathological desire to control, and who find it unacceptable for a woman to book the tickets, drive or buy the popcorn.

There are advantages for men too. Sure, men are ambivalent. They're absolute beginners in this new sexual world, and they don't always mean what they say. A man who says he adores sexually assertive women may indeed want a woman who'll be deliciously uninhibited – but at times and in ways of his choosing. A man who says he loves the idea of equality may protest that he's being treated as a walking dildo when a woman he doesn't fancy invites him into her bed. But increasingly, as men come out about how tough it is to be male, there's a recognition that the traditional script has costs for them too. Having to do what a man's gotta do doesn't always feel like a freedom. Shy men may miss out on relationships altogether – and any man may be reticent about initiating with a woman who is richer, older or out of his class. And those men who've been asked out and said yes know exactly what's so good about women making the moves: 'Because she'd said what she'd said, I knew she liked me'.

LOVE IN THE AGE OF AQUARIUS

Our courtship styles are Janus-faced: they look to both past and future. And that's true too of our stories about courtship – those narratives, both public and private, that we use to make sense of what happens to us.

We need to be wary about the stories we tell. Stories can be treacherous. And at present many of our sexual narratives are backward-looking and full of warnings; they come with a subtext about the risks of initiating for women – or even with an explicit injunction: Don't. Courtship backlash books and articles tell women they'll only get hurt if they make the moves. Films and novels warn us that women who initiate have highly ulterior motives. And stereotypes of instrumental masculinity and receptive femininity rampage unchecked in the evolutionary psychology paperback.

In courtship backlash writing, in books like *The Rules* and articles like 'Why I don't call men', women are advised to be cool and inaccessible: don't talk to a man first, always end the date first, keep a timer by the phone. The old ways protect us from pain, say these advocates of 'Grandma-knew-best' sexual styles: rights for women never meant the right to get hurt.

This superficially appealing proposition needs looking at closely. Women should always be sceptical when we're told we need protecting, for the safety that dependency seems to offer us is invariably illusory. Those time-honoured images of containment and mystery that can seem so seductive – the princess in her tower, safely encircled by the walls that signify the chaste hymen – had their origins in an era of cruel patriarchal oppression. There's never been any safety in passivity and withdrawal. As Audre Lord put it, 'Your silence will not protect you'. Ask women what they hate most about the traditional game, and they all say the same: the worst part is the most passive part – waiting for the phone to ring.

There's also a denial in courtship backlash writing of the anarchic nature of sexual attraction. There's an underlying assumption here that we can school our emotions so we'll only fall in love with men who'll pursue us, and switch off from those who aren't looking our way. Yet most women's love lives don't feel like arenas of infinite possibility; few of us find the world to be teeming with desirable men. And if a woman does meet someone she falls in love with, and approaches him and is rejected, why is her hurt any worse than the hurt of a woman who really wants a man but never makes a move – and who later thinks that maybe, just maybe, they could have got together if she'd asked him? The hurt of the woman who asks is only worse if she feels *shame* as well as loss – the shame that we feel if we violate our new slimline fat-free version of the old sexual code, which tells us that it's great for women to be sexually bold – but not at the very start of relationships. But this shame isn't obligatory: we can learn to think differently. Ditch the shame, and the woman who at least tried, even if it didn't work out, surely has less reason for regret: she did what she could.

As though to drive home the message of the courtship back-lash articles, there have recently been a lot of re-tellings of the oldest story about the woman who initiates, the story that goes back to Sumer and that warns us that women who do are up to no good. Bad sexual women like Alex in *Fatal Attraction*, Catherine in *Basic Instinct*, and Brigit in *The Last Seduction* – all dazzlingly amoral and impeccably elegant – make marvellous entertainment, but their influence is thoroughly retrograde. These stories serve profound psychological purposes: that's why they're so persistent. They give form to men's fears about women who take control. And they soothe women's fears about sexual competition, reassuring us that those women who are ultimately sexy – who make the boldest moves, who wear the tightest frocks and can demonstrate the most devas-tating sexual skills – don't in the end get their man – or not to keep. Yet every time we buy into the story that the woman who initiates is or should be punished – whether conclusively with a bullet through the heart, or more stealthily, by a phone that stubbornly refuses to ring – we're really punishing our-selves. This sexual value system constrains us all.

At Relate, the marriage guidance service, they seem to be particularly fond of antique ideas about initiating women. But the Relate mythology isn't about the thrilling if wicked sexual woman with the fuck-me shoes and the devious schemes, who sashays around causing trouble in all directions: in the Relate consulting room, the initiating woman is cast instead as the robber bride who steals the man's erection. In a news item on male sexual dysfunction, under the headline 'Assertive women "make men impotent"', a Relate counsellor recently suggested, 'Perhaps one of the biggest changes (over the past fifteen years) is that women have started to say that sex is important for them. Women have begun to say, hang on, there's someone else in the bedroom – their sexual satisfaction is important too. It may be men are perhaps having trouble coming to terms with that . . .'.[1] There are a number of more plausible explanations for the increase in men seeking help for impotence – from the greater availability of sex therapy, to the alarming research linking all kinds of problems in the sexual functioning of males in many species to exposure to environmental oestrogens. Yet Relate spokespersons choose instead to blame the woman who likes to have orgasms and knows how to ask for them. That's how powerful our simple stories are.

Some of our most stereotypical stories about sex have recently been given a spurious scientific validity with the popularization of evolutionary psychology. Genetic arguments bolstered by animal studies are adduced to prove that the 'natural' way is best because it's how things are meant to be – women are there to be looked at, male pursuit and female responsiveness are implicit in heterosexuality, and for women to say 'Come up sometime and see me' is to oppose yourself to Mother Nature's great scheme. Evolutionary psychologists are mostly men – and it's surely no coincidence that the world they conjure up is a perfect male fantasyland, a world in which promiscuous men with an instinctive drive toward power and money pair up with women who are effortlessly monogamous and who work really hard at looking good – and who forgive the men their 'natural' promiscuity.

But in reality, sexuality in the natural world takes many forms and can be used to prove almost anything. The animal studies that evolutionary psychologists use to support their theories also contain instances of female initiative, and evidence that females have their own genetic agendas that may be quite different to those of their male partners. A female swallow, for instance, may choose a genetically average mate and take advantage of his parenting skills to help her rear her chicks, but then sneak off to have sex with a more desirable male – one with longer tail-feathers – in order to improve the genetic endowment of her offspring. But studies like this rarely feature in popular articles on evolutionary psychology.

These females with genetic purposes of their own, lured into infidelity by the promise of those exceptional tail-feathers, simply don't fit with the familiar old formulae – male polygamy/female monogamy, male activity/female passivity. And we overlook what doesn't fit – which is one reason why the stereotypes persist, and only need tiny bits of evidence to keep them going.

The evolutionary psychologist, the advice columnist and the scriptwriter all seem to be pushing us back towards the traditional routines. But to oppose to all this, there are also progressive influences on our courtship styles.

In particular, the shifting economic balance between men and women looks set to have a profound impact on our love lives. Money and sex have an intimate relationship. And sometimes there's a startling precision about the way money shapes sexual initiative – as in the study that found women initiating sex much more often once they earned at least sixty per cent as much as their partners. It's because of this connection between money and sex that it's possible to predict with confidence that a move towards more equable courtship styles is inevitable. The financial dynamic between men and women is changing fast: new sexual patterns are sure to follow.

These changes are coming about right through the socio-economic spectrum. Where the traditional male industries have disappeared – where men can't get work but women can – the old pattern of male providing is undermined, and women start taking more control. But because these changes are predicated on the man's loss rather than the woman's gain, the women involved may be secretive about their sexual and economic stratagems, like the Leicester hairdressers who were dating men who were unemployed, and who took control from the first moves of the game, but covertly, to protect the men's self-esteem: 'You can't let on what you're up to but you've got to give them a little push haven't you?'

The love lives of those at the top end of the labour market

are also being re-structured by women's relatively greater
earning power. Think of those women who are moving ahead
in the workplace and earning good money, and who start
acting out the *Cosmopolitan* fantasy, in control in the boardroom and in bed, like the cool accomplished women Annette
Lawson describes, who worked in the financial centres of
New York and San Francisco, and who'd developed a more
emotionally independent and masculine sexual style – with
more partners, more affairs, and more initiatives. These
women exemplify one of the fundamental rules about female
sexual assertiveness. More power means more initiatives. If
a woman is of higher status or has more money than the man
she wants, she's far more likely to ask him out.

When the bill arrives on a first date, what follows is a little
enactment that gives lots of clues to the sexual meanings of
money for the couple. Spending money on women can cause
a lot of male bitterness, as Kinsey showed in the fifties, when
he totted up how much it would cost to get a nice American
girl into bed, and concluded that prostitution had much to
recommend it. And where the man pays for everything, the
financial agenda can distort the erotic one: he may doubt that
he's wanted for himself, she may feel she 'owes' him sex, or,
at worst, he may feel she 'owes' him sex and act on that
assumption. But the woman who pays for herself takes a first
significant step towards a new courtship pattern.

In spite of the retrogressive elements in our culture, many
of us find these ideas appropriate or inspiring. We pay for
ourselves: it feels right. We'd love to be one of those powerful
women who slip on more masculine sexual styles along with
their Armani jackets: it sounds exciting. And when we feel
this sense of rightness or excitement about shifting gender
patterns, we're taking our inspiration from the ideal of the
androgyne – who is 'male and female in one'.

The androgyne is an archetypal image that goes back to
Greece but that has a fresh appeal today. He/she is the symbol

for the astrological age we're now entering, and at present – to the delight of astrologers everywhere – there are examples all around of that blurring and dissolving of gender boundaries epitomized by this archetype. Transsexual images that once disturbed have been domesticated and incorporated into the mainstream – k d lang on the cover of *Vanity Fair* being shaved by Cindy Crawford, drag queen RuPaul as the face of MAC cosmetics. Styles of self-presentation for young people mix masculine and feminine signifiers: our ideals of youthful physical perfection encompass flat-chested women in vests and jeans and pouting men with long hair and long eyelashes. And in the virtual world, there are particularly striking instances of the cross-over between the genders, and the pleasure people can take in playing around with sexual identities: heterosexuals who flirt – or even have orgasmic relationships – on the Internet often choose to appropriate an opposite sex persona.

Away from the cutting edge of stylistic and psychosexual innovation, androgynous ideals have been an enriching influence on men's experience of parenting and women's experience of work. Many of us have found our lives enhanced as we've transcended the old gender boundaries and learnt to express that more hidden side of ourselves that might once have been given an opposite gender label. For men this has meant both exploring the inner emotional land-scape, and re-inventing themselves as nurturing and playful parents: for women, the challenge has been to find ways of empowering ourselves in the public world. There are plenty of men today who take delight in parenting tasks that their fathers would have been embarrassed to perform – and many women who've come to relish the expression in the workplace of that instrumental aspect of femaleness that's so apparent in the delectable bossiness and dynamism of three-year-old girls but that often gets hidden or suppressed as girls grow up.

But it's when we articulate our hopes and dreams for our love lives that the presence of the androgyne is most deeply felt. Today our ideal is companionate marriage. In the past the man's marriage was quite different from the woman's – but now we generally enter into lasting partnerships in the hope that we'll both be free to express our talents, that we'll take equal responsibility for finances and share domestic tasks, that we'll become more intimate by disclosing our feelings in a mutual way, and that we'll enjoy and initiate sex on equal terms.

Over the next few years, we'll be seeing this ideal in action in the very first moves of our love relationships, as women learn to adopt more assertive styles at the start of our sexual negotiations just as we have in the workplace. Some women of course are doing this already. Take Alice whose story we heard in Chapter Five. She meets someone she likes at a party, and she sets herself the challenge of asking him out. She picks up the phone and makes the moves, and then, when his phone is disconnected, defies the advice of her friends and travels right across London to see this man she wants. Here, Alice lives out the courtship mythology that used to be the prerogative of men. 'I was into doing new things. I thought, Haven't done that one before – I'll give it a go'. Getting her man is all about setting herself challenges, taking risks, overcoming obstacles, making the moment: and it all works out beautifully.

WHAT KIRSTEN DID

So what's the secret of women like Alice? What's different about the women who do?

Of all the women I talked to, Kirsten was the one who'd adopted a new courtship script in the most thoroughgoing way. Kirsten is tall and blonde with an engaging manner and an enviable bone structure. She's Danish and was brought up in Denmark, but has lived here since her twenties. She's divorced and has two children, and works as an art lecturer. And she often makes the moves.

'I'm puzzled and intrigued the way women don't ask men out,' she told me. 'I certainly do. I've done it often. I've met someone at a dinner party and thought, I really like that person, and rung my friends afterwards and asked for his phone number so I could ask him to an exhibition or out for a drink. I've never picked someone up just for sex. But I suppose I'm not looking for long-term relationships either – though it would be lovely if it happened . . . .'

I've suggested that in their sexuality women who ask men out follow a pattern – and Kirsten certainly fitted this sexual profile. She's often been attracted to men who are younger than her, and it doesn't matter whether or not they have money: that classic female eroticization of male power, and its expression in an exclusive attraction to older, richer, higher status men, simply isn't part of her sexuality. 'If it doesn't feel good when the two of you are together and being intimate, why bother?' she said. 'Money doesn't make the slightest difference at times like that.' And her willingness to initiate at the start of relationships is reflected in other aspects of her sexual behaviour. She takes initiatives right through the sexual sequence. 'I've certainly been the one to suggest going to bed for the first time,' she said. 'And I'd certainly ask for what I want in bed. If you can't communicate in that intimate situation, there really is no point in carrying on. And I'd ring up the next day. Oh yes! I'd say "Wasn't it good?" or "Wasn't it nice?" or "I enjoyed it". I could certainly do that – because I enjoy it when men have said that to me, and I'm sure they enjoy it as much if I do the same for them!'

But in the rest of her behaviour she's no different from most women: she certainly isn't uniquely self-assured. Forget the old stories: women who do are every bit as insecure, diffident and plain scared as the next woman. Alice recalled that first phone call she made to the man she asked out and later married: 'I was shaking so much I nearly dropped the phone,' she said. Women who make the moves are just as afraid as anyone else. But they *think* differently. What is distinctive about these women is the way they conceptualize risk and rejection. They feel the fear and do it anyway.

'Of course there's always a risk of being rejected,' said Kirsten. 'But I don't think it's any worse for a woman to make a first move and be rejected than it is for a man. When I'm thinking of asking a man out, I'll certainly be apprehensive, but I don't think it's any worse than when you apply for a job. You take a risk – it happens with so much you do in life. It would be the same as when I stand in front of a group of students, and think, How am I going to get through these five hours with so many students? If you don't get up there and make contact, you'll never know, you can't move on. A man is not some sort of god-creature. He's not a judge of your character. If he doesn't go out with me, it doesn't mean there's a shortcoming with me, it may mean he's got appalling taste!'

Kirsten takes a lot of risks in her romantic relationships – and she thinks about risk like a man. Daring to do things that might go wrong is part of life. Of course you'll feel apprehensive – but if you don't try, you'll never know how he feels, you can't move on. And when men do reject her approaches, this never makes her think, I shouldn't have done that, or stops her from doing it again. There's no sexual shame here: Kirsten would never say, I went too far, It was a mistake to hurl myself. She feels entitled; she believes she has the right to do this. She doesn't reflect men at twice their natural size: no man is allowed to become the ultimate arbiter of her worth. If he turns her down, it might mean he's got appalling taste . . . .

Once we get rid of female shame and come to believe, like Kirsten, that we have every right to make the moves, the only hurdle is our fear; we can do anything if we dare. Our new female courtship mythology must encompass that sense of daring, as we explore new styles of sexual behaviour that include the taking of risks and the exercise of initiative, and as we learn about the sexual rewards that come from courage and clarity. Only then will our courtship styles fit with the pattern of relationships we now aspire to, in which we go out to work, make money, care for our children, and make love, all on equal terms. If we're looking for a kind of loving that is reciprocal, tender and equable, then surely that ideal of reciprocity should be guiding our behaviour right from the very beginning. And for most of us today, that's the only kind of loving that will do.

REFERENCES

Chapter 1 Courtship Today

1 Katie Roiphe, *The Morning After*, Hamish Hamilton, London, 1984, p. 80.

2 S. Rose and I. Friez, 'Young singles' scripts for a first date', *Gender and Society*, 3, 1989, pp. 258–268.

3 Susan Sprecher and Kathleen McKinney, *Sexuality*, Sage, Newbury Park, 1993, p. 27.

4 S. Green and P. Sandos, 'Perceptions of male and female initiators of relationships', *Sex Roles*, 9, 1983, pp. 849–852.

5 Wendy Dennis, *Hot and Bothered*, Grafton, London, 1993, p. 92.

6 Warren Farrell, *Why Men Are The Way They Are*, Berkley Books, New York, 1988.

7 Beth Bailey, *From Front Porch to Back Seat*, Johns Hopkins University Press, Baltimore, 1988.

8 *Ladies Home Journal*, May 1909.

9 Cecil-Jane Richmond, *Handbook for Dating*, Westminster Press, Philadelphia, 1958, p. 11.

10 John Gillis, *For Better For Worse: British Marriages 1600 to the Present*, Oxford University Press, New York, 1985.

11 ibid.

12 *Guardian*, 18 November, 1995.

13 Gillis, op cit., p. 31.

14 *Guardian*, 11 September, 1995.

15 Annette Lawson, *Adultery*, Oxford University Press, Oxford, 1990, p. 295.

Chapter 2 Women Who Do

1 *Guardian*, 15 September, 1994.

2 *Guardian*, 27 May, 1994.

3 *Sunday Times*, 12 December, 1994.

4 *Tales from the Thousand and One Nights*, Penguin, London, 1973.

5 Bruno Bettelheim, *The Uses of Enchantment*, Penguin, Harmondsworth, 1978, p. 285.

6 Robin Norwood, *Women Who Love Too Much*, Arrow, London, 1986.

7 *Njal's Saga*, Penguin, Harmondsworth, 1970, p. 39.

8 Christopher Badcock, *Psychodarwinism,* HarperCollins, London, 1994.

9 Sheila Kitzinger, *Woman's Experience of Sex*, Penguin, London, 1985.

10 Matt Ridley, *The Red Queen*, Penguin, London, 1994.

11 Mark Ridley, 'Paternal Care', *Animal Behaviour*, 26, pp. 904–932, 1978.

12 Susan Faludi, *Backlash*, Chatto and Windus, London, 1991, p. 142.

13 ibid., p. 86.

14 Harold Bloom (ed.), *English Romantic Poetry*, Doubleday, New York, 1963.

15 Bram Stoker, *The Lair of the White Worm*, Arrow, London, 1975.

16 Angela Carter, *The Bloody Chamber*, Penguin, Harmondsworth, 1981, pp. 93–96.

17 Matt Ridley.

18 Camille Paglia, *Sexual Personae: Art and Decadence from Nefertiti to Emily Dickinson*, Penguin, London, 1990, p. 338.

19 ibid., p. 342.

20 Samuel Taylor Coleridge, *Poetical Works*, Oxford University Press, Oxford, 1971.

21 John Cleland, *Fanny Hill: Memoirs of a Woman of Pleasure*, Penguin, London, 1985, p. 39.

22 Lynn Hunt (ed.), *The Invention of Pornography: Obscenity and the Origins of Modernity, 1500–1800*, Zone Books, New York, 1993, p. 230.

23 Angela Carter, *The Sadeian Woman*, Virago, London, 1979, p. 63.

24 Marina Warner, *From the Beast to the Blonde*, p. 221.

25 Suzanne M. Sgroi and Norah M. Sargent, 'Impact and treatment issues for victims of childhood sexual abuse by female perpetrators', in Michele Elliott (ed.), *Female Sexual Abuse of Children: The Ultimate Taboo*, Longman, London, 1993.

26 *Guardian*, 20 April, 1995.

27 Carter, *Sadeian Woman*, op cit., p. 60.

28 *The Kalevala*, Oxford University Press, Oxford, 1989, p. 42.

29 Paula Weideger, *Female Cycles*, Women's Press, London, 1978.

30 Gabriel Garcia Marquez, *One Hundred Years of Solitude*, Pan, London, 1978, p. 30.

31 *Guardian*, 24 May, 1994.

32 Laurie Lee, *Cider with Rosie,* Penguin, London, 1962.

33 ibid., pp. 208–209.

34 W. H. Auden, *Selected Poems*, Faber, London, 1979.

35 Hanif Kureishi, *The Buddha of Suburbia*, Faber, London, 1990, pp. 199–204.

Chapter 3 Women's Fears

1 *It's Bliss,* June 1995.

2 *Fast Forward*, 10 November, 1993.

3 *Just 17*, 29 June, 1994.

4 *Company,* June 1994.

5 *Cosmopolitan*, February 1994.

6 *Guardian*, 20 January, 1996.

7 Steve Humphries, *A Secret World of Sex*, Sidgwick and Jackson, London, 1988.

8 C. T. Hill, Z. Rubin and L. A. Peplau, 'Breakups before

marriage: The end of 103 affairs', *Journal of Social Issues*, 32, pp. 147–168, 1976.

9 Celia Cowrie and Sue Lees, 'Slags or Drags, in Feminist Review' (ed.), *Sexuality: A Reader*, Virago, London, 1987.

10 Leo Tolstoy, *Anna Karenina*, Penguin, Harmondsworth, 1976.

11 Gustave Flaubert, *Emma Bovary*, Penguin, Harmondsworth, p. 44.

12 Lawson, op cit., p. 146.

13 Margaret Leroy, *Pleasure*, HarperCollins, London, 1993.

14 Sue Miller, *The Good Mother*, Pan, London, 1987.

15 Kate Saunders, *Night Shall Overtake Us*, Arrow, London, 1994.

16 Erica Jong, *Fear of Flying*, Minerva, London, 1994, p. 9.

17 Dalma Heyn, *The Erotic Silence of the Married Woman*, Mandarin, London, 1992, p. 19.

18 Deborah Tannen, *You Just Don't Understand*, Virago, London, 1992.

19 Carol Gilligan, *In A Different Voice*, Harvard University Press, Cambridge MA, 1982.

20 Faludi, op cit.

21 Germaine Greer, *The Change*, Hamish Hamilton, London, 1991, p. 337.

22 Brigid McConville, *Sisters*, Pan, London, 1985, p. 64.

Chapter 4 Men's Doubts

1 Shere Hite, *The Hite Report on Male Sexuality*, Optima, London, 1990, p. 609.

2 ibid., p. 612.

3 *Cosmopolitan*, December 1994.

4 *Guardian*, 7 July, 1995.

5 Warren Farrell, *The Myth of Male Power*, Fourth Estate, London, 1993, p. 222.

6 Hite, p. 615.

7 Farrell, *Myth of Male Power*, op cit., p. 207.

8 D. Symons and B. Ellis, 'Human male-female differences in sexual desire', in *The Sociobiology of Sexual and Reproductive*

Strategies, (ed.), A. E. Rasa, C. Vogel, and E. Voland, Chapman and Hall, New York, 1989.

9 Nancy Friday, *My Secret Garden*, Quartet, London, 1975.

10 *Sun*, 27 September, 1994.

11 Hite, op cit.

12 Helen Fisher, *Anatomy of Love*, Simon and Schuster, London, 1992.

13 Barbara de Angelis, *Secrets About Men*, Thorsons, London, 1990.

14 C. L. Kleinke, F. B. Meeker and R. A. Staneski, 'Preference for opening lines: Comparing ratings by men and women', *Sex Roles*, 15, pp. 585–600.

15 L. Jensen-Campbell, W. Graziano and S. West, 'Dominance, Prosocial Orientation, and Female Preferences: Do Nice Guys Really Finish Last?' *Journal of Personality and Social Psychology*, 1995, 68, 427–440.

16 Bailey, op cit.

17 June M. Reinisch and Ruth Beasley, *The Kinsey Institute New Report on Sex*, Penguin, London, 1990.

18 Andrew Stanway, *Why Us?*, Thorsons, Wellingborough, 1984, p. 43.

19 Fred Belliveau and Lin Richter, *Understanding Human Sexual Inadequacy*, Hodder and Stoughton, London, 1980, p. 137.

20 'The Pulse', Channel 4, 15 February, 1996.

21 A. Kinsey, W. Pomeroy and C. Martin, *Sexual Behaviour in the Human Male*, Saunders, Philadelphia, 1948, p. 545.

22 Robin Skynner and John Cleese, *Families and How to Survive Them*, Mandarin, London, 1983, p. 196.

23 K. Kelley, E. Pilchowicz and D. Byrne, 'Response of males to female-initiated dates', *Bulletin of the Psychonomic Society*, 17, pp. 195–196, 1981.

Chapter 5 Mythologies

1 C. S. Lewis, *The Allegory of Love: a study in medieval tradition*, Oxford University Press, London, 1936.

2 Georges Duby, *Love and Marriage in the Middle Ages,* Polity Press, Cambridge, 1994.

3 Fisher, op cit., p. 49.

4 Joseph Campbell, *Creative Mythology,* Penguin, Harmondsworth, 1976.

5 *Company,* August 1995.

6 C. Hendrick and S. S. Hendrick, 'A theory and method of love', *Journal of Personality and Social Psychology,* 50, pp. 392–402.

7 Lawson, op cit.

8 *Guardian,* 11 September, 1995.

9 Cowrie and Lees, op cit.

10 *The Mabinogion,* Penguin, Harmondsworth, 1976.

11 Farrell, *Myth of Male Power,* op cit., p. 213.

12 *Guardian,* 28 September, 1994.

13 Campbell, op cit., p. 37.

14 Yvonne Roberts, *Every Woman Deserves An Adventure,* Macmillan, London, 1994.

15 Robert May, *Sex and Fantasy,* Norton, New York, 1980.

16 Lawson, op cit.

17 Josephine Hart, *Damage,* Arrow, London, 1991, p. 177.

18 Lawson, op cit.

19 P. Frazier and E. Esterly, 'Correlates of relationship beliefs: gender, relationship experiences and relationship satisfaction', *Journal of Social and Personal Relationships,* 7, pp. 331–352.

20 Hite, op cit.

21 Nick Hornby, *High Fidelity,* Indigo, London, 1995, p. 25.

22 Margaret Forster, *Daphne du Maurier,* Chatto and Windus, London, 1993, p. 18.

23 A. Kinsey, W. Pomeroy, C. Martin and P. Gebhard, *Sexual Behaviour in the Human Female,* Saunders, London, 1953.

24 Lasse Hessel, *Window on Love,* Crawford House, Australia, 1994, p. 42.

25 'The Architecture of the Imagination', BBC2, 27 August, 1993.

26 Alfred Lord Tennyson, *Poems Published in 1842*, Oxford University Press, London, 1929.

27 Dorothy Parker, *The Collected Dorothy Parker*, Penguin, Harmondsworth, 1977, p. 119.

28 Laurel Richardson, *The New Other Woman; Contemporary Single Women in Affairs with Married Men*, Free Press, New York, 1985, in Lawson.

29 Clarissa Pinkola Estes, *Women Who Run With The Wolves*, Rider, London, 1992.

30 Sylvia Plath, *Ariel*, Faber, London, 1965.

31 Parker, op cit., p. 122.

32 Valerie Flint, *The Rise of Magic in Early Medieval Europe*, Oxford University Press, Oxford, 1993.

33 *Cosmopolitan*, March 1996.

34 *Just Seventeen*, 14 June, 1995.

35 Sir James Frazer, *The Golden Bough*, Chancellor, London, 1994.

36 Irving Goffman, *Gender Advertisements*, Harper and Row, New York, 1979, p. 8.

37 Bailey, op cit., pp. 112–115.

38 Laura Martin, *A Life Without Fear*, Rutledge Hill Press, Nashville, 1992.

39 Milan Kundera, *The Book of Laughter and Forgetting*, Penguin, Harmondsworth, 1980, p. 36.

40 Sigmund Freud, *On Sexuality*, Penguin, Harmondsworth, 1977, p. 256.

41 H. Walker and N. Buckley, *Token Reinforcement Techniques*, Engelmann-Becker, Eugene, Oregon, 1974.

42 Thomas Mann, *Death in Venice*, Penguin, Harmondsworth, 1955.

43 Lawson, op cit., p. 17.

44 Rachel Swift, *Women's Pleasure,* Pan, London, 1993, p. 35.

45 Desmond Morris, *The Human Animal*, BBC Books, London, 1995, p. 123.

46 Jensen-Campbell, Graziano and West, op cit.

Chapter 6 Looks and Smiles

1 *Sunday Times*, 20 March, 1994.

2 *The Penguin Book of Women Poets*, Penguin, Harmondsworth, 1979, p. 43.

3 I. Broverman, D. Broverman, F. Clarkson, P. Rosenkrantz and S. Vogel, 'Sex Role Stereotypes and Clinical Judgments of Mental Health', *Journal of Consulting and Clinical Psychology*, vol. 34, 1970.

4 Katherine V. Forrest, Silver Moon Books, London, 1994, p. 72.

5 ibid., op cit., p. 147.

6 ibid., p. 116.

7 Irma Kurtz, *Irma Kurtz's Ten-point Plan For An Untroubled Life*, Fourth Estate, London, 1995, p. 31.

8 Fisher, op cit.

9 M. Moore, 'Nonverbal Courtship Patterns in Women: Context and Consequences', *Ethology and Sociobiology*, 6, pp. 237–247, 1985.

10 B. Murstein, 'Stimulus-value-role: A theory of marital choice', *Journal of Marriage and the Family*, 32, pp. 465–481, 1970.

11 Fisher, op cit., p. 20.

12 ibid, p. 22.

13 Pauline Reage, *The Story of O*, Corgi, London, 1976.

14 John Nicholson, *Seven Ages*, Fontana, London, 1980, p. 116.

15 Farrell, *Why Men Are The Way They Are*, op cit., p. 127.

16 Antonia Abbey, 'Sex Differences in Attributions for Friendly Behavior: Do Males Misperceive Females' Friendliness?' *Journal of Personality and Social Psychology*, 42, pp. 830–838, 1982.

17 Timothy Perper, *Sex Signals: The Biology of Love*, ISI Press, Philadelphia, 1985.

18 Sue Townsend, *Adrian Mole: The Wilderness Years*, Methuen, London, 1993, p. 76.

19 *Elle*, March 1995.

20 *Elle*, March 1995.

21 *Elle*, July 1995.

22 *Cosmopolitan*, November 1995.

23 *Sunday Times*, 2 April, 1995.

24 *Women's Journal*, August 1992.

25 Mary Spillane, *The Complete Style Guide*, Piatkus, London, 1991, p. 139.

26 Matt Ridley, op cit.

27 Naomi Wolf, *The Beauty Myth*, Chatto and Windus, London, 1990.

28 Matt Ridley, p. 285.

29 ibid., p. 288.

30 *Guardian*, 24 July, 1993.

Chapter 7 Do Women Say No and Mean Yes?

1 C. L. Muehlenhard and L. C. Hollabaugh, 'Do women sometimes say no when they mean yes? The prevalence and correlates of women's token resistance to sex', *Journal of Personality and Social Psychology*, 54, pp. 872–879, 1988. *See also*, C. L. Muehlenhard,'"Nice Women" Don't Say Yes and "Real Men" Don't Say No: How Miscommunication and the Double Standard Can Cause Sexual Problems', *Women and Therapy*, 7, pp. 95–108, 1988.

2 R. L. Shotland and B. Hunter, 'Women's "Token Resistant" and Compliant Sexual Behaviors Are Related to Uncertain Sexual Intentions and Rape', *Personality and Social Psychology Bulletin*, 21, pp. 226–236, March 1995.

3 Helena Kennedy, *Eve Was Framed*, Vintage, London, p. 111.

4 Catherine MacKinnon, *Feminism Unmodified*, Harvard University Press, Cambridge, 1982, p. 178.

5 Andrea Dworkin, *Letters from a War Zone*, Secker and Warburg, London, 1988, p. 14.

6 Martin, op cit.

7 Muehlenhard and Hollabaugh, op cit.

8 Shotland and Hunter, op cit.

9 Janet Malcolm, *Psychoanalysis: The Impossible Profession*, Pan, London, 1982, p. 6.

10 *Guardian*, 30 January, 1996.

11 Lewis, op cit.

12 Andrew Marvell, *The Poems of Andrew Marvell*, Routledge and Kegan Paul, London, 1969.

13 Cowrie and Lees, op cit.

14 Ellen Fein and Sherrie Schneider, *The Rules*, Thorsons, London, 1995, p. 172.

15 *Cosmopolitan*, September 1995.

16 Fein and Schneider, op cit., p. 78.

17 Hill, Rubin and Peplau, op cit.

18 Fein and Schneider, op cit., p. 82.

19 D. F. Hurlbert, 'The role of assertiveness in female sexuality: A comparative study between sexually assertive and sexually nonassertive women', *Journal of Sex and Marital Therapy*, 17, pp. 183–190, 1991.

20 Fein and Schneider, op cit., p. 161.

21 C. L. Muehlenhard and S. L. Andrews, 'Open communication about sex: Will it reduce risk factors related to date rape?' Presented at the annual meeting of the Association for Advancement of Behavior Therapy, Houston, 1985.

Chapter 8 Money

1 *Guardian*, 18 September, 1991.

 2 Fisher, op cit.

 3 Gillis, op cit.

 4 ibid.

 5 Bailey, op cit.

 6 Rose and Friez, op cit.

 7 Lawson, op cit.

 8 *Guardian*, 11 September, 1995.

 9 Morton Hunt, *The Affair: A Portrait of Extra-Marital Love in Contemporary America*, World Publishing, New York, 1969.

10 D. Buss and M. Barnes, *Journal of Personality and Social Psychology*, 'Preferences in Human Mate Selection', 50, pp. 559–570, 1986, and D. Buss, 'Sex Differences in Human

Mate Preferences: Evolutionary Hypotheses Tested in 37 Cultures', *Behavioural and Brain Sciences*, 12, pp. 1–49.

11 Linda Sonntag, *Finding the Love of Your Life*, Piccadilly Press, London, 1988, pp. 30–35.

12 *And Then He Kissed Her*, audiotape from Mills and Boon, Richmond, 1991.

13 Matt Ridley, op cit., p. 259.

14 *Options*, August 1995.

15 Judith S. Wallerstein and Sandra Blakeslee, *Second Chances*, Corgi, London, 1990.

16 Matt Ridley, op cit.

17 Farrell, op cit.

18 'Everyman', BBC1, 19 November, 1995.

19 *Guardian*, 12 August, 1995.

20 Christos S. Mantzoros, Emmanuel I. Georgiadis and Dimitrios Trichopoulos, 'Contribution of dihydrotestosterone to male sexual behaviour', *British Medical Journal*, 310, pp. 1289–1291, 20 May, 1995.

21 *Guardian*, 13 April, 1994.

22 Gillis, op cit., p. 51.

23 Lawson, op cit., p. 43.

24 Senior Scholastic, 1948.

25 1950s marriage text quoted in Bailey, op cit.

26 Senior Scholastic, 1945.

27 Teen advice book, 1954, quoted in Bailey, op cit.

28 Kiowa Costonie, *How to Win and Hold a Husband*, Kiowa Publishing Company, New York, p. 71, 1945.

29 *Ladies Home Journal* teen advice column, 1942.

30 Nina Farewell, *The Unfair Sex*, Simon and Schuster, New York, 1953.

31 C. Muehlenhard, D. Friedman and C. Thomas, 'Is Date Rape Justifiable?' *Psychology of Women Quarterly*, 9:3, pp. 297–310, 1985.

32 Hite, op cit., p. 759.

33 Kinsey, Pomeroy and Martin, op cit., p. 607.

34 Barbara de Angelis, *Secrets About Men*, Thorsons, London, 1990, p. 203.

35 *Sunday Times*, 14 August, 1994.

36 Hite, op cit., p. 760.

37 *Ladies Home Journal*, March 1955.

38 *Woman's Journal*, February 1995.

39 *Sunday Times*, 24 May, 1994.

40 Ginie Polo Sayles, *How To Marry The Rich*, Berkley Books, New York, 1992, p. 56.

41 Gillis, op cit.

42 George Eliot, *Middlemarch*, Oxford University, Oxford, 1988.

43 Lawson, op cit., p. 80.

44 ibid., p. 81.

45 Naomi Wolf, *Fire With Fire*, Chatto and Windus, London, 1993, p. 257.

46 Astrid Lindgren, *Pippi Goes Aboard*, Penguin, London, 1977, p. 10.

47 Kristine Beuret and Lynn Makings, 'I've Got Used to Being Independent Now: Women and Courtship in a Recession', in *Women and the Life Cycle*, ed. Patricia Allatt, Teresa Keil, Alan Bryman and Bill Bytheway, Macmillan, Basingstoke, 1987.

48 Gillis, op cit., p. 43.

Chapter 9 Danger

1 N. B. McCormick, 'Come-ons and put-offs: Unmarried students' strategies for having and avoiding sexual intercourse', *Psychology of Women Quarterly*, 4, pp. 194–211.

2 C. L. Muehlenhard and A. S. Felts, 'An analysis of causal factors for men's attitudes about the justifiability of date rape', unpublished raw data, 1987.

3 R. L. Shotland and L. Goodstein, 'Just because she doesn't want to doesn't mean it's rape: An experimentally based causal model of the perception of rape in a dating situation', *Social Psychology Quarterly*, 46, pp. 220–232, 1983.

4 Estes, op cit.

5 *Guardian*, 21 August, 1995.

6 *Guardian*, 3 March, 1995.

7 *Guardian*, 24 July, 1993.

8 *Guardian*, 18 January, 1996.

9 Helen Benedict, *Virgin or Vamp,* Oxford University Press, New York, 1992, p. 147.

10 *New Internationalist*, February 1994.

11 *Guardian*, 3 January, 1996.

12 *Leicester Mercury*, 19 July, 1994.

13 Kennedy, op cit., p. 121.

14 ibid., p. 149.

15 *Observer*, 25 April, 1995.

16 Kennedy, op cit., personal communication.

17 *New York* magazine, 10 November, 1986.

18 Benedict, op cit., p. 179.

19 ibid., p. 162.

20 Muehlenhard, Friedman and Thomas, op cit.

21 Judith Rossner, *Looking for Mr Goodbar*, Cape, London, 1975.

22 S. Copenhaver and E. Grauerholz, 'Sexual victimization among sorority women: Exploring the link between sexual violence and institutional practices', *Sex Roles*, 24, pp. 31– 41, 1991.

23 J. Belknap, 'The sexual victimization of unmarried women by non-relative acquaintances', in M. Pirog-Good and J. Stets, *Violence in Dating Relationships*, Praeger, New York, 1989.

24 Belknap, op cit.

25 C. Muehlenhard and M. Linton, 'Date rape and sexual aggression in dating situations: Incidence and risk factors', *Journal of Counseling Psychology*, 34, pp. 186–195, 1987.

26 Muehlenhard, Friedman and Thomas, op cit.

27 Martin, op cit., p. 32.

28 D. Follingstad, L. Rutledge, D. Polek and K. McNeill-Hawkins, 'Factors Associated with Patterns of Dating Violence

Toward College Women', *Journal of Family Violence*, vol. 3, no. 3, 1988.

29 Rodney Cate and Sally Lloyd, *Courtship*, Sage, Newbury Park, 1992, p. 100.

30 Nancy Friday, *Women on Top*, Hutchinson, London, 1991.

31 M. P. Koss and K. E. Leonard, 'Sexually aggressive men', in N. A. Malamuth and E. Donnerstein (eds), *Pornography and Sexual Aggression*, Academic Press, Orlando, 1984.

32 Martin, op cit., p. 31.

33 ibid, p. 73.

34 ibid, p. 74.

35 ibid, p. 110.

36 ibid, p. 80.

37 Iona and Peter Opie, *The Classic Fairy Tales*, Paladin, London, 1980, p. 123.

Chapter 10 How To

1 *Guardian*, 16 April, 1996.

INDEX